The Long Way Home

Bonnie Ridley Kraft

Photography and cover design by Jesse Kraft

Technical advice on weapons, motorcycles and angst – Alan Ridley

First published by Dog Ear Publishing
4010 W. 86th Street, Ste H
Indianapolis, IN 46268
www.dogearpublishing.net

ISBN: 978-145750-729-8

This book is printed on acid-free paper.

Printed in the United States of America

Also by Bonnie Ridley Kraft

The Kámen

For my sons, the brothers Kraft — Adam and Jesse
Y para la hija de mi corazón, Narda Lucía

CHAPTER **1**

Sylvia Duncan should have been paying better attention when she crossed the street. After all, she was a uniquely experienced traveler. At what might have been considered young at only twenty-two years old, she had been abroad and completely on her own for well over a year, intentionally staying apart from her country of birth, the United States of America. When living and working in a major international city, she knew to keep her valuables limited and close to her person, carrying only a small bag from her hotel with a notebook and pen, the tools of her trade. She knew to walk briskly and with intent, even if, in truth, she had no intent to anything. She knew to stay in that part of the city that was alive with people, and well-lighted at night. So truly it was just a matter of becoming familiar with the city itself.

Amsterdam. She'd never been here before, and she had always thought she would never get lost as much in any city as she had during a brief stay in London. She had been wrong. In London, she couldn't keep her directions straight, and she'd blamed that on the fact that she could barely distinguish right from left, perhaps due to the insistence of the British for driving on the left-hand side of the road. Never mind distinguishing north from south. But that was not the problem here in Amsterdam. Amsterdam was, well, just complicated, criss-crossed with one hundred sixty-something canals and over twelve hundred low arched bridges. Fortunately, her hotel was near the Station Amsterdam Centraal, Centraal Station for short, where trains, buses, trams and ships converged, and she always managed to keep its location where it should have been, at the edge of the water of the River IJ. But it seemed she never arrived via the same rough, cobbled street, or the same curving bridge, or the same murky canal!

The city was a spider's web of street after narrow street of brick and cobblestones, with the façades of the buildings leaning in over her, like an ancient forest closing out the sky. The store fronts and living spaces were tall and narrow and gabled over the canals and over the streets, hovering protectively.

And the bicycles! More dangerous than the trains and trams, than the buses, than the speeding cars, she thought, were the bicycles. She had gotten bumped by one and she had stammered out an apology to the rider's bent back, already half a block away. He was apparently either unaware or uncaring that she had just got all the breath knocked out of her. But after only a few days, she had absorbed the feel of the city and its nuances, and had learned how to cross the streets where there were no marked walkways or signal lights, judging how fast the trams might be coming, or ducking among heedless bicyclists. And then even signal lights were ignored, as she calculated how to anticipate when cars would turn or would start up, nearly running over her heels. When there was a pedestrian light, the funny little lighted figure that jerkily mimicked walking would turn green and presently would blink on and off, then turn red. As quickly as a native of the city she figured that out, too, knowing when she could step off the curb and make it – barely! – to the other side, so as not to have to await the next signal.

Not that she had any reason to be in a hurry. She was here for a few days to meet a friend, Nico DiCapelli. She had come early, just to savor the city. For the past three months, she had ridden out the political changes in 1990 Czechoslovakia in the mountains of the northern part of that country, staying at an ancient estate, the Kámen, just a few miles out of the village of Tatra. A jubilant time it had been, the people throwing off the heavy yoke of communism with exuberance, lifting the poet-revolutionary president Václav Havel to *hrad* Pražské – Prague Castle – in a joyous enthusiasm unrivaled in the rest of Eastern Europe, or anywhere else in the disastrously collapsing Soviet empire.

Before that she had been a few months in the tiny mountain hamlet of Asolo in the Alps of northern Italy, and then two more months in Trieste, a city that huddled at the edge of the Adriatic Sea and couldn't quite decide whether or not it was indeed Italian. And right after leaving the United States, she had resided for nearly four months in Edinburgh, Scotland. And a misty, grey four months they had been, too, in spite of the stony, austere beauty of that city. There she had girded herself against the raging anger at the betrayal she had suffered. There she had held the world at bay by the force of a desperate will. All the things she had loved were far away – her parents, her two brothers. And except for them, the rest of her past was a bitter nightmare of ghosts that were no longer cherished. It had been a solitude that she had needed as she had borne her heavy burden alone and had come to terms with the bleakness of her future.

But just now she was not thinking of the lonely pain of that seemingly distant time. Rather, she was thinking that Nico DiCapelli would arrive on the next day. She was pondering an enigma: how could she look forward to seeing him again at the same time that she also harbored a great deal of trepidation about being with him?

The truth was, she was not paying attention to how long the pedestrian light had been blinking its insistent warning before she stepped into the frantically busy intersection of Oudezijds Achterburgwal and Damstraat.

She was halfway across the vastness of the wide avenue when the red flashed on. She quickened to a run, but even as she sped up, time suddenly seemed to slow. Just by a hair she missed the truck in the traffic lane nearest the sidewalk but one. A few more steps and she would have the curb! She heard the throbbing roar of a motor. She heard a dull thud and she felt the air leave her body. She heard the sound of tires screeching on pavement and a quick exclamation that would pass for profanity in any language. She felt a hand reach out and grasp her by the arm to balance her, dragging her forward, holding her so firmly that it hurt. And then she heard her own voice, absurdly apologetic. "Sorry!"

Then time picked up again to its proper pace and she finally saw what had struck her, or to put it more accurately, what she had struck. A motorcycle. This was not a bicycle or a scooter, but a motorcycle, black and solid and loud, with a black-clad rider. She could see nothing but his eyes, as a black helmet covered all else of his features. Not just his head, but also most of his face, concealed by a bar that extended out from the chin, leaving just a slit of a few inches for vision.

She thought it odd. No one wore a helmet in Amsterdam, just like no one used an umbrella when it rained. Except the tourists.

Then she chided herself. A ridiculous observation, when she was standing in the middle of the busy intersection with traffic streaming by on her heels and with those fierce eyes boring into her, eyes nearly as black as the helmet itself.

He switched to English from whatever language he had used to swear. "Get on," he ordered.

She blinked. "I beg yours?" she said. He was stopped midway into the intersection where he had half-dragged her, apparently ignoring the blaring of indignant horns, and the traffic streaming past on both sides of them like water parting for a rock. She was standing next to him, and he was still grasping her arm. Too hard. It was going to show a bruise. Matching bruises, she thought dryly, feeling her leg beginning to sting from her encounter with his motorcycle just a few seconds ago.

"Get *on*," he repeated roughly, giving her arm a jerk.

She was brought sharply back to reality. "Oh! Have you gone daft?" she gasped, trying to pull back from him.

Then the light changed again, and the driver in the car behind the motorcycle began to sound his horn in furious impatience, and the one behind that as well, until a turbulent cacophony resounded across the intersection and echoed up the narrow alleys. Sylvia was suddenly confused and her leg hurt, and she couldn't get around the blasted motorcycle without getting run over.

"Now!" he snapped, his dark eyes as commanding as his voice.

She obeyed. Stupidly, she would recall later. But at least she finally moved. It was not toward the curb, to safety. It was not away from him into the speeding traffic. Rather, it was where he had told her to go. She stopped her resistance and he jerked her towards him. She swung up on the motorcycle behind him, clinging to her small bag. He took one of her hands and drew it firmly to his waist. "Hold on," he said, and released her to grasp the controls. He let the clutch fly and gunned the motorcycle through the intersection, darting in front of the cross traffic in an arrogant disregard of the now-red light.

She saw none of it. She heard only the roar of the motor and felt her long hair lift with the sudden wind. She clung as he twisted open the throttle. The machine dipped and leaned as if it were actually as alive as a wild beast, and not a mere piece of steel.

However, she had managed to retrieve at least a few of her wits by the time they reached the next major intersection, and she peered around his shoulder. He deftly managed the motorcycle ahead of a car and around a truck, speeding down the cobbled street. His elbows he kept clamped to his sides so as not to knock them against the objects that they flew past.

She did not utter a sound. Indeed, the roughness of the street surface jarred away most of her breath, and the wind snatched what little was left. She pressed her body against his back to avoid being flung off. The motorcycle continued to weave through the traffic and then straightened, emerging into a small clearing and flashing directly towards an oncoming tram. Head-on. She saw the tram coming, saw that it could not possibly swerve and could not stop, and saw the disbelieving engineer drag at the cord of his warning bell. She wanted to scream but there was no time, not even to draw a breath. At the last possible second, the motorcycle swerved onto the sidewalk, sending pedestrians scrambling and cursing.

She caught her breath and felt a rush of fury at his carelessness. Well, she was safe enough talking to his back. He wouldn't hear anything with his helmet on and the engine roaring and the wind sweeping past. "I don't have a helmet, you idiot," she said, clinging for her life. "I would appreciate if you would be more careful. You may be willing to stake your life on your absurd driving skills, but I am not."

They kept on flying through the streets and so she kept on berating him. "You go through traffic lights as if you are colorblind. And there is a speed limit, you know, even in Amsterdam. This is, after all, not a road race." He could not hear her, but it made her feel better to scold him. She drew another breath to continue, difficult to do at this speed. "This is tantamount to kidnaping! Where do you think you are taking me?" she demanded into the wind.

His voice whipped back to her, surprisingly clear. "To your hotel," he replied.

She was mortified. He had heard everything she had said! And she shouldn't have been so flippant. After all, he had literally snatched her right off the street, and she had no idea of his intent or his temperament. Suddenly it registered *what* he had said, not just that he had answered her, and relief swept through her. He was taking her to her hotel! She was so grateful that she allowed herself to lean into his back with a shaky sigh.

Five seconds later, reality struck, and her relief fled. "But you don't know where I'm staying!" she cried, flinging out her arms and sitting up so straight that she nearly lifted herself from the rear of the charging machine.

This time he didn't answer, but a strong arm snaked around behind him and grasped her firmly against his back, preventing her from flying off. She wondered how he could possibly have the perspicacity to make such a move and still manage the insane drive through the city at top speed on this ferocious beast of a machine.

She could determine nothing of his thoughts from the straight line of his back and the arrogant set of his shoulders, and indeed, that was all she could see. In that moment she felt imprisoned, and the beginnings of genuine fear began to stir. "Stop this motorcycle at once," she said as firmly as she could manage. "And let me go!"

He accommodated her immediately. In the middle of the intersection of Oudezijds Voorburgwal and Oudezijds Achterburgwal and Grimburgwal, with its odd angles and myriad of streets pouring into it and a full contingent of every form of transportation in the suddenly overwhelming city. He brought the motorcycle to a shrieking, sliding, sideways halt, and brought all the traffic around him to the same state. It had the predictable result of outrage expressed in sounding horns and Dutch profanity. She started to slide off the motorcycle and then realized where he was depositing her. Traffic was flying by on all sides and the sidewalks might as well have been on the moon. She righted herself on the machine and gave his back a resounding thump in reproach.

He shrugged, dropped a hand to hers at his waist to ensure she was holding on, and revved the engine. He released the clutch abruptly. The front tire lifted off the ground as the motorcycle pitched back into motion, with her clinging to him as her only lifeline. "Make up your mind," she heard him mutter into the racket, and she loosed a hand to thump him again.

Leaning the motorcycle so low to one side that she thought it would skid right out from under them, he suddenly turned away from the main roadways and hurtled up a narrow cobbled alleyway. The entire street could not have been more than ten feet across, building to building. She glanced up. Oh, yes, the buildings were still looming over her, but now they seemed to have a threatening leer. The echo of the motorcycle's screaming engine against the narrow stone confines was deafening.

Later she would think that the sound surely must have been just a roar, the same roar they had left everywhere else in their wake on this mad journey. But in that moment, everything seemed magnified to her. The sounding of horns by annoyed motorists at the intersections, the clatter of the cars on the rough stones as they slid by, mere inches from her knee, the racket of the motorcycle engine ricocheting off the tall gabled brick buildings, to be thrust back at her. The brick and stone bridges that she had thought so lovely were now lurking menaces, graceful arches turned to hunchbacks, with every one leaving her heart and stomach at the top of the rise as the motorcycle flashed up one side and plummeted down the next.

It suddenly struck her that she had gotten herself into trouble. Serious trouble. She was flying down the obscure back streets of Amsterdam with a total stranger who seemed bent on killing them both with his wild driving. Her mind began to plot her escape, even as she clung to him.

When she had demanded that he stop, he had. Never mind that it was in the middle of an intersection swarming with trains, trams, cars, and bicycles, for heaven's sake! But at least he'd stopped, so perhaps he would again. However, she wasn't sure she wanted to issue the same command just now and be dropped off on this remote alleyway with no idea of where in the city she might be.

The motorcycle dipped again and roared down another side street, pedestrians fleeing to take refuge behind the black phallic-shaped metal posts that were inserted along the roadway specifically for that purpose. The shops and restaurants flashed past in a dizzy blur of color. Then the machine careened around yet another blind corner and at last came to a screeching halt.

A flick of a thumb killed the engine. The motorcycle trembled and stilled, and silence descended. Then the driver sighed as if in relief, and twisted his head and body so that he could turn his dark eyes onto her face. "Here you are," he announced.

She gathered her wind-blown wits and looked around. The now-quiescent motorcycle was parked on Korte Niezel, directly in front of her hotel, the Amstel Grand.

CHAPTER **2**

Astonishment would come later. Sylvia was too relieved to be aston-ished just now. To suddenly turn up at her hotel by such a round-about, hair-raising route was at first incomprehensible. The motorcycle and the stranger seemed real. The hotel did not.

She slid from the bike and nearly collapsed as her legs were, inexplica-bly, like jelly. His hand shot out and caught her at the waist to balance her. For a brief moment she thought he would order her back onto the machine and begin the entire wild adventure all over again. But instead he flashed a grin. At least, she thought he must have, because his dark eyes, the color of black coffee, sparked with amusement. "I think you need to comb your hair," he observed, sounding apologetic but with humor hinting at the edge of his voice, the same humor that had touched his eyes. She caught a musi-cal accent in his English, but it was very light and its origin eluded her.

Automatically a hand went to her head, but she was used to her wild waves being in disarray, so she ignored them in favor of looking over the stranger who waited before her, still straddling the motorcycle. Apparently deciding that she was steady enough, he released her waist and reached a hand to the strap under his chin. He pulled it loose, yanked the helmet from his head, and shook his dark hair like a dog just coming out of the water. She thought all his movements slightly abrupt, or perhaps just focused to the point of being almost fierce.

The first thing she noticed was his nose. That was only because she had already locked gazes with his compelling dark eyes. And lost!

His nose. It was straight. It did not indent between his eyes. Rather it started at his brow and kept the same straight line all the way. No concessions.

No compromises. Straight from his brow, until the nose stopped. Just like that. Indeed, a remarkable nose.

She continued her inventory. Lips that had a certain firm stubbornness, in spite of the smile that was playing at one corner. And a chin that matched the lips for stubbornness. She definitely recognized stubbornness. She had a good measure of it herself.

His hair curled just past his nape, nearly as dark as his eyes, just now damp and disheveled from the helmet. His complexion was deeply tanned, but golden rather than swarthy. He was lean, and a good bit taller than she, although that was nothing to remark since she was, herself, quite petite. All in all, rather well put together, she decided. A frown creased her brow as she calculated his age. Late twenties, she would guess.

Her gaze returned to his eyes, meeting an unmistakable flicker of amusement. He had been watching her as she had conducted her survey. "Am I all right?" he asked dryly, and again she heard the touch of an accent that she could not immediately place. "Am I at least passable, then?"

She blushed slightly but overrode it with fierce determination. He might intimidate her with his reckless driving, but he certainly would not with his intent dark gaze. After all, she had caught the quick amused twinkle just a moment ago. "You'll do," she said impertinently.

She watched as he scanned her own slight frame. Again she put a hand to her hair, expecting it was even wilder than usual. She wondered what he was seeing. Nico had compared her hair to the beauty of pure Wyoming clover honey when it was fractured by the sunlight, and declared that her hair came out the winner. He had named her fair skin a Celtic shade of pale. She knew her eyes were a deep sapphire blue, but otherwise thought herself quite unremarkable.

The stranger's gaze came back to her face and he grinned. "And you also, *cariña*," he said. He reached over and snatched a handful of her long curls. "But it will take you the rest of the day to work out the tangles from this –" he tripped over the words for a moment, "– this mass of silk," he finished.

He switched on the motorcycle once more. The engine whined as it turned over a few times and then engaged. She took a step back from the low grumble. He slid the helmet onto his head and adjusted the strap under his chin with one swift jerk. Then he gave her a small salute, and was gone.

Sylvia stood still, staring after him long after he had disappeared, the quietness descending around her like dry autumn leaves that had been disturbed by an errant breeze and then settled to rest again. At last she allowed herself to give in to the inevitable astonishment. How very remarkable he was! She shook her head in thoughtful amazement and turned to walk through the massive wooden doors into her hotel.

The Hotel Amstel Grand was a huge old thing, two hundred years old this year, first completed in 1790. The entryway was recessed with polished, delicately carved wooden columns on each side, marching upward with the white marble stairs. Six steps there were, narrow and with a very steep pitch, not unusual here in Amsterdam, and then more columns to lead into the lobby.

The lobby and reception were open and airy but with a feeling of opulence that was nearly overwhelming. Everywhere the polished wood shone with an almost satiny sheen so that in spite of its dark tones, it gave the impression of light. The floor was an intricate parquet in hardwood of varying shades, covered with a few rugs of red and black and gold in a coat of arms pattern, but only where necessary to protect against the trample of visitors' shoes. The immense area was graced by a feeling of intimacy as the furniture and plant arrangements had the effect of separating it into a series of smaller rooms. Overstuffed chairs were arranged in groupings around low tables, with high-backed chairs facing the fireplaces. There were four fireplaces in all, not lit just now because of the warmth of the September season. Gleaming crystal chandeliers, likely Bohemian in origin from the Czechoslovakia she had just left, hung from the high ceiling, and the low tables were graced with tall, exotic lamps of black and gold porcelain with simple cream-colored shades. Huge oil paintings of both portraits and landscapes – originals, not replicas – were reminiscent of the Dutch masters, and were hung in massive gilded frames.

Sylvia was normally quite observant, but she saw none of it as she tripped past, turning over in her mind the afternoon's strange twists, searching for some logical sense to them, as strange as the twists and turns of the speeding motorcycle. But when the spicy aroma from the restaurant floated past her nostrils, she suddenly remembered that she had eaten no lunch. It was nearly three o'clock already and she was not inclined to bother just now. However, a cup of tea would be rather nice.

She collected her room key at reception and then dashed up the two flights of stairs to her room. Running fingers through her tangles with one hand, and reaching for her brush with the other, she glanced into the mirror. No wonder the stranger had been so fixated on her hair! It was immeasurably wilder than usual, and that was saying a great deal. It was thick and fell past her waist when it was wet, pulling up three to four inches as it dried in natural waves. It did precisely as it pleased. In one of his tongue in cheek observations in a letter, Nico had pointed out that it matched her personality rather well, as she usually behaved in the same fashion. She decided she would rather have tea than take the time to brush out the tangles, so she snatched up her bag with her notebook and pen. She could not sit still for long without writing, not even over tea!

Back downstairs she went, the elegant curve of the wooden banisters and the wide, sweeping fall of the steps unheeded, her mind still wrestling with the problem of the stranger. Why had he picked her up? He could have let her pass by him and the motorcycle and make the curb. Why had he taken her on that long and wild ride? It had seemed to last forever, and she knew she had not walked so far from the Hotel Amstel Grand as to require such a long ride back. But most perplexing, how had he known in what hotel she was staying? She wasn't sure whether it intrigued her or disturbed her. In any case, she had finished her tea with a bit of milk and sugar, and a small biscuit, hardly tasting any of it, and still had not solved the riddle.

So she gave it up. She took out her notebook and pen, and began to paint in words the motorcycle, the man, the mad drive. It flowed, as her writing nearly always did, and she was at the same time both aware of and oblivious to her surroundings. She worked best when she was in a center of activity but undisturbed, and so it was past six-thirty when she realized with a start that the restaurant personnel were good-naturedly working around her to get the place set up for the evening meal. Perhaps she should have been embarrassed, but she was rather used to losing herself in time and writing. She signed the charge to her room and opened the bag to place her notebook inside.

She stopped mid-movement and stared. The bag! The Hotel Amstel Grand! It was immediately clear where the stranger had gotten his information. Her small bag was from the hotel, and the name was printed in bold letters, along with the address of Korte Niezel 674. He must have noticed it and gambled – and won! – that it was where she was lodging. How very clever of him! And nothing so disturbing, after all. The stranger apparently had talents for analysis and deduction that would rival Nico himself.

Nico. She left the restaurant and once more ascended to her room. Again she was deep in thought, but this time regarding Nico. He would arrive tomorrow afternoon and she would take the train from Centraal Station to the Schiphol International Airport to meet him. Only twenty minutes it would take, but just now any minute seemed long.

Oh, how she had longed to see him during these past two months! They had been together only a few short weeks in Czechoslovakia but it had seemed a lifetime in a microcosm. She had been suspicious and wary of relationships. She still was. Or more exactly, if more bluntly, she had turned the avoidance of relationships into an art form. But their circumstances had been unusual, hers and Nico's. They had been thrown together in mystery and danger and violence. And they had both, in the extremity of the situation, let down barriers in a way that was not usual for either of them. Nico, because he was naturally reserved and reticent, absorbing information but not giving out much. And she, Sylvia, because she had been betrayed and abandoned and had resolved not to expose herself again to that kind of pain. And yet they had each been open with the other. But afterwards, when the danger was past, and the remembered terror was a wisp of an errant, disturbing cloud of memory, they had been uncomfortable and embarrassed and, strangely enough, seemingly even further apart than they had been before.

She had been quite sure she would not hear from him again when he left Czechoslovakia and she had stayed, even though his words and actions had certainly contradicted that notion. She had been hopefully – and regretfully! – certain she had seen the last of him. But she had been wrong. He had written often, his letters somewhat self-conscious, but always with an undercurrent of his wry sense of humor. He revealed little more about his secretive job than what she already knew, and absolutely never dropped a hint of where he was assigned. And he divulged even less about his thoughts or feelings regarding her. So she had kept her own letters in the same tone, responding gently to his tentative overtures and his teasing, but giving away no more. She had already given away too much to Nico DiCapelli.

And then, two months after she had parted from him, he had rung up right out of the blue and asked her to join him here in Amsterdam. She was quite ready to leave Czechoslovakia after having been there for over three months, but had not decided where to go next. And so she had agreed to meet him. He would arrive tomorrow, and she was anxious to see him. However, she was also nervous about seeing him. She was certain that she still was not ready for a relationship, whatever that meant. But perhaps he had no thoughts himself along those lines, and she was just letting her imagination play havoc with her emotions. She could keep herself safe and separate. God knew she'd had enough practice this past year.

She didn't sleep well that night, tossing in the big bed for what seemed like hours. At last she gave it up and rose from the tangled covers, switching on the lamp next to the bed. The light cast somber shadows even as she studied her room once again. Compared to her place at the county inn in Czechoslovakia, the Kámen, it was opulent. Nico had insisted that they stay at the Hotel Amstel Grand, as it was central and it was comfortable. He also had insisted that he pay for her room as well as his own.

Smiling slightly, she glanced around her room. It was painted in a soft green, accented by cream wainscoting and trim that ran all the way around the edge of the lofty ceiling. The curtains were heavy, but a darker green, and pulled back by intricate belted ties. A small radiator stood against the wall should heating be necessary, not likely this early in September. The floor was covered by a red and cream rug, and the bed coverings matched.

She had played over and over in her mind a hundred variations of how she would meet Nico the next afternoon. It would help if she knew his thoughts and feelings for her. At their abrupt parting two months ago, he had been more than clear. "You are mine," he had whispered as if he would not be denied. "You are *mine*."

But he had given her no more clues of his feelings since their time together at the Kámen, where they had been imprisoned and left to die in an ancient hillfort in the mountains, so she knew nothing of what he might be anticipating. And even worse, much worse, she did not know her own thoughts and feelings. Should she allow her excitement and pleasure to show? Should she reveal her uncertainty, her tentative reservations? Or should she take her usual, practiced pose, that of polite but distant conversation? Nico was a man who was a stranger and yet not a stranger at all.

By half-past six in the morning, she was relieved to have the long night behind her, and was downstairs having her breakfast. As always, she passed by the tempting variety of breads and cheeses and boiled eggs and chose a bit of fruit. There was a selection that reflected the autumn season: crispy, sun-kissed apples and the more demure pears, as well as some citrus that had been imported from the south. Black tea with milk and sugar. Thirty minutes later she stepped outside into a mist-like rain that had settled gently upon the city and cast a grey pallor over the canals, making the streets seem narrower and the tall, hovering buildings appear to loom even closer.

In spite of the drizzle, it was warm, and so she set out to walk for a few hours. She headed into the Jordaan Quarter, the old working class part of the city, now being transformed by artists and artisans who were moving into the area to live and work. The streets here were constructed with ugly, rough asphalt rather than being cobbled, the stones having been paved over some decades ago. During protests and riots of the recalcitrant laborers, the bricks had become handy weapons to use as projectiles, so they had been covered with the black, tar-like substance. She thought it an interesting way to address the problem – paving over the crude weapons rather than dealing with the underlying social causes. Cheaper and easier, she supposed cynically. She wondered if Nico would agree.

Already a line was forming on the Prinsengracht in front of the Anne Frankhuis, the house where the young Jewish girl, Anne Frank, had lived in hiding, concealed from the cruelty of the Second World War. There she had written her poignant adolescent diary. And there, she was ultimately betrayed to the Germans and deported to a concentration camp, where she died of typhus just a few days before Allied troops liberated the camp. Sylvia skirted the groups of people to get past, her intent ear picking up the babble of several different languages. By late morning she was quite damp and entirely tired of walking.

She passed the Rijksmuseum, a palatial building well over one hundred years old that housed the art of the grand old Dutch masters, including works by Rembrandt, such as his famous painting *The Night Watch*. Even without the draw of the marvelous artwork, the building itself was like an old mansion and worth seeing, with its two towers reaching to the heavens, just now the very drizzly heavens. The walls were red brick accented with white and the roof was grey tile. Gardens stretched out on all sides, their well-tended splendor just beginning to fade as if in a reluctant concession to the encroaching end of summer. Inside, soaring arches ran the length of the building, giving a sense of vastness that perfectly displayed the massive old paintings in their heavy, gilded frames. She had spent an entire afternoon there only a few days ago.

Dodging a bicyclist, she realized that she was directly in front of the Vincent van Gogh museum, and on an impulse, she ducked inside. She paid her few Dutch guilders for admission and darted up the stairs to the first floor, where she began to make her way through van Gogh's magnificent works. The paintings were displayed in chronological order, but in her admittedly unpracticed view, she thought it depicted more how his life had ebbed and flowed rather than a maturing of his art style.

She stood mesmerized in front of her favorite van Gogh painting. *Crows over the Cornfield*. In spite of the dark clouds threatening at the horizon, she thought it bright and airy and determined, giving the sense of a stubborn autumn breeze heavy with the scent of harvested grain and a wonderful ability to withstand the impending threat of a long and bitter winter. She was not one to linger long in a museum, but she was quite alone, and the solitude and dry warmth appealed to her, and so she stood and gazed, hands clasped behind her back.

Her reverie was broken by a softly-accented voice behind her. "Beautiful, no?"

She started slightly, not having realized anyone else was around. She turned. To her astonishment, there he was, leaning on the rail that encircled the open foyer, watching her. The outrageous stranger from her outrageous motorcycle ride of the day before.

She glanced at the painting again, and then back to him. He looked rather less disheveled than he had yesterday, and his dark eyes were somehow not as penetrating. The stubborn edge was still apparent in the mouth and chin, however. "Yes," she said. "It is a beautiful painting."

"Not the painting." He smiled. Pushing away from the rail, he stepped close to her. "Your hair."

"My hair!" What was it about his obsession with her hair! She nearly asked and then decided she would prefer to maintain her reserve.

"Yes. Your hair. Does the rain make it curl?"

She put a hand to it. Indeed, the dampness did make it curl more fiercely. Had she given it any thought, she might have checked in a mirror upon entering the museum. She gave him a faint frown. "Yes. I suppose it does," she said.

He reached out and grasped a handful, much as he had done the previous afternoon. It seemed a natural gesture. She wondered why it didn't make her feel as if her private space was being invaded.

He didn't give her time to think about it or to pull away. He dropped his hand. His gaze left her face and went to the painting. "You like this one, then?"

She turned back to the painting. "I do."

He gave a brief frown that somehow clouded his dark eyes more than it creased his brow. "Why?"

She smiled. "Because it's warm and bright, and I can feel the sun and wind and breathe the scents of the harvest. And I can sense that the cruelty of winter is being held at bay indefinitely. Or perhaps even permanently."

He looked slightly taken aback. "*This* painting? *Crows over the Cornfield?*"

"Yes."

He studied the painting for a moment and then studied her in turn. "*Conoces –*" he began, and then caught himself. "Do you know, it was one of Vincent van Gogh's last paintings before he died? Most interpreters of art believe that it foretells his suicide, at the age of only thirty-seven. The black birds circling and the sky heavy and oppressed and overcast. The autumn of his life, fast fading into winter and death. *La muerte.*"

Briefly, his accent sounded a bit heavier and her brows drew together slightly, marring the smooth skin. She stared at the painting, trying to see it from that darkly shrouded point of view.

"They say it reveals the advanced stages of his mental illness, his insanity. And his hopelessness, and despair."

She chewed her bottom lip, her face screwed up in thought.

"In Vincent's own words in a letter to his brother, Theo, he described how it was not difficult to show 'sadness and extreme loneliness' in this place where he painted. He described the sky as 'troubled.'" He gazed at the painting and then back to her. "Can you not see it?" he persisted.

Still she frowned, assessing the painting. Suddenly, her expression cleared. "No," she announced. "I cannot. It still feels light to me. With a natural warmth from the sun. No matter how deteriorated his mental state, no matter how deep his despair, he must have still had a spot of brightness in his soul, a bit of light and warmth, to have painted it."

He looked startled, and then as if he would like to burst out laughing, but in deference to the solemn place where they stood, he chuckled softly instead. "You're a stubborn one, are you not?" he said. "I can see it in your chin."

It was her turn to be startled. "My chin?"

"And your mouth. Stubborn."

"Oh," she said. It was exactly the way she had described him to herself and to her notebook. Stubborn.

"Perhaps you are thinking instead of van Gogh's *Starry Night?*" he suggested. "Or even *Sunflowers?*"

"No. I know both of those paintings. They feel bleak, even cold. Not as bright, nor as – as tenacious as this one."

"Tenacious," he said, as if puzzled either by the word itself or its context. Then his brow suddenly cleared. Completely unexpectedly, he said, "We shall have lunch now."

Automatically she answered, her voice cool and her body already turning away from him in a practiced rejection. "Oh, no. I cannot. But thank you." Her defense mechanisms were finely tuned and time-tried, and her response was given almost without thought. She took one short step away from him.

"Why not?" he asked, apparently unperturbed.

She stopped and frowned, surprised at his insistence. Usually her stand-offish attitude and her chill demeanor worked the first time around. She had no follow-up ready. "I'm not hungry," she said. It was weak, and she knew it. And she knew that he knew it.

"You will be soon," he argued.

"No, really –"

"Do you often skip meals?"

"I suppose so."

He looked over her slender figure. "You should not," he said earnestly.

"Oh, indeed," she began to protest, the imposing colors and bold brush strokes of the troubled genius momentarily forgotten.

"You are quite slim enough," he said.

"Listen, Mister – Mister whoever you are –"

"Salvadore," he said. He pronounced his name in four syllables. Sal-va-dor-e. He put out a hand as if they had just been introduced. She took it.

"And you?" he prodded.

"Sylvia," she said.

"Sylvia." He tested the name in his gentle accent, giving the 'y' a heavy 'ee' sound. "Sylvia." He grinned. "We shall have lunch now, Sylvia?" he said.

She gave in. Afterwards she didn't quite know why. But for now he took hold of her hand and led her down the curve of polished wooden stairs and out of the building into what was now an unexpectedly bright and sparkling day. The clouds had rolled away and the sun exploded prisms from the mist-drops that still clung to the late summer leaves in the gardens that graced the museum. Indeed, it was much as she had imagined van Gogh might have seen the autumn. Bright, optimistic, enduring. And denying the existence of winter and its inevitable bringing of death.

Still holding her unresisting hand, he led her along Pijlstees and into one of the many *bruine cafés* – brown cafés – so called because of their dark woodwork and walls made dirty-looking by age and the residue of years of cigarette smoke. This one was called *Wijnard Kalkhoven*. It was quite crowded but he managed a small table for them in a back corner. The café was not a place she might have visited alone, as the press of people and the chatter of voices and the overly-loud music were too daunting even for her. She looked around curiously, taking in the small space.

The ceiling was high, as was standard in these ancient buildings, and the pipes for plumbing were hung from the darkened ceiling in a maze of metal angles. The room was narrow and the fans that twirled lazily above did little to dispel the haze of blue smoke from the many smoldering cigarettes. It looked as if it could comfortably seat about twenty people, but there were nearly double that number crowded around the small, well-worn tables. There were several windows with lace half-curtains, but they were high and narrow and somehow tinted or covered – or dirty, she thought – so that not much light came in by that way. The subdued brown walls were thick with old black and white photographs of Amsterdam as if depicting its unique ambience throughout history. The place was cheerful chaos, with the nondescript music throbbing beneath the hubbub of human voices in conversation and laughter. The floor repeated the dark unpolished wood of the walls, also showing signs of long years of rough boot heels. The chairs and benches were plain wood and uncomfortably hard, and were crowded cheek by jowl, and the table tops were covered by what appeared to be ancient Oriental rugs.

With sudden shyness, she realized he had been watching her as she methodically reviewed the room. He smiled at her discomfiture. "This place," he said, *"Wijnard Kalkhoven,* has been a *bruine café,* a brown café, since, I think, 1679. Some are even older. One claims to date from 1574." He gestured with one hand. "If you look over towards the bar, you can see a collection of liquor bottles. They have paintings of every single mayor of Amsterdam since 1591."

She glanced across the room at the bottle collection, and then back to him. "You are a veritable guidebook, aren't you?"

He was amused, and pleased. *"Bruine cafés* provide a place for *gezellig.* A cozy atmosphere, conversation, good cheer. It is quite untranslatable to any other language, as it is in fact nothing more than a nuance." From his lips, the word 'nuance' had three syllables. "The bartenders draw the beers extra frothy, and then behead them with a knife before they are served. Do you see?" Again he pointed towards the bar to draw her attention to this apparently amazing phenomenon.

She took her focus away from her surroundings and returned it to her companion. She frowned at him for a moment. "Have you been following me?" she asked abruptly.

His expression remained unchanged. "It was, how do you say, it was a coincidence," he said. In spite of the din of the place, their table was small and she had no problem hearing him, or being heard.

She said, "First the motorcycle yesterday, and today the Vincent van Gogh museum?"

He picked up on her wry skepticism and gave her a cheeky grin. "I could hardly have arranged for you to crash into my motorcycle in the middle of Oudezijds Achterburgwal and Damstraat, now could I, *cariña?"*

"Possibly not," she said. "But meeting in the museum seems a bit contrived, don't you think?"

He lifted one shoulder. "I saw you walking and so came upon you in front of *Crows over the Cornfield."*

"Mmm," she said, not convinced, but thinking that in fact it really did not matter.

His level dark gaze was distracted by the slightly impatient blond waiter. Understandably, the man was in a hurry, given the crowded place. So Salvadore glanced at the tattered, one-page menu on the table and ordered for both of them, in Dutch.

She watched the waiter's rotund retreating back and then frowned in Salvadore's direction. "How would you know what I might like to eat?" she said. "Or to drink?"

He looked slightly put upon. "I do not mind doing that for you," he said, obviously missing the point.

And, she thought, probably deliberately. She let it pass.

He was silent for a time, studying her until she felt slightly uncomfortable. Unexpectedly he took her hand again. "From where do you come?" he asked.

"I am from the United States," she said.

His dark brows hitched up. "The United States?" He sounded disbelieving.

"Yes."

"Are you certain, then?"

How extraordinary! "Quite," she said dryly. "I think I'd know, wouldn't I?"

"But you speak with a Czech accent in your English," he protested, his brows still skeptical.

She was surprised at that observation, as she was quite sure it was not the case. It was true she had been in Czechoslovakia for three months, and that she picked up accents rather quickly and thoroughly. As a dog picks up fleas, Nico had observed solemnly in one of his letters. Still. She made a mental sidestep. "From where do you come?"

He grinned at her. "Quick you are, no?" he said. "I am getting to know you rather well."

"Where?" she persisted.

"And stubborn," he added. "Quick and stubborn."

She smiled. "Where?" she repeated yet again.

The waiter brought the drinks and meal all at once and deposited them onto the table with a series of solid thumps. Salvadore released her hand and gave the waiter an approving nod. "Now, Sylvia," he said. "You will tell me if you wish something else and I will order it for you."

A glass of red wine and herb-speckled potato dumplings with vegetables, a large serving. "This will be fine," she said.

"*Claro*," he said confidently. "Of course." He also had been served the dumplings in their thick broth, but instead of wine, he was having the Dutch beer, *pils*, appropriately beheaded.

He was too sure of himself by half, she decided. "Except that it's too much food," she added.

"It is not so very much," he argued.

She shrugged and smiled. "From where do you come?" she said.

He gave an appreciative laugh at her persistence. "Where do you think?" he said, lifting his *pils* to her in a tiny salute.

She raised her wine and touched his drink with a light *chink* of glass meeting glass, and took a sip. The wine was dry and robust, a perfect complement to the heavy-looking dumplings. She rarely drank wine with lunch as it made her sleepy and she didn't care to write when she was less than alert. But this day she had no intention of working. This day she was meeting Nico. "Why should I guess?" she said. "Is it a secret, then?"

His fork in the left hand and his knife in the right, he tackled the dumplings even as he looked at her thoughtfully, as if taking her measure. He spoke at last. "Perhaps I am Italian."

The dumplings were light and more liberally spiced than she might have expected. She was suddenly hungry after all. But even as she sampled her meal, she contemplated him. Italian. It was possible. Maybe even likely. His coloring, his slight accent. His name, for all she knew. But something was not quite right. It could likely be his reticence that had put her on her guard. "And perhaps you are not," she said.

"Why do you think that?" He grinned again, apparently unflappable.

"You're not Italian, not from Italy. Where?" she persisted. She was no longer teasing. For some reason, she wanted the truth. She sensed that with her change of tone he was suddenly on his guard.

"Why not Italy?" he countered.

But she had tired of his game. "Keep your little secret," she said dismissively, giving a small shrug of indifference and taking another bite of dumpling. "It doesn't matter to me. If you wish to be Italian today, then certainly you may have your charade."

Salvadore was momentarily distracted by the waiter checking on their satisfaction, then he turned his attention back to Sylvia and switched topics. "What are you doing here in Amsterdam?" he asked.

He sounded casual and conversational, but Sylvia was more than a little perceptive, and she sensed a current underneath. "What am I doing in Amsterdam? Having lunch with an Italian," she said with a light touch of sarcasm mixed with levity. She saw a darkness flash across his face and vanish so quickly that she wondered if it had been real.

"So you are," he said lightly, but the glint in his coffee-colored eyes belied his tone. He was not amused. He kept on eating, but silently.

She fell silent as well, and picked at her food, the spicy dumplings barely touched. She was no longer hungry, so she watched him eat, patiently waiting for him to be finished so she could be on her way without appearing rude.

After several long moments, he noticed that she was not eating. "You do not like your meal?" he asked, sounding concerned.

"I do."

"Then why have you not eaten? Oh, *cariña*, I do apologize! I have been poor company."

"True," she said.

He put down his knife and fork and took her hand again. She nearly pulled away, but he held it firmly and she did not particularly care to make a scene in the crowded restaurant.

"What will we do after lunch?" he said.

"I shall return to my hotel," she said bluntly. "You remember it, I'm sure. The Hotel Amstel Grand."

"Now, see here, Sylvia –"

"I have a prior commitment for this afternoon," she said.

"Do you?"

She could tell that he did not believe her, that he wanted to ask more, but he knew better. She gave him no satisfaction. "I do. So as soon as you are finished, I should go."

"Perhaps you will join me for dinner?" He sounded tentative, for the first time since she had met him the day before. For some reason, it did not seem natural on either his face or in his demeanor.

"I cannot," she said.

"Prior commitment." He provided the excuse for her.

It annoyed her. It was clear that he thought she was brushing him off. Well, she was, wasn't she? "Yes, that's right," she agreed. "A prior commitment."

"*Qué lástima*." he said. "A pity. I had hoped to make amends."

"There is nothing to amend," she assured him, almost sharply.

He sighed and signaled the harried waiter to bring the check.

The walk back to her hotel seemed long with the tension between them, in spite of the sunshine and warm breeze gusting off the canals. He attempted to revert to his easy, conversational deportment, but she deliberately gave him no openings. She pondered on his strange reluctance to tell her about something so straightforward as his nationality, and about the fleeting darkness she was sure she had observed when she challenged him. What was it? Annoyance? It had seemed more. But she did not know him well enough to decipher his moods. Nor did she care to know him so well as that.

In fact, as they neared her hotel, she thought on him less and less as her mind turned to Nico. She would go to her room to freshen up and then head for Station Centraal, and catch the train to the Schiphol International Airport. A small thrill trembled through her. Just a few more hours and she would see him again. Nico.

She climbed the steep stone stairs to the hotel lobby ahead of Salvadore. Stopping at the top, she turned to where he stood two steps below her. "Thank you for lunch," she said.

"Sylvia." He sounded more urgent than regretful.

"I must go."

"Shall I escort you to your room?"

"That won't be necessary." He already knew her hotel. She would not have him knowing her room as well.

He put out his hand and she gave him hers. He didn't shake it. Rather he lifted it to his lips.

She nearly jerked away but then willed herself not to react. Instead she smiled down at him.

He smiled back, as if he were relieved to be on good terms once again.

Then she let fly with her best parting shot. "One of your little Italian customs, no doubt?"

He tried to laugh at her impertinence, but she knew that his attempt was completely without humor.

"Once again," she said. "Thank you for lunch."

He gave a small shrug, as if conceding a point to her, albeit reluctantly. "Enjoy your afternoon," he said.

She turned away from him and crossed the vast lobby to the wide staircase. She climbed two flights and then stopped and looked down. He was still standing where she had left him, as if rooted to the spot and intending to stay awhile. She fervently hoped that he would not be there when she left for Station Centraal.

She needed not to have worried. When she reached her room, the red message light on her telephone was blinking on and off, ominously insisting that she access it. Nearly she ignored it and made her way to the train station. But instead she lifted the receiver to her ear and pushed the button for messages.

"Yes, *het blauwtje de* Duncan," said the voice with a heavy Dutch accent. "At half-past twelve you receive a message from *meneer* Nico DiCapelli. He say that he is – he is to be detain until tomorrow. He is to be at Schiphol Airport at the same time and on the same flight as he was to come this day."

Her stomach pitched from the sudden let-down. It was rather like being on an airplane that takes an unexpected dip into an air pocket. And she had just gotten her nerve worked up to meet him. "Is that all?"

"That is all." The accented voice might have been sympathetic.

She replaced the receiver onto the telephone. Her first reaction was to be concerned for Nico. His was a dangerous profession, meddling in the political and economic concerns of other countries, and she had no idea where he might be assigned at the moment. She hoped that he was all right. Then, strangely, her thoughts turned to Salvadore. She had told him that she had a commitment. She had taken the commitment seriously, but apparently Nico did not feel strongly enough about it to honor it. A sharp twist of old-remembered pain touched her deep within. She shook it off and picked up her pen and notebook and set to work.

CHAPTER **3**

But the pain did not easily shake off, and her concentration was ruined. The blank white page before her remained blank, staring back at her even as she gripped her pen harder than necessary. Absurdly, she felt like weeping. It was most annoying. She was not a weeper!

The afternoon was a long one. She chose not to go out in spite of the lovely weather, unwilling to admit even to herself that she did not want to run into Salvadore. By evening, her cozy but lonely room felt like a self-inflicted prison, and she was hungry and wishing she had eaten her dumplings at lunch.

Just before seven, she changed from her jeans and shirt to a pair of dark slacks and a blue sweater. She descended to the streets, intending to walk until she discovered a restaurant that appealed. The evening was cool and calm, the murky canal waters slithering silently past. She wandered past the *Oude Kerk* – the Old Church – which was undergoing an extensive renovation. The vast brick and stone edifice faced onto Voorburgwal, on the east bank of the River Amstel, the quiet waters of the canal reflecting its reddish-grey brick and stone splendor. She recalled that it had been built sometime in the 1300's. And that it had been added to and extended over the centuries, and that a very famous and huge organ had been installed sometime in the early 1700's. Ruefully she thought of Salvadore and his sounding like a guidebook. Well, perhaps she was no better!

The buildings at the sides of the *Oude Kerk* and behind it were a mere six feet away from the church and seemed to encroach upon it as if to strangle it. They housed part of the city's bustling prostitution business. But even here she felt safe. The narrow cobbled streets were crowded with passersby, a few here to do business, she supposed, but most not. Some of the shorts-clad tourists glanced sideways and tittered self-consciously when they saw the women who displayed themselves in the windows in varying states of undress. Others stared outright, appraisingly. The natives strolled past, oblivious to either the merchandise or the tourists.

Sylvia kept pace with the natives, stepping through the winding streets and relishing the warmth of the September evening and the activity around her. Suddenly, it felt good to be out of the closeness of her hotel room and mingling anonymously among the crowd, and her spirits lifted. Just when she was becoming tired of walking, and the need to choose a restaurant seemed to be more compelling, she heard a familiar drawl behind her. *"Cariña!* Shall we have dinner?"

She stopped short and turned. "Salvadore!" she stammered, astonished.

Smiling, he took her firmly by the arm, and led her directly into a small Indonesian restaurant with the strange name of *Kantjil en de Tijger.*

She had to explain!

He did it for her. "I can see your prior commitment did not work out?" he enquired politely.

"Yes. He – well, no, not exactly. He could not –"

"Never mind," he said with an enigmatic smile.

"But Salvadore, I –"

He shrugged. "It does not matter. You will have dinner with me instead. You like Indonesian food, I hope?"

She looked around the small place. It was simply appointed and very clean, with pristine white tablecloths. "I hope so, too," she said with a smile.

He declined the menu and ordered for them both. She thought his dictatorial manners mildly annoying, but didn't bother to protest. At least dinner should be interesting, if only for the surprise of it.

They were both silent until the waiter brought two glasses of a light white wine. Salvadore lifted his glass to her in a small salute and took a drink. "Sylvia," he said then. "You were angry with me earlier."

She shook her head. "Not angry. Annoyed, perhaps."

"Because I did not tell you my nationality?"

"It seemed an absurd bit of information to withhold."

"Well, yes. I suppose it must have seemed so."

She nearly asked him the question again, but decided it was not worth ruining yet another meal.

He told her without her asking. "I am from Argentina. From Buenos Aires." From his lips, it sounded like *Buenos Eye-rees.*

She kept her astonishment to herself. "So why didn't you just tell me that?"

"Well, because many Europeans look down upon South Americans."

"I'm not European."

His brow furrowed as if he still believed her to be Czech. "North Americans as well," he said.

"I have not observed that. But I'm not from South America, and you are. So I'm sure you would know better than I." She was surprised that such a concern would even faze him. He seemed to be so self-assured. Well, who could tell? People reacted differently. Perhaps he'd been treated poorly in the past because of it.

Their meal began to arrive, dish after tiny dish of a vast variety of food, placed in groupings on warming plates. She looked at Salvadore in astonishment.

"It's called *rijsttafel*," he said. "Rice table. It is a little bit of everything with a variety of sauces so you can try many things. I am hoping you will find something among all of this that you will eat."

She smiled at his impertinence and proceeded to serve herself. Even by taking minute portions of everything, her plate was soon full. As she spooned up a bit from each dish, he gave a cheerful running dialogue of what she was about to eat. "*Loempis*, that's Chinese-style egg rolls. *Sateh*, tiny kebabs of grilled pork with spicy peanut sauce. *Perkedel*, meatballs. *Gado-gado*, vegetables in peanut sauce. *Daging smoor*, beef in soy sauce."

He then served himself, still talking nineteen to the dozen in his musical accent. "The idea is to present different tastes and textures. Conflicting. Contrasting. Bland vegetables and spicy meats. Sour and sweet. Textures both soft and crunchy. And all to be eaten with a bit of steamed rice. Hence the name, *rijsttafel*. Rice table." His narrative didn't slow down until he himself had started to eat.

She found everything to be delicious and told him so.

"I am most happy that you finally decide I am a success at something," he said. "You did not like the motorcycle ride yesterday and you did not like your lunch today."

"I did not appreciate your obstinate refusal to tell me your nationality," she reminded him sharply.

"Yes. *Claro*. Of course. Well. I have remedied that."

She smiled to herself at his disconcerted stammer and applied more spicy peanut sauce to her plate. "I would like to live for awhile in Argentina," she said. "In fact, I had debated whether to travel there when I leave Amsterdam, or perhaps to go to Turkey instead. Istanbul."

"Surely not alone?"

"Of course alone. That's how I travel. I stay in a place for several weeks or months rather than trying to see a lot of places in a short time. And I stay alone."

"But here you are not alone," he said.

"Except for you this evening," she said, "I am alone."

"But you are meeting someone here?"

She stopped eating and looked directly into his eyes. "Have I said so?"

"Yes," he said around a mouthful of spiced pork.

"Indeed. How so?"

"You said you had a commitment."

"So I did." She was not giving over. Not much, anyway.

"Well?" He was still on a fishing expedition. It put her on her guard.

"And you interpreted that to mean that I was meeting someone?" she said, taking a sip of her crisp white wine.

"I did."

"What of it?" she said more sharply than she had intended.

"Now, *cariña, no te enojes.*"

She lifted a brow. "I beg yours?"

His lips split into a broad grin, exposing white teeth. "Don't get testy. Again."

She smiled and let it go.

He continued to grin. But he didn't let it go. "You are meeting a man here." It was a statement, not a question.

"Am I?"

"Yes."

"Why do you think so?"

"Because when I first met you tonight, you started to say something about *him.*"

"Aren't you observant?" Her sarcasm was gentle.

"I am," he said.

She did not respond.

"Is he still planning to meet you? Perhaps he was just delayed."

She put down her fork and moved both hands to her lap. Her back straightened ominously and her chin came up. But he didn't know her well enough to detect this particular minefield. "I hardly see why that is your concern, considering you were reluctant to tell me even your nationality," she said somewhat sharply.

He was not at all put off. "Of course it's my concern," he said pleasantly. "If this man, your friend, does not meet you here, then I can have you to myself for awhile longer."

She raised a brow at his insolence. "You do not have me to yourself," she said.

"But I do." He gestured around the small room, empty now except for the patient waiter who was clearing the nearby tables.

"You know what I mean." She was getting annoyed with him again.

"Apparently I do not."

"I am just having dinner with you," she said. "That is all."

His unfathomable eyes suddenly snapped with humor. "And a museum and lunch earlier today, and a motorcycle ride yesterday. Oh, yes, I most certainly do have you to myself."

Then her sense of the ridiculous overcame her temper and she laughed, relaxing a bit and letting down her guard.

But in spite of his light demeanor, he persisted. "Is he still planning to come?"

His persistence was annoying, but harmless. "He is."

"When?"

"Really, Salvadore –"

"Tomorrow?"

She sighed in exasperation. "Yes. Tomorrow. Are you satisfied?"

"Qué lástima."

"What a pity," she said.

He nodded. *"Sí.* A pity he is coming so soon."

In her mind she was uncertain whether she agreed or disagreed with him. Her reaction to Nico's message had dismayed her. She smiled at Salvadore. Perhaps she should spend more time with him since he seemed so interested in being with her. It might take her mind off Nico and relieve the rawness of her emotions. Those emotions were a warning to her that she had let herself slip by caring more than she should, and certainly more than she had ever intended. Nico was just a friend. If that. That much was clear from his letters. But it had not been clear from his words and his touch when he had left her in Czechoslovakia. She trembled again to recall them.

Salvadore's fingers on the back of her hand returned her to the present. "What is it?" he said, concerned.

She shook her head. "Just someone dancing over my grave," she said.

He frowned. "I do not know that English – *el modismo.*" His brow wrinkled and then cleared. "That English *idioma.* No. I mean, that English idiom."

"Never mind. It was just a fleeting remembrance of a confusing time."

His sharp eyes seemed to reveal more knowledge than he could possibly have gotten from her. "What is his name?"

She looked away. "I don't wish to speak of it," she said.

He might just as well have not heard her. "Is he a friend? Or do you care for him?"

This time he truly had crossed over the line. Never mind that she didn't know the answer. "Really, Salvadore, I hardly think that is any of your business."

He was not put off. "I suppose not," he said agreeably. "But you might tell me just the same."

She turned the tables. "Are you here in Amsterdam to meet someone?"

"No," he said quickly.

Too quickly, she decided. She felt the undercurrent again but understood it no better than she had earlier in the day. "What are you doing here, then?"

"Just visiting. Like a tourist."

Still she felt the tension in him and could not make sense of it.

He picked up her hand and put the back of it to his lips. Then he grinned at her. "An Argentine custom," he said.

She smiled back at him, suddenly grateful to have him with her, flatteringly attentive on the very evening that she should have been with Nico.

Nico. Salvadore took some of the ache from her bruised feelings. His flattering attentiveness, the light white wine.

"Shall we go?" he said, and when they emerged onto the street outside she did not resist when he slipped his arm around her waist. They walked slowly along the canal, the warmth of his body pleasant against hers.

CHAPTER 4

The next morning, Sylvia was sure the pain of the previous day was gone. She had appreciated Salvadore's company, but her attention and her energies were now back on Nico. The same trepidation, the same excitement. The same emotional roller coaster.

A quick glance out of her window as she opened the curtains to the morning told her the day was going to be beautiful. No mist, unusual for a nearly-autumnal Amsterdam morning. And no indication of impending rain. Just brilliant light, Vincent van Gogh-type light, bold and intense, reflective on the canals. Too impatient to wait for her just-washed hair to dry, she combed out the wet tangles and let it go for the moment. It could dry at breakfast. She donned a simple yellow sundress and slipped on white sandals.

Then she bounded down the stairs for her tea and fruit, her exuberance reflected in the faces of her fellow guests and the hotel employees as they returned her bright smile. She had intended to linger over her tea, to make the morning seem not so long, but her energy would not be contained for more than a short time.

So she went outside and sat on the front steps, soaking up the sun. Then, thinking her hair was sufficiently dry to brush, she headed back upstairs to her room.

She burst into the room and scarcely had the brush in her hand when her eye caught sight of the telephone. The message light. Blinking off and on like the pedestrian sign just before it turned to red and released the torrent of traffic. *No!* Not again!

In some trepidation she forced herself to retrieve the message. It was the same voice which had delivered the bad news yesterday, she was sure.

And it was the same bad news. Identical, except this time *meneer* DiCapelli did not commit to coming on the next day. Rather, he would come when he could. And would Sylvia please wait?

She was not given to tantrums or gratuitous fits of fury. But she would make an exception. She wanted to slam down the receiver. Instead she replaced it with an exaggerated carefulness. And then she let fly with the hairbrush and watched it bounce off the opposite wall. The damp towel she had used to dry her hair she caught up and heaved after the hairbrush. It hit the wall with a soggy *thunk*, not half as satisfying as the sharp crack made by the hairbrush.

Really, glass would be so much more gratifying, so she picked up a wine goblet from the side table. Then she sighed and put it back down. Shards of crystal were apparently beyond the limits of her capabilities to pitch a fit.

She sank onto her bed, first sitting on the edge, then flinging herself across it, face down. Yesterday's sense of rejection, of having re-injured an old hurt, all those feelings were back in force. It was a sad fact that it took only that flashing red light on the telephone to turn a bright morning dark with unhappiness.

Sitting bolt upright on the bed, she started to think through what she should do. She would leave! She had planned only a short time here in Amsterdam. At Nico's invitation. Well, she had obligations, too. She would go to a travel agent near the hotel and get a booking for Istanbul. Or Buenos Aires. *Buenos Eye-rees*. Wherever. But with no forwarding address for Nico DiCapelli, that much was certain.

She bounced off the bed and placed her room key in the pocket of her jeans.

The telephone rang.

The jangling sound scraped her nerves, and she felt her heartbeat quicken. Nico! Oh, was he going to get an earful! She steeled herself. She was ready.

But when she lifted the receiver and said, "Hello?" she thought her voice sounded breathless and vulnerable. It irritated her. She did not want Nico to know how she felt.

She needn't have worried. It was not Nico.

"*Cariña!*" Salvadore's musical drawl came through the wire. Her heart plummeted. Again. He paused. "*Cariña?*" he repeated, this time somewhat cautiously. "Are you there?"

"I am here."

"Is your man coming today as planned?"

"He is not my man, Salvadore. And no, apparently he is not coming today." She was shocked at how easily she had revealed what she preferred to keep close to her heart. She would have taken it back if she could. This was none of Salvadore's business.

"I am sorry." He sounded genuine.

"Yes. So am I." She sounded furious, not sorry.

"In that case, may I see you today? At breakfast, perhaps?"

"I've had breakfast."

"Oh. Well. *Claro.* I see." Not at all his style. He was practically stammering again.

She felt immediately guilty for unloading her disappointment onto him. He, at least, seemed pleased to spend time with her. Unlike Nico, who was apparently too busy with other commitments. "But I would be pleased to sit with you while you eat," she said.

"Would you?" His apparent pleasure lifted her mood.

"Of course," she said.

"And perhaps afterwards we can take out one of the canal boats?" he suggested. "It is a brilliant day."

He could have been inviting her to join him in a visit to a local pig farm. Her response would have been the same. "Oh, thank you, Salvadore. I would like that."

"Sylvia."

"Yes?"

"Perhaps I shall ask you for the entire day."

"And perhaps I shall agree to that."

"And dinner as well?"

"Perhaps. No. Yes. Dinner as well." Let Nico show up now. She'd tell him that *she* had a commitment, and he could just wait for her.

"*Excelente!* When can I expect you downstairs?"

"When can you be here?"

"I am here now." There was a smile in his voice that warmed her.

She threw caution to the winds. "In that case, I am coming right down."

And down she went, running her fingers through her still-damp hair and abandoning her notebook and pen in her room.

CHAPTER 5

The day was truly a delight. The sun was warm, the winds were calm, unusual for this low, flat terrain. Salvadore seemed set upon charming her, and she let him. She managed to keep her thoughts off Nico, and onto the lively city around her. Salvadore hired a small canal boat which he piloted as expertly as he had controlled that beast of a motorcycle, but in a substantially more moderated fashion. They glided through the confusing morass of canals, beneath the arched brick bridges and past the vast open air markets, including the famous Albert Cuyp flower market. And, of course, past row upon row of houses, narrow and tall and all attached one to the next in order to save the precious land that had been reclaimed – or more accurately, claimed – from the sea with the unflappable Dutch gift for poldering. No mere river or ocean would deny the Dutch their prime real estate! The newly created islands in the basin of the River IJ were, in fact, completely artificial. Stolen from the river.

She was easy with Salvadore, just enjoying his company, just taking him and, indeed, the day at face value, not probing below the surface.

In the afternoon, after a quick lunch of shrimp salads at a canal-side café, she consented to ride behind him on his fierce black motorcycle, with a firm agreement that he would terrorize neither her nor the poor pedestrians and the other drivers. He kept his part of the bargain and she was content to keep her arms around his narrow waist and her body pressed to his back as they rumbled out of the city and into the flat, below-sea level countryside. They flew past farms of nearly-spent flowers, and fields where the stubble of the harvested grains had dried golden. Black and white sandwich-cookie cattle grazed in square pastures with grey stone fences. Permanent-looking houses of the same stone as the fences and a windmill here and there completed the picturesque stereotype of Holland. Indeed, it looked more like a postcard than the postcard itself.

They both enjoyed the day, neither attempting to tread into the other's private territory or thoughts. He touched her rather more often than she was used to or would normally allow. Her hair – often! – her arm, her hand, a light pressure at the small of her back. So she did allow it, deciding it was yet another Argentine custom. But in truth, she liked the warmth, the closeness of him, and thought his touch was welcome and non-threatening.

In the evening she left him in the lobby for a bit and dashed upstairs to brush the tangles from her hair. The moment she entered the room, her gaze went automatically to the telephone.

No message from Nico.

The brightness of the day dimmed, and her eyes stung with tears.

Damn him! She was determined not to feel anything. She had learned that when one blocks out an emotion, its loss immediately dims the brilliance of all others. Perhaps it is the lack of comparison of the extremes. How can one have great joy if one refuses to suffer great sorrow? Or perhaps the act of blocking out cannot be confined to only one emotion. If she blocked one, she blocked them all. In any case, she had learned to suppress pain and vulnerability and had relinquished joy and caring in the process. And thought it well worth the cost. At least for today.

Well, *this* was why she had denied the damnable pain. Although she had been married very young and for only a few months, her former husband's infidelity and cruelty and death had scarred her, and had caused her to build fences around herself. No, not fences. Walls! Thick walls, made of the granite rocks of sheer determination, and sealed by the mortar of a relentless pain. She had built it, stone by cold grey stone, in the months she had spent in the lovely but bleak city of Edinburgh, Scotland immediately after her cheating husband's death, and her dutiful attendance at his funeral. Yes, she had put herself back together again. But at what cost? As Nico had said, she had built a fortress against the world, constructed with stones as formidable as those of Edinburgh Castle itself, high upon the hill overlooking that ancient city.

And now Nico had breached that wall, and to her cynical lack of surprise, he was bringing through the rift pain rather than joy.

Damn him for making her care. Damn *her* for allowing him to make her care.

Resolutely she turned to the mirror and brushed the wind from her hair, the honey-colored waves shimmering gold and red. She changed her jeans for a light dress of a blue that matched her eyes, the hem of which skimmed a few inches above her knees. She slipped on a pair of strappy white sandals that she had found in Prague and bought just for this trip. Checking the mirror one more time before she left her room, she smiled at herself in satisfaction. "You may not be enough of a woman to bring Nico DiCapelli to Amsterdam," she told the pale face that gazed back at her. "But you are apparently more than enough to keep Salvadore interested."

She descended the stairs slowly, wondering whether it were really a good idea to be with Salvadore when she was in this vulnerable state. She stopped wondering when she saw him. He waited at the bottom of the wide, wood-carved staircase. He wore blue jeans and a plain dark green t-shirt and was leaning on the banister in an apparently negligent manner. His dark eyes watched her descend to him, his face touched with a smile of appreciation and greeting. When she returned his smile, her own was genuine.

"*Cariña*," he said, raising her hand to his lips in the gesture that she had earlier found annoying but now found endearing. His eyes went from her face to her body and his smile widened. "Indeed, you are beautiful," he said. "*Mi cariña*."

She flushed slightly in pleasure, wondering what the translation was, but he didn't enlighten her.

He grinned at her discomfiture and, tucking her hand under his arm, he led her outside.

The mild weather held into evening. Warm, but not hot. No wind, not even the hint of a breeze. The streets were lively with passersby and he led her down one alley so narrow it was barely wide enough for a single car, or even for two pedestrians side by side unless they were walking very close. And certainly not both cars and pedestrians at the same time.

Salvadore guided her past vehicles and around pedestrians, undaunted by the closeness of the walls. They meandered by shops, one after the other, most still open for business. The street curved in such a steady manner that Sylvia was sure they would eventually circle around to where they had begun, at the Hotel Amstel Grand.

But just before the narrow way opened onto yet another canal, Salvadore drew her to a halt and turned into a small restaurant.

"What is it tonight?" she asked, having become used to his dictatorial surprises.

"*Portugués*," he said, opening the door for her. "Portuguese. Although the name certainly is not. This is *Café Carpershoek*. That's about as Dutch as you can get."

She stepped inside ahead of him. The room was nearly vacant, and the hour was the main time for dining for the Dutch, who preferred to take their evening meal early. It didn't bode well for the quality of the place, she thought as she took in the small room with its few tables to the left and a bar with a line of empty stools on the right.

The proprietor was a hefty blond man with very pink cheeks and a pristine white apron. He greeted them heartily, as well he might, she thought. Any customer would be welcome here! With a flourish of the napkins, he seated them at a table for two – barely large enough for two, in fact – that was directly in front of the bay window that jutted into the street. It was spread with a crisp white tablecloth as clean as the apron, and a single candle in the center of the table wavered and danced a spark of light into the emptiness of the room.

"We will be *el anuncio*, the advertisement to the rest of Amsterdam that his restaurant is open and worth trying," said Salvadore with a grin.

The strategy, if indeed it had been a strategy, must have worked. By the time Salvadore had ordered – for both of them! – the place was filling up. And by the time the proprietor brought their *piri piri* chicken, even the stools at the bar were taken, and the place rang with the cheerful din of a popular dinner place.

She was glad to be with Salvadore rather than alone. Alone was all right. She liked to be alone, to eat alone. Indeed, often she preferred it. But this night, alone seemed too painful. And Salvadore was better than average company. So she ate her spicy meal and drank the robust red wine he poured for her.

Instead of just ordering a glass of wine for each of them, this time he had ordered the entire bottle. With his teasing, flirtatious company and the spiciness of her chicken, she drank more wine than she normally would have. In fact, she quite lost track of how much she had drunk because he unobtrusively kept her glass filled. She was quite astonished when he ordered a second bottle. The first had gone rather quickly, she thought.

Salvadore was entirely charming. He charmed the proprietor, who called him his good luck token for filling his establishment. He charmed the Dutch couple at the next table with his fractured pronunciation of their language. And he charmed Sylvia. In spite of his ongoing repartee with others in the room, in truth, his eyes were for her only, and his touch assured her of his attention.

He was casting a spell, and she knew it, and she allowed herself to be caught in his gentle net.

She was surprised at how quickly the evening had flown by when their coffee came and Salvadore eyed her over the rim of his cup. "We shall walk awhile?" he said.

She thought it sounded like a good idea. Perhaps it would clear the wine from her head. And so they stepped out into the still-warm night, with him keeping a firm hold on her hand.

They did not walk far down Voorburwal. Near the *Oude Kerk* he led her into a small bar, the *Bep Nieuwezijds*. There was only one stool available in the crowded, smoky place, and he seated her upon it and ordered for them both. All Sylvia heard was *"borrel."* The barman placed two small stemmed crystal glasses onto the bar in front of them and filled them with a clear liquid from a brown clay bottle until the glasses were so full they could not be moved without spilling the liquor.

Sylvia looked to Salvadore for direction.

"Gynefer," he said, leaning close so that she could hear him. "A Dutch liqueur, made from juniper. Dutch gin. It is called *kamelenrug*. Camel's back. It means 'filled to the brim.' You must take the first taste without removing the glass from the bar so as not to spill. Then before drinking any more, you must offer a toast."

"Please show me," she said.

He grinned at her and then bent to one of the glasses on the bar and took a sip without touching the glass with his hands. "Now, you must do the same," he said.

Holding her honey-colored hair back out of her way with both hands, she followed suit. The liqueur was powerful, with a bite. She felt the fumes go through her nostrils and into her head even as the liquid burned down her throat.

"A bit strong, no?" He was standing next to her where she was perched on the stool, and he had his arm around her waist. She realized that she had allowed herself to lean into him slightly, but before she could think on that he lifted his glass to her. "Now," he said. "A toast."

She lifted hers.

"I will say the toast," he instructed. "And then we both must drink it down."

"All of it?"

"All of it."

"At once?"

"Yes. All at once."

"Oh, I don't think so –"

He ignored her half-hearted protest. He touched his glass to hers and said, "To your beautiful hair, *cariña. Proost!* And *salud!*" And he downed his liqueur in one swallow.

She took another sip.

"Oh, no," he said. "No. You cannot do that. It is the custom in *Holanda*. You must do it properly." He picked up her glass, grasped her chin with his fingers, and put the drink to her lips. She thought to protest, but the glass tipped up and she swallowed, nearly choking on the strength of it. He grinned and ran his thumb along her lower lip.

He also must have motioned to the bartender for another round, because before Sylvia quite knew what was happening, the clay bottle had appeared once more and the clear liqueur trembled at the top edge of the glasses, threatening to spill over. The camel's back.

She pulled back from him. "Oh, no, Salvadore. I've had quite enough."

"Sorry, *cariña*. But you cannot have only one. Because you must make the next toast."

"Don't be absurd," she protested.

He leaned to the bar and took the level of the liquid in his glass down a bit. "Now," he said. "You."

She shook her head, knowing her limit.

He raised a brow and bent to her glass and sipped enough to make it manageable. Then he handed it to her and picked up his own. "There. I have helped you. Now, the toast."

"But, Salvadore –"

"The toast, Sylvia."

Perhaps it was the wine and the gynefer. Perhaps it was Salvadore's arm around her waist, and his warm breath on her cheek and ear. Without quite knowing why and completely against her better judgment, she lifted the glass to him. "To your motorcycle," she said. "And your nose. *Proost!* And *salud!*"

"My nose?" He laughed and put down his glass. He guided the other glass to her lips and tipped it up until the contents were drained. Then he downed his own.

She suddenly felt a bit unsteady on the stool and leaned into him. He pulled her closer. "Another one?" he murmured, smoothing her thick waves gently, sensuously, back from her face.

She shook her head, half-expecting him to ignore her response.

"It has a bit of a kick," he said. "And you don't have much body weight. Probably two is enough."

They did not have more to drink, but they did stay in the bar for a good while longer. It became even more crowded, and the other customers jostled against them. Salvadore moved closer to her, and they talked. It was small talk for the most part, and a light banter. She had shut her emotions away for a long time, so it was a good feeling to enjoy his company and to know that he enjoyed hers. He gestured as he spoke, with the hand that was not clasped at her waist. Like an Italian, she thought ruefully. Like Nico. And when he was not gesturing, he rested his free hand on her thigh. The hem of her dress seemed to climb a bit, and she was conscious of the warmth of his hand. Rather than alarming her, his closeness seemed natural and she did not resist when his long fingers moved to her throat and his thumb gently lifted her chin and his lips came down upon hers.

His touch was light but with an undercurrent of possessive demand. In her mind, she knew she should pull back, knew she should stop this game before it went any further. But her body ignored the warnings and her hands slid up his chest and around to his nape where the dark hair curled, and her lips responded to his.

Again the warning nagged at her. She had to stop. She had to pull away. But she didn't. She didn't want to stop.

Before she was quite aware that it had happened, he had slid her from the stool and held her against his side as he pushed their way through the teeming crowd and outside into the fresh air. She took a deep breath, clearing her lungs of the cigarette smoke. Still holding her close, he walked with her down Korte Niezel to the Hotel Grand Amstel.

Once inside the deserted lobby, he released her waist and interlaced his fingers with hers and led her up the stairs. Directly to her room he brought her, and she was too foggy to wonder how he possibly could have known her room number. She fumbled for her key and he took it from her and opened the door.

She started to step inside. "Thank you, Salvadore," she began. The next instant she found herself pulled hard against his body, his mouth on hers, an urgent groan in his throat.

She did want him. She did. She longed to feel a man's touch, a man's body. And Salvadore was attentive and fun and had a very fine body indeed. She felt his hands slide down her back to her buttocks and lift her. She felt him step just inside her room with her body held tightly against his own.

How she did want him. But even as she melted against him, she knew that he could not fill the emptiness within her. This would be nothing but a quick affair, soon over. A pleasant experience, no doubt. And somehow more enticing to her than a relationship where a commitment might be involved. Truly, she did not want to commit herself again, neither body nor heart. To commit herself to love, was to commit herself to pain.

If only it weren't for Nico.

Remembering Nico's touch caused her to draw back.

"*Cariña*," Salvadore murmured, his breath warm on her neck, one hand buried in her hair, and the other at the small of her back, pressing her body closer to his. "*Mi cariña. I want you.*" His voice sounded urgent.

Oh, yes. She did want him. Wanted him to assuage the emptiness within her. And knew that he could not. Damn her for being a hard-headed realist. "I cannot," she whispered. "Salvadore, I cannot."

She expected him to insist, to persuade. She half wished he would. He did so like to have his way. And she knew he did indeed want her. Her own body gave a quiver of regret as he pulled back from her.

"*Seguras?* Are you sure?"

She most certainly was *not* sure. In fact, the truth was that she *did* want him. Now. But her words betrayed her body's needs. "Yes," she whispered. "Yes. I'm sure. Salvadore, please."

"Never mind, *cariña,*" he said. "Not tonight, then?"

"Not tonight. Not –"

"Perhaps another night. You can be sure, I will ask you again and again until you are ready for me. I will ask until you come to me."

She started to shake her head. She knew that she had to stop this right now, and not raise any false expectations, for either of them. But he stopped further protest by taking her lips again, and then by tracing her jaw line with his mouth, down to the vulnerable spot at her throat. She tensed and trembled and wanted to feel him urgent against her again. But he pulled back and touched her lips with his own once more. "Sleep well, *cariña,*" he said, his voice hoarse with his own desire. "I will be waiting for you in the morning when you come down for your breakfast."

He turned and left her there, and she did not move for a long time. A sound and movement further down the hallway startled her back to her senses. She closed her door but still she stood there, her fingers touching her lips where he had last kissed her, and her body taut with wanting.

CHAPTER 6

Once again Sylvia didn't sleep well, in spite of Salvadore's admonition to do so. She decided it was the wine and the gynefer. She refused to allow herself to think it had anything to do with Salvadore and his coffee-dark eyes and ready smile and insistent warm touch.

Whatever it was, after about two hours of trying to force a reluctant slumber, she gave up all pretense of sleeping at four in the morning. She wrote for a few hours until her hand began to cramp. Then she showered and dressed in jeans and a blue shirt. Slipping on sandals, she descended to the breakfast room just after it opened at six, pen and notebook in hand. She did not expect Salvadore to be there, probably not until after eight, since that is when he had rung her the day before.

She entered the room with barely a glance around at the sparkling crystal of the chandeliers or the gilt-framed paintings. Not surprisingly, given the early hour, she was alone. Well, very nearly alone. There was one other person sprawled in a chair at a table in the far corner of the room, nursing a cup of coffee.

Her heart stopped entirely, and then started up again at a rate that surely was not healthy.

He was waiting for her at breakfast, all right, dressed in blue jeans and a black t-shirt. But it was not Salvadore.

It was Nico.

All her concerns regarding how she should greet him, all her plans and calculations and schemes, all those vanished with her shock at seeing him so unexpectedly.

Her first emotion was disbelief, followed hard upon by joy. All of her frustration and anger, all her hurt, all her determined reserve crumbled away, at least for this moment. "Nico!" she cried, but it came out a mere whisper.

He had seen her before she saw him, and he was already coming to his feet. She stepped towards him, the distance across the room feeling as though there were still miles between them, but miles that were brought to nothing in just a few steps.

"Sylvia," he said, and she heard pleasure and relief and something else that would not come to her in that second.

His arms opened and he reached for her in what seemed an almost involuntary gesture. Then a shadow passed across his face and a fine line creased his brow and he hesitated.

Her momentum kept her moving towards him even after his hesitation warned her off. "Nico!" she said again.

He took one of her hands. For a brief, sinking moment she thought he was going to grasp it and give it a firm shake, as acquaintances do. But then he pulled her close against his chest and wrapped his arms around her. She could feel his breath release in a sigh, and then he kissed the top of her head.

She started to pull back. She wanted to see his face. But he did not immediately release her and she forgot his earlier hesitation as he held her against his body, his chin resting in the honey curls of her hair.

At last, but far too soon for her, he relaxed his hold and she stood back and looked him over. "Nico," she said a third time as her eyes drank him in. Nico. He was tall, just over six feet – one meter ninety-three, he would have said – with a body that gave the impression of leanness masking a muscular strength. The lines and planes of his body and features were straight. Straight back, straight shoulders, straight jaw line, straight nose.

She knew that body. How very well she knew it. He had clutched her against its hardness in the face of certain death, first by murder on a narrow trail in the mountains of northern Czechoslovakia, and later near there in an ancient hillfort where they had been imprisoned and left to die of exposure and thirst. And he had held her, to protect her against not only the cold but also against the hopelessness of their situation. And then she had held him, to protect him from his fever and concussion and claustrophobia, and his ultimate outrage against their very rescuers. Oh, yes. She knew this body, better than a mere lover ever could have.

His hair was very dark, nearly black, from his Italian father, she remembered. It was a bit longer than it had been when she had last seen him, but even so showed no tendency to curl. His eyes were a greenish hazel, almost startling against his tanned Mediterranean skin. His mother's eyes. At the moment those eyes were fixed upon her with a hunger that confused her. She thought him handsome, with one of his greatest assets being that he did not realize himself that he was handsome. He had a formidably solid ego and an unerring self-confidence, to be sure, but it was tied in with his intelligence and scrupulous logic, not with his appearance.

Ah, yes, she thought him handsome. And she knew him to be kind and gentle. And brilliant and methodical. And hard-headed and stubborn and opinionated.

He was looking her over in turn, a smile pulling at one corner of his mouth. At last he spoke. "You seem surprised to see me."

Her sapphire eyes flew to meet his gaze. "And why wouldn't I be?" she said. "Given your last message."

He frowned. "My last message?"

"Yesterday morning. Saying that you were delayed but did not know for how long."

His frown deepened. "But I also called last evening to tell you I was coming very late on a flight from London's Heathrow airport. You didn't get that message?"

"No."

"Oh, Sylvia, I am sorry."

"I had intended to meet you at Schiphol." She thought she sounded reproachful.

"I know," he said gently.

She suddenly imagined his feelings when he had gotten off the plane and she had not met him as arranged. "What time did you get in?" she asked, subdued.

"I checked into this hotel around two in the morning," he said. "Since you had not been at Schiphol to meet me, I thought not to disturb you so late."

Last night at two. She thought of where she had been at that moment, and remembered the gentle rustle down the hall from her. She was grateful that she and Salvadore had not taken things any further than they did. Indeed, the morning light had given her an entirely different perspective. Salvadore was entertaining, and attentive, and made her feel – feel what? Made her feel the emptiness less sharply when she was missing Nico? In truth, more of her thoughts and feelings centered around Nico than she cared to admit.

She realized that she was still clinging to his hand. She released it quickly even as she flushed.

He grinned in response. "Ah, Sylvia," he said softly. "How I have missed you."

He was wreaking havoc with her heart rate. Good thing she came from strong stock. "And I have missed you," she said, surprised that the words came without hesitation.

His brow creased slightly. "Have you?" he said. His voice was warm but she thought she could detect something underneath. Then she chided herself for her overactive imagination. First Salvadore's fancied darkness and now Nico's innocuous question.

"I have," she replied firmly.

He took the notebook and pen from her and placed them on the table. "Still at it, I see," he said, referring to her writing as he held an upholstered chair with a straight back for her to seat herself. He sat next to her, his chair close to hers, and took her hand again.

"As are you, apparently," she replied. "Given your uncertain schedule."

"True," he said. "Sylvia." He paused for a moment, and then went on. "I was wondering, since I am so late in coming, I wonder if you could possibly extend your stay here in Amsterdam for a few days longer?"

She recalled her resolve of the day before to buy a ticket to anywhere and leave him with no forwarding address. He was presumptuous if he thought her time was so easily rearranged as that. "Of course," she said.

He looked relieved. "I don't deserve it, I know."

"Don't be daft," she said, but she smiled.

He signaled the hovering waiter to bring her tea and milk and more coffee for him, and they talked about nothing in particular for awhile. At length they both ran out of words. Nico laughed. "We're no better at small talk than we ever were," he said. "Tell me, Sylvia, how have you been occupying your time here?"

Unaccountably, she flushed again.

That fine line was back in his brow. "Writing, I suppose?"

"Of course. And wandering around the city admiring the architecture and going to the museums." She reached over and softly touched his face with one fingertip. "And you? I never know where you are."

"I know." He sounded apologetic. He hesitated, and then spoke again. "Sylvia, I have something to ask you and I don't want you to answer me until I have it all out."

Trepidation shot through her. She knew he saw it. He was still holding her hand, and now he gripped it more tightly so that she could not possibly have withdrawn it. "Yes, Nico?" she said, bracing herself for his next words, not knowing what to expect.

They never left his lips. Startling both of them, Salvadore's familiar drawl cut across the tension, if indeed it were tension. "Sylvia," he said. "I am here. As promised."

She flushed yet again and was furious with herself for that. After all, why should she apologize or feel embarrassment? Nico had no claim on her. He'd been the one who had not shown up for two days. Self-consciously, she pulled her hand from Nico's firm grasp. He let it go, one dark brow raised.

"Nico DiCapelli, this is Salvadore –" She realized for the first time that she had never learned his last name.

Salvadore smiled down on her. "Salvadore will do," he said, and extended a hand to Nico. Nico rose and took it.

Sylvia was horrified that Salvadore would make some reference to her waiting for Nico. No sooner had she thought it than he voiced it. "Sylvia has been waiting some days for your arrival, I believe?" he said.

"I was detained." Nico's voice was polite but somehow cool, perhaps even a bit frosty, and Sylvia imagined that she could see something in his face that she could neither identify nor understand. She thought that his eyes stayed locked on Salvadore's for an uncomfortably long time.

But Salvadore only shrugged. "Shall I join you?" he said.

"Of course," said Nico, gesturing to an empty chair opposite Sylvia. She thought he sounded annoyed. She herself was annoyed, unfairly, she knew. After all, she and Salvadore had agreed to meet at breakfast. At least Salvadore had shown up when he said he would.

"Nico DiCapelli," said Salvadore. "Are you Italian, then?" He caught Sylvia's eye and she laughed.

"One of your countrymen?" she said.

Salvadore grinned at her impudent humor. Nico was at sea, watching them both. Sylvia put a hand on his arm. "Salvadore is Argentine, but tries to pass himself off as an Italian," she said. She wondered at the brief shadow that passed over Salvadore's countenance like a cloud barely touching the edge of the sun.

Then she glanced at Nico, and thought Nico's attention was surely piqued. He turned those intense eyes, now more green than hazel, back onto Salvadore. "You are from Argentina?" He switched from English to Spanish, and Salvadore answered in kind.

Sylvia knew that Nico was fluent in several languages including Spanish. Even so, she was impressed. She thought his accent must be impeccable, as his speech was the rapid-fire roll-the-words-together delivery that made such music of the Latin-based languages. She knew enough to pick up a word or two, but not so that she could understand the gist of what they were saying.

Nico seemed more intense than necessary given the casual social situation. Perhaps he viewed Salvadore as a rival of sorts. She dismissed that as ludicrous, ignoring the contradiction of the previous night's activities. In fact, she felt as if last night were perhaps just a dream. It seemed too far from the reality of this moment.

Salvadore put away a sizable breakfast, but that did not slow his conversation with Nico. Nico continued to observe Salvadore and drink the thick black coffee until Sylvia thought he would surely float away.

Suddenly, Salvadore switched back to English. *"Cariña!"* he said. *"Disculpe!* I am so sorry to exclude you from our conversation."

Again, that faint line crossed Nico's brow. Sylvia did not know how to interpret it. Then suddenly Nico reached over and took one of her hands. Salvadore's gaze followed the movement, then he moved his eyes to Sylvia's face. *"Cariña,"* he said, this time deliberately, she was sure. Deliberately baiting Nico. *"Cariña,* I shall leave you to your *amigo."*

He rose and Nico did likewise and again they shook hands. Salvadore reached past and took Sylvia's hand that Nico had been grasping. He lifted it, and turned it, and kissed her open palm. But his eyes were on Nico, not Sylvia.

Nico gave not a tremor. Then Salvadore spoke. "Shall we meet for dinner as planned, Sylvia? You are also invited, DiCapelli."

Sylvia watched Nico, but neither his body nor his expression gave away any emotion. She knew that such restraint came from not only his inborn nature, but also from his intense training. "Thank you, Salvadore," he said.

Sylvia started to speak, intending to remind Salvadore that she had not promised to meet him for dinner, but Nico cut across her. "I would be pleased to join the two of you. There is an excellent French restaurant, *Le Maîson Descartes*, at the French Embassy on Vijzelstraat just past a major canal. Prinsengracht, I think. Shall I make reservations for eight o'clock?"

Salvadore looked momentarily caught off guard. His gaze went from Nico to Sylvia and back to Nico. *"Bueno,"* he said easily. "All right. Enjoy your day." He left the room without looking back.

Sylvia was acutely uncomfortable, but Nico appeared perfectly at ease. "Seems like a nice person," he said, sitting back down. "How did you run across him?"

"Oh, that's just about the right way to say it," she said. "I was crossing the street at Oudezijds Achterburgwal and Damstraat – that's a mouthful! – and ran into his motorcycle."

"Ran into it?"

"Yes. Literally. I was a bit late making the curb."

"Good lord! You should pay better attention!"

She remembered that at the time she had been contemplating Nico himself. "Yes, I should have," she said. "And I should have heard him approaching. The motorcycle was so loud. It roared. Actually, it throbbed."

"Harley," he said.

She was startled. "I beg yours?"

"Harley Davidson. American-made."

"How can you possibly know what kind of motorcycle it was?"

"You said that it throbbed. Harleys throb."

"Oh, indeed?" She sounded disbelieving.

He laughed. "Yes. Indeed." Still he held her hand. "What would you like to do today?" he asked.

"I don't know," she said. She wondered what he would prefer. It struck her that she knew him very well, but barely knew him at all.

"Let's walk," he said. "I still haven't worked out the kinks from my last long flight." He stood up and stretched, bringing her up with him.

"I thought you flew in from Heathrow." The words were out of her mouth before she had considered them. She knew better than to ask where he had been assigned.

But he did not react. "I did, last night," he said. "But the flight to London was a long one."

That could have been from anywhere, perhaps even the moon, for all she knew. But his job did not allow a sharing of any further information. She thought his work was clandestine, more like a work of fiction than a real job. All over the world he traveled, but his mail always came and went through a discreet London address. Perhaps her next novel would be about him and his job, not even needing the embellishments of her considerable imagination.

Nico used a hotel phone to call *Le Maîson Descartes* for a reservation, and then they went out into the early morning sunlight, again unstained by any mist, and strolled aimlessly, hand in hand, along the canals. Before Sylvia had realized what he was doing, somehow Nico managed to bring the conversation back to Salvadore. "Where did you say he was from?" he asked.

"Argentina," she said. "Buenos Aires."

"Argentina." He repeated it thoughtfully.

"Actually, it's a bit odd," she said. "First, he said he was Italian, but I didn't believe him. He got quite annoyed about that, although I don't think he knew that I noticed."

"Italian?"

"Yes. Like you, I'd guess."

He watched her closely. "Why didn't you believe him?"

"Something about the way he had hesitated when I asked him. He was too, well, too coy by half. So I called him on it."

"And then he said he was Argentine."

"Yes, but not immediately. It seemed as if he had to think whether or not to tell me the truth, but I don't know why."

Nico said, "I do."

She looked at him sharply. "You do?"

He lifted a dark brow, momentarily giving his expression a quizzical look. "Because he is *not* from Argentina."

She stared at him in astonishment. "How can you possibly know that?"

"He told me."

"When you were speaking Spanish?"

Nico grinned and squeezed her hand. "In a way."

"In what way?"

"He did not tell me outright where he was from. But he is not Argentine. The Argentine Spanish is quite different from the Spanish spoken in the rest of the countries of South America, and indeed, in the world. Especially the Spanish spoken in Buenos Aires by the *porteños*, the natives of the port." The city's name, Buenos Aires, came past his lips in the same fashion as it had come from Salvadore's. *Buenos Eye-rees.*

She was intrigued. "How so?"

"Well, first of all, his pronunciation of several words was not right. The most obvious difference was the way he said words with *ll*. Double '*l*'. Not terribly unusual, but much of South America would pronounce that with a '*y*' sound. In Argentina, it is distinctly different, more like '*zh*'. Same with the '*y*'. It is pronounced '*zh*' as well. Like *Plaza de Mayo* is *Plaza de Mazho*." He was warming to his subject. "And grammatically, the informal pronoun '*you*' is '*tu*' in most other Spanish-speaking countries, but is '*vos*' in Argentina. Well, and in Uruguay and Paraguay, but to a lesser extent."

"More like the Castilian Spanish of Spain, then?"

He shrugged and frowned. "Well, in a way. But even Argentine Spanish might sound provincial to a Spaniard. At least the Spaniards would say so. Argentine Spanish, as the Argentines will be quick to tell you, is actually *castellano*." He slurred the "*ll*" into a "*zh*". *Castezhano*. "Not Spanish at all. And they would most certainly deny that their *castellano* is provincial. One Argentine friend told me that it's Spain's Castilian that is provincial, that Argentine speakers have held more true to the origins of the language." He grinned and shook his head at the cheerful audacity of the Argentines. "But the vocabulary and the pronunciation apart, his accent was a dead giveaway. The language of the Argentines, especially in Buenos Aires, where he said he's from, has a very heavy, very distinctive Italian accent. Even though the area was originally settled by the Spaniards, and they certainly brought their own language, there are actually more Italian immigrants than Spanish there now. There was a huge influx of Italians in the 1800's, and they brought their culture, and their food. And their accents! Particularly from the Genoese dialect, as many came from that part of northwestern Italy. In some of the neighborhoods of Buenos Aires, they call themselves the *xeneize*. The Genoese."

Sylvia was mesmerized. "So when you spoke with him, did you speak the Argentine *castellano*?"

He gave a short laugh. "Oh, no. I did exactly what he would have expected. Being from the United States, I spoke like a northerner. Mexican Spanish. About as far from *castellano* as one can get and still be speaking the same language."

She frowned, intrigued by Nico's knowledge, but troubled by Salvadore's seemingly unimportant deception. "Why would he lie?" she asked.

"Why, indeed?"

If he had implied a question, she ignored it. "Do you know what else was odd? He thought that I was from Czechoslovakia."

Nico stopped short. Since he had a firm hold on her hand, she stopped short as well. The man walking behind them nearly ran them over and muttered an expletive as he passed by. Sylvia murmured an apology but Nico didn't notice. "Czechoslovakia? Why?"

"He thought that my English had a Czech accent."

She could see Nico's methodical mind working it through. "Czechoslo-vakia." He said it almost to himself. Then unexpectedly he reached out and dragged the fingers of his free hand through her long curls. "There's some-thing not right about this," he said, his brow lining in thought.

"Not right about what?"

"That he would lie about his own origins and then guess yours as Czech. Why not any Slavic country? The differences and subtleties in Slavic-accented English are too minor to pick up from just a conversation. With much accuracy, anyway."

"Unless it was just a lucky guess?"

"Perhaps," he said.

She could tell from his tone that he did not believe it. "Too coinciden-tal?" she said.

He shook his head and replied. "No." Then he said, "Yes. Too coinci-dental."

There was something on his mind that he was not quite willing to share. She thought it must have something to do with his work, but couldn't be sure. She never could be quite sure when it came to Nico. His natural reserve and the confidentiality of his work were a formidable combination. She let it pass, and he did not pursue the topic further.

The weather and city were accommodating, the rays from the brilliant sun moving over the buildings and keeping any chill at bay. Amsterdam was its charming self, its canals and bridges and cobblestones impossibly quaint. The day was long, like a drawn-out dream.

But paradoxically, the day was short, like being awakened too suddenly from that dream, and seemed to slip away too quickly, fading into the late afternoon. They were easy and comfortable with each other and Nico kept claim to her hand, or an arm around her waist for most of the day. He spoke of countries where he had been when he'd had a bit of time away from his work, a few days here and there in places that may have given a hint of where he was sporadically assigned. Perhaps. Or perhaps not. He mentioned the rugged, rocky beauty of the west coast of Sweden, and the tiny islands where people had lived for centuries and where the Swedes had matter of factly hidden their Jewish neighbors from the murderous Nazis during the Second World War. She remembered the two Swedes, Gunnar and Anders, who had been assigned with him in Czechoslovakia. And then he described the flaming volcano, *Volcán* Pacaya in Guatemala, spewing forth cinder and fire from its smoldering caldera as he had stood teetering on its rim looking down at the roiling, crimson spectacle, the intense heat searing his face and body even as the over-heated rocks were hurtled angrily past his head.

But he never spoke of his assignments, of his work, and she did not press him. She was content just to be in his company. She had imagined being tentative and uncomfortable but he seemed extraordinarily pleased to be with her, and it seemed so natural to be walking at his side that her trepidation was soon forgotten. She refused to allow herself to think ahead to any kind of future, or to worry about protecting feelings and guarding against any commitment. Rather she just enjoyed the day. And she enjoyed *Nico*. Salvadore had managed to ease the empty place within her. But when she was with Nico, there was no empty place to ease.

It was half-past six when they wandered back to the hotel. Her long hair was wind-blown and wild and she felt overly-warm and a bit weary from walking all day. Again she wished that she was having dinner with Nico, and Nico alone, that Salvadore would find other entertainment. She knew it was selfish of her and probably rude as well. Even so. Her time with Nico was fleeting and dear and she wanted to guard it jealously.

He took her directly to her room. His own was just one door down the hall on the same side as hers. "Can you be ready by seven-fifteen?" he said, grinning as he touched her irascible hair. "Or will it take longer to work out the tangles?"

She thought his comment was rather too near to Salvadore's on the same topic. She smiled up at him. "I can be ready," she said. "Where shall I meet you?"

"I'll pick you up here at your room." He hesitated. "Sylvia –"

Inquiringly, she looked up at him. He took her face in both of his hands. He bent to her and kissed her. Gently, lightly, with no possessive demand. More like a tender promise, but with a barely-constrained passion. "See you in awhile," he said softly.

She took a quick shower to wash away the dust of the day, knowing her hair would not be dry by the time Nico came for her, but not caring. It could dry as they walked. She had only just stepped out of the shower and wrapped a towel around herself and made a turban of another on her wet head when there was a sharp knock at the door. Before she could reach it, the knock came again, more insistent.

There was no security peep, so she stepped close. "Yes?" she said.

"Sylvia." It was Nico. "Let me in."

"I'm not dressed. Just a minute."

"Sylvia!" He sounded more urgent. "Come on. I need to see you. Now."

She hesitated and then unbolted the door and opened it.

He shoved it open and stepped inside and closed the door with a snap. Then he looked at her. His intense green-hazel gaze raked from her turbaned head to her face to her towel and surely to her very toes before returning to her face. "Good lord," he breathed, the words catching in his throat.

She was flooded with an embarrassed self-consciousness. "I *told* you I wasn't dressed," she said in weak protest.

He took a step towards her. Then to her relief – and dismay! – he stopped. "Sylvia," he said, a hunger in his voice.

"Please. Sit down." Her own voice was trembling. She pointed to the chair at the desk.

He shook his head, still watching her. "I can't. I just need to speak with you."

"Go ahead. I will start my hair drying while you talk, if you don't mind." She pulled the towel from her head with one hand and began threading her fingers through the wet curls to ease out the tangles. He watched her every move, the hunger in his face not easing in the least.

Then he seemed to regain his senses with a great effort. "I need to leave," he said abruptly.

"What?" Her fingers halted midway in her long tresses.

"I've been called back to London."

Her heart stopped, and her insides froze. The icy pain shot through her breast, a familiar sensation. But just for a breathless moment. Then she steeled herself. A bit late, yes, but effective, nonetheless. "I see." Her voice sounded as cold as her heart.

He heard it. "I'm sorry. Sylvia, you can't know how sorry. It's for a very short time."

"How short?"

"Out tonight. Back tomorrow. Late morning or early afternoon. I promise you."

She shrugged. "All right." She tried to sound as if she didn't care.

His eyes showed his hurt, and his voice was pleading. "Sylvia. Please understand."

She had no choice but to distance herself. Her very survival was at stake. "Oh, I do understand." Truly she did not mean it in a sarcastic fashion. Even so, it came out that way.

He flinched. "It's an unusual – well, it's an unusual circumstance. Or I would not be called back just now."

"I don't know how much longer I can stay in Amsterdam, Nico," she said. "You aren't the only one with obligations."

She could see in his face that he wanted to challenge that statement. He didn't. Perhaps he didn't care enough to challenge. Perhaps he was afraid that she would reject his words, would reject him. Or perhaps he just didn't want an argument.

He got one in any case with his next statement.

"I want you to stay away from San – well, I mean from Salvadore while I'm gone."

His tone, his words set her off. "Oh, really?" Her chin lifted.

She saw that he knew her well enough to recognize the warning in her straight posture and stubborn chin. Still, apparently he had no choice but to forge ahead. "Yes. Really."

"I don't suppose Salvadore to be any of your business."

He looked taken aback at her sharp response. "Salvadore is most certainly my business," he said.

"How so?"

He scowled. "I don't want him around you."

"Don't be absurd. If I didn't see anyone else when you weren't around, I'd never see anyone at all."

He gestured impatiently. "You're missing the point."

"Suppose you tell me what the point is?" she challenged him. She had forgotten that she was standing there clad only in a towel, her damp hair drying in wild disarray without her attention.

"The point is that you don't know anything about him and yet you're – you're spending time with him."

"Really, Nico. I've known him for a few days, and we've walked around Amsterdam and had a bit of lunch."

"And that's all, is it?" The moment the words left his lips he looked as if he'd like to snatch them back.

She stared at him. "What on earth are you talking about?"

He let out his breath in an exasperated sigh and looked away. "Never mind," he said.

"I *do* mind." She was on a mission now. "Tell me what you meant."

He brought his gaze back to her. "All right," he said. "I'll tell you. I saw you and Salvadore in the hallway when I arrived last night. Well, actually today. Around two in the morning. *This* morning."

She flushed in embarrassment. And in fury. "Were you spying on me?"

Anger flashed across his face. "*Dio!* I most certainly was not. I had just checked in and was going to my bloody room."

She wanted to explain to him what was between her and Salvadore. She wanted to describe to him the empty place within her, and her pain at his absences and delays. But she could not expose such raw feelings, such vulnerability. "I had no way of knowing whether you would actually show up," she said.

"I *told* you I was coming," he said, his voice intense with determined control.

"And I was to sit in my room alone until you finally decided to arrive?"

"Of course not. Sylvia, you know, well, you know that I – that I –" His voice trailed off.

She felt a sharp pain inside of her. So little time they had, and they were wasting it in a squabble. Over nothing. But he couldn't know it was nothing.

"Ah, *merda*," he said suddenly. "Shit. I have to go."

"I understand," she said, but she didn't understand at all, and it was in her voice.

"Sylvia." He grabbed her bare shoulders. "Don't see Salvadore again. Don't. Not unless I'm with you."

She trembled at his touch. But she flared at his words. "No matter what you think you saw in the hallway last night, you've no right to give me such orders."

"Sylvia, I mean it." The urgency should have warned her. Instead it angered her.

"Surely you do not resent Salvadore so much."

"It's not that."

"I don't believe you."

"And I can't tell you enough to convince you." She thought he sounded somehow desperate. "You'll just have to trust me."

She challenged him. "You're hiding behind your work."

"You are wrong."

"Then tell me why."

"*Merda!*" he swore again in his father's Italian. "I would if I could."

"You can. But you won't. Nico, you've told me before about your work." She hoped that she didn't sound pleading.

"I know. But – but that was in, well, in extenuating circumstances. And I can't just now."

"Why not?"

"I would be placing you in danger. Possibly very great danger."

"Telling me what is going on would do that?"

"Yes."

Her voice sharpened. "What arrant nonsense!"

She could see in his face that he wanted to plead with her. It would do him no good. She saw that he knew that as well.

Suddenly, unexpectedly, he gave way. He ran a hand across his face in resignation, looking tired and world-weary. "All right. But take care. I'll be back tomorrow. Please, take care."

He pulled her to him and she did not resist, suddenly heartsick that he was leaving yet again and that they would argue in this fashion just before he left.

He bent his head and kissed her gently. With regret, she thought.

Almost involuntarily, her arms reached up around his neck. If she had just a bit less pride she would ask him to stay. She felt the towel start to give way and let it go unheeded.

But Nico didn't let it go unheeded. He pulled back from her and gave a great sigh. He grasped the edges of the towel and held it snugly around her. "I'll see you tomorrow," he said. He released her and stepped away toward the door.

"Nico," she said.

He turned back to her.

"Shall I go to the airport with you?"

"No." He sounded abrupt.

She flinched.

"But thank you," he added, his mind clearly somewhere else.

She screwed up her courage. "Why not?"

"It would not be safe," he said.

She wanted to challenge that, to accuse him of hiding behind his work. Again. But if he did not want her with him, she would not push it.

Then she saw that his mind was suddenly back with her. "Dammit, Sylvia, it's not what you're thinking."

"How could you possibly know what I'm thinking?"

"It's all over your face."

She could manage no more. "Please. If you're going to go, just go."

Wordlessly, he stepped back to her and pulled her close, wild hair and damp towel and all. And he kissed her once more. She tasted a deep, poignant sadness but didn't know whether it was hers or his. And then, to her despair, he released her and turned away.

He let himself out of her room and then closed the door firmly behind him. She heard him give the knob a sharp twist to test that the door was indeed locked.

She held herself still until she heard his footsteps retreating down the hallway towards the gleaming wooden staircase. Then she sank down onto her straight-backed chair and stared at the closed door through which he had just disappeared.

CHAPTER 7

For the love of heaven. What in the world had gotten into her? Last evening on the verge of being persuaded to spend the night with Salvadore. And tonight, clinging to Nico, clad only in a towel. What was giving way within her, that she would allow such behavior? Had her self-imposed loneliness reached such a saturation point that she would do anything to be held and touched?

She thought perhaps she should pack her things and get out of Amsterdam. Surely if Nico had wanted to be with her, he would not have gone so suddenly, not without a better explanation. It struck her that whatever he had been about to tell her at breakfast had never gotten said. She wondered what it was. Perhaps that he no longer wished to see her? That made no sense. If he did not want to see her again he would need only to drop out of touch. Well, maybe it was the so-called danger that he was referencing, implying that it somehow involved Salvadore.

Salvadore! She shot a quick sideways glance at her clock on the table next to the bed and leapt to her feet. Quarter until eight. He would soon be waiting at the restaurant, wondering why Nico and Sylvia had not shown up. And here she stood as if having grown roots into the carpet, wearing only a towel, and with her hair curling every which way. She jerked off the damp towel and, tossing it across the back of a chair, she dressed quickly in a light yellow dress and the same strappy white sandals she had worn the night before. Her wild hair she salvaged by tying it back out of her way with a bit of brilliant blue ribbon that matched the sapphire of her eyes. She snatched up her small white cloth bag and headed out the door.

She made her way down the stairs and dropped off her room key at reception. Then she stepped out onto the street, thinking on Nico's words.

Stay away from Salvadore. She might have actually considered it if he had given her a valid, believable reason. But the whole idea that Salvadore might be any danger to her was ridiculous. She knew him better than Nico did. Surely Nico was just reacting to having seen her in the hallway with Salvadore, as well he might.

She frowned as she remembered that episode, and how she had allowed Salvadore to kiss her and hold her. She did not want to hurt Nico. She knew that she would have been hurt if the tables were turned and it had been Nico who had been holding someone else. On the very eve of when she was supposed to be meeting him.

But then she reminded herself, as she followed Vijzelstraat and crossed the murky, restless waters of the Canal Prinsengracht on the arched brick bridge, it was Nico who hadn't bothered to show up when promised. And he had been with her for only one short day before leaving again.

She was quite aware that her formidable stubbornness was not her most enviable trait. But she had agreed to meet Salvadore for dinner. And so she would do just that.

The restaurant, *Le Maîson Descartes,* was in the same tall wooden building as the French Embassy, as Nico had mentioned earlier. If she hadn't already known where it was, she never would have found it, as its sign was high and small and weather-beaten, nearly impossible to read.

But by all appearances, it didn't need a sign. As she entered via the arching, carved doorway and climbed the narrow, ill-lit stairs, she could hear the babble of conversation in the hallway, a jumble of French and Dutch and English and god knew what else. She was only a few minutes late, the time being barely past eight. She looked around for Salvadore's dark head, but could not spot him in the small crowd that packed the narrow hallway. The throng obscured a brightly colored runner patterned in the red, white and blue of the French flag.

With several murmured *pardons,* she made her way through the warm press of bodies to the maître d' at the small reception desk. She gave Nico's name, telling the man that after all there would be only two. He informed her that the table was nearly ready. Perhaps *mademoiselle* would like to see the pen and ink exhibit in the room next door while she waited? No others of her party had yet arrived.

So she wandered back through the hallway and into the next room, looking at the row of ink drawings in severe, bold black strokes on heavy white paper. One followed the other along the austere walls. She thought them dull and without energy or substance or even breath. They reminded her of a toned-down version of the southwestern United States, and an ill-done version at that, with sweeping lines that were like wind-whipped sand dunes and lifeless, twisted shrubs. They left her feeling desolate and wind-whipped herself. She turned away, her heart as bleak as the drawings.

Ten minutes later she was seated at a small table by the back window overlooking a subtly-lit van Gogh-style garden one story below. Alone. No Nico. And no Salvadore.

Perhaps Salvadore had thought to give Nico and her some privacy. It did not seem to make sense, but nothing else did either. She waited for thirty minutes more, sipping a glass of an excellent, bold Bordeaux wine. Finally she gave up and ordered. She ate alone. And she was entirely miserable.

Sternly, she chided herself. She often ate alone. She liked to eat alone. But the two empty chairs at the table with her seemed so *very* empty. She wished Salvadore were here to fill the void. No. In truth, she wished Nico were here with her. Then there would be no void. She thought it an enigma.

Well, in any case, Nico had made a good choice of restaurants. The food was excellent, the service the same. She picked at her starter of curried prawns. With her knife and fork, she pushed around her entrée of pasta with mushrooms and garlic and leeks on the large blue and yellow china plate, from one side to the other until it was cold. If Nico had been at the table, he would have laughingly accused her of exercising her food. At last she gave it up and declined cheese and sweets and coffee. She paid, and then stepped out into the darkened streets, the night still warm. She did not want to return to her room. She did not want to walk around Amsterdam. She did not want to be here, alone. For a moment she wished she had stayed at the Kámen in Czechoslovakia.

Exasperated, she gave herself a smart mental smack. It would take some doing, but she would regain her equilibrium. She *would*. And she would re-occupy her self-built fortress to guard against the ravages of emotion. With resolution, she turned back to the hotel.

For the third night in a row she did not sleep well, her exhaustion no match for her gnawing loneliness. As she had the day before, she determined to leave. She would go to the travel bureau the next morning and arrange for a ticket – to somewhere! – and if Nico had not arrived by noon, she would leave.

It helped to have a plan. At least she felt more in control and less a victim to everyone else's whims. She was curious about Salvadore's disappearance, and she worried about Nico's reference to danger. If she would have been imperiled by just being with Salvadore, then Nico would be at least as imperiled himself. Her last thought before she finally slept was that Nico, at least, had gotten his way. She had not spent this particular evening with Salvadore.

CHAPTER **8**

Sylvia was up early again the next morning, and at the travel bureau in a corner of the Amsterdam Station Centraal as soon as it had opened at seven. While she waited to speak with an agent, she browsed through the brochures until she fixed on one touting the medieval city of Bruges, Belgium. A three hour ride on the *snel trein* – the fast train – with just one change of lines at the station in Antwerp. Then in Bruges, two ancient town squares and equally ancient cathedrals. She could keep her room here at the Hotel Amstel Grand and stay in Bruges for a night or even two. Just having a plan lightened her mood and she decided to book an open ticket, if only to provide another option. Nico had said that he would return by late morning or early afternoon. She would give him the benefit of the doubt, a bit, anyway, and split the difference. If he were not in Amsterdam by noon, she would be gone, leaving no forwarding address.

The agent, a short and rotund man with thinning blond hair, was as cheerful as an elf, and he elevated her spirits a bit. "There are two ways to spell Bruges, you know," he said as soon as she had made her travel wishes known. And he recited them for her, spelling out the letters slowly so that she would understand. "Bruges, Brugge."

Sylvia was instantly intrigued. After all, she spent most of her time playing with words – their sounds, their rhythms, their interweaving one with the next. "So how do you pronounce each one?"

She thought that he, quite literally, twinkled. "Ah, well. There are really two pronunciations of Bruges, as you might assume," he told her, his blue eyes twinkling as he deftly managed the paperwork to process her request. "The hard *g* and the soft *g*. One is the Dutch pronunciation, the other is French."

"Which should I use?" she asked.

He stopped shuffling the papers for a moment and met her gaze. "Depends on whether you are speaking Dutch or French," he said with a teasing smile.

She laughed.

Thus encouraged, he proceeded to entertain. "A few years ago there was a newspaper article claiming that Belgium would soon cease to exist as a country. The southern, French-speaking part where the Walloons live would join France. And the northern, Dutch-speaking part where the Flemings live would join the Netherlands."

"But of course that did not happen," she said.

Again he twinkled. "We here in the Netherlands thought it made great sense, as did the French down in the south. So did the rest of western Europe. It was so logical that no one questioned the story except to wonder why they hadn't read of it sooner, if the changes were imminent."

"And?" she encouraged.

The agent sat back and gave a broad grin, resting his crossed arms against his jolly round stomach, enjoying his fun even more than Sylvia. "At last we realized that the newspaper's date was April first. The Fool's Day, all over the civilized world, apparently. We had, all of us, fallen for the prank, and only because it made such logical sense." He paused for dramatic effect and then added dryly, "Of course, the Belgians were not particularly amused."

He laughed, pleased at his own story, and Sylvia joined him. As he handed over her ticket, she said, "So when I am in Bruges, do I pronounce it with a soft *g* or with a hard *g*?"

He gave her a conspiratorial look. "Use whichever you like. If you say it improperly to a Dutch speaker, he won't mind. And if you say it improperly to a French speaker, he will take great joy in correcting you. You cannot go wrong." Again he received great amusement from his own humor and gave her a wink. "Have a nice trip," he said, and waved forward the next customer.

She returned to the Hotel Amstel Grand. She did not want to go walking, blaming it on the overcast day, with a blustery wind but no rain. This day felt like autumn to her, like endings, like Salvadore's version of van Gogh's *Crows over the Cornfield*, and she was in no mood for endings. She tried to write in her room, but it would not flow. Descending to the hotel lobby, she found an overstuffed chair with soft velvet upholstery as dark burgundy in color as the wine that she had reluctantly sipped alone the evening before. It was situated in the corner with a vantage point from where she could see the main door as well as four round-faced clocks that announced the time not only in Amsterdam, but also in London, New York, and of all places, Capetown. A token gesture to Salvadore's southern hemisphere?

She could not manage to write there, either, so she gave it up. She kicked off her white sandals and curled her feet underneath herself and watched the door and the four clocks. She wondered which would win by noon, and she was of a mixed mind regarding her preference.

Her exhaustion caught up with her at last and she fell asleep curled in the chair. She awakened an hour later, stiff and overly warm. Her eyes flew first to the clock with the Amsterdam time, and her heart plummeted as if reaching for the bottom of a pit. Nearly half past twelve. But in the next moment she realized that she was not alone. Nico was sprawled half-dozing in the chair next to her, long legs stretched out careless of any passersby.

She watched him for a moment, her own thoughts still lost in sleepiness. His face, darkened with a few days' growth of beard, was drawn and haggard, as if he had not slept at all the previous nights. She decided that he looked dangerous, the kind of man from whom mothers should warn away their daughters. She wanted to run her fingers over his cheek and feel the roughness of him.

It was some time before he became aware that she was watching him. "Are you napping?" she asked somewhat cautiously.

"I was just joining you." He gave her the crooked grin that she remembered whenever she thought of him, and he added, "Did you get kicked out of your room that you have to sleep here in the lobby?"

She smiled back. She thought of the ticket to Bruges. Nico was here. She wouldn't need it. "How did your business go?" she said.

He frowned slightly. "Could have been better," he said. "How about your evening?"

She knew what he wanted to know. In truth, she ought to hold out on him. He was so very impossible. But she was tired of the tension between them. "Terrible," she said. "I ate at the French restaurant, as planned."

"I see." His voice was flat but accepting.

"No, Nico, you don't see. I ate alone."

"Alone?" Relief flashed across his face, followed by a frown of what might have been concern. "Salvadore wasn't there?"

"No. He didn't show up."

"Did he leave a message?"

"Apparently he's like you in that regard. No message."

"Now, Sylvia, don't be impertinent," he chided her, but with another smile.

She returned his smile. It was such a good feeling to have him back. For the moment she forgot her resolve to allow no more good feelings.

He gazed at her intently for a moment, and she thought he seemed pre-occupied. "What is it, Nico?"

"Nothing really."

She rolled her eyes.

"What?" he protested.

She just shook her head.

"I just thought it rather strange that Salvadore did not show up," he said.

Suddenly she was exasperated with him. "You're never satisfied, are you? You tell me not to have dinner with him, but then you're concerned when I don't."

He quirked a dark brow. "It doesn't make sense, does it?"

"You're right. It doesn't."

"Want to walk a bit?"

Actually, what she wanted was to question him regarding the faint line of concern on his forehead. Maybe later. "I'm hungry," she said.

"So am I." He stood and reached down a hand for her. "We can find a sidewalk café overlooking one of the canals."

The afternoon passed quickly. Sylvia was content enough just to have Nico's company. She had taken it for granted the day before. No more. His arm was around her slender waist and he kept her close against his warmth as if he would never let her go. She cherished it; she reveled in it. She wished it were true, that he would indeed never let her go. She remembered how she had promised herself not to allow Nico close to her heart. But then she thought how easy it would be to become permanently suspicious of happiness, to taste no joy without glancing over the shoulder to check what pain was stalking.

At last they returned to the hotel to freshen up for dinner. They were barely half-way across the vast lobby when one of the front desk clerks caught up to them. "*Meneer* DiCapelli. You have a message."

Sylvia saw Nico's jaw tighten. "What message?" he said.

"It was delivered by hand. It was noted by the courier as being private, very private. And most urgent. An emergency. We have been searching for you for the past two hours."

Nico kept a tight hold on Sylvia's hand as he followed the clerk into the manager's office. Apparently the message was locked in a drawer, accessible only by the manager himself. The cadaverously-thin man peered appraisingly over his spectacles at Nico. His hair was yellow, but more of an ancient, stained white than a true blond. His grey suit was impeccable even though it was somewhat shiny with age. He painstakingly scrutinized Nico's proffered identification, a United Kingdom passport, as if Nico were some-how an imposter. Which, in point of fact, he was, Sylvia observed to herself, since his only two legitimate passports had been issued by Italy and by the United States. Finally, with some reluctance, the manager handed over a sealed brown envelope.

Still gripping Sylvia's hand, Nico went back to the chairs they had vacated earlier in the corner of the lobby. He sat down next to her, tore open the envelope, and glanced at the contents. He gave a gesture of frustration with two fingers under his chin that could have started a street fight in Venice even as he swore more prolifically – in Italian! – than Sylvia had ever heard from him.

"What is it?" she asked.

He turned to her, his expression troubled. "Sylvia –"

Her chest tightened. "You have to leave again, don't you?"

"Yes, but just for a short time. A very short time." His eyes begged her to understand.

Bruges, she thought instantly. I'm going to Bruges. Hard *g* or soft *g*, it doesn't really matter. I'm going to Bruges. She shrugged and mentally withdrew. Or rather, she attempted to withdraw.

He had no intention of allowing it. "Sylvia." Again she heard the bare edge of pleading. It did not sit comfortably with Nico's personality, or with the preoccupied and troubled expression on his face. It should have made it all the more believable.

She forced herself to ignore it. "Really, Nico. I don't want to hear it. This is simply not going to work." She rose and started to walk away from him, but he was too quick. He sprang to his feet in one smooth movement and grabbed her arm just above the elbow. She thought that she might have a bruise as a result of his hard fingers.

"Listen to me," he said urgently. Releasing her arm from that stern, commanding grip, he took her hand firmly and led her outside.

"Can't you just tell me whatever you have to say here in the hotel?" she protested.

"No. I need to be sure there is no one to overhear us."

She rolled her eyes heavenward as if for divine wisdom. Or perhaps in supplication for patience. "Oh, for pity's sake, Nico. Don't you think you're taking this spy thing of yours a bit too far?"

He declined to be amused. "It's not a spy thing, and you know it," he said sharply. "And I'm going to tell you some things that I should not be sharing with you. I haven't been sure whether you would be more safe or less knowing the information, but you seem to be in the middle of this so I think you are entitled to know what's going on."

She was astounded. He was serious!

"Two pieces of information, and quickly. I haven't much time." He shot a glance at the face of the watch on the inside of his left wrist and then at the space around them. The street was humming with pedestrians and traffic, but the two of them stood close together on the arch of the Oudezijds Voorburgwal bridge where no one could overhear them without being noticed. "First. Salvadore is mixed up in a business where he shouldn't be."

His brisk, hard tone made her think that this must be what he was like when he was working. She had not seen him this way before. Still she was cautious, studiously withdrawn from him. "What business?" she asked.

And still he was stern and serious. "That's not important. What is important is that Salvadore is playing a dangerous game. He's been trying to tail me. When he lost me, he started bird-dogging you in hopes of flushing me out."

"I don't believe you!" she said, astonished. "Not even my fiction is so outlandish."

"Don't be so naïve." Again his voice was sharp, and his green-hazel eyes commanded her attention. "I was called back last night to lure Salvadore out of Amsterdam and away from you. We had hoped to intercept him, catch him off guard. The hunter becoming the hunted, so to speak."

"So that's why he was not at dinner last night. You might have told me then, so that I could have known I was to be completely stood up."

It seemed impossible, but his voice sharpened even further. "That's *not* why he wasn't there."

She was shocked, both at this nearly-rude tone as well as at his information. "I beg yours?"

"We didn't take him. We think he picked up the trail and then either lost it or backed off, but we don't know why. After all these months we thought he would be very aggressive and not take chances on losing me. And then he just bloody disappeared!"

She digested this for a moment. "Why does he want you?" she asked.

"Please, Sylvia. Not now. Not until it's over. Then I can tell you everything, and I will. The problem now is that we've lost him entirely. That's why they've called me back."

"I see." She looked away from him. She did *not* see.

"Sylvia, promise me that if he turns up here again, you will stay away from him. He's more treacherous than you can know, a gambler of sorts. He's got high stakes on the table in a very dangerous game, and he doesn't like to lose."

"Nico, I can see that you truly believe this. But I do not. You don't really know Salvadore."

"Nor do you," he said flatly.

"I know him far better than you do."

"Trust me. You don't."

"Nico –"

"Sylvia." He caught her face between his hands and dipped his head so that he looked directly into her sapphire eyes. He was urgent now, emphatically so. "The time is slipping fast away and you must understand the seriousness of this." He took a deep breath, as if hating to continue. Then he went on. "The second thing I need to tell you is this. Do you remember Eduardo Fuentes?"

She was completely astonished now. "The Colombian drug lord that kidnaped us in Czechoslovakia?"

"The same."

"He would be rather difficult to forget, would he not?" she said. "After all, he left us for dead in the ancient hillfort."

Nico gave a short nod. "As you know, he was – is – a murderer and a drug lord and god knows what else. He tried to kill us, remember?" He moved his hands to her shoulders and gave her a small shake as if for emphasis. "Salvadore is involved with him."

"I don't believe it!" She thought of Salvadore's ready grin and gentle touch. She thought of Fuentes' oily, evil countenance. It seemed preposterous. It *was* preposterous. She pulled Nico's hands away from her shoulders, but still she clung to them.

He squeezed her hands so hard that it hurt, but just for a moment. "Believe it. Sylvia, Salvadore is not Italian and he's not Argentine. He's a countryman of Fuentes. His name is Salvadore, all right. Salvadore San Martín. He's from Colombia and he's involved in the export business. With Fuentes. Problem is, his product is illegal. It's hard drugs."

"Salvadore, a dealer?"

"Yes. No. More of a runner. Ah, well, an export-import person. We believe that he moves it from one country to another, one city to another. He doesn't sell it directly. Not on the streets."

"Truly, I don't think –"

His urgency was nearing a fever pitch. "*Dio!* What in bloody hell do you think a drug runner looks like?" he said, his voice rising dangerously.

She decided that she did not appreciate his tone. She freed her hands and took a step back from him. "That's not the point."

"That most certainly *is* the point. He's not going to have *'I'm a drug runner'* emblazoned on his forehead."

"It's not his looks that make me doubt you. It's his, well, his –"

"His what?"

She couldn't find the words. Finally she gave it up. "I'd as likely believe *you* were a drug runner."

"I?" He was at first astonished, and then, surprising her, he suddenly grinned. "I might be and you just don't know it," he said.

She started to argue and then she thought for a moment. "I wonder," she said, frowning.

He took another glance at the watch on his left wrist and swore under his breath. He snatched up both her hands again. "Will you wait for me? Here in Amsterdam?"

She wanted to say yes. But she had a bad feeling about this, a very bad feeling. "I don't know," she said. "Until when?"

"Until I'm back," he said flatly, without compromise.

She flinched, but held fast. "Which will be – when?"

"I don't know. But not long."

She wanted to tell him that she would wait. But she could not go through this yet again, whatever *this* was. "I don't think so," she said, feeling her heart twist even as she thought of the ticket to Bruges that waited in her room.

"*Merda!*" he swore. *Shit!* "Why not, dammit?" He was stubborn and blunt and hard-headed, and he was in a hurry.

"Nico, it's apparently difficult for you to believe, but I do have a life apart from you."

"I know." She heard his voice take on a desperate edge. "But do you have something pressing just now? A schedule that requires you to be some other place soon? You were in Czechoslovakia for three months, more or less. Where are you going from here in such a hurry?"

She strove for annoyance. "Are you implying that I have nothing better to do than wait alone in Amsterdam until you decide that I finally become high enough in your priorities to matter?"

He flushed, whether from anger or something else she could not know. But she did see a glimmer of pain flash in his eyes and then subside. "Stop it," he said. "It's not like that and you know it. Sylvia, you *know* it."

She could see he was torn between the need to stay and the need to go. She knew she should let him go. But she could not. "How do I know it?"

"*Merda!*" he exclaimed redundantly. "I'm telling you. I had left instructions not to be interrupted until I myself contacted London. Except for this particular – particular problem."

"So your organization contacted you?"

He was silent for a long moment as if uncomfortable with the question. At last he said, "Well, not exactly."

"What, then?"

"I contacted them."

She was taken aback. "When?"

"Last night. I thought I should inform my contact that San Martín was here in Amsterdam."

"And so they called you back."

"Ah, yes. They did."

"You knew Salvadore would be a problem, then?"

He gave a furious gesture of frustration, again on the edge of what would certainly pass for an insult in his father's homeland. *"Dio!* I had no idea that he'd turn up here. Hell, I didn't even know he was in bloody Europe. I've been working that *bastardo* Fuentes ever since he tried to murder us two months ago. Mostly I've been in the Colombian mountains where the product, the coca plant, is grown and harvested. Fuentes has proven difficult to approach, much less to apprehend, in other countries. But it's been completely impossible in his own country where he operates more or less openly, with payoffs to the officials so that they look the other way." There was an unmistakable contempt in his voice. He ran a hand across his weary face in frustration. "So far Fuentes has slipped the trap. And as disturbingly, for whatever reason, San Martín, your Salvadore, keeps getting in the way."

She frowned at the 'your' Salvadore, but said nothing.

"What's bothering me," he said as he slid an arm around her waist and pulled her closer, "is how San Martín picked you up here in Amsterdam. It still seems too much of a coincidence."

"I don't understand."

"I think he may have connected the two of us long before he got to Amsterdam and tried to run you over with his damned Harley."

Not a very accurate description of that particular event, but she let it pass. She was suddenly less aware of his words and more aware of his proximity. She thought he'd ask her again to wait for him.

He didn't. Rather, he changed topics. "Will you stay close to the hotel and not wander around alone in the city?"

She let out her breath in an annoyed sigh. Not only did he want her to wait, but he wanted to tell her where to wait. "I will not."

"Sylvia. Promise me."

"No, Nico."

He swore yet again. "Are you just being stubborn? Or do you really not understand the danger? Don't you remember who and what Fuentes is? *Cristo*, Sylvia, he tried to murder us!"

"I will not allow you to make me a prisoner of your own doubts and fears," she said very softly.

He gave a sound deep in his throat that was indescribable, but that could be interpreted as nothing other than the extreme edge of fury. "So you won't stay close to the hotel?"

She blinked, but she held firm. "That's right."

He sighed again and passed a hand across his tired, beard-shadowed face. "What am I to do with you?" he said softly, almost as if to himself.

"You might try spending some time with me." She thought that she must sound petulant and it embarrassed her, but her emotions were beginning to churn again. "You're the one who asked me to come here to Amsterdam."

The long arm around her waist tightened, but gently. "Don't you think I'd rather be here? With you?"

"You're the one making these choices, Nico. Not I."

"Dammit," he started, then he impatiently bit back his words. He didn't speak for a long moment, and when he did, his entire demeanor had changed. He pulled her as close as he could, one hand in her hair holding her face against the base of his throat, the other at the small of her back. "Sylvia," he murmured into her honey curls. "If I could choose to stay with you, I would. Why else would I have asked you to meet me here?"

She trembled at his sudden tenderness, his gentleness, trembled as he held her tightly against his body, trembled as he moved her head back a bit so that he could take her lips with his. He held her for a long time and she did not resist. But she was already feeling the emptiness that would descend as soon as he walked away from her. Which, in her heart, she knew without a doubt that he would do. He did what he had to do, not what he desired. For his job? For his father, who had been killed in a motorcycle crash when Nico was but nineteen? She did not know. But certainly not for her.

"Sylvia," he whispered, and kissed her again. "Sylvia. Please, will you stay close to the hotel?"

She returned his kiss, her fingers touching the dark hair at his nape. She felt the strength of his shoulders and arms, the hardness of his body. She felt the strength of his character, of his honesty and of his commitment. All those things that were important to her.

"Please?"

It was mesmerizing. His strong warmth. His persistent lips. His soft, deep voice. It was tempting. Just melt into his embrace and agree with everything he said.

"Will you?" He was gently persistent.

She was vacillating.

"Tell me you will." He pulled back a few inches so that he could see her face, could read her expression.

With his movement away from her, the vacillation stopped and the emptiness, the coldness, set in. And her stubborn will resuscitated itself with a vengeance. "I'm sorry, Nico," she whispered. "I am. But I will not stay." And the words slipped gently from her lips and into her numbed mind. *Not close to the hotel. Not close to Amsterdam. Not close to you, Nico. Not close to you.*

He tensed, and she wondered what it was she saw in his face. Fury? Concern? He was very self-contained and thus very difficult to read. Then the practiced façade began to slip, to melt away, like butter beneath a hot sun. He tipped his head back and lifted his weary face to the slate blue sky, closing his eyes against a seemingly bitter pain. Then his shoulders came forward as if he were willing the last of the coiled tension from him. He returned his gaze to her face, those eyes still concerned, but oh, so very sad. His voice was soft, so soft she barely heard it. "If I have gotten you into something where any harm comes to you – again! – I'll never forgive myself." He kissed her one last time and this one was filled with longing and passion. And the fury she thought she had glimpsed in his demeanor earlier. It left her trembling again, very nearly breathless. "Goodbye, Sylvia," he said, a world of regret and pain in his voice. And something else, but she could not possibly know what it was. He released her and turned away.

She stared after his tall, straight form. To see the confident, purposeful way he moved, a stranger would never guess at the turmoil and pain that she knew were churning within him. Yes, she stared after him until he disappeared into the mass of people that meandered along the dark canal. At last she moved, but slowly and reluctantly, as if she carried with her a great weight. "Goodbye, Nico," she whispered. "Goodbye." In her mind it sounded so very final. And in her heart at well.

She turned and started her slow, regretful walk back to the Hotel Amstel Grand. It was time to fetch the open ticket to Bruges.

CHAPTER **9**

Sylvia had the ticket, but no plans to accompany it. Just herself and the *snel trein*. The fast train. No hotel reservations, no sense of how long to stay, not even a map of the city of Bruges itself.

Well, the ticket would have to be enough for now. She sat in the chair at her desk in the Hotel Amstel Grand and studied the timetable. There was a departure just before midnight, but it made no sense to arrive in Bruges at three in the morning with no accommodations. The first train out of Centraal Station the following morning was at seven. She'd be in Bruges by close to ten.

So. There it was. Her plan.

It felt empty. But it felt necessary, and perhaps after all, inevitable. She was a realist, if nothing else. It was a somehow barren admission. She gave a sigh and prepared for bed.

There were no surprises in store for her in that regard. She could not sleep. She twisted and turned until well past midnight, reminding herself that she had to be up by five-thirty, to catch the seven o'clock train. It did no good. It was nearly one in the morning when she at last conceded defeat. She tore herself up from the bed in a frustrated movement, wrapped the coverings around her shoulders against the night coolness, and went to work.

What had been so reluctant to come earlier in the day now came like a dam giving way in the face of the violent assault of a cloudburst. But it was not her latest piece of fiction, not her novel. Rather, it was her heart breaking again, surging free of her self-imposed prison, those fortress walls. All the longing poured out of her, line after trembling line, page after agonizing page, until a long two hours later she was spent, with her head resting on her crossed arms atop the desk and her face wet with tears, her hand aching with the furious effort. She saw the pages that had been born of her pain, and with an anguished cry she swept them from her desk and watched them float and flutter to settle onto the floor. She wept then, her body shivering with the chill, and her heart at last shattered, surely this time beyond repair. Oh, yes, this was how despair felt. She recognized it; she had been in this place before. No stubborn resolution here tonight, no firm determination to carry on, untouched by feelings, behind her grey fortress walls. No internal fire. Only the damnable cold.

The birthing pains of the night came forth with a new morning at last, and the fire-tested dawn that resulted should have been purified and crystal and beautiful. But in truth it was nothing more than just another day. She awakened at her desk, stiff and cold, with her grief still gripping at her chest and at her throat. She gave scarcely a glance to the papers strewn across the floor in a wild disarray. She dragged herself up. After a quick shower, she dressed in jeans and a sweater and carelessly threw a few things into her rucksack.

She made for the door and nearly missed a small envelope that had been thrust underneath. It lay face down on the floor. She picked it up and started to toss it onto the desk, but then caught the one word scrawled on the front of it. *Cariña.* She dropped her rucksack and tore open the envelope. A small card, an unfamiliar scribble. She read it in a whisper, not believing. "*Cariña.* Please take care. Stay in the hotel." There was no signature.

Nico! If this was his idea of a joke, she was not amused. If he thought this would dissuade her from going out, he was so very wrong.

But she knew it wasn't from Nico. Salvadore, then. What was this about? Had he heard Nico's warning to her? Impossible! But why this, why now?

She had no one to ask. She was completely alone. Now she had to worry not only about Nico's safety, but apparently also about Salvadore's. He must be in some kind of danger himself, to send her such an urgent warning. Perhaps Nico had been right. Perhaps Salvadore's danger was self-induced. Nico was so certain that Salvadore was a drug runner. And in his line of business, Nico should know.

Then it struck her. She sat heavily on the edge of her bed. Colombian. Salvadore San Martín was Colombian. But more disturbing was that Nico must have known it all along. So why the elaborate charade with South American Spanish? *Castellano?* He already knew from where Salvadore hailed, and that he was somehow tied in with that murderous drug lord, Fuentes. She remembered his joking reference to himself as a drug runner and wondered how much was a jest and how much hinted at truth. It was an observable fact that Nico had a strange, clandestine job. And a lot of readily available cash.

The thought made her shiver. Fuentes had exuded an evil, savage power. Salvadore displayed a nature that was irrepressible but still somehow kind. And, no doubt about it, he was charming.

And Nico? Nico was just himself. Just honestly and completely himself. One couldn't judge him by the surface. However, she had seen beneath that surface. So she knew, she *knew* the depths within him. The pain for his mother's great loss and his own, when his father had been killed some six or seven years ago. Killed by a man high on drugs who had run a stoplight and crashed into the motorcycle that Nico's father was riding. The unrelenting fury that drove Nico in his covert, dangerous job to stalk the drug lords, the drug runners. She gave a small shudder as she wondered what he might do if he caught them, when he caught them. So what exactly was this game that Nico was playing now?

Nico and Salvadore. They had both warned her. And with very little thought on the matter, other than being even more worried for each of them than for herself, she decided to ignore them. Both of them.

She left without a backward glance at the clutter of papers scattered about the floor of her room. As she left the key at reception, she told the clerk that she would be gone for a few days and nights.

It was barely dawn, and the morning was damp and overcast, matching the heaviness of her mood. Ignoring lights and crosswalks, she crossed the street and then cut across the open square in front of Centraal Station. She entered into the maze of the vast place and passed through the turnstile. Then she ascended to the level where the trains came and went, and waited on the nearly-deserted platform. The train rumbled in, echoing in the emptiness and rattling the metal floor under her feet, giving a whooshing whisper as it trembled to a stop. She boarded the nearest car and made for the upper deck, as yet the only passenger in this area. Tossing her rucksack onto the empty place beside her, she curled up in her seat, her sandaled feet underneath her body, and stared at the clock on the platform outside her window. The train tensed in readiness like a wild cat preparing to spring. Nearly seven o'clock. Those formidably punctual Dutch trains! The second hand hit twelve straight up and the train jerked and strained and smoothed and slipped from the station.

Amsterdam slid past, all dark, obscure canals and tall, leaning buildings, and then the misty Dutch countryside opened into a muted landscape of grey-green. It was more like the gentle watercolors of a French impressionist, Monet, perhaps, rather than the bold colors and authoritative brush strokes of van Gogh. Soft *g*, hard *g*. She did not smile to herself at her whimsy. She stared out of her window, seeing only the dull sameness of the terrain, the flatness, seemingly even more horizontal than the very ocean and river from where the land had been poldered. Her thoughts were miles away, and so she was startled when a young, dark-haired conductor asked for her ticket. She searched in her bag and at last produced it.

He moved his punch professionally, efficiently into place on the thin white cardboard and then stopped, his narrow black mustache thinning even more. *"Mademoiselle,"* he said. "This is a first class ticket."

"Oui?" She knew very well that she hadn't paid attention to either the ticket or the car.

"You should be in the first class car," he said, waving her ticket, a slight frown of admonition on his brow.

"Merci." That was very nearly the extent of her French. Except, of course, for Bruges with a soft *g*. "I'm fine here."

"Non, non, mademoiselle. You have a first class ticket." He stood resolutely, one hand on his blue uniformed hip and the other pointing to the next car, determined that she should see the error of her ways.

She gave a sigh and picked up her rucksack and rose. Balancing herself as the train swayed, she followed him as he descended the stairs to the lower level. She watched his slender, straight back, straight as a soldier's.

They entered the first class car, and then ascended the stairs once more. The seats were larger and had upholstery rather than hard plastic, and there was more leg room. Not that she needed it, petite as she was. Nico's long legs would certainly have approved of it, though. The car was as empty as the second class accommodations had been. The conductor led the way to her assigned seat. She thanked him and sat down. Staring out of the window once more, she thought that the early morning was still as grey as it had been from the second class car. Apparently money could buy neither decent weather nor peace of mind, never bother that elusive fiction of happiness or joy.

She scarcely noticed when the train flashed from Holland into Belgium, with no border crossing delays due to the relaxed relations between the two countries. The terrain was much the same, flat and stretching into monotony. Grey stone farmhouses formed unwieldy lumps against the horizontal landscape and the spent crops were bedraggled, now only brown, parched remains of the abundant summer. The nearly-autumnal harvest colors reminded her of van Gogh's *Crows over the Cornfield*. Again she thought that perhaps Salvadore had been right in interpreting the painting. She could find no brightness, either in the landscape or in her mood. There was no avoiding the beginning of winter, with its blighting, freezing chill.

At last she tumbled into a hard sleep, to be awakened by the same young, dark-haired conductor with the bearing of a soldier, now apparently her self-appointed guardian. They were nearly to Antwerp, and *mademoiselle* needed to change trains. She thanked him yet again and stirred herself awake. She was no longer alone on the train, more passengers having boarded at other stops along the line. They looked as sleepy and disconnected as she felt.

She thought the brief wait in the chilly dampness of the train platform at the Antwerp station would bring her awake. It did not. The west-bound train pulled in and she stumbled on board, taking care to choose the first class car this time so as not to be remonstrated with again, climbing up the steps to take her seat, once more on the upper deck. How a train could be so sleek and fast and still be a double-decker was beyond her.

She sat quietly, ignoring the passengers around her, and looked again at the timetable. Beyond Bruges was Oostende. She knew there was a ferry from Oostende to Dover, on the coast of Great Britain. The white cliffs. It was tempting! If she had checked out of the Hotel Amstel Grand and brought along her few things, she might catch the ferry and leave the Netherlands and Belgium behind. And more importantly, leave Nico behind as well. Or perhaps she would go on to Paris. Just a few more hours south of Bruges and she could be there. And Paris was indeed a large enough city in which to lose oneself.

But she had not checked out of the Hotel Amstel Grand, and she had not brought her things. She would return to Amsterdam and collect her belongings in a few days hence and then decide where to go next. Nico wouldn't hang around for long without her being there, of that she was certain. After all, he didn't hang around even when she was there.

When the train halted at Sint-Niklaas to load and unload passengers once again, she watched as a group of young people crowded into a tourist class car, chatting and laughing and pushing good-naturedly, tossing their rucksacks carelessly into the overheads and sprawling merrily onto the hard orange plastic seats. They must have been about her age. But her widowhood and her husband's betrayal had left her more mature. She corrected herself. *Not* more mature. Older. She didn't feel that she was even of the same generation as those cheerful young men and women, and she closed her eyes against the painful isolation of it.

Like a huge, lazy snake, the train slithered into Stationsplein, the Bruges station, at precisely thirteen minutes before ten. Right on schedule. The place was old and very large, and at the moment, quite empty. With her rucksack dangling from one hand, she stepped down from the train, noting that the group of young people in the tourist class car did not disembark.

She wondered briefly where they were bound. She took the escalator down from the platform to the main floor, her footsteps echoing on the grey tiles until she emerged into a vast asphalt parking lot, stretching forth like a huge, still lake. Shrugging her rucksack onto her back and untangling her long curling hair from the straps, she started walking, following the signs to Bruges, ignoring the line of waiting black taxicabs at the curb. It looked to be a long hike, and the day was still cool but clear. She felt bone-tired and hardly wanted even to expend the energy to find a hotel. Her step, normally light and questing, seemed to have lost its spring.

It appeared that the only way out of the station area was to follow the street that headed east and north, ducking under the Buiten Beginjnenvest motorway, crossing two canals and turning into Oostmeers. She didn't have a city map and given her penchant for getting lost, she probably should have looked around the station for one. But when she reached Sebrachtsstraat she spotted a large blue and yellow sign in the shape of a triangle. *VVV* it read, *Toerisme Brugge*. And then, it added helpfully, *TI*. The tourist information office. She wondered, as she had in other countries, why it was called the *TI*, as if English was the language here. It must be the same strange reason that other countries marked their toilets as *WC*. Water Closet. About as English as one could get! In any case, surely the *VVV* or *TI*, or whatever, would be located near the center of the city. So she made a right and continued on her way, the morning sunshine warm on her face.

Just as the huge lake Minnewater came sparkling into view, the street made a sharp left. She walked awhile longer beside the lake, admiring the green expanses of neatly trimmed grass and the towering downy birch and red oak and elm trees, their leaves not yet beginning to turn color in deference to the impending autumn. And then her eye was caught by a movement on the lake, and the resulting ripples that shimmered diamonds on the surface. The swans! They glided in pairs, graceful necks arched like the bridges that crossed the canals. She stopped short, remembering that the brochure had mentioned some political figure or nobility from centuries ago who was held here against his will. His "vengeance" when he was finally freed was to decree that swans would forever be kept in the canals of the city. What a delightful legacy! She surely would have to return here.

Shifting the rucksack on her shoulders, she continued on for a short distance. Another *VVV* sign commanded her to cross the canal that connected to the lake. And immediately the street became narrow and cobbled and plunged into the maze of buildings.

The brochure had described Bruges as a charming medieval city and from that she had imagined a large modern city with a small medieval heart. How wrong she had been! It was large, all right, but it seemed that the entire city was ancient. The narrow streets twisted and turned, the tall stone and brick buildings blocking out any landmarks that might have assisted her in keeping her direction. Every canal she crossed had a few swans displaying their finery with gracefully arched necks. And now her spirits began to lift in anticipation. This would be a grand place in which to get lost, and find oneself, only to get lost once again. Like the pattern of her own life. Her mood brightened and she was suddenly glad she had come. She decided to focus on finding a small hotel so that she could forsake the pulling weight of her rucksack and explore in earnest.

The way to the *Toerisme Brugge*, the tourist information office, was clearly marked now and again, so she kept herself headed in the general direction that they pointed as she made her way down Peperstraat. But she was brought up short by a massive, ancient stone church, its inexpugnable grandeur vanquishing all competitors and establishing it as the center and soul of Bruges. She recalled what she had read about it in the brochure. *Eglise d'accueil de notre-dame. Onze-Lieve-Vrouwe Kerk.* Church of our Lady. All different languages, but one behemoth of a church. It was undergoing renovation similar to the *Oude Kerk* in Amsterdam. But this church was not hemmed in and strangled by the city and the bustling business of prostitution. Rather, the medieval city kept its respectful distance from the reigning monarch, as it had for centuries.

Very nearly she went into it, but then remembered that she was tired and hungry. First things first. She continued down the street for a few blocks and then turned right, still following the *VVV* signs. Suddenly she realized that there were no cars on the streets. She had crossed into the pedestrian area.

At last she emerged into the city square, or rather one of the two main squares. This one was Burg Square, she thought, as it fit the description in the brochure. It was dominated on one side by the Stadhuis, the city hall dating back several centuries, and by the Heilig-Bloedbasiliek, Basilica of the Holy Blood on the other. Like so many other of the old buildings, it was also being renovated.

Not far from the basilica was yet another huge building, with the unmistakable blue and yellow *VVV* sign. Finally she had run to earth the tourist information office. It was apparently on the ground floor and there was a short flight of stone stairs up from the street. She climbed the rough sand-colored steps and ducked inside. September was just past the busy season, with the European holiday month of August behind, and the schools and universities back in business. Even so, there were three or four persons in the line ahead of her, and only one clerk.

Her stomach was reminding her of how many hours it had been since she'd had her last meal. Perhaps the tourist office would be cleared out a bit after she'd had lunch. Back down the stairs she traipsed and out into the square. The clouds were breaking up and the afternoon promised sunshine. She stopped by an exchange kiosk and changed some of her Dutch guilders into Belgian francs. She had spotted a tiny French restaurant on her walk through the square so she made for it and was promptly seated at a round metal table near the back of a garden in the shade.

It was a bit early for lunch, but she was hungry. She was working her way through a rather large but tasty salad of a variety of greens with tomato wedges and a dressing of olive oil and fresh basil, when the tall and gangly and very young waiter suddenly noticed her rucksack lying at her feet. "Are you just now leaving Bruges?" he asked in a bright, gentle accent as he cleared the table next to hers.

Bruges with a soft *g*, she thought. Must be French. She glanced at his clean-shaven face and dark brown eyes that seemed to be the same shade as his dark brown hair. "No," she said. "I've only just arrived."

He arranged the condiments on the table he was clearing and flicked an imaginary speck from the tablecloth. "Where do you stay?"

It seemed an innocent-enough question. She could spot an ulterior motive from at least a kilometer. "I haven't gotten a place yet," she said. "I will go to the tourist office after I finish my lunch."

He grinned, entirely pleased. "The owner of this restaurant also owns the hotel next door," he said. "He has many rooms available since this is not the high season."

She hesitated.

"It is an old hotel and very nice," he persisted. "Right here on the square."

She did prefer extremes, either way out in the country as was the Kámen in Czechoslovakia, or in the very center of a city, nothing in between. On the square. Very central. Or in Dutch, *centraal*. Or in French, *bien situé*. Convenient. She smiled up at him. She might at least check out the hotel lobby to see if it would be a good place to write.

"All right," she said. "I'll have a look."

A smile lit his youthful face once more and she thought he must get a commission for every booking he sent over. "Finish eating and then I will take you," he said.

"I am finished," she said even as she pushed back her chair.

He looked at her still half-full plate of salad in blatant disapproval, and then apparently remembered that she was also a potential hotel customer. She paid for her meal with some of the Belgian francs she had just gotten, even as he picked up her rucksack. "Come along then, *mademoiselle*," he said, and he led her next door.

The hotel was small. And it was certainly old. But the lobby area was cozy with a great deal of natural light and privacy from the street's pedestrians and city noises. It was in dark wood tones as so many of the old European lobbies were, but with a stunning display of blown glass from local artisans that flung a shimmer of prisms in sapphire and ruby and emerald and diamond-white crystal around the room. It reminded her of Nico's purloined jewels and antiques from *hrad* Pražské – Prague Castle – as they graced the church in Tatra with their brilliance, as described to her by Nico and the Czech patriot, Myslbek. Like a miniature, intense stained glass window, holding not only the beauty of the pure colors, but also the flashing reminder of history, of patriotism, of heart and soul and courage.

The young, self-satisfied waiter turned Sylvia and her rucksack over to the proprietor of the hotel with a brief explanation in French and then disappeared back towards the restaurant, sending a quick, over the shoulder smile to Sylvia.

The proprietor was an elderly man, entirely French, with thick dark hair. He was short and slight and smartly dressed, and he was immediately apologetic. With broad gestures and shaking his head sadly at the charming waiter's confident pronouncement that just the perfect room would be available, he announced that the only space he had was on the fourth floor, a bit of a climb for *mademoiselle* as there was, of course, no lift.

"May I see it?" she said, and obligingly he led the way up the steep wooden stairs, cautioning her along the way. If the room was as uninviting as the plain staircase and the narrow halls, she thought she would not stay here. The unadorned dimness would only exacerbate her persistently bleak mood. Four long staircases they climbed, beginning at zero in the European fashion, at last emerging onto the fourth floor.

The room bore no resemblance to the way up. It was very large and looked to be one of only four on the top floor. Situated as it was on the corner of the building that faced the square, there were windows in two walls to brighten the space. It was French and frilly in blue and yellow flowers and plaids with an old-fashioned four-poster bed dominating the space. But most compelling to Sylvia was the huge antique oak desk placed so that one could gaze out onto the square.

Again the proprietor apologized for the inconvenient location, but she swept away his concerns with a smile and a wave of her hand. "*Très bien.* It's lovely," she said. "It will do very well."

He beamed and then showed her *le toilette* that she would share with the other guests on the fourth floor. Returning to her room, he began pointing out sights of the square below.

She barely heard his French-accented English as he described the view, so lost was she in the vast stone city's charm. It did not dissuade him.

Then the bright tinkle of a bell downstairs startled her and brought him back to his business. He left her, calling back over his shoulder, "You can sign in when you come down. *Rien ne presse.* No hurry."

She thanked him again and closed the door and returned to the window.

In spite of the restoration project, the twelfth century basilica looked even more imposing from here than it did from below. At the moment, the midday sun was directly above the city, painting it in a golden glow. Yes! Vincent van Gogh! The skies! The light! But she imagined how the stone building would subtly change as the light shifted ever westward. Pink to cream to grey to dusk. And from her lofty height she could see restaurants and shops and other small hotels. But she could make no better sense of the layout of the city than she had from the street. Even as she thought it seemed haphazard, she knew it was not.

Ancient cities, without the cadre of modern urban planners to design them, grew in a natural and rational fashion rather than in a contrived, orderly way. The roads followed the streams. The industries, such as mills, were located on the river, the life's blood of the settlement, to take advantage of the power harnessed from the water. Houses were built with living quarters above and shops below to provide smithing and baking and a plethora of other services that every city needed. Efficient and economic and practical.

Brugge with a hard *g*, Bruges with a soft *g*. She imagined that the church before her in the direct light of midday with the sun chasing away all shadows and all subtleties would be Brugge with a hard *g*. And the church at dawn or at dusk, with its shadings and soft muted colors, the stones softened and accessible, that would be Bruges with the soft *g*. This time she did smile at her own whimsy.

Without unpacking her rucksack, she drew her notebook and pen from the side pocket and settled herself at the scarred, ancient desk. A portrait of words flowed from her pen, painting the scene that stretched out before her. Images, feelings, colors, scents. Brugge with a hard *g*. Brilliant tones, bold strokes, a cacophony of colors, of deeply-felt emotions. The Dutch. The genius, the despair of Holland's tormented son, Vincent van Gogh. And then Bruges with a soft *g*. Muted colors, delicate strokes, gently drawing out pastel hues, a sigh. The French. Surely the bearded old man from the lovely gardens of Giverny, Claude Monet.

She smiled to herself even as she wrote, entranced by her own considerable talent that sprang from her being like the pure, endless water from an artesian well. The outside world, its pain and confusion and hurt, was at bay as she lost herself in her words.

Indeed, down on the square van Gogh was transforming into Monet when Sylvia at last lay down her pen on the sturdy, battered desk. She spread her fingers and rubbed her hand to ease the stiffness. She was drained, but she was content. Unlike the urgent, agonized words she had left on the floor of her room at the Hotel Amstel Grand, this time the page after page of small, neat scrawl was cleansing. It was exhausting, too, but in a relieved sense, a catharsis.

She rose and stretched and, taking a towel, went down the hall to the toilet. No one else was about so she took her time and bathed away the long day. When at last she got out of the antique bathtub and pulled the plug, she imagined her tiredness swirling and flowing with the water that was gurgling down the drain. She returned to her room in her turquoise silk robe with the towel turbaned around her head. Shaking out her hair, she ran her fingers through the wet tangles even as she opened a window and tested the weather. Warm with no wind. She could go out with her hair still damp and carrying only a light sweater in case the evening cooled too quickly.

On her way out of the hotel, she stopped at the reception desk and signed the guest register. Name, nationality, passport number. Then she stepped out into the evening.

Since she did not yet have a good sense of the city, she stopped at a restaurant close to her hotel, a small, nondescript place with dark interior and questionable service, but excellent *tomates aux crevettes* – tomatoes stuffed with a light mayonnaise sauce and tiny shrimp – and a glass of a well-chosen, crisp white wine. The place was not busy, so she lingered for some time, absorbed in her surroundings and trying not to think about the chaos of the past few days.

Again she felt a strong sense of independence and self-sufficiency. She would spend a few nights here in Bruges and then return to Amsterdam for her things. No regrets. She had enjoyed Nico. She had enjoyed Salvadore. Now it was time to get on with her life, wherever it might lead her.

She gathered her notebook and pen and paid the waiter in Belgian francs. Then she climbed up to her room, hoping to be able to sleep at last.

CHAPTER **10**

How long does it take to get over a woman? Hell, Nico DiCapelli didn't know. He knew it must take longer than two months, because that was how long he'd been carrying Sylvia Duncan around in his heart and on his mind. It was extraordinary, considering he'd been in her company for a such short time.

If she had given him just one indication in her letters since then that she cared for him – just one! – he'd have seized upon it. But there was nothing but a polite acquaintance, a recitation of events and activities, rather than thoughts and feelings. Rather than emotions. Two months ago in Czecho-slovakia, his imagination had convinced him that there was something between them, something beyond friendship, something born of a shared affection and a shared terror. But her letters had since caused him to doubt. Maybe there was nothing there, after all. And so his own letters had mir-rored hers, casual and conversational and, on his part at least, a gentle teas-ing, rather than revealing his own very real, very perilous feelings. Even so, when he had at last worked up the nerve to ask her to meet him in Amster-dam, she had readily acquiesced. But *porco mondo*, damn it all. Now that drug-running *bastardo* Salvadore San Martín had somehow gotten in the middle of things and mucked them up.

Nico had arrived back at the Hotel Amstel Grand much later than he had hoped, at half-past four in the afternoon following the ill-fated evening when he had been summoned back to London. He was exhausted, his only sleep having been a quick nap on the short plane trip between London's Heathrow and Amsterdam's Schiphol airports. Less than an hour, for god's sake! The only redeeming factor of the night's and day's activities was that he had gone both ways via private jet and so had been able to stretch out and get a very small bit of rest, and avoid the hassles of immigration and customs. His organization was rather adept at getting around such minor nationalistic details. But nothing had been accomplished with regards to Salvadore San Martín and Eduardo Fuentes, so everything else related seemed to be a great waste, including the row with Sylvia and then the long night and day away from her.

A quick survey told him that Sylvia was not in the huge hotel lobby, so he made directly for the dining room. At this hour, much too early for dinner, it was nearly deserted. He searched the room for her, but with no success. Well, this was not the kind of place where she would likely be at this time of day, anyhow. He stopped at the desk of the maître d' on the way out and inquired whether Sylvia Duncan in room twenty-six had been down for breakfast that morning. A convenient habit, he thought, this custom of breakfast being served as part of the room tariff, because the waiters kept track of the room numbers of the diners. He was somewhat taken aback to learn that she hadn't been down at all that morning.

For her tea and fruit, he said to himself as he retrieved his key from reception and mounted the stairs two at a time. Plain black tea, none of that anemic herbal stuff, or the flowery flavored blends either. Milk and sugar in the tea, and then perhaps a bit of whatever fruit was in season. Her morning repast. No wonder she was so bloody slender.

He planted himself firmly in front of the door of her room and knocked. There was no response from within. He frowned and knocked again, more sharply this time. Still nothing. No stirring, no voice. Nothing. His hope dissolved into disappointment and then concern. *Merda.* Oh, shit. Where in bloody hell could she be? Had she deliberately ignored his advice to remain at the hotel, or had something happened to her? His vague fears began to take form and substance, going from grey and wavering to a solid black and white.

He strode on down the hallway and let himself into his own room. The bed with its soft pillows and cozy eiderdown comforter should have been inviting, given his lack of sleep over the past several days. But he ignored it. He shrugged his rucksack from his shoulder, dropped it to the floor with a thud and began pacing. And thinking, calculating. He forced himself to shed emotion, the knife-edge of concern, and concentrate on the facts. What was normally an easy and automatic process was somehow distorted by the intense feelings he had for her. He shook his head and started again. This time he focused on her safety and her potential danger, and this time he had more success. His logic was methodical and relentless, and he put his mind through its paces. Where in *hell* could she be?

The easy explanation was that she'd gone for a late afternoon walk. That explanation was not only the easiest but was also the most likely. Her habits, including her sleeping and eating and working habits, were quirky. Even so, he felt compelled to know where she was, and to know right *now*. He bent to his rucksack that he had carelessly tossed onto the carpeted floor and fished for a ring containing small metal devices. He much preferred to go from window to balcony to window like a cat burglar, but this particular hotel was devoid of balconies or even a narrow ledge between his window and Sylvia's. So it left him with just one other option. He was only moderately adept at picking complex locks, even after all his training, but the ones on the doors of this hotel seemed pretty old-fashioned and straightforward. If he could get a bit of time without interruption, he could let himself into her room in just a few minutes. It was, no doubt, breaking and entering. Well, entering, at least. But, he thought grimly, as his trainer had said in Latin, *Necessitas non habet legem.* Necessity knows no law.

He stepped back out into the hallway and gave a quick glance up and down. At the moment there was no one about, so he strode directly to her door and went down onto one knee on the carpet. Out of the corner of his eye, he watched the hallway for anyone approaching, and at the same time he fiddled with the lock and listened for the works to give.

Well, apparently in this old place, they did not give so easily.

He swore softly and then came abruptly to his feet as he heard someone approaching. He stuffed his hands into his pockets and strolled nonchalantly toward his room with an absent-minded nod to the couple that made their way past him. He waited until the door of their room had opened and closed and then returned to Sylvia's door to try once more.

This time the lock gave way, so immediately as to be almost alarming. He heard the satisfying click and turned the knob and pushed the door open even as he retrieved his small tools. He stepped inside and closed the door softly behind him.

His first glance at the room was disquieting. It was a bloody mess! Sylvia was normally rather neat, he remembered from her room at the Kámen in Czechoslovakia. But his trepidation eased when he saw that it was just a scattering of papers that were strewn about, and his heart rate slowed back to normal as he set to work, searching for something that might tell him where she had gone.

He sat down cross-legged onto the carpeted floor and began to sort through the mess. But completely out of character for him, he was immediately distracted, and found himself reading the neat, gently sloping scrawl that filled the pages. He knew it was none of his business what was written here, that he was invading her privacy. Even so, he managed to convince himself that he had to look, to find a way to locate her and make certain she was safe. But in truth he was hungry for something more of her, a clue to what made her mind and heart work the way they did. A hint about how she might feel about things. About people. Well, perhaps, about him.

He realized that he'd never before read anything that she had written except her somewhat vague and general letters to him, and he was completely taken aback at what was before him now. He thought the intense words and emotions on these pages were very powerful and poignant. Somehow, it allowed him to see through her carefully constructed walls, her fortress against the world, to her bared soul, and feel her – her what? Not her joy. Not her gentle, observed happiness. Rather to feel her pain. He wished he had been here to hold her as she had written these words, to somehow buttress her against such anguish that had resulted in these pages of outpouring. He determined that when he found her again he would say the words that he'd tried to say to her that first morning he was in Amsterdam, before Salvadore San Martín had unexpectedly materialized at the breakfast table like a freaking hurricane, twisting Nico's very thoughts and sending his carefully practiced words into an unspoken chaos.

Nearly half an hour had passed when with a start he realized that he had become distracted from his search for her by her very words on the paper. He stood up and stretched, and then his eye caught the flash of white of an envelope on the desk. Again feeling as though he were invading her privacy, he picked it up and turned it over.

Cariña.

He sank into her chair, feeling the breath go out of him as surely as if he had been kicked in the belly. All of this outpouring, all of this painful feeling, this unrelenting emotion, had been on account of that *bastardo* San Martín. Only Nico's ego and his absurd wishful thinking could have interpreted it otherwise. With a lurch of his gut, he remembered her slender form in the hallway pressed closely against the Colombian. It hurt the same now as it had then, like a knife thrusting into his heart.

He hurtled the envelope from him without looking inside, not caring if it ended up on the desk or on the floor with the rest of the damnable papers.

His first instinct was to get the hell out of Amsterdam, to put as many miles between Sylvia and himself as he could. As many hours and days. And *years.* But now she was somehow involved in his dirty, dangerous business – again! – and he could not leave her to the designs of San Martín, whatever they might be. Or to Fuentes, or to anyone else related to this interminable battle in which he was engaged. He knew who and what San Martín was, and he would never abandon her to him.

San Martín had charmed her, there was no doubt. And she may hate him, Nico, forever, but he was not going to let her become further involved with the Colombian, emotionally or otherwise. She would undoubtedly blame it on his jealousy. A fair deduction, he had to concede, since he was indeed jealous. Painfully so. As close as they had been in Czechoslovakia, he certainly had never held her in that passionate way that San Martín had the other night, even as much as he might have desired it. The picture came to him again, unbidden. He shied away from it in his mind and shook his head as if to deny what he knew he had seen.

Well, then, let her place the blame where she might, where she wanted, where she needed. He would let her go, as difficult as that may be. He would let her go, but he would not let her go with a *bastardo* like Salvadore San Martín.

He had not needed Sylvia's awkward, uncomfortable introduction at breakfast. He knew bloody damn well who San Martín, her Salvadore, was. Every time he thought he was closing in on Fuentes, that murdering *figlio di puttana*, the son of a whore, he would catch a glimpse of San Martín. As if in a dark or cloudy vision, somehow unclear. Like an antique mirror that was shadowed and bent and distorted, but nonetheless the image was there, unmistakably there. Nico had watched in impotent fury as the massive drug deals had gone down, observing but not intercepting, as were his orders, a part of his assignment from his organization.

And always, San Martín had been there in the shadows. If Fuentes was slippery, San Martín was nearly invisible. Like the light from a star that vanished if one looked at it directly. But there, every time. Always there.

Nico forced himself up from the chair and dropped to his knees to continue through her papers. *Merda*, she was prolific. He wished he had the time to just sit there on the floor for hours and read her small, neat handwriting, even though he knew how it would make him ache in the very center of his being.

Then without warning, he found what he had been seeking there in the mass of papers and his troubled thoughts were preempted. The receipt for a train ticket. He scanned it for the information he needed. The date purchased. Yesterday. He scowled. She had planned to leave even then? It made no sense. He'd have to think on that later. He noted the destination. Bruges, Belgium. He smiled grimly as he found the address of the travel bureau and the agent's name. Centraal Station. *Meneer* Hans van der Straaten. How very convenient. At least she was not trying to cover her tracks. Now all he needed was to find out exactly when she might have left, if indeed she had already left. The receipt didn't tell him whether it was an open ticket or for a date certain.

He made a half-hearted attempt to straighten her papers and then gave it up. He had left no bigger a mess than she had, and it was likely she wouldn't even notice that he had rummaged through her poignant musings.

He was halfway to the door, his strategy already formulating in his mind, his emotions resolutely pushed below the surface to deal with later.

But he found that he could not resist. He would have a bit of her, for a short while, at least, since it seemed that was all that would be left to him. He snatched up a handful of her scattered papers and folded them into his jacket pocket as he slipped out of her door and down the hallway to his own room.

Within fifteen minutes he was in Centraal Station with his rucksack and Sylvia's receipt, looking for the agent who had sold her the ticket by which she had fled him. He took a little scrap of paper with a number from the dispenser and watched as the agents on duty served one customer after the next. Finally his number was called and he approached one of the desks. "I need to speak with *meneer* van der Straaten, please," he said.

Getting an agent in a place of this kind was much like a lottery, with winners and losers. Apparently mostly losers. He had the misfortune to have his number called by a pudgy middle-aged woman with brown hair that made a tightly curled frame around her face and accented her disinterested demeanor. But she came to life when she realized she had an opportunity to pass off some of her work to someone else. She gestured to the empty chair behind the desk to the left of hers. "That is *meneer* van der Straaten's desk," she said. "He will be back in ten minutes. Wait there." She waved him away and called the next number as if glad to be rid of him. As he moved aside and leaned against the counter to leave the way clear for the next unfortunate victim, Nico wondered whether she got paid by the number of customers serviced or dismissed, rather than by client satisfaction.

He waited. Patience never had been his long suit and he knew it. His Italian father, now seven years dead, had pointed that out to him, but gently, at the tender age of five. His trainer with the organization that paid him to seek justice and deliver freedom by whatever means, legal or illegal, had pointed out the same, albeit less gently.

Ten minutes passed, then fifteen. Then twenty. Nico was on the verge of accosting the woman who had handed him off to nowhere, when a short, rotund man with receding blond hair emerged from a door behind the desk. He seated himself and arranged his papers with a studied air of efficiency, and then looked up to where Nico was hovering anxiously near the counter in front of his desk. "Well, young man," he said. "How can I be of assistance?"

With relief at the friendliness of the greeting, Nico handed over the receipt for Sylvia's ticket for the agent to study even as he seated himself in the chair indicated.

Nico might not be particularly comfortable with relationships and the elusive rules of romance, but he certainly knew how to play a rôle. Just now he was a heartbroken young man trying to find his girlfriend after a flaming row. It shouldn't be too hard, he thought, since it wasn't too far off target. At least he had the emotions right, if not the facts. He regretted having lost his temper with her, which he had done to exhaustion and no effect. He never lost his temper!

Meneer van der Straaten was suitably convinced, and anxious to help such a dejected young man. Yes, he remembered *het blauwtje de* Duncan. A pretty little thing, wasn't she, with all those wild curls? He had a great many customers in a day but he especially remembered her because she had such a wonderful sense of humor, being amused at all his jokes. He laughed at that, and Nico smiled, but weakly. *Porco mondo,* dammit to hell, what had she been thinking that she would have been so bloody cheerful?

Going to Bruges, Belgium, she was, the agent continued. With an open ticket.

An open ticket. Nico's heart sank, and his face must have reflected his dejection.

Sadly, the agent shook his balding round head and agreed that this was a dilemma. But then he added that it was an open departure for only three days, so if she were gone from Amsterdam just now, it was possible she had left this very morning. He had no way of knowing when she would actually travel, of course. Most likely not at night, though. Today's first train had left at seven o'clock this morning, to arrive in Bruges at thirteen minutes before ten. He smiled at his own preciseness and Nico found himself wondering if *meneer* van der Straaten might be a closet comic.

Nico thanked the agent and purchased his own ticket for Bruges. "Good luck to you," the agent said as he handed over the paperwork. "Your train leaves in ten minutes at the Papeneiland platform. Eighteen thirty-two exactly."

Nico was well aware of the formidable precision of the Dutch rail system. He grabbed a Bruges guidebook at the newsstand and, shoving through the turnstile, he ascended immediately to his platform. He was aboard the train barely five minutes early, anxious to be on his way. Predictably the train pulled out of the station on the second, exactly six thirty-two. Well, all right, eighteen thirty-two.

The *snel trein* might be the fast train, but it felt slow to Nico as he watched the minutes drag by and the countryside flash past even as the dusk began to settle. *Snel trein,* snail train, he thought, impatience coursing through him. Perhaps he should have taken a flight from Schiphol Airport to Bruges. Or perhaps he should have commandeered one of his organization's private jets. They certainly owed him a favor. But he really didn't want them to be able to locate him. Not for any reason, any emergency.

He ignored the flat countryside that shimmered by, gradually fading as evening descended like an oppressive shroud, and again tried to understand Sylvia's actions and motives. It was not like her to go off just because she was in a snit. As soon as that thought crossed his mind, he had to admit that he did not know whether or not she even had snits. Certainly he could not imagine it. Even so. Either she was in a snit, or some harm had befallen her. The latter was a very real possibility with that damnable Salvadore San Martín hanging about. Or she had been deeply hurt by his inexplicable actions over the past few days and had interpreted them to mean that he just did not care. A logical interpretation it would be, too, albeit a wrong one. How so very wrong.

Ah, he was weary! Trying to get comfortable, he twisted on the orange plastic seat, every movement restless and impatient. He stretched out his long legs into the aisle, unmindful of the potential hazard to other passengers. At last he dozed. Sylvia's face haunted his restless half-conscious thoughts, her hurt apparent, and her expert distancing herself from that hurt just as clear.

He was startled awake by the conductor, a young Frenchman. "Ticket, *monsieur?*"

Drowsily he dug into his rucksack for the ticket he had bought from the jovial *meneer* van der Straaten. The conductor made to punch it, and then burst out laughing.

Nico stared up at him as if he had gone daft. Ah, *Dio*, he thought. Good god! Not another one!

"Two times in one day!" the conductor exclaimed.

"I beg your pardon?" Nico said.

"Two times in one day, a passenger sits in second class after buying for first class! Usually I have the different problem, the opposite! *Mon dieu!*"

Nico shrugged. He was too weary to care.

But the conductor was insistent. "*Non, non, monsieur.* You are just as the young lady earlier today on the morning train. I tell her she must move to first class as she pay for first class."

Wearily, obediently, Nico stood and picked up his rucksack, and followed the slim, determined Frenchman with the very straight back. They passed through three cars before reaching the first class car, the conductor talking all the way. "Today I work the many hours – how do you say in *anglais?* – a long shift," he said. "Two times from Amsterdam to Antwerp and back today. But I remember my passengers." He shook his finger at Nico as if impressing upon him how seriously he took his job. "Especially the young *mademoiselle.* A pretty little thing she was, *petite.* Hair the color of autumn sun, and long with curls."

Nico came fully awake in an instant. "Sounds like my girlfriend," he said. "She came down to Bruges without me and I am following her. We had a, well, a disagreement, and –"

"Ah," said the Frenchman nodding his dark head wisely as he pointed Nico to his seat. "A lover's quarrel. *Oui,* she could be your girlfriend. She was very sad."

"Sylvia Duncan?" asked Nico, mournfully, he hoped.

"*Oui, monsieur. Mademoiselle* Duncan it was."

Nico's heart quickened. "She was sad, you say?" he said as he slid onto the upholstered seat.

"Oh, *oui.* Very sad. The blue eyes no smile when her lips smile." The Frenchman leaned a hip into one of the seats, bracing himself as the train took a wide turn. He was now completely engrossed in the conversation. "She sleep as if she is very tired. I have to awake her so she must change trains in Antwerp. I hope she is awake by the time she arrive in Bruges." He ran the tip of an index finger over his thin black mustache.

"Oh, I hope she was," Nico said fervently, and it was not at all a rôle. "Else I may never find her."

The conductor nodded, as if to impart great wisdom. "You will find her, *monsieur,*" he said solemnly. "She is a *petite fille* who wants to be found."

It was a ridiculous statement. The man could not possibly have had any such knowledge about Sylvia. Out of hand, Nico's logical mind rejected it. But his heart did not. His heart lifted in a foolishly ridiculous hope to match the Frenchman's equally ridiculous statement. "Do you think so?" he said.

"I am French," the man said as if stating the obvious. He waved his hand with an airy conviction. "We Frenchmen know the women. The little Sylvia wants to be found."

Nico slept not at all the rest of the way. He bade the Frenchman good-bye at Antwerp and watched the darkened Belgian countryside slide past, barely lit by a sullen, gibbous moon just rising. He reached the Bruges station at nineteen minutes past nine. Twenty-one nineteen. Once inside the station he quickly changed some of his British pounds to Belgian francs.

Under normal circumstances he would have walked, but this night he was both exhausted and in a hurry so he shrugged his rucksack over his shoulder and hailed one of the black taxis waiting in the huge, nearly-empty parking lot. In his pack was the guidebook for Bruges. He already knew it was a fairly large city, and he knew it would be difficult to find Sylvia. Except that Sylvia was a *fille petite* who wanted to be found. He smiled even as he directed the taxi driver towards the main squares in the heart of the city. Fifteen minutes later they rolled to a halt several blocks from Burg

Square, the driver explaining apologetically that he could drive no closer as the streets in the center were closed to traffic. Nico paid the driver in francs and, retrieving his rucksack, he strode off down the cobbled lane until it opened into Burg Square.

He paused to check out his surroundings. The square was softly lit, the ancient stones absorbing the gentle rays of light from the street lamps rather than reflecting them. The basilica towered above all the other buildings, as a benevolent protector. Then his gaze went directly to a small hotel above an Italian restaurant and market. It was a faded little place made of stone and wood, but he was not particularly picky. He requested a room that faced the square. It was a request easily granted, as the hotel was nearly vacant. Two dim flights of stairs later he deposited his rucksack onto the narrow bed. He ignored the dark, cool room with its shabby furniture and went directly to the window and flung it open.

Oh, yes, this would do very well indeed. The darkness was nearly absolute except for the gentle glow of the church, beautiful even in its prison of wooden and metal scaffolding. The pedestrians were thinning out across the square. He scanned the place, cataloging shops and restaurants in his mind, filing away the city with precision for future retrieval. He yawned. Directly across the square from him, opposite the old church, was another small old hotel with a French restaurant next to it.

That would be just the ticket, he decided, knowing that he had to be quick, as many Belgian restaurants took the last orders at ten, and it was very nearly that. He headed for the washroom to splash water onto his face, wishing that there was a shower in this creaking old place. He would eat, and then bathe, and sleep. And then he would worry about the rest of it tomorrow.

CHAPTER **11**

For the first time in several nights, Sylvia knew that she would sleep well. Perhaps it was the long, tiring train ride and the circuitous walk to the Burg Square at the center of the city. Or perhaps it was the intense bout of painting the portrait of Bruges with her pen, tracing its history, its colors, its rhythms, and its very soul, word after word. But most likely, she thought, it was that she was no longer subject to either Salvadore's intense scrutiny and imagined undercurrents, or Nico's whims of appearing and disappearing at will. No, neither of them could disturb her sleep this night. They were hours away in Amsterdam or wherever else they had both taken themselves. And no one knew that she was in Bruges but herself. It was a satisfying feeling.

Tomorrow she would explore Bruges, taking her notebook along and again painting the city in words. Bold words and decisive colors as van Gogh would have painted it on a canvas, and this time from the street rather than from her bird's-perch at the top floor of her hotel. Bruges with a hard *g* tomorrow!

Already a plot for a new novel and with new characters was taking shape in her mind, weaving in and out of the Bruges she already knew from the window of her room. She toyed with it even as she drifted off to sleep, forming its rhythms and how they might fit into the nuances of this city. Her only dream that night was of Nico, and he was earnestly explaining to her just what it was he had wanted to say when he had first come to Amsterdam and they had been interrupted by Salvadore. In her dream, what he had to say made perfect sense and moved her to a gentle joy. When she awoke, she could remember none of it, but the joy remained with her even as she bounded down the dingy stairs to find a place for her morning tea.

She emerged from the twinkling prisms of the artisans' glass in the quaint lobby of her hotel into the early morning sun, and stopped to survey her surroundings. She was always amazed at how a place looked and felt different depending on the time of day, the weather, and her mood. This morning Bruges seemed to have its own light source rather than relying on the sun to illuminate it. A Monet painting it could have been, muted but bright, unfocused but sharp. An enigma. No. A paradox. She smiled even as she thought of it, and gazed around the square. Places that had seemed dominant last night from her fourth story window were now more retiring, more subdued, and other places were now demanding a place of greater importance. She wished for a brief moment that her talent was expressed in lines and shapes and colors rather than in words.

A small café beckoned, its front all shining windows with blue and white patterned curtains tied back. The wooden chairs and tables were small and plain and spilled out onto the brick sidewalk. It was still a bit cool to be outside so early but she wore jeans and a light shirt and had brought a sweater. She stepped into the café and ordered tea with milk and sugar, and a round, plain roll with a light glaze. She made her request in not very fluent French, wondering how Nico managed to be so expert in several languages. It must be a gift, she thought, an inborn talent. Like painting or music. Or like writing. The idea pleased her. The blond girl behind the counter encouraged her fractured pronunciation and cheerfully served up her tea and roll on a small white wooden tray.

Outside she went and seated herself so that she was facing her hotel and the French restaurant. The brew in the small blue porcelain teapot was hot and strong, nestled into a tea cosy against the coolness. The roll was exquisite, warm and only a bit sweet. She left her notebook and pen alone for the moment and let her body and mind absorb the morning.

She lingered until she had put away two pots of tea, and then determined her plan for the day, such as it was. She would walk, and she would write. Indeed, the city begged to be captured in meanderings and in words.

After leaving a few francs on the table, she rose and started her sojourn, determined to lose herself in the labyrinth of ancient cobbled streets. It was so very clean! Every street, every brick, every stone. The walls of the buildings were thick and the antiquity of the place was evidenced by the architecture rather than the state of decline. She took herself away from the high-end row of shops near the square and spent the morning on the back streets. Impossibly small shops offered fresh fruits and vegetables, or newly-cut flowers, or smelt of freshly-baked bread. The natives were cheerfully doing their morning shopping even as they stopped for a gossip with the shopkeepers and the neighbors. Now and again a small park would surprise the stern stone buildings by providing a merry spot of green relief.

By lunchtime, she was thoroughly lost and quite ready to put up her feet and give them a rest. She asked directions back to the center of the city. Once she was directed, then twice, each time making it a bit closer before getting caught in the tangled web of cobbled streets and changing her direction.

On her third query, a young man cheerfully insisted that he escort her to her hotel so she would not get lost again. He was tall and blond and very Dutch, and he spoke no English. Sylvia spoke no Dutch, so they stumbled along in a discombobulated French that would have surely horrified a Frenchman. In fact, she could have found the square quite handily by herself, as it was only six or seven blocks from where she had asked directions. But he delivered her to the doorstep of her hotel on the square and left her there with a wave of his hand and an admonition not to get lost again that day. At least that's what she thought he had said.

She found a quaint Italian restaurant just a few blocks from the square. It was hidden away rather than being on a main street, but it was busy and bustling. With locals, she decided. A good omen.

Surprisingly hungry she was – for her! – so she put away a sizable portion of pasta primavera, delicately seasoned, the vegetables with just the perfect crunch. It might have been prepared and served up in southern Italy! She declined the tempting red wine as she intended to spend the afternoon working in her room. But the fine weather seduced her and she wandered again through Bruges, this time keeping fairly close to the center, strolling to the nearby Markt Square to admire the towering Belfry and listen to its forty-seven bell carillon peal out over the city. She sat for a time on a green wooden bench near a sculpture of two Flemish heroes, a butcher and a weaver who had led the common people in a stalwart resistance against a French invasion. By the end of the day she felt quite the expert on how to make her way through the maze without taking a wrong turn.

Again she wished she had checked out of the Hotel Amstel Grand in Amsterdam. She would like to stay in Bruges for a few weeks, she thought as she slipped up a long, narrow alleyway that opened onto Burg Square right next to her hotel.

CHAPTER **12**

From Nico's perspective, the day was not nearly so bucolic. For hours he haunted the city center, alternating between the Burg and Markt squares, convinced that Sylvia would not be able to resist this part of the old city of Bruges. He despaired of ever finding her, and tortured himself by imagining that she had not come to Bruges at all, that she had ridden the *snel trein* straight through to Oostende and caught a ferry from there to Dover, on the south coast of England. Or that she had arrived at Bruges and then realized her mistake and gone directly back to Amsterdam, and was even now waiting for him to come to her. Or – no, dammit! He would not let his thoughts go in this other direction. He could not begin to contemplate that she could be with Salvadore San Martín even now. Or that Fuentes might have her. God knew where the drug lord might be. But it was a good bet that he was not far from here, if San Martín was in the neighborhood. Fuentes had a nasty habit of turning up unexpectedly and apparently without logic or reason. It made him no less lethal.

Twice during that long day Nico rang up the Hotel Amstel Grand and asked for Sylvia. Both times he was told that *het blauwtje de* Duncan was not in. Would he like to leave a message? Both times he declined and hung up in frustration at not reaching her, and in relief that she had not yet checked out and left Amsterdam for good.

He wondered whether there might be another central point in Bruges that would have captured her interest before she could make her way here to one of the squares. But he studied the tourist maps once more and decided that was unlikely.

He sat outside in the heat of the sun at a small café on Burg Square and downed one thick black coffee after the next until he was so wired with caffeine that he could barely sit still. As the sun reached its zenith he decided he was too warm to remain at his table. A third time he called the Hotel Amstel Grand to find Sylvia still not in. But this time he left a message. "This is *meneer* Nico DiCapelli. I have room twenty-eight in your hotel. Please inform *het blauwtje de* Duncan in room twenty-six that I am in Bruges, Belgium, and will she please wait for me in Amsterdam?"

No sooner had he hung up than he chided himself. "*Wait for me,*" he muttered mockingly. "She must be bloody tired of hearing that."

He left the telephone kiosk and sauntered off eight or ten blocks to explore the Church of Our Lady on Mariastraat. It was magnificent with its soaring, vaulted ceilings and intricate wood and brass work, all delicately illuminated by the sunlight that was filtered and subdued by the stained glass windows. The colors danced along the stone walls in intense sparkles of emeralds and rubies. And sapphires, like Sylvia's eyes! Surely she would be drawn to this stately cathedral in the same way that she had been seduced by the ancient, well-tended church in the village of Tatra when he had first met her in Czechoslovakia.

He wandered past the painting of the *Madonna and Child* by Michelangelo. The first work, and one of the few by that great but impetuous genius to leave Italy. Astonishingly, poignantly beautiful. He realized then that he didn't even know what kind of art, what kind of paintings, that Sylvia might like.

Frowning slightly, he examined the painted sepulchers from the thirteenth century, still in beautiful condition. The ancient carved wooden statues caught his attention for awhile as he studied the intricate details. And then he strolled slowly past the sixteenth century tombs with the sculptures of Mary of Burgundy and Charles the Bold, whoever in hell they had been. He couldn't remember. Charles the Bold? Or Charles the Bad? Perhaps it depended upon one's perspective. But then, he thought with sour humor, Charles the Bad might as well be Salvadore the Colombian.

At last he planted himself on a bench in the very back of the cathedral, determined to soak in its lofty and holy ambiance. But he caught himself watching for Sylvia rather than absorbing the beautiful arches or the vast expanse of the architecture, or the massive, ponderous paintings that dominated the walls. With an exasperated sigh, he returned to the sunlight and headed back to Burg Square where he reclaimed his table at the café and ordered a late lunch of Belgian mussels cooked in a buttery broth.

What an interminable day it was, so slow in passing! He took no enjoyment in this ancient city. He ached to have Sylvia appear before his eyes, honey-colored hair curly and tousled, pen and notebook in her hand, sapphire eyes smiling. Or snapping! He closed his eyes and imagined her before him, her slender frame, her height just at his shoulder. Then he remembered seeing her with Salvadore in the hallway of the Hotel Amstel Grand, that slight body pressed close to the Colombian's, and in great annoyance he threw the thought from him and rose. He had paid for his lunch some time ago so he spent the next few hours wandering around the two squares.

On Markt Square he poked around the Belfry for awhile. On a whim, he decided to climb to the tower's summit. A breathless three hundred sixty-six steps later he was rewarded by an unparalleled panoramic view of Bruges. Then his gaze was drawn across the still-green countryside all the way to the flash of light on the restless water of the sea.

He brought his attention back to the maze of streets and buildings below him. *Merda!* It would be easier to find a squirrel's hoard in a forest than to unearth Sylvia here in this vast old city! Again doubts assailed him, and the only thing that kept him from leaving here was his complete lack of options. He would not give up his search. He *could* not! But he knew no other place to look. Either his formidable logic had forsaken him entirely or he had not enough information to reach a conclusion.

Leaving a muttered obscenity floating at the top of the tower, he descended back to the Markt Square. His dinner of *steak-frites* – steak and fried potatoes – was at another café where he could watch Markt Square as he had watched Burg Square. For whatever good it did. In a short, impotent temper, he kept his place until the night turned late and chilly, and then he returned to Burg Square and went directly to his dark, empty room. Unable to sleep, he paced the floor. At length, with an Italian expletive directed at nothing and no one in particular, he remembered the papers he had taken from Sylvia's room at the Hotel Amstel Grand. He flipped on a light. From his jacket pocket, he drew out the pages that were covered with Sylvia's gentle scrawl and settled down to read them.

His mood could not have been more foul. So he would deliberately intrude into her privacy and gauge her feelings for that *bastardo* San Martín.

He sprawled uncomfortably on the straight-backed chair, his long legs crossed at the ankle, and began to read. The words tortured him, so poignant was their message. He ached for her, even as he was beset by an intense longing. How had San Martín, in such a short time, become so involved with her, so controlling of her feelings? How had he been so bloody fortunate, taking the place that Nico coveted as his own?

It was only gradually that it came to him, seeping into his consciousness. So gradually that he hardly knew how or when it had happened. He had been wrong, so very wrong. The words Sylvia had written with such passion were not for Salvadore, but for him, Nico. He sat back, stunned, his breath catching. Then he started reading again. At last he came to what seemed a nearly desperate attempt for her imagination to send her heart's message.

> *"All my poetry,*
> *all my prose,*
> *all my heart and soul*
> *I pour it out,*
> *I pour it out*
> *'til it trembles in fullness.*
> *Fullness of myself.*
> *And I hand the cup*
> *to Nico."*

His heart stopped.

Hands unsteady now, he went on to the next page. The words swept over him like a tidal wave off a wild and rocky northern Oregon coastline.

> *"I want to write the ending*
> *I want to see again, through the mist of my tears*
> *I want to turn my back on my fears*
> *I want to gaze upon the future."*

Here there was a streak of ink on the paper where it had been unmistakably dampened, leaving a blue smear. Tears?

> *"I would live all the pain again*
> *just to hold you*
> *to have you*
> *to touch you*
> *to breathe you.*
> *I want to write the end of the story*
> *with you.*
> *With Nico."*

He slid slowly from the chair and settled to his knees on the hard planks of the floor. *With Nico.* *"Gesù Bambino,"* he whispered. This outpouring was to him, not to San Martín. And such an admission it was, from the careful, reticent Sylvia. From the vulnerable, still-afraid Sylvia. Such a confession. He blinked as his eyes stung. Gentle God in heaven, he had not wept since he was six years old, not even when his father had been killed.

He blinked again. He would not let Sylvia withdraw from him now. Oh, no, not now that he knew her feelings, and knew they were for him. He knew this was a mighty and unwitting acquiescence from her, and one she would be loath to admit. But the evidence was at his fingertips, and he would cherish it. Sylvia cared for him, as deeply as he cared for her.

"Sylvia," he whispered, still on his knees as if in worship. "Sylvia. You are *mine*."

He would sleep well this night.

CHAPTER **13**

As for Sylvia, again she slept well enough, her feet tired and her very being sated with the fresh air. But once more Nico waited for her in her dreams, and when she awoke in the early morning, her hair was tangled and her cheeks were wet with tears.

Perhaps it was the waking with tears on her face. But the fragile comfort, the sense of satisfied aloneness and aloofness of the day and night before had vaporized, and had left her but an empty shell. She sternly pushed all thoughts of Nico from her mind, and made her decision. She would walk a bit this morning, and then she would pack her few things and take a late train back to Amsterdam. Once there, she would contact a travel agent and be on her way. To somewhere.

"To nowhere," she said aloud and was startled to hear her own voice. "Goodbye, Nico," she whispered, picking up a desolate echo of their parting in Amsterdam. She pulled on a pair of jeans and a long-sleeved blue shirt, and left her room to find some tea for her breakfast.

CHAPTER **14**

Nico's desperation to find Sylvia was ten-fold this morning. Again he was at the same café on Burg Square with a hot, thick coffee at hand, brought by the long-suffering waiter who had come to view Nico as just another permanent fixture, like the doors or the tables or the chairs. Or the basilica itself, for god's sake! He still could not believe it, after feeling the burning hurt when he had thought her impassioned words spoke of Salvadore. Instead, they were of him. They were of her. She was *his*. "Ah, Sylvia, love," he muttered into the tepid dregs in his nearly empty cup. "Come to me, Sylvia."

He was turned to stone with shock when at that very moment she appeared, as if conjured up by his plea. *Sylvia!* Emerging from the *petite* hotel next to the French restaurant, her long curls catching the early morning sunlight and splitting the reflection into brilliant shades of chocolate and golden honey with a touch of crimson sunset. He couldn't move. He *had* to move! He stared even as she turned from the square and started down a narrow alleyway next to the hotel.

As if in a trance, he came to his feet and dropped a few Belgian francs onto the table. Then, in stunned disbelief, he froze once again. Coming across the square from the direction of the basilica was Eduardo Fuentes. *Fuentes!* That bloody Colombian drug lord who had occupied his waking hours for the past two months, who had left him and Sylvia for dead in a Czechoslovakian hillfort. *Merda!* Shit! And damn the *figlio di puttana,* the son of a whore. It was *impossible!* What in bloody hell was he doing here?

Nico turned his face toward the café windows so that Fuentes would not see him or recognize him. As soon as the Colombian started away from the square, Nico would follow him. Indeed, Nico thought, chiding himself, he should not have been surprised. If Salvadore San Martín were as close as Amsterdam, it followed that Fuentes would turn up in the same vicinity sooner or later. But what a great opportunity to gain information on the drug runners! He could observe them at his leisure, as they didn't even know he was here in Bruges.

Fuentes lingered for what seemed a very long time at the window of one of the expensive international brand-name shops as if browsing. Nico kept his face averted, but continued to watch intently. Finally the Colombian began ambling toward a side street. Nico started forward, smoothly as a stalking cat, intense and ready.

Then he abruptly halted. Damnation! Every time he was close to Sylvia, his job came between them. Fuentes was his job, and he had to do his job. And this was a rare and unexpected opportunity. But in fact, his organization didn't even know he was here in Bruges. He was on leave, *porco mondo*, damn it all. This time Sylvia would come first. She had to come first. She was his future. He should have put her first well before this.

He stared longingly in the direction where Fuentes had disappeared. Then he gave an exasperated sigh. He set across the square at a determined trot and ducked into the dimness of the alley where Sylvia had vanished some moments before.

CHAPTER **15**

In spite of her general propensity for getting quite lost – directionally impaired, Nico called it – Sylvia thought she knew her way around this part of Bruges rather well by now, and decided to take a shortcut through the narrow cobbled alley next to her hotel. There was no one about in the dim byway, but there were passersby on the busy street at one end and at Burg Square on the other, so she felt safe enough. She walked rapidly, thinking, planning her escape to nowhere, paying no attention to her surroundings. Indeed, the impending encounter was much the same as the one she had had in Amsterdam, when she had inadvertently crashed into Salvadore and his monster of a motorcycle. She did not see the lean, dark-haired man striding purposefully towards her until she was nearly upon him. Even then she noticed him only peripherally and distractedly, and shifted her direction a bit to pass him by.

But he intentionally side-stepped directly into her path and she drew up short, startled. "Pardon," she said, and made to slip past him. Then she looked at him, at last actually seeing him. She stopped, completely still, at once aware of the remoteness of the dim alley and the looming, unbroken grey line of ancient stone buildings. She looked into his face. Salvadore!

In the next instant she knew that this man was *not* Salvadore. "Who are you?" she said, the words coming involuntarily. She was aware that she sounded breathless, but could not seem to alter that. "Who are you?"

He did not seem surprised or put off. Nor did he move from where he had planted himself, deliberately blocking her way. "I ask *lo mismo* – the same, maybe," he said, his accent heavy, certainly much heavier than Salvadore's.

She wondered if he were insulted by her forwardness. She was never forward! But just now she was. "Who *are* you?" she repeated yet again, even more firmly. Truly, his eyes, his carriage, his very looks reminded her of Salvadore. She had a sudden flash of insight and spoke from impulse rather than thoughtfulness. "Are you looking for Salvadore?" she asked.

He started back as if she'd slapped him, his cool demeanor dissolved. But only for a brief moment. Then a controlled mask descended upon his face, and his eyes bored into her. Coffee-dark eyes, so like Salvadore's. But cold. Salvadore's eyes had never been cold, not with her. "Salvadore?" he said shortly, even contemptuously, she thought.

"Don't act as though you did not recognize the name," she said, her admonishment clear. "Because you did."

"*Sí?* Did I?" He said it as if she were somehow daft.

"Oh, yes. You did," she replied. She said it as if he were hiding something.

She hit a nerve with her insolent tone.

"You have *una imaginación grande*," he said sardonically. "*Es de los Estados Unidos?* You are from United States?"

The intended insult was unmistakable. Undeterred, she gave a slight smile. *En garde!* And attack! "I am from the United States," she said, and then added in her most mordant tone, "How very observant of you!" She paused to watch the disdain flit across his countenance. Then she thrust. Not parried. Thrust. "And you must be Colombian."

It was a shot true to the mark and she knew it. And she knew that he saw her knowledge. With impossible swiftness, his left hand snaked forward and grasped her wrist before she could jerk back from him. His grip was brutal.

"Let me go. You are hurting me." She was surprised at the calm coolness of her voice. And impressed.

Apparently he was impressed as well. He stared at his hand on her slender white wrist as if the sight of it shocked him. He released her abruptly.

She wanted to pull back her hand and rub her bruised wrist, but willed herself to stillness. He observed her without speaking, and she did the same with him. So sure she was now, so very sure. He had indeed recognized Salvadore's name. She still had no understanding of this situation, whatever it was. She was sure Salvadore was in some kind of danger from this man. But it sounded so very fantastic, so theatrical.

At last he gave her a short nod. "*Sí.* I am of Colombia. *También,* and also is Salvadore. Where is he?"

Although she had been certain that he knew Salvadore, even so it was a shock to hear the name fall from the stranger's lips in this bizarre conversation.

So. Nico was right. Salvadore was Colombian. She wondered what else that Nico had told her might be true. Well, knowing him, probably all of it. Then she collected her whirling thoughts and stared up at this man's face, considering how she might extricate herself from this alley with its menace.

Their gazes were locked for some time. Then in annoyance, he gave over first. He threw up his hands. "What is that you do in Bruges, *brujita?*" he said. "You little witch."

His tone was oddly conversational, but his words stung.

Her thoughts changed direction abruptly. "Why do you call me such a name? Little witch?"

He grinned unexpectedly, a dimple flashing in his left cheek. The threatening demeanor had dissolved, at least for the moment. The resemblance to Salvadore was uncanny – white teeth against the olive skin, the crinkling at the corners of his dark eyes. "Well," he said. "You are not much big, no?"

She found him outrageous and she wanted to take him on, but held herself in check. Barely. "You are rather rude, aren't you?" she said as coldly as she could manage.

"*Sí,* I am," he agreed, still grinning that charming Salvadore grin.

"And rather proud of it." She observed to herself that his command of the English language was not nearly as adept as Salvadore's. Not only was his accent much heavier, but his vocabulary was considerably limited, even primitive, especially his use of the verbs, nearly all in the present tense. The sure mark of a beginner in any non-native language.

He gestured impatiently, suddenly finished with the lightness he had exuded for a few brief moments. "You have a – a something that I need."

"Do I?"

"*Sí.* You do."

"And you think that speaking to me in such an insolent fashion will get you what you want?"

She could tell that he had barely understood her words, but he seemed to manage the intent. "What I *need*," he corrected.

"Whatever." She knew that it sounded rude, even as she gave an eloquent shrug of disinterest that would have made Nico's Italian father proud. But indeed, this man's overbearing demeanor offended her.

"You will give to me."

"Will I?"

"*Maldición!* Damn you! *Sí,* you will."

She arched a dismissive brow at his expletives. "You will excuse me. I am leaving now." She made as if to turn back towards the square.

But he was quicker. "No, you are not." He gripped her wrist again, but not as hard as before, at least not so hard as to hurt her. Not to hurt perhaps, but to frighten. She felt her nerves jump. He must have seen it on her face. "I need some – how you say – some *información*," he said, pressing his advantage.

"Let me go," she said evenly, and much more calmly than she felt, but she did not attempt to struggle away. Something inside told her it would be in vain.

He changed his tactics. *"Por favor.* Please," he said. "Please stay."

"I'd rather not."

"Sylvia. Please."

She stared at him, the question falling from her lips before she had considered it. "How is it that you know my name?" she asked. In the next instant she thought that perhaps she should have denied it.

He looked momentarily dismayed, then his hard, impassive gaze returned. "You are Sylvia, no?" He said her name with the same accent and the same inflection that Salvadore had used.

"That's not the point," she retorted. "It's my name, and I don't recall having given you permission to use it. How is it that you know it?"

His dark eyes narrowed again and his forehead creased in a frown. He considered her words for a moment as if trying to make sense of her meaning. Then his brow cleared as he apparently understood. "From Salvadore," he said. "I know how you are called from Salvadore."

She frowned, not understanding.

"Salvadore know you – know about you from DiCapelli. Nico DiCapelli."

"Nico DiCapelli?" she said blankly. She hoped.

He wasn't buying. "Nico DiCapelli," he said firmly. "And you know the name of DiCapelli, the same that I know the name of Salvadore. Where is he? Where is DiCapelli?"

"How would I know any DiCapelli?"

"You tell me. *Ahora!* Now!" His grip tightened.

"No. *You* tell *me.*" She was completely aware of her formidable stubbornness and intended to employ it to its fullest extent. A liability suddenly turned into an asset. "Tell me who DiCapelli is. And tell me how you know Salvadore."

His eyes narrowed. Evil, she thought. Definitely evil. In the next instant she thought she was, perhaps, wrong. She usually was when it came to judging the character of a man. Good lord, look at her now-dead husband. She'd thought he was a good and honest and kind person. Well, she had thought that for the first few months she had known him, at least.

He hesitated, and then answered half of her question. "Salvadore *es mi hermano.* My brother."

She tried not to react. She raised a brow skeptically. "Your brother." She hoped she sounded disbelieving, because she was not. His brother! A very close family resemblance. The stubborn line of his mouth. The dark eyes. The nose! That formidable nose!

"He is my brother," he repeated. "And I am – I worry for he – him – to be safe. I do not see him from – no, – *since* he come to Bruges."

"Oh," she said. Perhaps her thoughts of danger threatening Salvadore had not been so theatrical after all. But what in the world was he doing in Bruges? It made no sense.

He gave an impatient jerk on her wrist, and she knew she would have a lovely bruise as a souvenir. "Tell me where he is," he said, his voice now a low, threatening growl. *"Ahora!* Now!"

She thought he sounded vicious and pulled back. If she were not alarmed, she ought to be, and she had sense enough to know it.

But his mercurial demeanor changed abruptly once again. This time it did throw her off balance. *"Por favor,"* he said, an unmistakably pleading tone in his voice. "I must find him. Is important. He is not, *eh*, safe."

Almost involuntarily, she responded to his apparent emotion. "Why do you think I can help?"

"Tell me where he is."

"I don't know."

"Por favor! Please!"

"I am telling you the truth. I don't know. He was to meet me and Nico for dinner a few nights ago in Amsterdam."

A quick, self-satisfied grin flashed across his face and as suddenly vanished. So. A point to him, this mysterious stranger. He had gotten her to admit that she knew who Nico DiCapelli was.

"But he didn't show up," she added.

Now he frowned in confusion. "Show up?"

"Yes. He didn't come to the restaurant in the evening as he had intended. I haven't seen him since that same morning, at breakfast." That was the truth. But she didn't bother to mention the note that Salvadore had left under her door. She still wasn't certain what was going on.

He glanced around the cobbled alley as if he expected Salvadore to materialize at any moment.

The inconsistencies of this conversation and of this man's odd behavior were beginning to gnaw at her. "Why would Salvadore speak to you of me?"

He shrugged. "Just we are talk – talking."

"When?"

He gave her a guarded look that disturbed her, but didn't answer.

"I thought you said that you had not seen him since he came to Bruges," she said, closely watching the frowning face for a reaction.

"*Es la verdad.* Is the true," he admitted, seemingly reluctantly.

"So, I ask you again. When?"

He still held her wrist, but more gently now. "He tell me about you, *eh,* some weeks ago," he said.

She stared at him, not comprehending. "Weeks ago? I don't understand. I've only just met him since I came to Amsterdam."

"*Sí. Yo sé.* I know."

"So how would he know anything about me?" She frowned in concentration. "Or why would he care to?"

He sighed, as if the entire conversation had spun out of his control. Then he spoke, but answered only her first question. "He know you, who you are – in *Checoslovaquia.*"

"Czechoslovakia!" She was astonished. She suddenly remembered that Salvadore had thought she was from Czechoslovakia. It left her even more confused.

"You are at the Kámen, *la mansión vieja,* the old mansion near to the village of Tatra, no?"

"Yes, but –"

"Salvadore is – no – he *was* there."

"I never saw him, nor met him there."

"*Por supuesto que no.*" He shook his dark head. "Of course not. He did not want that you see him. Or know him."

Her brow creased again. "But why?"

He looked away and then back to her. "We go to a place and to talk?" he said. "*Por favor?*"

Her first inclination was to refuse. Her next inclination was to accept. A table at a public café with several other patrons close by would feel much safer than this dim, deserted alleyway. "Yes, of course," she said.

"*Entonces.* Come, then." He kept his grip on her wrist, even more tightly than before. She wondered at that, but walked quickly to keep up with his long stride as they headed in the direction away from the Burg Square. But just halfway down the narrow alley, he pulled up abruptly and opened a side door on the left. Suddenly alarmed, she hesitated and then protested. It was both too late as well as ineffective. He had dragged her inside and slammed the door shut before she could even cry out. Not that there would have been anyone to hear her.

She struggled to pull away from him but he gave her an impatient jerk. "*Para!*" he said sharply. "Stop! I do not to hurt you."

She forced herself to calmness. "I don't wish to be here," she said stiffly.

"I think is best to have some – how you say? – some alone. Some private."

"I am not comfortable here. I will go now." She tried to pull away, but his grasp was firm.

"No," he said flatly. "You stay."

"You will force me to stay?"

He looked, of all things, affronted. "No! *Sólo te pido.* Only I ask. I think you are not safe on the streets of this Bruges."

She stopped her struggle. It was useless in any case, her slight size no match for his lean strength that certainly equaled Salvadore's. But she would not submit. He might be able to overpower her, but she would not give over. "And why would I not be safe here in Bruges?"

He ignored her question, and pointed to a dark, narrow wooden stairwell, obviously well-trodden. "Now we go up for a coffee."

"I don't care for coffee." She planted herself stubbornly, her free hand on her hip. "I don't like it. Not at all. It's bitter."

He rolled his eyes as if in exasperation, but a reluctant smile twitched at one corner of his mouth. Well, at least she apparently had a bit of entertainment value, if nothing else. "*Bueno.* Not to have a coffee then. But you go up."

"I'll scream," she threatened.

He looked her over appraisingly. "You, Sylvia, I no believe. You not be a woman to scream."

She was startled for a moment. "Oh. Why not?"

"If you be with Nico DiCapelli, then you – you no *nerviosa* – your nerves not be so weak. And also with Salvadore. No *nerviosa*. Not with nerves, not you."

She suddenly regretted having dropped Salvadore's name.

"Come. *Ahora.* Now. I no like to waste this time." He again gestured up the narrow stairwell.

She took her hand from her hip and motioned in the same direction. "After you," she said.

"I do not think." But he gave a half-grin at her persistence. The dimple flashed, and for a brief moment he looked almost boyish. "You go? Or perhaps I put you on my arm, I mean, on my shoulder, and carry you?" His dark eyes gleamed as if he might enjoy doing just that.

With ill-grace she preceded him up the stairs, but only because she had no choice. She scrambled up the steep incline, with this stranger right behind, his hand at the small of her back. The top of the stairs revealed only one door, and he reached past her with his left hand and shoved it open.

"*Bueno.* Here you are, *amiga,*" he said.

"I am most certainly *not* your friend," she said even as she stepped inside. The room where she found herself was austere. There was a cot on one side, with a few threadbare blankets tangled upon it. Two well-worn wooden chairs and a small battered table comprised the only other furniture. An alcove provided a makeshift kitchen, with a few cracked cups and plates scattered haphazardly about, desperately in need of a good wash. A closed door was set into the wall to the left of the cot, and Sylvia wondered briefly if there might be a means of escape there.

"You sit," he said, pointing to one of the rickety chairs. He made the blunt order sound like a polite invitation. Then in another of his disconcertingly quick movements, he snatched her small bag from her hand. She made no protest when he upended it onto the floor. He picked up her tablet and pen, her passport, and a few francs. *"Bueno,"* he said as he dropped the few items back into her bag and handed it over.

She took it. "Expecting a gun or a knife?" she asked with a caustic edge to her voice.

His only response was to turn away. "I make the coffee now," he said.

"I told you. I don't care for any of your nasty coffee," she said tartly.

He shrugged and made for the alcove. *"Bueno.* But still I make," he said. Then he glanced at the door from where they had just entered. "Do not think to try to run from me, because I stop you before you come the stair of the top."

She sighed and settled herself onto one of the hard chairs, eyeing the door. No doubt he was right. She could not escape, not just now at least. And so she watched her captor cautiously, but with a measure of curiosity. Salvadore's brother. Yes, the resemblance was startling, even though this man somehow seemed older. He was tanned and lean, clad in blue jeans and a denim jacket over a black t-shirt. His dark hair was slightly longer than Salvadore's. And, as she had already noted, his eyes and nose and stubborn mouth were definitely from the same family.

Busy preparing the coffee, he scarcely seemed to notice her. "Older or younger?" she said suddenly, breaking the silence between them.

"Cómo? What you mean?" He looked up from the battered pan on the small gas range where the scent of boiling coffee rose with the cloud of steam.

"Are you Salvadore's older or younger brother?"

He grinned, a flash of white teeth splitting his face and the dimple appearing. Again he looked almost boyish. "More young," he said. "Younger. By one year only."

"That's odd," she said bluntly. "I'd have thought that you were older."

"Hard living, you say in *inglés,"* he said, smiling briefly in evident satisfaction at his command of this idiom in the foreign language. "Hard living," he repeated, almost as if he were proud of his hard living. Apparently deciding that the coffee had boiled long enough, he poured out two cups and handed one to her.

She took it and held its heat between her two hands, not drinking. The scent of the coffee was heady and rich. She breathed in deeply. But really, she preferred tea. Nico was the one who favored the horribly strong coffee, nearly strong enough to chew, she had told him once. And he had laughed at her when she wrinkled her nose in mock distaste. In Turkey, he had told her, they don't brew their coffee. Rather, they cook it. Thick and sweet and never to be stirred, else the sludge would never manage to slide down your throat.

Her captor settled himself onto the other unremarkable chair, facing her, and took a cautious sip of the hot brew. He wiped his lips on the back of his hand and grinned again. This time, rather than looking boyish, she thought he looked feral. Somehow predatory – on the hunt and relentlessly seeking. For what, she could not know. He leaned forward, bringing his face closer to hers. "So say to me, little Sylvia. For what you come to Bruges?"

"I'm on holiday."

"*Sin compañia? Sola?* Alone?"

"Yes."

"Or with DiCapelli?"

"No."

"Or maybe Salvadore?"

"Alone."

"Where is DiCapelli now?"

"I don't know."

"And Salvadore?"

"I told you. I don't know where he is."

"Is important I find him. And soon."

"Why do you need him so badly?"

He sat back a bit, scowled at her and took another drink of his steaming coffee. "How much you know Salvadore?" he said.

"Not well. Just as a friend."

"And DiCapelli?"

"The same."

"A friend." He sounded as if he did not believe her.

Unaccountably, it annoyed her.

He looked at her, his gaze speculative. "I no can believe," he said slowly, "that you think to spend time with both – with either them. DiCapelli or Salvadore. Why want you to be see Salvadore?"

She shook her head at his clumsy use of the English language, but she did understand what he was trying to say. Nico would argue that understanding was all that was really necessary. To communicate. After all, that was the most basic purpose of any language, wasn't it? Not that she had agreed with him, not in her line of work. As important as the basic need to communicate were the rhythms and the shading that added nuances to the meaning, providing a poetry of sorts. And this man's use of the English language was nearly devoid of either rhythm or poetry. "Why would I not want to see Salvadore?" she said. "Or Nico, for that matter. It's my business, after all, not yours."

"Salvadore is *el narcotraficante*. The drug trafficker," he said bluntly, watching her closely for a reaction. The word "trafficker" was apparently a well-practiced one.

She stared at him, startled to hear that particular word fall from his lips. It felt incongruous. And if she knew anything, she did know words. Salvadore, a drug runner, a drug trafficker. It was exactly what Nico had said. And bless her for blind, but she didn't believe either of them. She shook her head in denial.

He responded with more intensity. "Salvadore, my brother, and DiCapelli have a, how you say, a fall out. About a drug shipment," he said.

She looked at him blankly.

He scowled at her. "Do not play to be the, *eh*, the naïve with me," he said. "You know this fall out. And you know that DiCapelli is *igual* – the same – like Salvadore. They are both drug traffickers." He shrugged eloquently. "I no care of DiCapelli. But Salvadore, I need help him. He is my brother."

But her mind had skipped past his words. Truly, she could not have been more astonished. Nico, a drug runner! She knew better, even with his half-joking remark that he might be one, for all she knew. And she knew what he really did, knew from their time together in Czechoslovakia. But she couldn't share any of that. Who was this man, anyhow? "Who are you?" she said, an echo of her question in the alley.

This time he gave over. "I am Raúl," he said. "Raúl San Martín. The brother of Salvadore San Martín. The same I say you."

"And you're telling me that your brother, Salvadore, is a drug dealer?"

"A drug trafficker. *Sí*. I am." He scowled again. "I am not proud for my brother Salvadore. I try to make him to stop before is too late. But with *amigos*, friends, the same like DiCapelli, is a battle – how you say – a battle up the hill."

Normally she would have found his phrasing intriguing, or at least amusing. Not just now. "I don't believe you," she said, shifting the cup in her hands.

"Oh, you believe," he said intensely. "You believe. You – you *will* believe." His voice had an inflexible edge. "Salvadore not only is trafficker, he is user. I want find him, take him to home."

"Salvadore is not a user," Sylvia said. She knew that the charming man with whom she had spent time was not a drug user.

"How you know?" His voice was a challenge. "Do you know a user of drugs? Before – until now?"

"Well, no," she said, biting her lower lip, remembering what Nico had said. It wasn't emblazoned on the forehead, was it?

"When Salvadore is with the drugs, he is very reckless, very – how you say – outgoing. No. Very *loco*, very crazy."

Sylvia thought back to that mad motorcycle ride in Amsterdam. It was reckless, all right, and even a bit crazy. But Salvadore had seemed to have his wits about him, and he had been in perfect control of that dangerous, noisy machine.

"Do you see that?" said Raúl, watching her intently. "When you are with him, do you see him in this way?"

"No," she said resolutely.

Shaking his head as if in great despair, he rose from the chair to pour himself another cup of the strong brew from the battered pan. "Not is good. You are see – you are seeing, you are knowing, with two men of danger. Very danger," he said as he returned to his chair and sat down. "You are – how you say – have luck I find you soon. In time."

"Have luck!" she said sharply. "You as good as kidnaped me!"

He shrugged. "Is better for you. And I must stay you here for a time, until I find Salvadore and that DiCapelli. Only then I know you are safe."

She was incredulous. "Safe? With you?"

He nodded. "Safe with me." Then he sighed. "Only I wish I trust you to stay here when I go."

"Of course I won't stay here."

Exasperated, he rolled his eyes dramatically upward. *"Disculpe.* I am sorry. I am very much sorry, but I think you stay. I lock the door, I lock you in. Here."

She glanced around the room once again, contemplating her escape. With dismay, she noticed for the first time that the place was windowless. Locked in she would be completely trapped and at his mercy.

She stood and carried her untouched coffee to the alcove. "I am responsible for my own safety," she said. "I do not need you as my care-taker."

He frowned. "Caretaker?"

"My guardian. My jailer."

He ignored the last jab, which he obviously had understood. "Oh, yes, you need the caretaker," he said impassively. "You no understand what is happen, how you are in danger. But I do." He pressed his palm to his chest for dramatic emphasis and then he stood up, finished his coffee, and deposited the empty cup next to her full one. "I go now. I bring food when I come. If you need *el baño*, the toilet, is to that door." He pointed across the room to the narrow door next to the cot.

She nearly groaned. No way of escape there. Not that she really had expected one. "You must let me go," she said, not knowing what else to say, or how to move him to change his mind and release her from this shabby prison.

"No. Is for your best good," he said shortly. He turned toward the door. "I am not to be away for a much time – for a long time."

Sparing her one last glance, he opened the door, stepped through, and closed it firmly behind him. She heard the unmistakable metallic click of a key in the lock, then the sound of his retreating footsteps as he made his way down the creaky wooden stairs. And then silence.

CHAPTER **16**

Nico was halfway down the alley at a dead run when he realized that Sylvia had, quite literally, vanished. She did not have that much of a lead on him, and he was quick once he started moving, after pausing to consider that damnable Fuentes. So where could she have gone? There were no storefronts here, just residences with their low-beamed entrances off the alley. No natural light came along this street, only subdued shadows of varying degrees of greyness. Where in bloody hell was she?

He followed the alley to its end, where it opened out onto a wider street, De Garre. Glancing both ways, he realized that he didn't know which direction to go looking for her. He walked quickly first one way and then the other. Nothing. He turned back to the alley where he searched carefully, but there was no one and nothing to find. Bloody *damn* bloody hell!

Nico returned to the square, frustrated and very concerned. Where could Sylvia have gone? How could she just disappear like that? And what in *hell* was Fuentes doing here in Bruges? It made no sense. Amsterdam, perhaps, since that is where Salvadore San Martín had been. But Bruges? He lowered himself heavily into a chair under the gaze of the bemused waiter at the same café to consider his next move.

He was sprawled with his elbows on the table and his head resting on his hands, when the unbelievable happened. With a mind-numbing roar, a black motorcycle debouched from one of the pedestrian-only streets and shot into the square, coming to a skidding halt right in front of the café where Nico sat. *Merda!* Think of the devil! Salvadore San Martín! Nico leapt to his feet and took one long, menacing step toward the noisy machine. So. Not a Harley after all. A Buell. Hence the same blasted racket. Lighter, quicker, faster, but with the turbulent throb of a Harley.

He cursed even as Salvadore switched off the motorcycle and leaned it onto its kickstand. The Colombian was not wearing a helmet, in blatant disregard for Belgian traffic laws, and his dark hair was blown back from his forehead. He seemed not to give a damn that he had just roared along pedestrian streets and into the square. He was clad in jeans and boots and a dark t-shirt.

"What in the devil have you done with her?" Nico demanded, his frustration metamorphosing into a barely controlled fury.

"With *her?*" said Salvadore, giving a slightly puzzled frown even as he rubbed the wind from one eye with his fingers.

"You know bloody damn well who I mean."

"Sylvia?"

Nico let out his breath in exasperation. "Yes. Sylvia."

"I left her in Amsterdam, with a note telling her to stay at the Amstel Grand." Salvadore swung off the motorcycle and planted himself in front of Nico, eye to eye.

"Oh, did you?" Nico could see the note even now. *Cariña.*

"Why would I tell you different?"

"Because she's not in Amsterdam."

"Where is she, then?"

"As you bloody well know, she's here in Bruges."

"Sylvia? Here?" Salvadore sounded genuinely astonished. And, perhaps, concerned.

Nico wasn't buying. "I got a glimpse of her, and she just as quickly disappeared."

"Maybe she does not wish to see you." Salvadore's expression could only be interpreted as a smirk.

Nico ignored the implication. And the smirk as well, even though he was sorely tempted to knock it off the Colombian's face. "She didn't notice me," he said.

"Where did you spot her?"

"It would be helpful, San Martín, if you would stop acting as though you know none of this."

Salvadore said, "But I do not. I followed you here after checking on your train ticket at Centraal Station in Amsterdam. I had no idea she also was in Bruges."

"You followed me?"

"I did."

"Why?"

"I was quite sure you were coming into trouble. Well, into danger."

"Indeed?" Nico's skepticism was obvious. As was his sarcasm. "So you are here to protect me."

"You likely don't know it yet, since you've spent all of your time sitting in this square – how do you say? – oh yes! Cooling your heels." Salvadore grinned at the absurdity of the idiom. "Well, Eduardo Fuentes is also in Bruges."

"Eduardo Fuentes." Nico watched Salvadore through narrowed eyes, trying to read his face for the truth.

It was Salvadore's turn for sarcasm. "You remember Eduardo Fuentes? The drug, *eh*, drug lord from Colombia?"

"Whom you know very well," shot back Nico.

"I do know him well," Salvadore acknowledged agreeably. "Or I know *of* him at least. And what I know is not very pleasant."

"But none of this has anything to do with Sylvia," Nico said.

"Sylvia. No!" Salvadore was suddenly alarmed as though he had just thought of something. "Oh, no! Sylvia!"

"I have already told you that she has gone missing. You acted surprised the first time, too."

"Believe me, DiCapelli, I did not know she was here. I have seen only you, and Fuentes, of course, and –" He abruptly stopped himself.

Nico's instincts sharpened. "And?"

Salvadore was quick. He adroitly shifted direction. "With Fuentes here, Sylvia could be in danger."

Nico knew in an instant and with utter certainty that Salvadore was holding out on him. "With *you* here she could be in danger," he snapped.

"How so?" Salvadore actually managed to look injured.

"You're no better than Fuentes."

"Now, see here, DiCapelli –"

"Maybe you're even worse. Fuentes, at least, acknowledges who and what he is."

"What is that supposed to mean?"

"You're a drug runner, San Martín. A *narcotraficante*. A trafficker."

"I?" This time Salvadore was clearly and honestly astonished.

But Nico ignored his reaction. "Further, you are not from Argentina as you claimed. You are as Colombian as that *figlio di puttana*, that son of a whore, Fuentes."

"You assume that because I am of the same nationality as Fuentes that I am also a drug runner? How *very* creative of you." Salvadore sneered. He did it rather well.

"It has nothing to do with your nationality. It has everything to do with your proximity to Fuentes every time a major drug deal is coming down."

Salvadore's dark eyes were slits. "I could say the same of you," he said, his words clipped.

Nico figured that in about five seconds more they would be at each other's throats. Literally. And ignoring the real concern. With a great effort of will, he squelched his ardent desire to plant a solid, street-fighter's punch into Salvadore's handsome, sneering face. "So you could," he said, forcing his voice to less intensity. "We'll hash that out later. For now, we need to find Sylvia."

Salvadore blinked in the face of Nico's abrupt change of tone and direction. "All right," he said slowly. "All right. We will first find Sylvia. When and where did you last see her?"

"I was sitting at this very café here on the square. She came out of the *petite* hotel next to the French restaurant, do you know it?" Nico pointed. "She turned immediately into the alley on the left. I followed her, but by the time I had reached the alley, she had disappeared."

Salvadore's brow creased. "So quickly?"

Nico had not intended to mention Eduardo Fuentes again. But no matter what he thought of Salvadore, just now the only important consideration was Sylvia. "She had a few minutes on me. Just when I started after her, Fuentes appeared."

"Fuentes was following her?" Salvadore said sharply.

"No. He crossed the square and went down another street. I was going to go after him, but changed my mind and decided to follow Sylvia instead."

Salvadore regarded him. "I see you are finally getting your priorities straight," he said.

Nico heard the sarcasm and wanted to tell him to mind his own bloody damn business, but kept his tongue in check. "Well, perhaps I am," he said, a tad ruefully. "So I am. But apparently not soon enough."

"She can be quick, no?"

"I know. But there is no way she could have just disappeared. I went the length of the alley and checked up and down the next street. And there are no shops or cafés along the alley. Just residences, all one long line of buildings with no breaks in between."

"So she could not have taken an unexpected turn or ducked inside a store front." Salvadore contemplated that. "Which alley?" he said.

"Come, I'll show you." Nico turned back to the place where he had emerged moments before.

Salvadore scowled as he followed Nico into the alley.

Nico picked up an uneasy nuance. "What is it?" he said.

Salvadore shook his head. "It is nothing."

Nico stopped walking and faced the Colombian. "What *is* it?" he said again, more sharply this time.

"Are you quite sure it was this alley?" Salvadore asked.

"I'm entirely sure. I just left it, didn't I?"

Still Salvadore scowled.

"For Sylvia's sake, come clean with me, San Martín. Why does it disturb you that she disappeared from this particular alley?"

The Colombian turned away.

Nico nearly grabbed his arm to jerk him around, but stopped himself. "Not even for Sylvia," he said bitterly. He shook his head in frustrated disbelief. "Your damnable drug business comes even before her."

Salvadore was silent.

Nico let fly with a string of Italian expletives. When they were exhausted along with his breath, he said, "I'll find her without your help. Strangely enough, I thought you cared for her. But now I can see you were only using her."

Salvadore suddenly came alive, his controlled dispassion vanishing. "You are right in thinking I care for her. I am not the one who kept deserting her in Amsterdam. And god knows where before that."

Nico ignored his acidic, baiting tone. "That is irrelevant. For now, will you help me find her, or not?"

"Of course I will."

"Then tell me. What is it about this alleyway that disturbs you?"

Again Salvadore scowled.

Nico said suddenly, "Is Fuentes staying here?" He could tell from Salvadore's fleeting reaction that he was close to the mark. "So Fuentes might have snatched her? How could that be? I saw him go down a different street, at a ninety degree angle from this alley. He couldn't possibly have gotten over here in time."

"Not Fuentes," said Salvadore slowly as if feeling his way through an oppressive darkness.

"Not Fuentes? Then who?"

Still Salvadore hesitated, and then at last he spoke. "There is another Colombian here, besides Fuentes."

"And yourself."

"Yes. A third."

"Also a drug runner?"

Salvadore ignored the shot. "He is someone I have been tracking off and on for a very long time."

"Who is he?"

"His name is Raúl."

"Is he here in concert with Fuentes?" asked Nico.

Salvadore frowned as he tried to understand what Nico was trying to say. "In concert?" he said.

"In business with Fuentes. Working with Fuentes."

"Oh, yes. I see. Well, yes. In a way."

"So you think this Raúl has her?"

"Did I say so?"

"Yes. Just not in so many words."

Salvadore started up the alley, walking slowly and inspecting each doorway.

"Does Raúl have her?" prodded Nico again even as he searched alongside Salvadore.

"I believe he might," said Salvadore. "I've seen him come in and out of this alley a few times. He must be staying in a private residence along here."

"What would Raúl want with Sylvia?"

Salvadore sighed and stopped walking. He turned to face Nico. "He would use her as bait."

"Bait? For what? Or whom?"

"I'm not certain."

"Fuentes? She would not be bait for Fuentes."

"Not Fuentes."

"Who, then?"

Salvadore was silent, and now he refused to meet Nico's sharp questing eyes.

"For me?" said Nico, his mind working quickly, logically, eliminating all but the relevant facts.

"Or for me," said Salvadore at last. "I cannot be certain which of us is the target. Or perhaps both of us."

"I don't understand," said Nico.

Salvadore glanced once more around the alley. "We can do no good here. Let's go someplace where we can talk."

Nico shrugged his agreement and they made their way back to the square, going slowly so as to check every step of the way for any sign of Sylvia. There was none. But neither did they find any indication of a struggle.

"Would she have gone willingly with this Raúl?" asked Nico.

Salvadore frowned. "I shouldn't think so. Unless –"

"Unless?"

"Unless he caught her off-guard. It would only take a moment, one quick second of surprise."

"You mean if he startled her?"

"No. I mean if there was something about him that she thought – that she thought she recognized." Salvadore blinked against the sunlight as they emerged onto the square. "Something that confused her for a moment."

"You're speaking riddles." Nico led the way back to the café, entirely frustrated. He knew that Salvadore was holding back some very important information. Without being asked, the resigned waiter stoically brought his coffee, thick and black, and Salvadore ordered the same. When they were settled at a small table with no one nearby, they resumed their conversation.

"What would confuse her so much that she would allow herself to be abducted without a struggle?" asked Nico.

Salvadore looked away, then back at Nico. Nico could not decide whether the Colombian was just uncomfortable, or somehow dealing with a private agony. Or trying to think of a way to deceive him, to send him down the wrong track. *Damn* him!

"I need to tell you something," Salvadore said at last. "And you will have to trust me." He caught Nico's look. "I know it will be difficult, as it is for me to trust you."

Nico was silent. "All right," he said at last.

Salvadore turned his cup of steaming coffee between his hands without tasting it and frowned in concentration. "I have been tracking Fuentes for some time," he said.

"Tracking him? I'd think you would always know where he is, given that you –"

"Will you let me finish before you argue?" snapped Salvadore furiously.

"Go ahead," said Nico, and settled back to hear out the Colombian. He told himself to be silent and not to interrupt again, as difficult as that was, given the high stakes.

"I had lost his trail, but picked him up again when he went to Czechoslovakia over two months ago. I was closing in. It would have been a fine place to take care of him, to take care of him *permanently*, if you know what I mean, with Czechoslovakia being in a bit of turmoil with their transition as they shed their Communist oppressors. Surely no one would have noticed if a *cabrón*, a bastard of a drug lord had suddenly gone missing. But then he slipped the noose, so to speak, when he ducked out of the Czech authorities' control and disappeared. After I left Czechoslovakia and returned to Colombia, you always seemed to be around whenever Fuentes turned up. So I thought that in addition to tracking Fuentes, I would track you as well, and you would help to keep me close to him."

Nico thought that was hugely ironic, maybe even humorous. No wonder he had felt like he was going around in circles with Salvadore the past few months. Apparently they had been trying to track each other! "Ring a ring o' rosy," said Nico softly. "Ashes, ashes, we all fall dead."

Salvadore ignored this apparent irrelevance and continued. "I saw how you and Sylvia had become, well, friends at the old inn, the Kámen. So I decided to keep an eye on her whenever I lost you."

"You have been in Czechoslovakia for the past two months?" In fact, Nico knew better, as he had spotted Salvadore now and again in the dim shadows and the mists of the Northern Andes.

Salvadore shook his head. "No. I can't tell you how many times I've made the trip between Bogotá and Prague." He shook his head. "I know every connection and every airline schedule. *Cristo*, I've been through Lima and São Paulo and Paris and Zurich and Munich and New York – well, you get the point. It's a wretched, bloody long way. From time to time I would get word of you or of Fuentes. I would react immediately, but you would have already, *eh*, slipped the trap."

Nico frowned. "And all the while I thought it was you who slipped the trap."

Salvadore shrugged and took a swallow of his cooling coffee. "Very nearly I missed Sylvia's departure from Czechoslovakia. I had been gone a few days and returned to discover that she had checked out of the Kámen. But I picked up her track at the Ruzyne Airport in Prague and came to Amsterdam on the same plane that brought her."

"I can understand how you used her to find me. But why would you want to? You could find Fuentes without me."

"Fuentes, yes. Off and on. Fuentes is actually not all that difficult to track, especially in Colombia. He operates quite openly there, as I am sure you know by now. But Fuentes is not the one I have been hunting, not really."

Nico's eyes narrowed. "Raúl," he said slowly. "You were searching for Raúl."

Salvadore ran one finger under the neck of his black t-shirt as if the day had suddenly and unexpectedly warmed. "Yes," he said at last. "I was searching for Raúl."

"And just exactly who or what is Raúl?"

Salvadore looked away for a long moment. When his gaze returned to Nico, it reflected an intense personal pain. "Raúl is my brother."

"Your brother!"

"Yes."

"What has he to do with Fuentes?"

"I will tell you that later, after we find Sylvia. For now, I tell you only because Raúl and I are just one year apart in age and we look much the same."

Nico was quick. "So Sylvia may have come across him and thought that he was you?"

"For a brief moment, yes. But that brief moment would be long enough to take away any advantage she might have had when he accosted her. *If* he accosted her."

Nico surveyed his companion. Even though Salvadore's story was compellingly told and his carefully controlled emotions seemed real enough, Nico knew he could not trust him. He knew anyone connected with Fuentes was likely dangerous and even more likely to be somehow involved in the drug business.

Salvadore might as well have read his mind. "Remember, DiCapelli, you are near Fuentes whenever I am. I could as likely believe that you are involved in drug trafficking."

"Do you believe that?"

"I did."

"What changed your mind?"

"Well." For a moment the tension left Salvadore's face and he grimaced ruefully. "I haven't exactly changed it. Not yet."

Nico raised one shoulder. "Nor have I. But I can put it aside for the moment, until we find Sylvia, at least."

"*Igualmente.* Likewise." Salvadore hesitated and then spoke again. "Listen, DiCapelli, if you are to trust me, I suppose you should know a bit more of my truth."

"What is it?"

"I didn't follow you here. I actually left Amsterdam the same night we were to have dinner with Sylvia."

"To come to Bruges?"

Salvadore nodded.

"But why?"

"I have a contact in Colombia with whom I am constantly in touch. When I called him that day, he told me that Fuentes had been spotted in Bruges."

"So you came here?"

"Immediately."

Nico thought of the white envelope in Sylvia's room. As if reading his mind, Salvadore said, "After I came here and confirmed the sighting, I returned to Amsterdam to leave a message for Sylvia to stay in the hotel. I didn't want to risk leaving a telephone message, but I had to do something. I was worried that she was so close to this danger."

Nico finished his coffee and a new cup was brought immediately. Normally he would have relished the strong, hot liquid, but just now everything seemed in slow motion, unreal. He kept his emotions under tight control, but with great effort. Only by tamping down his nearly-overwhelming concern could he tackle this problem with his mind. He forced himself to concentrate. "So Raúl, your brother, is staying in a private residence on that alley." He scowled towards the place where Sylvia had disappeared.

"I don't know that for certain, but I believe it must be true."

"Assuming he has Sylvia, would he harm her?"

Salvadore hesitated for just a moment and then said, "Well, that depends."

Nico's gut clenched. "Depends on what?"

Salvadore sighed and then gave over. "On what his orders are."

Nico paused and then said, "Is Raúl one of Fuentes' drug runners?"

A shadow crossed Salvadore's face, a deep and lasting pain. Nico felt strangely touched by it. "He's not a drug runner at all," the Colombian said haltingly. "Not in the normal sense of what you might think. He does, well, he does special assignments for Fuentes."

"Special assignments? What sort of special assignments?"

"Well, I don't know exactly how to phrase it. Deliveries, perhaps."

"Of drugs?"

"No. Not drugs. I think he is probably more – more specialized than that."

"Money?"

"Sometimes. Not often."

"Well, what else is there, in Fuentes' business?" Nico said, impatient now. "That's about it. Drugs and money."

Salvadore said, "People."

Nico raised a brow.

"Roughing up," Salvadore went on, his voice both blunt and brutal. "Killing." Now he looked Nico straight in the face, still unwavering. "*Secuestro*."

Nico flinched even as he felt his heart turn over. "Kidnaping," he said.

"Yes. Kidnaping."

"So Raúl is in Fuentes' employ?"

Salvadore's words were measured, and delivered with a relentless precision, as if to mask a very strong emotion. "My brother, Raúl," he said steadily, "is also known as *la mano izquierda*."

Nico's chest felt as if someone were gripping his heart in a cold fist. "*La mano izquierda*," he said on a breath. "The left hand of Eduardo Fuentes."

"I see you know this name?"

"Oh, yes. Of course. Anyone connected to the drug trafficking business knows of *la mano izquierda*." In truth, the reputation of this appellation was notorious to the extreme in the drug circles. Lethal, emotionless, thorough, relentless. A machine without heart or soul. Truly the right hand of Eduardo Fuentes, but his odd nickname was due to his in fact being left-handed. "And he is your brother?" Nico gave a low whistle and swore. *"Gesù, Maria e Giuseppe."*

"It gets worse. You see, DiCapelli, it's not widely known, but Raúl also uses drugs. Fuentes supports his habit, keeping him supplied with the strong, pure stuff and a lot of money. He's extremely talented, is Raúl, and very good at anything he does. He's been an incredibly effective strong arm for Fuentes. He says that he's not an addict, that he controls the drugs rather than the drugs controlling him. And I must admit, he's a very atypical user. He picks and chooses when he will work and when he will, well, decide to take flight with the drugs. But to me, his brother, he is more like a slave. Unable to break free from either Fuentes or his compulsion to fly. As I told you, he is only a year younger than I am. I have attempted many times to bring him back to our family. I have begged him. I have forced him. But in the end, Fuentes' hold, and the hold of the drugs, are too strong." Salvadore paused for a moment as if he could not go on. Then he said very softly, "Sometimes I get the feeling that Raúl thinks he can turn his back on anything that threatens him, and it will somehow go away. Even death."

There was a heavy silence. Nico thought that this admission, this long recitation of pain, had been incredibly difficult for Salvadore to admit to a stranger like him. At last he spoke. "I would have thought, given his reputation, I mean, that *la mano izquierda* would be much older. He has quite a string of exploits attributed to his name."

"Yes, I know. His reputation has grown at an almost exponential rate. But I'm afraid he has earned every bit of it."

Nico drew a breath. "And this – this brother of yours, *la mano izquierda*, has Sylvia?" he said, giving voice to what he hoped, what he prayed, was inconceivable.

"It is just one possibility," said Salvadore slowly, sounding despondent. "But I think perhaps a likely one."

Nico ran a hand over his beard-stubbled face. "Do you know which residence might be his?"

"Not precisely. But I know the general area, I think. And it's down that alley."

Nico shoved back his chair with a scraping sound of wood on flagstone and rose. "Let's go, then."

Salvadore made to follow, but Nico stopped him with one raised hand. "I think perhaps you had better bring your Buell," he said.

Salvadore stared at him. "Why?"

"If we find her, you will have to get her out of here. Fast."

"You would trust me with her?" Salvadore said doubtfully.

"I must. I have no other choice just now, do I?"

Salvadore watched him, considering. "And leave you to Fuentes? Or, perhaps worse, to Raúl?"

"I can take care of myself," Nico said. "It's Sylvia that we must get free of this tangle. I've got to know that she's safe."

So Salvadore made his decision. He shrugged and stepped over to the shiny black machine. With a scowl, he shoved it off the kickstand and pushed it silently towards the alley without starting the engine.

CHAPTER **17**

Sylvia stared at the lock on the shabby door. She crossed the room and tried the handle. The door was definitely locked. Well, she knew that it would be. Again she scanned the windowless room and sighed in frustration. She went to the alcove and took a tentative sip of the now-tepid coffee that she had earlier disdained. Pulling a face, she replaced the cup on the cluttered counter. The brew was as awful as she had imagined. Then she tried the door once more, to no avail.

Wanting to leave no stone unturned, she crossed to the door where the bathroom was. She pulled it open and blinked. The room was small and dingy like the rest of the place, the grey walls oppressive. The toilet looked as if it hadn't been scrubbed for weeks. But she saw none of that. Rather her gaze was captured by a shaft of anemic light from high in the wall. A window! Narrow and filthy it was, and near the ceiling, but a window nonetheless.

A tentative spark of hope flickered in her breast. She slipped the long strap of her small bag around her neck. Might as well choose the side of optimism and be ready to go at a moment's notice. She dragged one of the battered chairs into the bathroom, and with some difficulty squeezed it between the sink and the toilet, directly below the window. Then she climbed onto the chair.

The edge of the window sill was still several inches above her groping fingers. With a grumble of frustration at her lack of height and one ear tuned to the sound of possible footsteps on the stairs, she fetched the second chair and stacked it onto the first. Again she clambered aboard, this time with more caution as the chairs tilted perilously. The window had a dusty metal latch that looked as if it had not been opened in years. She tugged at it, nearly losing her balance. It didn't give. She pushed at it with both hands, feeling vulnerable in her precarious position as the chair beneath her feet creaked and shifted yet again.

Just when she thought she would have to risk breaking out the dirty glass, the latch gave way with a metallic screech, and the window swung wide.

Not knowing when her captor might return, she acted quickly. With some difficulty she scrambled up into the window, clawing with fingers and feet and hearing the overbalanced chairs crash to the floor below her. For a breathless second she hung suspended, but then her weight shifted forward and her shoulders were lodged in the small opening. It was a tight fit but she was slender, and so she managed to squeeze herself through with just a scratch on one arm and a small rip in the knee of her jeans. She climbed out onto the dark red tiled roof.

Without hesitating, she followed the roof line down toward the alley side. The curving, overlaid tiles were slippery with moss and age, and she was grateful that she was wearing sneakers rather than sandals. She made her sliding way down the steep slope, taking painstaking care and keeping one hand on the tiles slanting on the roof above her for balance. At last she reached the edge of the roof, and looked down into the alley.

Oh, no. It was a very long drop.

Indecisive, she leaned over the brink and scanned the rough side of the stone building. And then she spotted it. A rusty drainpipe. She reached out cautiously with one hand and tested the pipe. Well, she thought, it seemed relatively stable. Slowly, gingerly, she swung her legs off the edge of the roof, and then turned onto her belly. She slid a breathless inch at a time down the rough tiles, scrabbling for a toehold. A chink in the stone wall supported and balanced her until she could get a grip on the ancient drainpipe. Hand over hand and with her toes seeking purchase on every rough stone along the way, she eased herself down until she was within about eight feet of the roadway beneath her. Then she held her breath and closed her eyes. Releasing her grip on the drainpipe, she let herself drop like a cat onto the cobblestones below.

CHAPTER 18

Nico and Salvadore halted abruptly, as if the cobblestones had split asunder, opening a chasm at their feet. Sylvia had just fallen from the heavens – literally! – only twenty feet in front of them. Nico started forward, but Salvadore grabbed his arm and pointed.

At the other end of the alley was a man whose resemblance to Salvadore was astonishing. "Raúl?" Nico said, knowing the answer.

"*Maldición!* Oh, damn!" said Salvadore. "He's got a gun."

"Will he use it? Even on his own brother?"

"As I told you. It depends on his orders. He's like a machine when he's working, focused and centered, completely absorbed."

Nico said, "Get Sylvia." His tone was intense, brooking no argument.

Salvadore recoiled and jerked his gaze to Nico's face. "*Cómo?* What?"

"Get Sylvia out of here, on that damned Buell. Take her back to Amsterdam," snapped Nico. "Now! I'll take care of things here."

"Oh, shit," said Salvadore, without any accent at all. "Holy effing *shit!*"

CHAPTER **19**

Her heart pounding wildly and adrenalin burning her veins, Sylvia scanned the narrow roadway to determine which way she should run. But there were dark shadows of men looming both ways in the alley, and she felt surrounded, blocked in, trapped. There was no obvious solution. She knew only that she had to move. *Now!* She had just made up her mind which way to go but hadn't taken even a step when the familiar Harley-throb of the Buell told her that Salvadore was bearing down upon her.

She was sure he would run her down, that she had somehow managed to get between him and his drug profits. Very nearly he did. He brought the motorcycle to a sliding halt a mere inch from her, in the process spraying her legs and feet with pebbles and dust and jerking the machine around so that it faced in the same direction from which it had come. She stumbled backwards.

"Get on," Salvadore ordered in a bizarre replay of their introduction in Amsterdam.

She stared at his stern countenance and dark eyes, frozen in her place. Nico was sure he was a drug runner, in league with Fuentes and perhaps now Raúl. She was as sure he was not. Indecision gripped her as she struggled to get past her paralysis and to make a choice. And quickly.

The decision was made for her. Before she could move or before Salvadore could repeat his command, she heard Nico's familiar voice. He sounded as if he were in a rage. Calm, cool Nico DiCapelli was livid, and of all things, he was apparently directing his fury at her! "Get on that bloody motorcycle, Sylvia!" Nico roared, his command echoing off the narrow stone walls and reverberating past the din of the motorcycle. "Now!"

She could not possibly have heard him correctly. He wanted her to go with Salvadore? It made no sense! But on the strength of his ire, and as an instinctive reaction, she obeyed. She was no sooner aboard, clinging to Salvadore's narrow waist, than she realized this was not what she had either wanted or intended.

With his left hand, Salvadore released the clutch in the same instant that he twisted the throttle wide open with his right. The motorcycle jerked sideways and then shot forward violently, spraying gravel and flashing past Nico in the narrow alley. She twisted to look back and saw Nico standing in the middle of the cobbled street. Raúl was just beginning his advance with the handgun raised and threatening, his face dark with fury at having been thwarted.

"Salvadore!" she cried. "Take me back!"

His response was to bend forward, forcing her to do the same. The motorcycle picked up speed with such velocity that she could scarcely breathe. They shot across the square and down one of the cobbled pedestrian streets evoking curses in both French and Dutch as passersby scrambled out of the way. She knew she'd be killed if she slid off. She knew he wouldn't stop. She made her decision.

She slid off.

Or very nearly. At least she meant to.

Salvadore slammed on the brakes at the same time as he reached around and gripped her with one hard hand. The motorcycle veered out of control, skidding sideways with a screech of protesting tires on the rough cobblestones. As if in slow motion she felt the muscles of his body contract in a great effort to bring the beast back to balance.

The motorcycle slid and hung at a precarious angle for seemingly an eternity, and then righted itself as it quivered to a stop at last. He swung on her then, his black hair blown back to reveal his sculpted forehead and high cheek bones and dark eyes. Just now those eyes snapped fury. "*Maldición!* Dammit, Sylvia, don't you ever do that again!" he shouted over the throb of the Buell. "You'll kill us both."

If she'd had her wits about her, she would have reminded him of the long, wild ride in Amsterdam where they might have crashed at any moment. But the sharp retort didn't come to her just then. All that came was an entreaty. "Please, Salvadore. Take me back to Nico."

He glanced behind them, gunned the engine, and again the machine swept forward. "I cannot, *cariña*," he said into the wind.

"Don't leave him there alone," she pleaded.

"DiCapelli can take care of himself," he said, even as he nosed the motorcycle into the now-legal traffic, intending to head directly for the

E403 expressway, which would bear northeast towards Amsterdam. She could plead, but he wouldn't stop, she knew. She could beat on his back and protest and still he would not take her back. And even if she could go back, what good would she be to Nico?

She knew that Nico was a dead man. Why else would he send her away with Salvadore, of all people? Raúl would not make the mistake of letting Nico slip away as she had done. All the words she had intended to say to Nico, all the time she had meant to make up. She was on a first name basis with grief, and grief came upon her in full force. A sob shuddered through her, and she collapsed against Salvadore's back, clutching him even as the wind whipped away her tears. He dropped a hand to hers and kept it there for a long time, a gentle pressure of comfort. And insurance that she would not release him again and push away and disappear from the motorcycle, vanishing into the vagaries of the wind.

She had no idea of how long they flew down the motorways at high speed, weaving in and out and around and ahead of the slower traffic, reminiscent of the wild ride in Amsterdam. Flashing ahead from one motorway to the next. E40, E17, E19, A16. They meant nothing to her, and she didn't even wonder how Salvadore seemed to know exactly where to turn, where to change routes. She had no knowledge of their crossing from Belgium to the Netherlands. She saw none of it. Her eyes tightly closed and her emotions churning, she clung to Salvadore, leaning with him when he dropped the machine into the curves, pressing forward against him when he bent low to the motorcycle on the long flat stretches of highway that she thought they must be nearly horizontal with the machine.

There was no way she could have fallen asleep on the back of that screaming motorcycle and still have stayed aboard. But when she realized that at last they were slowing, she was shocked and disoriented to discover they had somehow exited the motorway and were on the outskirts of Amsterdam. The ride had seemed interminable and she was exhausted. But she must have somewhere lost track of time, because it did not seem possible they could be so very far away from Bruges. From Nico.

The thought of Nico roused her from her stupor at the same time the motorcycle rumbled up to a red stop light and at last jerked to a halt. "Salvadore," she said.

He seemed startled to hear her voice. "*Cariña*," he said. "Are you all right?"

"Please, Salvadore. Please take me back to Bruges."

He planted a booted foot on either side of the still-throbbing Buell and twisted to see her better. He shook his disheveled head. When he spoke, he didn't use Nico's name. They both knew who he meant. "He told you to go with me, *te recuerdas*? Do you remember?"

Yes, of course she did. She remembered Nico's urgent command. She remembered her mindless obedience. She remembered his receding form in the roadway, with Raúl advancing, the handgun that was pointed at Nico flashing like a silver spark of menace even in the dim alley. It was an image that would stay with her forever. "Where are we going?" she asked, subdued.

"I'm taking you to your hotel in Amsterdam. The Amstel Grand."

"Salvadore –"

"And then I'm going back to Bruges."

Oh, god. It had to be Bruges with the hard *g*. "No, Salvadore. Please."

"I thought you were concerned about DiCapelli."

"I am. I want to go back with you."

"No. It's not safe for you there."

She was desperate, knowing that this mattered. "Nor for you," she argued.

"Sylvia," he said gently. "Eduardo Fuentes is in Bruges."

Her heart stilled in her breast. "Fuentes?" she whispered in horror even as the light turned to green. They shot forward, not speaking again. The Buell roared along Amsteldijk following the Amstel River, and then turned sharply down Korte Niezel. They slid to a gritty and authoritative stop at the front of the Hotel Amstel Grand. Salvadore did not kill the engine.

Unsteadily, she slipped off and prepared to take up her argument. He was having none of it. He immediately cut off her pleas. "*You* are staying. *I* am going." He said it with a very deliberate enunciation as if she might not otherwise understand.

"I cannot bear to lose you both," she cried.

He snatched her to him then and held her and smoothed her wild hair and whispered unintelligible words in Spanish. Unintelligible, but their meaning was unmistakable. And then he spoke in his beautiful, melodic English. It was a murmur, but she heard it all, even over the dull, impatient grumble of the Buell. "But I think you especially cannot bear to lose Nico DiCapelli," he said.

She knew it was true. And yet – "Please, Salvadore. Don't go back there."

In response he took her face between his hands and kissed her. It was quick, but it was hard and powerful, with a full measure of regret. "*Adiós, cariña*. Go with God. You will please stay in your hotel until DiCapelli or I return. Just this once, try to obey. *Por favor*." He reached a hand to tousle her already-wild hair and then gripped the throttle. He raised his booted feet and shot away, leaving her at the front of the indomitable Hotel Amstel Grand. Alone.

Well, she was rather used to being alone. Good lord, she'd had enough practice. By choice, but even so. Alone.

She thought to walk along the canals to clear her mind and then remembered Salvadore's admonition. And Nico's warning, how many long hours ago. Stay close to the hotel. Stay *in* the hotel.

It seemed an eternity ago that first Nico and then Salvadore had given her identical instructions. She had ignored them both, and by doing so had dragged them into the middle of this mess. Oh, yes, she would take all the blame. The fact was, though, Nico had a finely-honed talent for getting himself into tight spots. Apparently Salvadore did as well.

While we're at it, she thought, it must be her consistently warped judgment, her bad taste in men. Then she smiled to herself. All right, the truth was, she liked Nico and Salvadore just as they were. Well, maybe she had been wrong just the one time, after all. Her dead husband, who would now have been her ex-husband if he hadn't managed to tumble into a crevasse in the mountains near Lolo Pass in western Montana and finish off both himself and the ill-conceived marriage. The faint smile carried her on inside the hotel, past the bell desk where the very Dutch bellman caught her eye and smiled and afterward felt rather smug about his blond good looks.

Never mind that she'd given him not even a passing thought. Just a smile.

It was enough.

For him, maybe. Not for her. Even as she collected her room key at reception along with a small envelope with a message, the smile dissolved. As she slowly climbed the stairs, she tore open the envelope and removed the card. It was a telephone message from Nico, dated two days ago. *I'm in Bruges looking for you. Please wait for me at the Hotel Amstel Grand.*

Her mind was in an agony of turmoil. She couldn't stay in her room. She needed to be in Bruges. A *snel trein* from Centraal Station, and just under three hours later, Bruges. Or off to Schiphol Airport, perhaps.

Even as she contemplated it, she knew she had to stay in Amsterdam. Nico and Salvadore had enough to worry about without her getting in the way and being used as a pawn by Fuentes or Raúl. A pawn to draw in Nico, or Salvadore. She did not know which of them might be the ultimate target. In any case, it was too high a price to pay. In spite of her anxiousness to be gone from here, she had to stay, until one or both of them returned.

She unlocked and opened the door to her room and slipped inside. She would write. She would fill the hours with places and people and events, with sounds and scents and energy. She would paint a picture of her own future, awash with color and with light and with joy.

And with Nico.

CHAPTER **20**

Nico stared after the motorcycle's vanishing form, its throbbing roar diminishing second by second. He felt every muscle in his body clench. How very close he had been to Sylvia. And yet how very far. As he always seemed to be. Hellfire and damnation. Sending her away with Salvadore was one of the hardest things he'd ever done. With *Salvadore!* What in bloody hell had he been thinking in the heat of the moment?

Well, it was done now. A decision made under pressure and in an instant, yes, but based on whatever feeble facts he had. Perhaps. But more likely it had been based on raw emotion. Sylvia had to be safe at all costs even if it meant sending her with Salvadore. He had cast his lot with the Colombian. God help him – and Sylvia! – if he had been wrong.

These thoughts took all of two split seconds, suspended in an eternity. Then, forcing himself to relax his muscles and concentrate on the urgent matter at hand, Nico turned to face the threat that was inexorably advancing down the alley. A tall young man, long-limbed with a muscular leanness. Intent and intense. Nothing about him indicated the unsteady dissipation of a user of hard drugs.

Nico's first impulse, his gut instinct, was to make a run for it. It had worked innumerable times in the past, in the dense jungles of Colombia and elsewhere. But he focused on the raised handgun, a SIG Sauer P225, that glinted in Raúl's left hand – *la mano izquierda!* – and decided against a bullet in the back. With a cool deliberation, he spread his feet in a menacing fashion and folded his arms across his chest, planting himself directly into the path of the approaching Colombian.

Oh, yes. This was Salvadore's brother. If Sylvia had been momentarily confused, Nico could understand why. Raúl bore an uncanny resemblance to Salvadore. Dark good looks and a confident, arrogant carriage. Except that there was a kind of hard, focused intensity about Raúl's young features that Salvadore's animated face didn't have. The killer at his work, Nico surmised. At least Salvadore must have told the truth about that. Inexplicably, the idea cheered him.

Nico's eyes narrowed in speculation as he watched the man stride towards him. Raúl's demeanor seemed to display a bizarre combination of rage and exhilaration, and Nico wondered whether he was high on drugs even now. In his left hand was the handgun, in his right a fat brown paper bag.

Raúl spoke first. "The little Sylvia go. She get away," he said. His anger was obvious and he was waving the gun a bit wildly.

Nico kept a cautious eye on the weapon. "So it would seem," he said.

"With that *cabrón,* that bastard Salvadore."

Nico merely nodded.

"Quién estás?" said Raúl. "Who you are?"

"I think you know."

"Nico DiCapelli?" Raúl sounded tentative.

"The same," said Nico, nodding his acquiescence.

"Bueno. Now I have you," said Raúl, his edge of anger abruptly giving way to a grim satisfaction. "The little Sylvia is escape, but now I no need she." He shook his head. "Her. I no need her."

"Raúl San Martín," said Nico. "Salvadore's baby brother. So. At last we meet." He stuck out one hand as if to greet the Colombian.

Raúl looked taken aback. He stared at Nico's outstretched hand and then back to his face. "You know *nada* of me," he said.

Nico dropped his hand. "I know what Salvadore has told me."

Raúl sneered. Nico thought that his sneer was remarkably like Salvadore's. *"Sí.* I know what that to be," he said, "because I know my brother."

"And your brother seems to know you rather well, too," said Nico.

Raúl shrugged as if dismissing whatever Salvadore might have said. "I know he talk – he say bad things to me, no? I mean, about me. Maybe he think to know. But he know nothing. *Nada.*"

Nico shifted his feet slightly, keeping a sharp eye on the restless movement of the handgun. "He knows you work for Eduardo Fuentes," he said.

"Ah," said Raúl, now looking a bit wary. "So you know the *señor* Fuentes?"

"I know Fuentes very well," said Nico, deliberately avoiding the use of the more polite *señor.* Not for that *bastardo* Fuentes, he wouldn't.

Raúl must have heard the deliberate disrespect, because he frowned slightly and the weapon became still for a moment. "He wait you," he ventured.

"And so you will take me to him?" Nico deigned to look hopeful.

"*Claro*," Raúl said. He was back to gesturing with the handgun. "I take you to him."

Nico suppressed the urge to duck. "Stop waving that bloody thing around," he snapped. "You'll shoot someone."

The Colombian nodded as if pleased. "*Sí*. I shoot you, if you be the trouble."

"So does Fuentes want me alive or dead?" said Nico. "Or perhaps it doesn't matter?"

Raúl frowned, not understanding. Nico repeated his question, but this time in pure Colombian Spanish. Raúl looked startled for a moment, and then doggedly continued struggling on in his fractured English. "Very alive. But I do what I have do."

"And what is your reward for delivering me to Fuentes?" said Nico. "More drugs?"

Raúl's face flushed to a dull red, and Nico half expected him to shove the barrel of the gun against his chest. "*Basta!*" the Colombian said. "Enough! No more to talk. You go with me. *Ahora*."

Nico glanced down the alley, hoping that someone or something would appear to distract Raúl. He hoped in vain. There was no one.

"We no can to stay here," said Raúl. "Peoples come. Maybe." He gestured with the handgun. "You walk," he ordered.

"How about a café on the square?" suggested Nico cheerfully. "We could have some coffee and a nice chat."

Raúl scowled. "No! Of course, no!" he said. "You go with me, where I say you." He shoved the brown paper bag at Nico. "Here. You take."

Nico took.

Waving the gun again, Raúl directed Nico further down the alley, towards the place where Sylvia had so unexpectedly materialized from the heavens.

Apparently completely agreeable, Nico started strolling down the alley in the direction Raúl had indicated, away from the square. The Colombian walked behind him, the barrel of the weapon pointed directly at Nico's spine.

They had made their way to about the halfway point of the alley when Raúl spoke again. "*Para*," he said. "Stop. We to go here. *A la izquierda*." He waved the gun at a tall wooden door on the left.

Nico shrugged and shoved open the door, revealing a single flight of steep stairs. "Go," Raúl said tensely, prodding Nico's back with the pistol. "Up."

Nico started up the dimly-lit stairs even as Raúl closed the door behind them. At the top of the stairs was another door. Carefully keeping the handgun leveled, now at Nico's chest, Raúl unlocked the door and pushed it open to reveal a small, dingy room.

As if suddenly smelling something rancid, Nico wrinkled his nose as he stepped across the threshold. "Nice place," he said with lethal sarcasm, even as he heedlessly tossed Raúl's paper bag onto the floor.

Raúl took no offense to either Nico's tone of voice or blithe action. *"Es bueno.* Is okay," he said.

"Is this where you kept Sylvia?" said Nico.

Again a flush diffused across Raúl's face. *"Sí.* Is the place."

"It didn't keep her very well," Nico observed laconically.

Raúl's face darkened even further. *"No es importante.* She no is important. I keep her until she go. But I get what I come, why I come. I get," said Raúl.

"You wanted me?"

"Sí."

"Not Salvadore?"

Raúl blinked as if this made no sense. "Why I want my brother? My own brother?" He smiled, the dimple denting his left cheek. "I see him when I want, no?"

Nico wondered at that. Had Salvadore been tracking Raúl, or not? "Why do you want me?" he said. "You don't even know me."

Raúl's smile turned predatory. *"Señor* Fuentes want you."

"Ah. Fuentes. Of course."

"And now he have you." Raúl all but crowed over his success, and the weapon remained steadily pointed at Nico's chest.

Too steadily, Nico thought, for Raúl to be high on drugs. But he was certainly high on power, which was at least as dangerous.

Suddenly Raúl's demeanor changed. "Turn," he ordered, pointing toward the opposite wall. "I search you."

Nico complied, turning his back to his captor and then lifting his arms overhead and spreading his feet in an exaggerated fashion.

Raúl clearly had considerable experience in this particular duty. Expertly he patted down his hostage, ensuring that Nico had no weapons. *"Bueno,"* he said, apparently satisfied.

"Happy now?" Nico said. He turned back to face the Colombian and then glanced around again. "How did Sylvia escape from here?"

Raúl shrugged. *"No es importante."*

"Of course it's important," Nico said. "I might just decide to escape the same way."

Raúl's dark eyes narrowed. "I think she maybe to go from the window in *el baño."* With his right hand, he gestured toward the narrow door that was standing open on the opposite side of the room. "You go there."

Nico stepped across the room, Raúl at his heels. The grimy bathroom revealed two tumbled wooden chairs and a small window that gaped open to allow a faint breeze to draught through in an unsuccessful attempt to freshen the stale air. Nico grinned. "She's pretty resourceful," he said as if amused. Actually, he *was* amused, picturing her lifting off of the toppling chairs as she slipped away to freedom.

This time Raúl had a scowl to match his shrug. "I say you. Your Sylvia no is *importante*. I have you, why I come. But you no can go also. No. You no to go in the window. You too big. Not like the little Sylvia." Now he was angry again. "Your little Sylvia can go *al infierno* – to hell, and with Salvadore *también*. And she – she will go."

Nico nearly missed the reference to Salvadore, and he did not take the time to analyze just what its significance might be. His thoughts were only for Sylvia. Why would Raúl be damning her to hellfire? "What do you mean?" he asked, allowing himself a scowl.

Raúl suddenly looked sly. And just as suddenly, he looked nothing at all like his brother. "You send her with one of the *narcotraficantes* of *señor* Fuentes," he said with a feral grin. It wasn't Salvadore's grin, and it was ugly, threatening. This time that capricious dimple in his left cheek did nothing to soften it.

Nico felt his insides twist. "Salvadore?" he said, he hoped nonchalantly.

"*Sí*, Salvadore. He work with Fuentes."

"As do you," said Nico.

Raúl's lips twisted into a grimace. "In some way," he said.

"You are an enforcer. And *un secuestro*. A kidnaper." Nico paused, then finished. "And a drug user."

"*Mierda!*" Raúl swore. *Shit!* "I no have this talk – this talking in *un baño*." He jabbed the handgun in Nico's direction as if to punctuate every word. "You know *nada!* Nothing! Here. You take the chairs and we talk in the other place."

Nico complied, picking up the overturned chairs and depositing them with a thump onto the gritty wooden floor of the dingy room. He seated himself, and stretched out his long legs like a casual visitor. "Please," he said to Raúl with a smile. "Seat yourself."

Raúl scowled again at his captive's cool demeanor, but he sat. The handgun remained leveled at Nico's midsection, now completely still.

"So," Raúl said. "You think I am to be the drug trafficker?"

"No," said Nico. "I think you are a drug *user*, on Fuentes' payroll."

This time Raúl did not rise to the bait of Nico's taunt. He flashed a white-toothed smile, again reminiscent of Salvadore. "Is what my brother say you?" he said. "And you – you believe! Is why you send your Sylvia with my brother on the motorcycle?" He grinned again, apparently enjoying himself. "Maybe is Salvadore that is the drug user. You think about that? And now, now you think to where you send your Sylvia with Salvadore!"

"Away from here," said Nico. He wished desperately that he knew which brother to believe, Raúl or Salvadore. But it hardly mattered now. Sylvia was away to Amsterdam with Salvadore. Or she was still in Bruges and under Fuentes' control. The latter thought made him want to smash something, but he forced himself to suppress the urge. What if his instincts had been wrong regarding Salvadore? Because instincts were all he had to go on just now. He did not trust Salvadore, but he was inclined to believe Salvadore over Raúl, if only because it would mean that Sylvia was safe. Not very logical, from a man who prided himself on his logic.

"I think, I wonder, where is now, the little Sylvia?" said Raúl. He was clearly relishing the tone of the conversation.

Nico didn't answer. Again he contemplated what he knew, what he suspected. What he believed. At no time in the past few months had he glimpsed anything about Salvadore that indicated he might be a drug user, neither in his behavior nor his actions. Nothing. There were signs, after all, although the hard drugs affected people differently. But Salvadore had seemed confident and alert, vividly alive. Hell, now that he considered it, Raúl wasn't behaving much like a user of the hard drugs, either.

Had Salvadore lied about that? If so, why? In any case, Salvadore had seemed genuinely concerned about Sylvia's welfare. Too concerned, perhaps, Nico thought, remembering the scene in the dimly lit hallway of the Hotel Amstel Grand. But part of that was his own fault. He should have gone to Amsterdam when he had said he would. He should have put Sylvia first, as Salvadore had intimated.

Hell, he *had* put her first, but for that *bastardo* Fuentes. And now, in an ironic turning of the tables, she was gone and Fuentes was back in control of the game. After two months of tracking the *figlio di puttana,* the son of a whore, it was he, Nico, who was trapped. His organization had no idea where he was, so there was no help forthcoming from that quarter. And he had no way of knowing whether Sylvia was headed for Amsterdam, courtesy of Salvadore's damnable noisy motorcycle, or in Fuentes' murdering grasp.

Nico shook the thoughts from his head, knowing them to be useless, and knowing that he needed to concentrate on his own immediate situation. He turned his attention back to Raúl, who had been watching him intently as if trying to read his mind. "When do I meet Fuentes?" Nico said, apparently casually.

Raúl shrugged, but Nico could sense the quickened tension in him. "Soon," he said. Then his dark eyes shifted and he looked thoughtful, as if he had forgotten something important and then had suddenly remembered it at an inopportune time. *"Eh.* Well, no. *Ahora.* Now. Now I go and you stay and then I come back and then you see *señor* Fuentes."

Rising from the chair, he backed away from Nico. Still holding the handgun pointed at his captive's chest, Raúl let himself out of the door. Nico heard the click of the key in the lock. The door might be old and scarred, but the lock that glittered there was most definitely a new one. He stared at the door even as he listened to Raúl descending the narrow steps.

Then he went directly to the bathroom to check the window. It hung open as they had left it, the bit of fresh air still not making much of a difference. Raúl was right. He would never fit through it. It was a miracle that Sylvia had managed it, even as slender as she was. Remembering the tumbled chairs, he smiled to himself. Ah, my Sylvia, he thought. You do manage, don't you?

And just now she was on the back of a fleeing motorcycle, clinging to Salvadore's waist. Again. His smile faded. What if he had placed her directly into danger by way of his actions? What if Salvadore really were in league with Fuentes? Or with his brother, Raúl?

Well, he would know soon enough, and for now he would have to believe that she was safe. He *had* to believe. Returning to the main room, he crossed to the door. Locked, as he knew it would be. He imagined Sylvia going through the same routine. He inspected the door carefully, thinking that perhaps he could take it off its rusty hinges.

He made for the alcove that served as a makeshift kitchen and started jerking open cupboards and drawers in search of a knife or something else he could use to remove the screws from the hinges. And perhaps use as a weapon, if necessary.

He swore in frustration. There was nothing, not even a spoon. Raúl didn't keep much of a household. Of course, these were transient lodgings, no doubt. If Raúl moved around as much as Fuentes, he wouldn't be here long. He wished briefly that he had his rucksack, with his small hoard of tools. But it waited for him at his little hotel room on the square. He wondered for a moment when, if ever, he might retrieve it. Then he remembered the brown paper bag. Picking it up, he removed bread and cheese and meat that had been carefully wrapped. No knives or forks. *"Merda,"* he muttered as he tossed it all back onto the floor in a disorderly heap. *Shit.*

Nico began to pace the small room. He felt cornered and he didn't like it. Being without some control had the effect of making him a bit claustrophobic. Surely there had to be a way out of here! But he could think of nothing, so he turned his thoughts back to Sylvia. How he wanted to see her, to tell her what was in his heart. Why hadn't he done it sooner? Why hadn't he told her in Amsterdam during that lovely day they had spent together, just the two of them? He smiled again to think of it. Her hand in his, the honey of her hair in the sunshine, the feel of her soft lips when he kissed her, the very scent of her. He sighed. He hadn't wanted to risk altering the mood of that day. He had just wanted to cherish the time, the talking, the sharing. The touching. Well, none of that mattered now. All that mattered now was her safety.

He did not pace for long. He froze in his place at the sound of heavy footsteps on the stairs and felt his pulse quicken in anticipation.

But when Raúl unlocked the door, Nico was lounging negligently with one shoulder propped against the battered wooden door jamb of the bathroom, his arms folded casually across his chest as if he hadn't a worry in the world.

Raúl slid the door open cautiously and entered first. His left hand flashed up, with the muzzle of his SIG Sauer handgun pointed directly at Nico's face. Then he stepped aside and another figure entered the room.

Eduardo Fuentes. Nico would never forget this man who had tried to kill him and Sylvia in the mountains of northern Czechoslovakia. Fuentes was dressed to the nines as always, in a dark suit and blue shirt with a blue and yellow tie. His clothes were perfectly tailored to his slender, fit physique, and his black leather shoes had been polished to an impossible sheen. The drug lord ran one palm across his immaculately groomed hair. He was in his mid-fifties and had swarthy skin and a rounded face. His basilisk eyes were black, with deep lines at the corners as if he had spent his life squinting against the sun. Nico thought that the man was handsome enough, and then, more uncharitably, he added in his mind, handsome in a greasy sort of way.

"*Señor* DiCapelli," Fuentes said, coldly enough to lower the temperature in the dingy room by several degrees. "It has been a long time." His English was precise enough, but with a heavier accent than Salvadore's.

"Indeed it has," said Nico. He grinned as if in welcome. "But perhaps not long enough. It has only been two months since you left me and Sylvia to die in the mountain fortress above Tatra in Czechoslovakia."

"I was very surprised to learn that you had escaped," said Fuentes. "And vastly annoyed. How did you manage that?"

"Some friends found us."

Fuentes scowled. "This time there will be no friends to interfere," he said. He slammed the door closed. "Where is Salvadore San Martín?" he demanded.

"I expect he's in Dover," said Nico, sounding matter of fact. "Or at least on his way."

Fuentes gave a sharp gesture and turned to Raúl. "I thought you said he was here in Bruges," he said.

"He is – eh – he was," said Raúl, shifting his weight from one foot to the other and sounding rather hesitant. "He take away with the woman."

Nico thought that he exhibited a tentativeness that his brother did not share. But then his instincts kicked in and made him wonder if some of Raúl's apparent uncertainty might be feigned, perhaps for the benefit of Fuentes' massive ego. The young man was, after all, *la mano izquierda*.

"Bound for Dover, *señor* DiCapelli says?" said Fuentes.

Raúl shook his head slightly. He spoke in Spanish now. *"No estoy seguro."*

I'm not certain.

Fuentes sighed in exasperation. "You have bungled again, Raúl," he said, still speaking in English.

Raúl did not understand all the words, but he did understand the danger behind the baiting tone. He shrugged as if Fuentes' observation was irrelevant. "But I bring DiCapelli." His dark gaze met the predatory one of Fuentes.

Fuentes nodded. "Yes, you have brought DiCapelli. And that will have to do. We can find Salvadore later."

"What do you want with Salvadore?" asked Nico.

"My relationship with Salvadore is my business," Fuentes said.

Nico shrugged as if it didn't really matter. But he was vexed. Damnation. He still didn't know whether Salvadore was working with Fuentes or not.

"So you think he's gone to Dover, do you?" said Fuentes.

"I do," said Nico.

"And the woman? Your Sylvia?"

"Also to Dover. With Salvadore. I think she likes his motorcycle."

Fuentes scowled again. "Well, never mind. I will take care of her later."

Nico was instantly on the alert. "What is Sylvia to you?" he asked.

As if irritated, Fuentes ran his fingers through his hair again, this time managing to disturb the studied black perfection. Oily, Nico thought.

"When I leave someone for dead, I expect them to stay dead," Fuentes said.

"She's no danger to you," said Nico.

"It's the principle of the thing," Fuentes said, as casually as if the issue were ethical or philosophical, rather than someone's very real life. Or death.

Nico's mind was racing. How could he possibly keep Sylvia out of danger? Hell, how could he keep himself out of danger? Fuentes could finish him off here and now and no one would be the wiser.

As if reading his thoughts, Fuentes grinned wolfishly. "You need not worry for some while, DiCapelli," he said. "I like to have my little game, as you probably remember from our contest two months ago. I will keep you alive until I have Salvadore and that Sylvia woman. Then you can all go straight to hell together."

His words were ominous, but a quick spark of hope ignited within Nico's breast. So. Salvadore was to suffer the same fate as he and Sylvia. A desperate exultation rose within him. Maybe Salvadore could, and would, keep her safe after all.

"Where we take him?" said Raúl. He was fidgeting with the weapon, his thumb restless on the safety. With an effort, Nico maintained his nonchalant pose. If this kept up much longer, Raúl would manage to shoot him, if only accidentally. Or maybe, Nico thought sardonically, Raúl would shoot himself. Better yet, he would shoot Fuentes. The thought momentarily cheered him.

Raúl's apparent restlessness did not seem to bother Fuentes unduly. "We certainly will not stay in this dump," the drug lord said, glancing around disdainfully. He slid one hand into the pocket of his suit jacket and pulled out a very small, very efficient-looking pistol. A Seecamp mousegun, Nico thought.

"Señor DiCapelli," Fuentes said. "We are going to transfer you to better quarters now. Both Raúl and I will have our weapons trained on your belly or your back. So I suggest that you attempt no tricks." He returned the gun to his jacket but kept his hand in the same pocket as well.

Raúl followed suit, sliding his own handgun into the left pocket of his denim jacket.

Might as well get to work, thought Nico. It was time to scratch and scrape around on that smooth surface that Fuentes wore so confidently. "Excuse me, Eduardo," he said, his calculated politeness a thin veneer of civility. "But I think a pistol in the pocket of that suit coat ruins the line of it. Don't you agree? It doesn't hang well. Absolutely undermines your careful efforts to achieve a *soignée* look." Nico shook a finger at him for emphasis. "Gentlemen's Quarterly would not approve at all."

Raúl shot a startled glance at Nico and then looked at Fuentes as if to judge his reaction.

"I'll just have to manage for now, won't I?" said Fuentes.

"Well, for god's sake, don't leave your hand in the pocket," said Nico. "That looks ridiculous. No one puts their hands in the pockets of a suit coat." He gestured towards Raúl. "Now with Raúl, it doesn't really matter. It's a denim jacket. More casual."

"I can do without your critique of my fashion sense," Fuentes said, this time with an edge to his voice. "Let's go for a walk." He motioned towards the door. "Keep DiCapelli here until I am all the way down the stairs," he said to Raúl.

After Fuentes had descended to the alley, Nico and Raúl did the same. Once on the cobblestones, Nico and Fuentes walked side by side while Raúl kept to the rear.

Fuentes kept up a rambling conversation, seemingly casual to anyone they might happen to encounter. "Beautiful old city, is it not?" he said.

"Indeed," said Nico. "I saw a good bit of it yesterday."

"What brought you here?" said Fuentes. *"Mi suerte buena?* My good luck?"

"Holiday," said Nico tersely.

"With that Sylvia woman."

Nico shrugged and thought of his last glimpse of Sylvia, clinging to Salvadore's back, her honey-colored curls streaming out behind like a tangle of brilliant sunshine. He wondered where they were now.

They emerged from the alley into the harsh brightness of Burg Square, Fuentes continuing his disjointed dialogue. "I don't believe for a moment that Salvadore and your Sylvia went to Dover," he said.

"Oh, really?" said Nico. "Where did they go, then?"

"I'd say in the opposite direction, well, actually north. Northwest. Back to Amsterdam."

"Interesting opinion," said Nico. He did not allow himself the luxury of a scowl. In retrospect, perhaps he should have sent Sylvia and Salvadore elsewhere. Well, that was the problem with split-second decisions, wasn't it? It was too bloody easy to second-guess them later. Like now.

The shadows of the old basilica were lengthening, and the crowds were thinning. Nico looked around, wondering whether he could create a diversion. But Fuentes was more attentive now, and a quick glance back at Raúl showed that he was following a few feet behind Nico, his left hand still shoved menacingly in his jacket pocket like a thug in a third-rate American gangster movie.

They crossed the square and sauntered down a narrow cobbled pedestrian street. "Here," said Fuentes, indicating a hotel on the right.

It was a large stone place and quite opulent, not one that Nico had noticed before. "A bit nicer than Raúl's place," he said wryly.

Raúl scowled his annoyance.

Nico was grateful that Salvadore had told him about his brother. Otherwise it would have been very easy to underestimate him. But Nico would never underestimate the likes of *la mano izquierda*. "Raúl," he said. "I wonder. If I ever see you without that scowl, would I even be able to recognize you?"

Fuentes waved one hand in impatience, and Raúl's scowl stayed firmly in place.

They ascended two rough, uneven grey stone steps and entered the lobby. It was an open room and large, but with several alcoves on either side that gave it an intimate feeling, not unlike the Hotel Amstel Grand in Amsterdam. The wooden paneling that accented the tall columns was a lighter color than might have been expected given the apparent age of the place. Oak, Nico decided, polished to a brilliant sheen. The ceiling was high, and it curved up from the columns to give the impression of several arches, again breaking the size of the room into segments that the eye could manage. The chandeliers were an intricate work of brass and hung with tear-shaped crystals, with a multitude of electric lights that were a remarkably accurate imitation of flickering candles. A single fireplace stood sentinel at the far end of the room, its veined black marble mantle mirroring the light from the chandeliers like a black and white negative or a reflection of diamonds that cast prisms of pure starlight rather than colors. The carpet runner was a dark chocolate hue, but with some kind of vines twisting about in an intricate but pleasing pattern, cutting a riotous swath against the parquet flooring. The numerous chairs were upholstered in a subtle grey and yellow-green stripe.

The room was exquisite and gently lit, as if trying for a mellow feeling. *Merda.* Nico felt anything but mellow.

"*El ascensor*," said Fuentes, directing Nico across the lobby to the lift on the right. Nico eyed the clerk at the oak registration desk, but that young man was earnestly occupied with the telephone. Nico stepped off the carpet runner and then listened to his own heels clicking rhythmically on the parquet flooring as he walked, a sound of finality to his ears. There was no way out of this one. Ah, *merda*.

It was an old-style lift, with a door that had to be operated manually. Nico pulled open the door and then slid back the metal safety screen. He stepped inside. It was quite small and faintly claustrophobic. The interior looked to be brass, and a mirror was fastened onto the back wall. Nico glanced at his reflection. A bit tense, but holding up well enough, he thought. Nothing untoward that Fuentes would notice. That *bastardo* would note only his studied nonchalance, Nico decided. He determined this with a force of will that had proven indomitable in other circumstances at least as awkward as this one. Awkward, indeed!

Raúl pulled the door closed and then the safety screen, and punched the button with the number six. With a screeching groan that caused Eduardo Fuentes to give a start, the elevator moved up slowly. They debouched onto the sixth floor and Fuentes shoved open the elevator doors and pointed the way once again. Nico noted that Raúl's handgun was out of his pocket now. No subtlety here, now that there was no one else about.

Fuentes' room turned out to be a two bedroom suite. The sitting area was lavish with two long couches and a Turkish rug on the floor between them. Kurdish, Nico surmised from the pattern and colors. A fully stocked bar was at a sideboard. The ceilings were high and paneled in white and gilt. The tall windows would have welcomed the light from out of doors, had the curtains not been drawn.

The doors to the bedrooms stood open. Fuentes directed Nico to the one on the left. "Your room for this night," he said, pleasantly enough.

Nico pointed to the other bedroom directly across the living area. "And that one is for you?"

Fuentes nodded. "That is correct."

"But where will poor Raúl sleep?" said Nico, with exaggerated concern. "On one of the couches?"

Raúl scowled. Again.

Fuentes gave a brief glance toward Raúl, then looked back at Nico. "Raúl will not sleep at all," he said. "He will stand guard to ensure you do not somehow manage to disappear, like the Sylvia woman."

"It's going to be a very long night," said Nico, grinning at Raúl.

Raúl waved his weapon threateningly. "Not so long if you not do I say you," he snapped.

"Now, Raúl," chided Fuentes. "*Señor* DiCapelli is our guest. You'll not forget that." He removed the little pistol from the pocket of his jacket and then slipped off the garment and draped it over the back of a heavily upholstered chair.

Raúl snorted, but stopped waving the handgun around. Even so, he did not put it back into his pocket, nor did he relax his vigilance.

"Drink?" said Fuentes, moving to the sideboard where there was an impressive array of liquor bottles. The attendant glasses stood in even rows like obedient crystal soldiers.

"Scotch," said Nico. "Teaninich, if you have it. On the rocks." He lowered himself casually onto one of the couches and crossed his long legs with one ankle resting on the other knee. He looked as relaxed as if this was his own suite, and Fuentes and Raúl were his guests.

Fuentes picked up the bottle of Scotch from the bar and glanced at the label. "Sorry. Looks like it has to be Dalwhinnie."

Nico shrugged. "That will do," he said.

Amiably, Fuentes poured. An expensive Mexican tequila for himself with coarse salt and wedges of lemon on the side, and a stiff Dalwhinnie with ice for Nico.

And nothing at all for poor Raúl, who stayed planted by the doorway, attentive but still scowling.

CHAPTER 21

Salvadore left Sylvia standing alone and bereft at the foot of the stairs of the Hotel Amstel Grand.

Cristo. He'd like to order her back onto the Buell and head north until he ran across Denmark, flew over the Kattegat into Sweden, and all the way to the bloody Arctic Circle. But he could not. Nico DiCapelli was in Bruges, facing down his brother, Raúl, and most certainly that *cabrón,* that bastard Fuentes. And while Sylvia might be here in Amsterdam where he had deposited her, without a doubt her heart was still in Bruges. With Nico.

Mierda. Shit. But there it was. Sylvia was not his. She would never be his. But just now Nico was in Bruges.

Ah, but so was Raúl. One more chance, perhaps the last chance, to bring home the prodigal son.

He had survived the brutal trip with Sylvia clinging to him, pressed against his back as if they could somehow become one. He had absorbed her desperate, silent grief as surely as if she had poured it out to him in words. With every kilometer that flashed past across the flatlands of Belgium and Holland, he had felt her metamorphose from irrational shock, to realization of the bleak truth, to mourning her impending loss. He knew as well as she did that Nico stood no chance in the hands of Eduardo Fuentes. He – Nico – had slipped from the drug lord's grasp once before, by whatever fluke. It would not happen again. Fuentes did not take lightly to losing.

Salvadore wondered for a brief moment whether he might just consider leaving Nico to the whims of Fuentes and thus secure at least a chance for himself with Sylvia, except for his resolve to extricate his brother from the grip of the drug lord and his poison. As quickly as the thought crossed his mind, he discarded it. Raúl or no Raúl, he could never turn his back on

Nico DiCapelli. Not now. The two of them fought in the same war, he knew. Salvadore was well aware of his own bitter motives for engaging the battle with the drug runners, the *narcotraficantes*. He did not know what DiCapelli's reasons might be, but it did not matter. It was the same brutal fight. And he would wage it shoulder to shoulder with Nico against the poison that Fuentes spread like so much dream dust. Perhaps together the two of them could accomplish what neither had managed alone.

If in fact Nico was still alive by the time Salvadore returned to Bruges. The odds of that were not good.

On the outskirts of Amsterdam, merging onto the motorway, he ruthlessly screwed open the throttle of the Buell, retracing the weary, harrowing journey he had just completed with Sylvia. *Snel trein*, fast train, indeed. He must have cut off nearly an hour from what the train managed from Bruges to Amsterdam. And he would do the same on his return trip to Bruges. He would find Nico DiCapelli, alive. And he would finish off Eduardo Fuentes. Then Nico could head for Amsterdam and his Sylvia. And Salvadore would once more, one last time, drag the protesting, angry Raúl back home to the heart of his family in Quinchía, to *la villa de los cerros*, the village of the hills. He knew it would be a last ditch attempt to reclaim the promise of the young man Raúl had been before Fuentes had sunk his depraved claws into that youthful innocence.

Salvadore was flying, at one with the motorcycle and the pavement, when the pulsing flash of blue lights and the shrill howl of a police siren jerked him from his troubled thoughts and his mindless attack on the motorway.

Ah, *mierda!* So he had at last managed to pry loose the attention of the stolid Dutch police. God knew how many kilometers per hour over the speed limit they had him for, and the equally obvious infractions of no helmet or whatever other safety gear might be required.

Well, there was nothing for it. He was five seconds away from the next exit, and it might be interesting to see how well the police car maneuvered on the narrow side roads. He twisted the throttle fully open, and with a screech of tortured tires, he laid the Buell nearly onto its side. The machine hurtled from the motorway, down the curving ramp, past a stop sign without even hesitating, and into unknown territory.

He heard the corresponding squeal of tires and the sharp wail of a siren as the police car reacted and followed him down the off-ramp, undoubtedly with a bit more caution through the intersection with the stop sign. But Salvadore paid no heed to what might be happening behind him. He was alert for side lanes and byways, certain that in minutes the entire police patrol within several kilometers would be alerted to the madman rocketing his way through their pristine and quiet domain.

Even as he imagined that he could hear another caterwauling siren join with the first, he saw his opportunity. Less than thirty meters ahead, a dirt road angled off to the left. Salvadore slammed on both the hand and foot brakes, and the machine slid sideways. When he released the brakes, the motorcycle righted itself and hurtled down the bumpy but bucolic lane. He rode the roughness of the grassy curb so as not to leave a telltale cloud of dust in his wake. Easing off the throttle, he slowed to a more reasonable and hopefully less noticeable speed.

So much for outpacing the *snel trein*. Here he was, suddenly on a country outing with sirens screaming on all sides, but with no one noticing his leisurely jaunt through this pastoral tranquility.

Oh, what the hell. As good a time as any to pull over for something to eat. He spotted a quaint café with two small tables outside. Pulling off the narrow excuse for a road, he parked the Buell unobtrusively behind a bush that was heavy with foliage still untouched by autumn. Running his fingers through his wind-blown hair, he sauntered over to one of the tables and planted himself onto the wooden chair, elbows on the threadbare but clean red and white checkered tablecloth.

In less than fifteen seconds, a sturdy Dutch housewife-looking woman appeared. She might have stepped out of a postcard for the countryside. Plump, with rosy cheeks framed by loose blond hair cut in a pageboy, she wiped her hands on her white apron as she advanced. He guessed her age at mid-forties, and gave her his most amiable smile.

She returned the smile, clearly delighted to have a stranger at one of her tables. He thought it likely that on a normal day she would have only the locals patronize her business in this out of the way place. She apparently had no menu but rattled off his three choices in Dutch. He grinned helplessly and raised both hands in bewilderment, so she waved reassuringly at him and headed inside the small building. In short order a basket of fresh bread and a tall glass of foamy Pilsner materialized in front of him. Even as she placed a small plate with a thick slab of golden butter next to the bread, a blue police car shot past on the dirt road, sirens giving full cry like a hunting dog on the scent. She clucked her tongue in annoyance at the cloud of dust it left in its noisy wake and waved her apron as if to ward it off, however ineffectually.

Salvadore sprawled on his chair with the cold beer in one hand and lifted his glass in a sardonic salute to the disappearing tail lights of the speeding police car. *"Proost!"* he said cheerfully. *"Salud!"* He sipped the refreshing brew and downed bread and butter until the woman appeared with a thick, meaty stew with boiled dumplings. He took his time eating, anxious to be on his way but knowing he had to give the police time to acknowledge that their quarry had slipped the trap and to call off the chase. Only then could he resume his charge back to Bruges. And this time at a more reasonable speed so as not to yet again attract the unwelcome attention from the now-alerted patrols.

As he swallowed the last of the cold Pilsner, he had only two thoughts. Keep yourself alive, Nico, until I get back to Bruges to join you. And Raúl, *mi hermano*, my brother, don't do anything too stupid until I can snatch you away to home and safety, one more time. For all the damned good it might do in the end.

He paid the smiling woman in Dutch guilders and left a hefty tip and then retrieved the motorcycle from behind the bushes. Wearily he climbed aboard and left the small wayside restaurant at a more sedate pace than the Buell had seen for a long while. He rode on the side roads but stayed as parallel to the motorways as he could manage so as not to lose his way, and thus traveled gradually south and east towards Bruges. This time, he suspected, the *snel trein* would arrive well in advance of him and his machine.

Dios mío, he thought in wry amusement. My god. It was damned embarrassing.

CHAPTER **22**

A weary Salvadore rumbled into Bruges on the Buell well after nightfall. His return ride from the small café just outside of Amsterdam had been exemplary, a model of how a proper Dutchman or Belgian should behave on the road. He was sporting a new black helmet that he had bought from a motorcycle shop on the way, as well as a protective black leather jacket that the French salesman had insisted was *de rigueur* for riding in both the Netherlands and Belgium. Resigned to being forced to treat his body with the proper respect for his own well-being, he kept the machine a fraction under the speed limit and observed both stop lights and stop signs as he meandered down the peaceful country lanes, still avoiding the motorways. He had snagged a roadmap when he had stopped to refuel, and so was quite comfortable with taking a more direct route rather than having to try to run parallel with the motorways in order to avoid getting lost.

But he had chafed at the slow pace, and his impatience was sharp. How he had longed to crank open the throttle and make short work of this interminable trip and the endless day.

His arrival in Bruges was so sedate as to resemble a severe case of boredom. He did not want to risk taking the Buell down the pedestrian streets as he had earlier in the day, and so parked it some five or six blocks away from the square where he had met Nico so many long hours ago. He pocketed the key and, removing the new helmet, he chained it and the motorcycle to an antique lamppost, ensuring that neither of them would wander off on their own, or more to the point, disappear at the hands of a clever Belgian thief with an eye for expensive motorcycles. Then he strode to Burg Square, keeping to the shadows.

Dios. What now? He didn't have even a clue where to begin. He leaned against a rough stone wall, hidden by the darkness, and watched the square for a time. It was still busy, with people coming and going from the restaurants and shops. Briefly, he wondered what Sylvia was doing in Amsterdam, whether she had stayed in the hotel and in her room, or if she had given in to the impulse to wander the streets and explore the museums and restaurants. He allowed himself a quick smile at the thought of her bright head of unruly curls haloed by the street lamps of Amsterdam. Then he turned his thoughts back to Bruges and the danger at hand. He had to find Nico, his unlikely partner in this desperate battle. And he must – he *must!* – find Raúl. The loved one, the lost one. His brother. He had promised his mother, who had smiled her trust in him from her beautiful dark eyes. She really believed that he could do it.

And he had promised his father, even though he knew that his father believed there was nothing left to redeem in the violent, murdering, unrepentant man that the once whimsical, charming Raúl had become. A chameleon, he was, this much-loved younger son and brother. Because of the poison, the damnable filthy drugs. Every time Salvadore was fortunate enough to happen across him, he never knew what he would discover.

Find him, his father had said. Find him, for your mother's sake, and for your sisters, who also believe. But I tell you, Salvadore, my son, your brother is a lost soul. You may find him, you may bring him back to his family, but you can never return him to who and what he was. The youth he was, the man he could have been, is gone, irretrievably lost as if he never existed. I have only one son now. But your mother cannot understand that. She still counts Raúl as her own, as our own. But he's not. He's *perdido*, lost. Lost to all of us. He's not even a prodigal son. He's no son at all. He's but an animal, living on base instincts and cruelty and with an obsessive dependence on the poison. Salvadore, he's broken. *Destrozado.*

Salvadore didn't understand exactly why, but the word sounded more poignant in the Spanish. *Destrozado.* Broken. Destroyed.

Coming from his normally reticent parent, it counted as an impassioned speech, a recitation of despair. And more important, and thus more devastating, a final acceptance of reality, of ultimate defeat.

The everlasting pain of it rode Salvadore without mercy. He never awakened to a new day but he felt the weight of it. Oh yes, it rode him, even as it spurred him on. He had brought Raúl home twice before, had faced down Fuentes and his murderous accomplices, had taken his brother violently and against his will back to Quinchía, the small village in the Colombian Andes where the exportable crop was coffee beans rather than coca. There he had imprisoned him, watched over him, weaned him from the poison, even as Raúl railed at him, cursed him, hated him. He had at last brought him back into the arms of his parents and three sisters, healed and clean and seemingly his old charming, devil-may-care self.

And then had lost him again. *Damn* Fuentes. *Damn* the poison that laced through Raúl's veins, bringing him comfort. But comfort from what?

Salvadore rested his forehead against the cool, rough stone of the wall of the ancient building and took a deep breath to clear his mind and his roiling emotions. He felt old and exhausted and drained of any will to move ahead. He was sick to the death of it, working against the odds, struggling ever forward, but never managing to win against his opponent, never to reach his ultimate goal. Like Sisyphus of the Greek myth, whose punishment in hell was for eternity to roll a boulder up a hill and then watch it tumble back down, so that he had to roll it up once again. Presumably, poor Sisyphus was still at it.

Is this how his entire life was to be spent? Year upon wasted year pursuing the unachievable? Losing his own self, his own soul, even as he sought to save the lost one? In truth, he wondered sometimes which of them really was the lost one, the broken one.

How he longed to turn his back on it all. How he longed to disappear into a normal life. Working at an honest job, having a home, raising a family. In what seemed a natural progression, his thoughts turned back to Sylvia. And he abruptly straightened away from the wall. There was certainly no future in those kinds of meanderings. Rescuing Raúl from himself would continue to be his obsession, and Sylvia would, in the end, belong to Nico DiCapelli. He didn't know Nico well, didn't know what might be the motivation behind his single-minded pursuit of Fuentes. But Nico had gradually made his way past Salvadore's defenses, first gaining a grudging respect and then the beginnings of a fledgling trust. Two people brought together by something as basic as a vitriolic hatred for one single man who made it his business to destroy others. Individuals, families, lives.

Ah, but tonight he had to find Nico and he had no idea where to begin looking. He watched Burg Square for awhile longer. Then, giving in to the pressing need to do something, anything, he skirted the square, staying in the shadows. At length he came to the alley where Raúl had apparently been staying. He glanced into the dimness. It was deserted. He doubted that either Raúl or Nico still was there, but even so he walked slowly down the cobbled street until he reached the midpoint. Cautiously, he began trying the doorknobs. The first two were locked. But the third turned in his grasp. Reaching his right hand into the pocket of his leather jacket, he withdrew a SIG Sauer P225 handgun. It was the same exact weapon that Raúl favored. Salvadore hated the thing, hated touching it, hated that he might actually have to use it. His ever practical and ever stoical father had reminded him of the trite but true cliché: One must fight fire with fire. Or firepower with firepower. Salvadore was proficient with the SIG Sauer. He could use it, and had, when bringing away Raúl. He knew he would use it again for the same purpose.

Slowly he pushed open the door. The place, whatever it was, had not even a glimmer of light. He felt against the wall for a light switch. His questing fingers found two round buttons, apparently the old style of switch. He closed the door, grateful for the silence afforded by the well-oiled hinges. Bending his knees slightly and raising the weapon, he pushed one of the buttons. Nothing happened. Bracing himself yet again, he pushed the other one.

It would be inaccurate to say that light flooded the small area. The low-watt bulb provided more shadows than light, but even so Salvadore blinked against the abruptness of it. There was nothing to see but a shabby narrow staircase with another battered door at the top.

He ascended the stairs, weapon at the ready. The door at the top was also unlocked, and the hinges oiled to ensure silence. He gently opened the door onto what was apparently a vacant room.

Less cautious now, he punched on the light, and the shoddy lodging was illuminated. The unkempt cot along the wall, the sink in the alcove with its few unwashed coffee cups. The stale odor of a little-used, confined place caused him to wrinkle his nose in distaste. Oh, yes, he could imagine Raúl lodging here when he was using the drugs. The same Raúl who loved the crisp mountain air of the Colombian Andes, the freshness of the mischievous breezes. The vast open space where the snow-capped volcanic peaks strained towards the embrace of the heavens, azure in the mornings and cerulean in the evenings. How could Raúl even breathe the stifling air in this room, or tolerate the closeness of the grey walls? Never, *never* would Salvadore come to understand it.

Salvadore crossed the room to glance into the small excuse for a bathroom. His gaze was drawn upward to the tiny, still-open window with the errant breeze tugging determinedly. As Nico had done before him, he gave a wry grin. The wild bird had taken her flight from here, there was no doubt. Ah, Raúl, my brother. You met your match in that one!

But apparently Raúl and Nico had flown as well, no doubt directly to Eduardo Fuentes' murdering breast. So. Where would the drug lord have taken Nico DiCapelli? Salvadore knew Fuentes very well by now. There was no way he would have stayed in a sordid place like this.

Assuming they were still in Bruges, which was by no means a certainty, they would be in much finer quarters. And perhaps close by, since Fuentes would not like the potential danger of exposing someone as resourceful as Nico to public scrutiny for long.

Well, he was forced to admit that it was quite a stretch, but he had nothing else to go on. So he would make the assumption that Nico was being held fairly close to the square in a hotel that surely must rival the Amstel Grand itself, if Fuentes were to maintain his usual standards of quality. Nothing but the best for that murdering *cabrón*, that bastard.

Feeling somewhat better now that he had a plan – never mind that it wasn't much, as plans go – he left the dingy flat, turning out the lights as he went. He strode quickly down the alley and paused at the edge of the square. He wondered what time it was, as there were now only a few people still milling about. Even so, he kept to the shadows like a stalking wildcat. Gradually he made his way around the perimeter, going several blocks down each street that intersected the square like a spider's web. In the end, he came across two hotels that might come close to satisfying Fuentes' taste for luxury. Unfortunately, they were at opposite sides of the square, and a few blocks into the pedestrian streets, making the already uncertain surveillance even more difficult. Well, there was nothing for it. He would find a room and catch a few hours rest, and then early in the morning he would resume this uncertain vigil. The hotel he settled on faced the square. It was a small, nondescript place, but clean and quiet. He took a quick hot bath and then stretched out on the bed to think.

CHAPTER 23

It was nearly six-thirty in the morning when Nico blinked himself awake. For a moment he was at a complete loss as to where he was and why he was there. The walls that seemed to close in around him were unfamiliar and dark, the only illumination coming from an open door. He did not move a muscle as he absorbed his surroundings. It was very quiet with no sounds of traffic or other people. From what he could make out in the dimness, the room where he lay was very well appointed. Ah, yes. The Hotel Amstel Grand, Amsterdam.

But in the next instant he knew. Not Amsterdam. Bruges, courtesy of the hospitality of Eduardo Fuentes himself. And the scowling Raúl.

His first thought, simple and straightforward, went to Sylvia. Where was she? And was she safe? And then to Salvadore. What would he do once he had delivered Sylvia to the safety of Amsterdam? Because at this moment he had no doubt that was exactly what the Colombian had done. But then what? He hoped Salvadore had stayed with her to protect her, perhaps had even taken her into hiding.

Stacking his hands behind his head on the pillow, he pondered that. He didn't know the elusive Salvadore very well, not yet anyway. He couldn't. But he had gotten some fairly insightful glimpses of the character of the man. Yes, he would have gotten Sylvia to safety. But then he would most likely come straight back to Bruges, where he had left Nico in mortal danger.

And where he had left his brother Raúl dancing dangerously on the strings that were manipulated by the master puppeteer himself. Fuentes.

The thought of Raúl focused his mind on his own situation. He threw back the bed coverings and swung his legs over the side of the bed. Standing, he slipped into the lush white terrycloth robe that hung in the closet, courtesy of the hotel. Then he silently padded to the open door, where he looked out into the large sitting area. Across the room, the door to Fuentes' room was closed. Raúl was propped crookedly in one of the upholstered chairs near the door to the outer hallway, the pistol still gripped in his left hand but now lying across one thigh. Nico measured the distance across the room to the Colombian even as he took a few gliding steps forward.

Raúl shifted and stirred and then came to full awareness with a jerk. He shot to his feet and raised the weapon, all in one smooth, swift movement.

Nico grinned. "Good morning, Raúl," he said laconically. "I hope I didn't disturb your rest."

Predictably, Raúl's scowl had returned. "Go back you room," he snapped.

Nico shook his head and went directly to the bar where Fuentes had poured the drinks the night before. He opened the small refrigerator and, taking out a bottle of fresh orange juice, he gave it a shake and then poured a glassful. With exaggerated politeness, he held it out to Raúl. "Care to join me?" he said.

Neither Raúl's scowl nor the gun wavered. "No," he said. "I no want."

Nico shrugged. "Suit yourself," he said even as he put the bottle back into the refrigerator. He walked to one of the couches and seated himself. In blatant disregard of the good manners his mother had taught him, he flopped his bare feet onto the low walnut table and proceeded to carry on his one-sided conversation with what had to be a grating cheerfulness. "Not much of a morning person, I take it?"

Raúl ignored the overture but seated himself onto the chair which he had abruptly vacated a few moments before, the weapon still trained on his prisoner.

Undeterred, Nico kept talking. "Can't say as I blame you, not this morning at least. It can't have been very pleasant whiling away the night in that chair while Eduardo and I spent a comfortable evening having drinks and friendly conversation, and then going to bed."

Still Raúl remained silent, watching his tormentor.

As if the thought had just occurred to him, Nico suddenly brightened. "Listen, Raúl," he said. "Why don't you go rest in my room for awhile and I'll stand guard."

This last goad got a response. "You no speak me more," the Colombian snapped, making a quick, stabbing motion with the pistol for emphasis.

Nico sighed. "All right," he said. "I was just trying to be helpful."

Raúl shot him a disbelieving look.

Finishing his orange juice, Nico put the glass on the table, ignoring the wooden coasters meant to protect the table's surface. He rose and, making directly for the telephone at the bar, he lifted the receiver.

Raúl was on his feet again in an instant. Damn, but he was quick. "What you think to do?" he demanded. "Put down that!"

Nico stood with the receiver in his hand and stared at the Colombian in mock astonishment. "For god's sake, Raúl! I'm just calling for room service. I'm hungry."

Raúl took one menacing step forward. "No! Put down!" The volume of his voice was rising steadily with his mounting fury.

Nico moved the receiver to his ear and with his other hand made as if to punch in a number. "Want anything?" he asked. "I'm having eggs and toast and black coffee."

"Put down now!" Raúl's order was nearly a shout. The Colombian began his threatening advance at the same time that Fuentes' door flung open.

The drug lord stepped into the room, not at all his usual dapper self. His black hair was disheveled and his hastily donned robe was askew. But the wicked-looking little pistol in his hand was steady enough. *"Mierda!"* he swore. "What the hell is going on?"

Nico managed to look aggrieved. *"Cristo!* I was only trying to order from room service." He gestured across the room at the young Colombian. "I think perhaps Raúl needs to rest. He's a bit testy this morning."

Fuentes took two long strides to where Nico stood. He jerked the receiver from his hand and slammed it back down onto the telephone.

Nico rolled his eyes and immediately headed for the refrigerator to search for other options. "I see that you aren't much of a morning person either," he grumbled at Fuentes, even as he rummaged through the small refrigerator. There was a bowl of chilled fresh fruit, and he took out a brightly burnished red apple and inspected it. "Well, it's not eggs and toast, but I guess it will have to do." He placed the apple onto the bar with more flourish than it deserved.

Then he removed two unappetizing-looking brown bananas. He frowned and shook his head reproachfully. "Everyone knows that you don't chill bananas," he chided. "It ruins their appearance." He put the offending fruit onto the bar next to the apple and returned his attention to the bowl. "Ah, here we go," he exclaimed. He grabbed an orange and tossed it towards Raúl, startling both Colombians. Reflexively, Raúl caught it out of the air as it flew past his head, even as Fuentes swore violently.

Nico turned away from them both and reclaimed his place on the couch where he settled himself and then took a sizeable bite from the crisp apple.

Fuentes was not amused. His black eyes were slits and his lips a thin straight line. "I may change my mind about you, DiCapelli. I am not amused at your antics. Perhaps I won't bother to keep you around after all."

Nico's gut clenched at the menace in Fuentes' demeanor and words. But he gave a careless shrug. "That's up to you, of course," he managed to say around another bite of apple. "But I think it's not likely you will find Salvadore and Sylvia without my help. Dover is a pretty big place, with a lot of nooks for hiding."

Fuentes' lethal fury gave way to a grudging exasperation. "Still singing that song, are you?" He shook his head. "Why not Paris? Or Madrid?"

"Why not, indeed?" said Nico agreeably.

"Or why not Amsterdam?" the Colombian added.

Nico shrugged again and finished off the apple. He dropped the core into the empty glass where the orange juice had been and stretched. Then he came to his feet under Raúl's watchful eye. "How about we all go down to the hotel restaurant for breakfast?" he suggested. "I'm sure it's included in the room tariff."

Raúl muttered a curse under his breath, the exact meaning of which managed to elude Nico, but Fuentes stepped to the bar and lifted the room service menu. He shoved it in Nico's direction. "Decide what the hell you want," he said. "Then Raúl will call down the order." He hesitated for a moment, as if remembering that they were in Belgium, and Raúl spoke neither French nor Dutch, and only a little English. Nevertheless, he was not about to call it in himself, and he clearly didn't trust Nico to do it.

Nico took the menu to the low table along with a pad and pen belonging to the hotel. He sat on the couch and studied the offerings as seriously as if he were translating the text of an ancient manuscript and made several notes on the pad. Frowning in concentration, he read his list to himself. Seemingly satisfied, he nodded. "Okay, Eduardo, my man, what will it be?" He held the pen in readiness like an eager-to-please waiter.

With a muttered expletive Fuentes snatched the menu and perused it briefly. "Omelette with onions and green peppers and cheese," he said.

Nico nodded wisely. "Southwestern omelette," he said as he wrote.

Fuentes looked momentarily confused but Nico ignored him. "Raúl?"

"The same," snapped that tense young man.

Now Nico looked confused. "The same as I am having?" he asked, pen still poised. "Or as Eduardo is having?"

Goaded beyond patience once more, Fuentes grabbed the pad from Nico's hand. "*Maldición!*" he swore even as he thrust the paper towards Raúl. "Damnation! Call this in," he said. "I'm going to take a shower." He strode to his room and slammed the door violently.

Raúl seemed unconcerned at Fuentes' abrupt departure. He placed his handgun on the counter next to the telephone. Keeping a watchful eye on Nico, he lifted the receiver of the telephone and punched in the room service number.

Nico could hear the precise French-accented voice on the other end of the line. "Yes, Mr. Fuentes? This is room service. How may I assist you?"

Raúl scowled at the pad that held Nico's barely decipherable scrawl. In his heavily accented English, he recited the lengthy, complicated order to the unfortunate person on the other end of the telephone.

There was a great deal of repeating and clarification, and when Raúl at last got to the southwestern omelette there was a long silence on both ends of the connection.

At last the French-accented voice inquired, "Southwestern? What is southwestern?"

Raúl glanced helplessly at Nico.

"Omelettes," said Nico with a grin. "Two of them. *Con cebollas, pimientos verdes y queso.* With onions, green peppers and cheese. Come *on*, Raúl."

That young man scowled again but dutifully repeated what Nico had said in both Spanish and English. At last the person on the other end of the line seemed satisfied enough. Either that, or he had finally reached the point of giving up.

"Oh, wait," Nico said suddenly. "And coffee. Sweet. And thick. Cooked in the Turkish style. Not that anemic brewed stuff."

Raúl repeated this request with ill grace. This was followed by a barrage of confusion from the telephone and another annoyed glare at Nico from Raúl.

Nico leaned back on the couch and again stretched out his legs and lifted his bare feet to the table. Well, if nothing else, the staff of this hotel should remember their unusual guests in the suite on the sixth floor.

Before the food arrived, Raúl herded Nico back into the oblivion of the comfortable prison of his room, so he took a quick shower and donned the same blue jeans and light shirt that he had shed the night before. He didn't give two seconds of thought to the clean clothes in his own shabby room in the little hotel on Burg Square. When one didn't know whether he would live thorough the day, a good breakfast seemed immeasurably more important than clean underwear.

Nico had learned through hard experience that perspective was a relative term. Given the choice of what his priorities might be for this day, should it indeed be his last, he would pick sweet Turkish coffee over a fresh wardrobe. And indeed, shouldn't that be the perspective for every day, whether or not Fuentes or some other lethal threat lingered on the horizon?

Shaved, showered and dressed, Nico was ready when the sharp rap reverberated through his door. He shoved it open, took one glance at Raúl's not very stoic countenance and strode toward the laden trays that lined the bar. He grinned.

A southwestern omelette for Fuentes, an omelette for Raúl, also south-western. And an entire spread of eggs – over easy, over hard, scrambled. Hot bacon and ham and sausages, cold meats, three different types of cereals with milk, assorted fruits and cheeses and breads. Ah, this was the satisfying result of Nico's exhaustive survey of the menu. But he stepped past it and made directly for the coffee – sweet, thick Turkish coffee. He picked up the tiny cup and brought it to his lips for a sample. Perfectly cooked, after all. He grinned at Fuentes and Raúl, raised the cup in a small salute, and said, "Well, then, *şerefe!*" the Turkish word for a toast. Cheers! For the benefit of the Colombians he added, *"Salud!"*

Raúl glowered. Even though Nico knew Fuentes was fuming at Nico's small coup of having ordered enough breakfast to serve the army of a minor nation, remarkably his impassive stare never wavered. And neither did Nico's determined but sardonic grin. It was, after all, not just a Turkish toast, but a recognition of the choice of properly cooked coffee over clean underwear. *Salud*, indeed!

Ignoring both Fuentes and Raúl, Nico picked up a large plate and started spooning up his breakfast, a bit of each dish until the offerings were barely touched but his plate was full, much like the *rijsttafel* that Salvadore and Sylvia had shared in Amsterdam. He looked at the vast amount of food still remaining and then to his captors. "Damn," he said. "I forgot to order tomatoes and cucumbers." He shrugged. "Well, never mind." He gestured towards the still full dishes. "Please," he said politely. "If your southwestern omelettes aren't enough, help yourself. I don't think I can eat all of it."

Raúl stood well back with his handgun trained on Nico and his dark eyes revealing the ardent desire to use it. But for some reason, Fuentes would not be baited this morning. What a disappointment. "You and I will eat," he said to Nico. "And then Raúl will have his breakfast."

"But the food will get cold," said Nico even as he took his heaped plate and Turkish coffee to the low table and proceeded to dig in. "Poor Raúl. First no sleep, and then a cold breakfast. Doesn't seem fair." He pointed his fork in Fuentes' direction. "Why don't you stand guard while Raúl eats?" he asked. Then he shoveled up a bite of the hot scrambled eggs.

Raúl glanced at the spread of food and then at Fuentes. But the drug lord ignored him. He took a plate, spooned up part of one omelette, and then meats and cheeses in turn. He seated himself on the couch opposite where Nico was and began eating.

Nico took another bite of the scrambled eggs. He chewed, swallowed, and then spoke. "So," he said. "What shall we do today?" He took another mouthful, this time of the fresh bread and a hard yellow cheese. "Have you seen the Michelangelo sculpture of the *Madonna and Child* at the Onze-Lieve-

Vrouwekerk, the Church of Our Lady? Really, you shouldn't miss it while you're here. It's quite unique, one of the few Michelangelo pieces outside of Italy. There's also a van Dyck painting there, I think the *Crucifixion*."

Fuentes shrugged. "I'm more interested in the artwork in Amsterdam," he said.

Nico did not miss his point, but he chose to ignore it. "The grand masters?" he asked, remembering Fuentes' passion for acquisition of rare and invaluable things, especially those that were rightfully owned by someone else. Whether they belonged to other persons, or to other countries, cultures or heritages, none of it mattered to the grasping drug lord. He would take what he could. Things of great beauty, and value, and importance. Nico blinked as he took the concept one more step forward. In his mind, he had been describing paintings, sculptures, ancient jewels of vast historic value. But now he was describing life. Human life. His life, and Salvadore's and even the volatile Raúl's. But most importantly, Sylvia's life. A thing of great beauty, and value, and importance. He jerked himself from this flight of fancy and back to the very dangerous matter at hand, and forced himself to speak on the topic that he himself had introduced.

"The Dutch grand masters," he repeated. "Vermeer? Jan Steen? Rembrandt? Or perhaps the more modern Vincent van Gogh?"

Fuentes sampled a bit of the ham with mustard sauce. "I have a van Gogh," he said.

"Do you?" said Nico, picking up his Turkish coffee and taking an appreciative sip. "I wonder, Fuentes, who really owns it? From what unfortunate collector or museum did you steal it?"

Nico felt Raúl's astonished gaze upon him. But Fuentes' response was casual and unoffended. "Well, since I happen to have it at the moment, I would suppose that it belongs to me."

"That's one interpretation," Nico said agreeably. "Another might be that your acquisition is so tainted by treachery and drugs and blood that the painting no longer has any beauty or meaning. Perhaps Vincent van Gogh, in his madness, saw the future for this incalculable beauty that he had created. Perhaps that is why he ended up taking his own life, to prevent further creation of that which would ultimately destroy. He would surely have been horrified that the beauty he created at such a great cost to himself could result in such ugliness."

Nico could sense the tension of imminent violence radiating from Raúl. But Fuentes merely grimaced. "Philosophical this morning, aren't you? Van Gogh's suicide had nothing to do with such nonsense as beauty creating ugliness. He was insane, and that's all there is to it."

"I'm sure you're right," Nico said with a shrug. "That particular artist, van Gogh, was incapable of ugliness. Unlike, say, Caravaggio." He was casually referencing that Italian genius who was also a murderer and worse. Not unlike Fuentes himself. "You, Fuentes, are a vestigial being. Degenerate, atrophied, worthless. Having no use, but somehow still remaining malignant and malevolent. Like an appendix, a useless organ that can turn to poison, destroying the very body where it lives."

Fuentes made a sharp gesture as if to shut him up, but Nico was not finished. "To get back to our conversation on art, the ugliness is what *you* create, Fuentes. Destroying lives to feed your own acquisitive nature, your greed. It's not enough that you steal and murder. You take human beings, and you twist and manipulate them with your filthy drugs until they are worse than dead. A living death." He gestured towards the young Colombian. "Like Raúl. Not even thirty years old, and already one of the living dead. Taken from his family, taken from all those who care about him. Destroying not only his life, but destroying the life of his own brother, Salvadore. Raúl is taking Salvadore down into the pit with him so that he won't have to suffer alone. It's a cruel and bitter thing to do to one who loves you."

Raúl stiffened at this sudden reference to him. He looked as if the earth beneath his feet had suddenly and unexpectedly shifted. He looked, in a word, stunned.

But Nico changed direction before either Raúl or Fuentes could react. He lifted his empty cup. "Raúl," he said. "Why don't you ring up room service again and have them send up another Turkish coffee? Sweet, like the last one."

His expression still one of dazed disbelief, Raúl automatically reached towards the telephone, but Fuentes gave an impatient gesture. "*Dios mío*, Raúl, don't be such a fool." He shoved away his unfinished breakfast, his temper finally ignited, and completely this time. "I've had enough of your mouth, DiCapelli," he said through his teeth.

"No problem," said Nico. He cut a piece of ham and chewed it slowly. He thought better of pushing Fuentes further, either on the topics of greed and drugs, or on the more mundane issue of a second Turkish coffee.

Fuentes lurched to his feet, abandoning the remains of his meal. He took the small pistol from the pocket of his robe and gestured towards Raúl. "Eat something," he ordered. "We're going to be leaving soon."

Obediently, the weary-looking Raúl filled a plate and ate quickly but as if without tasting the food. Nico noticed with mild amusement that he had taken none of the omelettes. He also noticed, with no amusement at all, that the Colombian's hand trembled slightly as he managed the fork. Odd, that, because when he grasped his pistol, his grip was rock-steady. Nico wondered when Fuentes had last supplied him with the drugs he needed to survive. Or, as Salvadore had somewhat enigmatically put it, to fly.

The poor *bastardo*. As much as Nico hated the drug lords and drug runners and yes, even the drug addicts, he hated them remotely, as an idea or a concept. And when confronted in person with a lynchpin like Fuentes, his hatred burned even hotter, intensely focused and tempered by the fire to a fine edge of fury and vengeance.

But to see Raúl's wrecked, poisoned life, a future destroyed, and to know the helpless, hopeless pain of Salvadore and his family, and their desperation to save the one who would not be saved. Ah, then his hatred had to be blunted and eased with a reluctant compassion and a bitter pity. He recalled the agony in Salvadore's eyes as he admitted his own failure to reclaim this lost brother from the depths of hell.

And at the same time he recalled the grief in his own mother's eyes as she knelt on the grass beside the open grave of his father, her beloved, forever-lost husband, and bade a tearless goodbye with a handful of soil that gave a hollow *thunk* as it dropped onto the lowered cherry wood casket. Over time she had come to learn how to forget and to remember at the same time, had come to learn how to let the memory walk at her side rather than having it block her way. But in that moment, at the graveside, she had bid farewell to a vibrantly alive man who had loved his family more than anything else in the world. A man who had been thrust into that cold, early grave by an out of control drug addict that could have been Raúl himself.

The young Colombian glanced up at Nico then. Looking startled at the intense scrutiny that met his eyes, he blinked, and his dark gaze, so like Salvadore's, slid away.

As if in shame, Nico thought for a moment. But in truth, he knew better. Whether Nico hated this young man or pitied him changed nothing. Raúl was Fuentes' puppet, his slave, and as such he was very dangerous not only to Nico, but to his own brother Salvadore. And ultimately to Sylvia. That made him an enemy, an obstacle that had to be confronted and taken out as surely as if the young man were Fuentes himself.

Nico's appetite was suddenly gone, and he picked at the remains of egg and cheese on his plate without interest. He was ready to get on with this day, whatever it might bring. It might be his last, that was true. But it might also be the day that brought him twenty-four hours nearer to Sylvia.

CHAPTER 24

To his utter astonishment, Salvadore awoke very early the next morning, rested and ready to face what the day might bring. Even the ever-present burden of his repeated failure to rescue his errant brother seemed lighter this day.

He bathed again, in cool water this time, to quicken his senses. Breakfast was not yet being served, and so he would just have to do without. He was determined to catch a glimpse of Nico DiCapelli, whatever his condition might now be.

He checked out of his hotel and then, with his light rucksack slung over one shoulder, he walked the six blocks to where he had left the Buell. It was waiting there, unmolested, the shiny new helmet still chained to the front wheel. Ready to go at a moment's notice. Okay, *bueno.* Then he went back to the vacant square and wandered around, keeping unobtrusively to the edges.

The plan he had made the night before, and the hotels he had scoped out as potential lairs for Fuentes, now seemed ridiculously naïve. How could he possibly have believed he could anticipate the next calculated move of such a master chessman as Fuentes? But having no other options, he doggedly stayed with his original plan. By god, he maintained with a determined obstinacy, there were only two possible hotels where Fuentes would deign to stay, and he was going to catch him leaving one of them, with the captive Nico in tow. And the slavish Raúl doing his part like any good soldier would. Just following orders.

Very nearly he missed them. He had stayed several minutes surveying the hotel that seemed the most likely of the two. But impatience chewed at him and so he nipped across the square and down the narrow, cobbled street to take yet another look at the other hotel. Coming down the pair of stone steps were three men. The well-groomed figure of Fuentes was first, and he was speaking to the man just behind him.

Nico DiCapelli. To Salvadore's relief, he seemed to be unharmed. For the time being, at least. And then his heart skipped, as it always did when he spotted the young man now following Nico. His brother. Raúl looked pale and tired, Salvadore thought, and he had a hunted, haunted look about him, something that Salvadore had not seen before.

He had time for only those few astute observations, made in a split second, before he took a quick step back out of sight. But he thought perhaps that Nico had caught the sudden movement from the tail of his eye.

He hesitated for a brief moment and then risked another look. The men had stopped at the bottom of the stairs and were looking up at a hotel worker, who was gesturing as if giving directions. Deliberately, Nico jabbed one forefinger in the direction opposite from where Salvadore watched. All of the men turned their heads to look where Nico was pointing. Except for Nico himself. He looked directly at Salvadore's shadowed form. Salvadore raised one hand in a quick thumbs-up gesture and again stepped back, but not before he caught the brief grin of relief that flashed across Nico's face. The message was unmistakable. If Salvadore was back in Bruges, then Sylvia must be in Amsterdam, and safe.

CHAPTER 25

Sylvia was safe in Amsterdam, all right. Safe but sleepless. Safe but worried, concerned, fretful, fearful. She tried all of the words that might sketch the outline of the suspended terror that consumed her, but none really described the knot of icy dread that was frozen in her breast, the insidious, nagging fear. This helpless waiting, not knowing whether Nico was harmed or safe, dead or alive. Knowing only that it mattered, how very much it mattered. He must survive this. He *must* return to her. She could not bear to lose him, not now, not like this.

Yes, she had borne pain before, but it was a pain that came from cruel deception and lies. There had been a loss, that was true. A loss of trust and love. And then the loss of a life, which in time she had come to admit to herself, had been substantially less hurtful than the former loss. In fact it had been a relief. Oh, yes, she had carried that bitter guilt at well. She could see herself standing at the graveside of her dead husband next to his mourning family, and instead of the grief that she should have felt for him, the grief that she had *owed* him, she could dredge up no feelings beyond a numb relief that it was over. Not even the woman who stood apart from the other mourners and wept copious and noisy tears could bring her from her steadfast refusal to be moved. And that woman had been her husband's mistress. Sylvia had never wondered how the woman had summoned the nerve to intrude on the family's privacy. In truth, it didn't really matter to her. Not then, not now.

But with Nico, the thought of impending loss was immeasurably more unbearable. It made no sense. He was not hers to lose, after all. There was nothing between them, not really. No relationship, no commitment, no professed or confessed caring.

Even so, she knew if she lost him now to Fuentes' murdering hands, she would mourn him more intensely and for a much longer time than she ever had her dead husband. With a bitterness, yes, but a bitterness that a future, her future and his, had been snatched away. Not with the acrid anguish of betrayal, but with the vast, echoing emptiness of an irreplaceable loss.

She pulled her thoughts away from such morbidity. Thanks to Nico and Salvadore, she was away from Raúl, away from Fuentes. She was safe. Safe but sleepless, safe but worried. Safe but claustrophobic where she waited in her room, time hanging heavy, an eternity from one moment to the next. She wrote. She paced. She gazed out of her window at the sleeping city, the night lights reflecting lazy ripples on the canal below. She paced anew, fretting against the narrow confines of her room. And she wrote some more.

It was perhaps the most prolific night of her life thus far, when it came to writing at least. She had laid aside her half-finished novel for the moment, and had abandoned herself to a new plot, new emotions, new characters, abandoned herself to the immediacy of Amsterdam and Bruges.

With her words she painted brilliance. Light, color, texture. She painted sensations. Sound, scent, taste. She painted people. Lives, loves, losses. It poured forth from her for hours, until the sky began to lighten at the window and the city began to live and breathe and move around her once again.

And still she wrote, as if the intense concentration could somehow hold at bay the dread that had settled into her consciousness, the foreboding that had seeped into her very pores. It was not until the sun raised itself high enough to fling its exuberance through her uncurtained window that she took her attention to the new day and realized that the interminable night was at last a dark memory to be stored away, buried with all the other tenebrous memories in the vault that she kept securely locked. Along with all the secrets of her heart.

The tension within her had eased, and she wondered why. Nothing had changed, not really. She still had no idea what was happening with Nico or Salvadore. But even as exhausted as she was, she felt able to face this fresh day with a new hope, and a new certainty that somehow Nico would return to her after all.

She tossed down her pen and, rising stiffly from her chair, crossed over to the window. A rare clear morning it was, with even the canal below looking peaceful rather than sluggish. The narrow buildings leaned over their shimmering reflections as if admiring their own antique beauty, their straight lines and rakish gables and varied colors.

She thought it a great shame to spend such a day indoors. But this time she took Salvadore's warning seriously. There was a real danger – she knew that now. She should have known it the very moment that Nico had dropped Fuentes' name. Even so, she might have ventured abroad in any case. But what if Nico or Salvadore should come here, or call? What if she somehow missed them?

With another longing glance at the beckoning sunshine, she sighed and headed for the bathroom, only then remembering that her toothbrush and other small necessities were at her hotel in Bruges, and that she had not checked out and paid. Well, there was a complication she had not considered. She snatched up the small handbag that she had come away with and rummaged for the card she knew was there. She always kept a card of her hotel with her, as she was nearly guaranteed to get lost sometime during her stay, no matter where she was.

Sure enough, there it was. The name of the hotel in French, the street address in Dutch. She punched in the international calling code and was shortly rewarded by the French-accented English of the proprietor. She explained that she had been unexpectedly called away, apologizing for any inconvenience. The man's relief was palpable, as he had been worried when *mademoiselle* had not returned last night or come down for breakfast this morning. He would be happy to send her bag to her hotel in Amsterdam, he assured her. She gave him the number of her credit card to cover the room charge and, thanking him yet again, she rang off.

That detail resolved, she called the desk of the Amstel Grand and explained her situation. The man at reception was confident that this was no problem for them. They often had overnight guests whose luggage was temporarily lost, or whose flights had been canceled, and the hotel had a nice package for that eventuality, with all the necessities for a day or two.

Sylvia thanked the man and then rang room service for a pot of tea and some fruit, not wanting to leave her room even for a quick breakfast.

Both the package of necessities and the tea arrived at the same time, so she poured a cup of the steaming brew and took it into the bathroom with her. She took a quick shower and washed her hair, and then untangled it even as she ate her orange sections and grapes.

All of that was finished in short order, and she was then at a complete loss. How on earth was she to pass an entire day holed up in this confining room with nothing to do but wait?

She looked at the stack of papers that were covered with her own determined scrawl, and sat down once more at the desk. She read over the last few pages she had written to recover her place and her thoughts, and then proceeded once more to lose herself in her writing.

It was astonishing. She was completely without rest, completely preoccupied, completely and frantically worried about Nico and Salvadore. Even so, her work consumed her. She wrote, page after page after page as the changing light from the passing day crept around her room, the hues and shadows muting and then brightening but always metamorphosing. The morning slipped past in a contorted portrait of a contrived city, contrived characters, contrived plot, but always with a true to the mark taste of the city and its people and atmospheres and ambience.

She was still writing, still pouring it out, still living what was coming forth from her pen. Ignoring the dull stiffness of her abused hand, ignoring the confusion of papers that floated from her desk and onto the floor, ignoring her protesting stomach that complained it had been too long since tea and fruit. She ignored it all, so intense was her concentration.

But when it came, she could not ignore the sharp, demanding rap on her door.

CHAPTER **26**

Okay, Nico thought. This is a day that I can work with, can make things happen.

It was true, after his perhaps ill-advised confrontation with Fuentes over breakfast, the morning had deteriorated rather abruptly. Nico's direct shots at Fuentes had left the drug lord in a foul mood. Not that Nico much cared. The truth was that the ultimate outcome of this little adventure had nothing to do with what Fuentes' mood might be at any particular moment. The showdown that was to come was a given no matter Fuentes' disposition, jovial or cantankerous.

But more disturbing, and infinitely more interesting, was Raúl's reaction to Nico's verbal attack on the drug lord. His entire demeanor had changed. Nico was aware that the young Colombian was watching him, trying without much success to be covert about it. Watching him, studying him, not as he had watched in his rôle as a captor and guard, but now with a slight line in his brow as if Nico had suddenly metamorphosed into some strange, unlikely being. As seemingly impossible as a mundane caterpillar turning into a monarch butterfly. Raúl seemed preoccupied and ill at ease. In the hotel suite he had been less inclined to wave the gun around and had shed his deliberately menacing posture. He practically ignored Fuentes' angry ill-temper and followed the drug lord's orders almost absentmindedly.

Nico didn't know what to make of it, and he didn't have a clue what might have precipitated it. Something about the blunt words that Nico had flung across the room at Fuentes, no doubt. He wasn't sure whether this odd change in behavior should make him more cautious or more hopeful.

He was still on the fence about whether Raúl's apparent shift in attitude was an occasion for more optimism or less, when the entire matter was decided for him. He was standing at the bottom of the steps of the hotel in the brightness of the morning sun, listening to Fuentes berate the unfortunate hotel clerk because a taxi would not traverse the pedestrian streets to fetch them to the train station. Not even for Fuentes, with all his money. Nor for his vile temper and rough words. The hotel clerk was sorry, very sorry indeed, but *Monsieur* Fuentes would have to walk the five blocks to where the taxi awaited. Just like everybody else. After all, they had no luggage to carry, did they? So what was the problem?

Nico was becoming bored with the entire episode until his observant eye caught a quick movement in the shadows. Salvadore? Could it be possible? He immediately inserted himself into the argument and created the brief diversion that took everyone's attention away.

And Salvadore had anticipated him. That quick gesture – thumbs-up! – immediately tipped the balance in favor of Nico's natural optimism. Sylvia was safe! And Salvadore, his partner, was on his trail. He knew then in a flash of insight that he could trust Salvadore completely. After all, he had trusted him with the one person who meant most in the world to him. And Salvadore had delivered. The two of them would sort out the confusion later, how it was that they both tracked Fuentes, how each one continually encountered the other in the most suggestive of circumstances. Nico now knew of Salvadore's pain for his lost brother. Salvadore did not yet understand the motives that drove Nico, but he would. Nico owed him that much. For he suspected that the force compelling each of them was much the same.

To Nico, Fuentes was a symbol of all that he hated. His father had been taken in such a mindless, violent fashion, in one suspended, breathless second of time. For Salvadore, it had to be even more personal. Raúl had been taken as well, but not in one terrible, screaming crash of twisted metal. Rather, his brother had to watch the slow, inexorable destruction of a young life, of a future, helpless to prevent it from running its unchangeable, inevitable course.

He glanced over at Raúl, this much loved, much despaired brother who was determined to self-destruct. And again he caught the Colombian studying him. Raúl flushed and looked away, but that small, perplexed line still marred his smooth forehead. Raúl had something on his mind, and Nico would have given a great deal to know what it was.

But just now he had no time to contemplate it further. The cranky Fuentes was on the march away from the hotel, hurling expletives back at the hotel clerk. Nico glanced behind and saw the transparent relief on the clerk's face at seeing Fuentes' retreating back at last. Nico gave an exaggerated eye roll and grin, and the clerk grinned in response. Nico knew that Raúl, who kept his place behind him with his left hand in his jacket pocket, had seen the exchange. He glanced at the clerk with a slight grimace that might have been embarrassment and then followed dutifully behind Nico, again very much the guard.

A few blocks later, they came upon the taxi that the hotel clerk had ordered. Nico and Fuentes climbed into the rear seat and Raúl into the front. "The train station," said Fuentes shortly.

Interesting, thought Nico. He would have supposed they would be taking a private car. He wondered what Fuentes was up to now.

CHAPTER 27

Salvadore was elated to have spotted Nico, and to know that Nico had seen him as well. He followed the three men at a discreet distance until they reached a street where vehicles were allowed. With dismay belatedly dawning, he realized that they were going to take a taxi. To god knew where, and with the Buell waiting on the opposite side of the square. He glanced around wildly for another taxi, thinking to follow them, but there was none about at this hour. With a groan of frustration, he watched as the taxi's red tail lights lit to slow for the corner and then disappeared from sight.

He stood on the cobblestones in the middle of the street and stared at nothing. Where in hell could Fuentes be headed? And with Nico and Raúl in tow. Airport? Train station? For all Salvadore knew, Fuentes could have hired the taxi for the entire day, to take them to any destination at all. Europe was a small place, but with big cities. It would be very easy to disappear unless one knew what Fuentes might be thinking.

Salvadore rubbed his hand across his beard-stubbled face. All right. What *might* Fuentes be thinking? Salvadore drew a complete blank. But then he remembered the unpleasant scene at the hotel. With a satisfied grin, he headed back down the pedestrian street and directly for the hotel that Fuentes had just vacated.

Once there, he took the two steps as one and entered the lavish hall. He glanced around as if overwhelmed and intimidated at such luxury, even as he kept a lookout for the hapless hotel clerk whom Fuentes had given such a dressing down. He spotted him at once. The dark-headed young man did not appear to be in the least disturbed at having just been abused. Rather he was laughing with a blond bellman, describing Fuentes' boorish insistence that got him nothing in the end, and Nico's ultimate if private siding with the clerk.

"Excuse me," said Salvadore, his English suddenly and conveniently acquiring a very thick accent.

The still-laughing clerk turned to him. "Can I help you?" he asked politely.

"Well. Maybe. I hope so." Salvadore gestured towards the door. "My friend, I mean, he was leaving, just a few minutes ago."

The hotel clerk hoisted one skeptical brow. "Your friend?"

"Yes," said Salvadore earnestly. "My friend." Then he looked taken aback as if he had just understood the clerk's sudden formality. "Oh, not the rude man! I heard him. He is that way always, treats people bad. I mean the other one, the one in the middle."

The clerk's grin was back. "Yes, of course. That one."

"I was to meet him here," said Salvadore. "But before I could see him, I think he had to work for the rude man." He managed a confused expression, as if he didn't quite understand what he had just said. "Well, I mean, I –" He trailed off, and then spoke quickly. "The rude man, he doesn't like me, you see, so I could not meet with my friend."

"I think the rude man doesn't much like anyone," said the abused clerk, but cheerfully. "But your friend seemed to be able to hold his own with him."

"Hold his own?" Again Salvadore contrived to thicken his accent and to look as if he were completely at sea.

The clerk gestured to the bellman. "Hans," he said. "Tell him about this morning's breakfast in the suite."

The bellman's face split into a wide grin, and he proceeded to describe the incredible banquet of food that Nico had ordered up, apparently unbeknownst to Fuentes, and then Fuentes' bad temper at learning the cost of all that wasted food. "And," the bellman added, laughing again, "you should have heard your friend when they were checking out and the rude one was protesting the cost. 'You're right to be upset, Fuentes,' your friend said. 'All that food, and no tomatoes or cucumbers. What kind of breakfast is that?'"

Now the clerk was laughing as well at the bellman's description of Nico's baiting of Fuentes, and Salvadore joined in. When they had quite exhausted the topic, Salvadore sobered. "But now I don't know where to find my friend," he said anxiously.

The clerk waved one hand dismissively. "They are taking a taxi to the train station," he said. "First class on the *snel trein*. I booked it for them myself. I warned that Fuentes person that they would never make the next train in time and would have to wait two hours more, but he wouldn't listen.

He was so sure that he could just order up a taxi to the door of the hotel, that he wasted even more time arguing." The clerk shook his head in bemusement at such a deserved comeuppance as missing a train due to one's own obnoxiousness.

"But where was my friend going then?" asked Salvadore, still maintaining his studied bewilderment. "I mean, to the train station, of course. But then to where on the train?"

The bellman nodded his understanding. "Amsterdam," he said. "Three first class tickets to Amsterdam on the nine twenty-five." But then he grinned at the clerk. "Which, once at the station, he will have to exchange for first class tickets on the eleven forty." He made a clucking sound with his tongue in mock concern. "Too bad. Very inconvenient."

"Ah." Salvadore nodded his understanding. "So I can go to the train station and find my friend, as he will miss the nine twenty-five."

"Right," said the clerk amiably. "Shall I call a taxi for you? It can meet you five blocks from here."

"No, thanks," said Salvadore. "Since I have more than two hours, I think I'll walk. That will mean less time that I have to spend around Fuentes."

Both the clerk and the bellman grinned at him, now that he was yet another partner in their complicity against all of the overbearing Fuentes' of the world. "Can't say that I blame you," said the clerk.

Salvadore thanked them and strode away from the hotel. But he didn't make for the train station. Rather he went directly to where the Buell waited. He spoke to the machine even as he unlocked the chain and freed both helmet and motorcycle. "We're going to Amsterdam," he said, pulling the helmet onto his head and jerking the strap tight under his chin. "And unlike the trip coming down here, we're going to outrun the *snel trein*. Both the nine twenty-five and the eleven forty."

He swung aboard, and with a flick of his thumb, he brought the motorcycle to life. Twisting the throttle open and releasing the clutch, he roared across the cobblestones, heading for the motorway and Amsterdam, with no intention at all of obeying either Belgian or Dutch traffic laws.

CHAPTER **28**

The sharp rap of knuckles on her door brought Sylvia from the spell she had cast upon herself and back to reality. It could not possibly be housekeeping, as the summons was too abrupt and demanding, not at all the style of this stolid and reserved hotel. It had to be Nico or Salvadore.

She leapt to her feet. Stepping quickly across the room, she had her hand on the doorknob, ready to pull open the door. Then she froze. Or perhaps it was Fuentes or Raúl.

"Yes?" she inquired cautiously.

A man's voice reverberated through the thick wood, simultaneous with another rough knock. "Sylvia! It's Salvadore! Let me in!"

"Salvadore!"

"Now!" he exploded, and she turned the key and jerked open the door.

He plunged into the room and slammed the door shut behind him.

She had taken a defensive step back, but now seemed planted to the floor. She stared at him. He looked disheveled and exhausted, but his dark eyes burned with a bright intensity.

"Salvadore," she said again, this time in a whisper, wondering what news he had brought to reduce him to such a state.

But then he caught her completely off guard, when his haggard face lit with a broad grin. "Nico is alive," he said. "Alive and well, at least when I last saw him."

She stared at him as if she had not understood his words. He reached out and grabbed one of her hands. "Sylvia! Did you hear me?"

Her lips parted, but no words came forth. The edges of the room seemed to be wavering, and tiny twinkle lights sparked in the periphery of her vision. She wondered if she might be going to faint.

"He is still with Fuentes, and Raúl. But he's fine. And he knows that you are fine, as well."

Finally his words penetrated the mists of her mind. "Did you speak with him?" she asked, at last finding her voice.

"No. But he saw me."

"Oh." She paused for a confused moment. "Where is he?"

"On the *snel trein*, headed for Amsterdam. Escorted by Fuentes and Raúl."

"So he is still in danger?"

"Oh, yes. He is."

A renewed concern shot through her. But then suddenly she realized how exhausted he must be. "Salvadore, please. Come sit, and tell me what is going on." When he did not move, she tugged at his hand. "Come," she repeated.

At last he obeyed. She drew him to one of the upholstered chairs and gently pushed him into it. Then she made directly for the telephone and ordered lunch for two. In a turning of the tables, she didn't ask him either whether he was hungry or what he might like to eat.

Then she pulled the other chair close to his and seated herself. "Salvadore, can you tell me what is happening? Or would you like to rest first?"

He shook his head. "Oh, I don't need to rest. I slept well enough last night. I'm just feeling a bit battered from dashing back and forth between Bruges and Amsterdam." Suddenly he scowled. "Especially the ride to Bruges yesterday afternoon. The police patrols apparently spotted me and put out an alert. I had to ride the back roads." His voice took on an aggrieved tone. "And drive the speed limit!"

Her eyes widened in mock astonishment. "And obey traffic signs and lights as well?" she asked, as if horrified at such a burden to bear.

"It's even worse! I had to buy a new helmet, and this thing." He gestured towards the protective leather jacket that he was wearing, and then immediately leapt to his feet and stripped it off. Tossing it onto her floor, he resumed his seat.

And he was as suddenly serious. "As I said, Fuentes is on his way to Amsterdam," he said.

"With Nico."

"Yes. And Raúl." His tone was off-hand and casual.

He did not fool her for an instant. "Your brother," she said gently.

He looked at her for a long moment, expressionless. "Yes," he said at last. "My brother."

"Tell me about Raúl," she said.

His gaze left her eyes and went to some place on the wall behind her that must have been at least a mile away. "Raúl," he said. After another long pause, he said, "You met him."

"Yes," she said. "I did meet him. My first thought was that he looks much like you."

"Does he?" he said, still not looking at her.

"Yes, he does. But then I knew in the next instant that I was wrong. He doesn't look like you, not really."

His gaze snapped back to her. "What do you mean?"

"I mean that he looks like you, at first glance. Startlingly so. But then he does not."

Salvadore frowned. "I don't understand."

She struggled to explain. "First impressions are the most immediate. Physical. But almost at once they are obviously inaccurate, replaced by the substance of a person, who and what that person was and is. Then you can really see what he is like."

He nodded as if he might understand.

She took that as encouragement and surged ahead. "Your brother is very like you, but there are some nuances that are, well –" She hesitated, searching. And then, as if still not satisfied with the word, she finished. "Some nuances that are *missing*."

Again he frowned. "Nuances? Missing?"

She was not dissuaded by the doubt in his voice. "I think that in many ways, Raúl's character is much like your own."

His gaze shifted again as he made to disagree. "There, Sylvia, you are wrong. At least, I hope you are."

"No, you don't."

He was startled. "What?"

"You do not hope I'm wrong. You only hope that Raúl is like you, rather than your being like Raúl. Or rather, like what you believe Raúl to be."

"Sylvia, if ever Raúl and I were much alike, we parted company some time ago. Even my father has come to terms with the loss of his younger son. Imagine how extreme, how complete a change would have to be for a father to give up on his own son. To abandon all hope for his redemption." The raw pain he heard in his own voice surprised him. First he had revealed this agony to Nico, and now to Sylvia. *Dios mío*. It was not a thing that he ever shared, not with anyone. He dropped his head into his hands.

When she spoke, her voice was very soft. "Abandon hope, all ye who enter here." She quoted Dante Alighieri, from the Divine Comedy. "But you have entered the very gates of hell, in spite of the admonition. You have entered, in pursuit of your brother. And thus you have not abandoned hope. Why not, Salvadore? Your father has. Why not you? You're not the father, after all. You're only the brother."

The truth tore from him, the words a reflection of his torment. "I cannot. I will not. Never will I abandon my brother."

"And I know why," she said, still softly.

Slowly he raised his head. "Why?" he whispered. "The fact is, I do not know myself. Tell me why."

"Because he has much of you in him. And you know it. You know what he could have been, what he still can be."

He shook his head, not so much in denial as against the pain of false hope.

But she gave him no quarter. "You *know*," she said. "And I know. Because I saw it in him. It is true, I saw his weakness, I saw his potential for cruelty, his desperation. But I also saw his courage, his inherent honesty. His humor and charm."

"Sylvia," Salvadore said heavily, "you have not seen Raúl under the influence of the drugs. The pure, hard drugs that Fuentes supplies to him. The poison. He's nothing but an animal then. Perhaps not even that." He hesitated, and then went on. "He says that when he's on the drugs, he's flying, that it's exhilarating. But he's not flying. He's crawling, wallowing in the gutter."

"I understand. But I could see who and what he is without them."

"Yes. So can I. But that's not who he is. Not anymore."

"But that *is* who he is. And you know it. And that alone is why you cannot abandon the cause, cannot abandon your brother." She stopped for a moment as if considering the wisdom of revealing the stark truth that she believed. Then she spoke it. "I am alone. Nico is alone. You are alone. But Raúl is not alone. Because he has you, his brother. So he is not alone, and he knows that he will never be alone. And that is why, Salvadore," she finished softly but with finality, "that is why Raúl will come to know the truth. The truth of his own strength. Because he knows that you will always be there at his side when he needs you. It is a source of power to him, even stronger than the seduction of the drugs, or the fleeting hold that Fuentes has on him. And he knows it."

Salvadore could not believe. He could not afford to believe. Ah, but believe he did, in the face of her mesmerizing certainty. "I have tried before to retrieve him," he said very softly. "To save him. He does not want to be saved."

"Yes, he does. But I think that he does not yet understand that you cannot do it for him. No one can. He has to do it for himself."

"I know that. But still I try." Salvadore shook his head. *"Why?"* The last word rang with a poignancy that was indescribable.

"Because you must. Because that is who you are." She reached over to touch one of his hands. "Because you love him. He is your brother."

There was a very long silence between them, during which neither moved. Then Salvadore said, "Do you have brothers or sisters?"

"Two brothers," she said. "One older, one younger."

"Then you understand," he said.

She had to be honest. "No, Salvadore, I don't."

He stared at her.

She said, "I don't believe that I would give up the living of my own life, that I would suffer so much as you do, for the sake of one of my brothers. I love them, but perhaps I believe that their lives, and thus their decisions, the choices they make, are their own. They are responsible for what they do, no matter the reasons or the provocation. And thus they should have to live with the consequences of their actions, just as I have to live with mine."

He was mute.

"So you see, Salvadore, I am not half the person that you are."

He raised one hand, but she cut across him. "And that is also because of choices and decisions I have made. Because of my – my own past. Past hurts. Past betrayals. I live within myself, not allowing myself to care for anyone as deeply as you care for Raúl."

He studied her for a long moment before he spoke. And then when he did, he caught her by surprise at his abrupt but astute observation. "That's not true, Sylvia," he said, his voice carefully neutral. "What about Nico DiCapelli?"

She could not bring herself to look at him. Nor could she speak. To her shock and dismay, her eyes flooded with tears. It gave her away entirely. The depth of her feelings for Nico. Her bottomless fear that something would happen to him, to snatch him away. The empty, endless future that stretched out before her if she lost him now.

She looked up and saw the understanding in Salvadore's dark eyes, and the sympathy. And an enduring pain that she could not begin to comprehend.

He was suddenly matter of fact. "Well," he said before the tears could spill down her cheeks. "I think we need to be making some plans for when Fuentes shows up here in Amsterdam. You can be sure that he knows that you and Nico never checked out of this hotel, so I'd guess he will come directly here."

She blinked at his sudden change in direction but was grateful for it.

He pressed on. "I think perhaps we should move you from here."

"Oh, no!" she protested. "However would Nico find me?" She was well aware that if she had not already given herself away, that statement would have done it. She didn't care.

"Not from the hotel," he said. "Just to a different room."

She didn't like it but she could see the wisdom of it. She gave a quick nod.

"I'll stay here in your room and we'll move you to another floor. But this room will remain in your name. Your new room will be in a name that Fuentes won't know. You will stay out of sight."

"But, Salvadore –"

"Completely out of sight." He shook his head. "If I let anything happen to you, Nico will have my neck for it. So like it or not, you *will* do as I say, even if I have to lock you in the room."

She rolled her eyes. "You are as bossy as Nico," she complained.

He eyed her for a moment. "Maybe. And it will probably do me about as much good as it does him. Poor old Nico."

That earned him a quick laugh and he grinned back at her. He glanced at his watch. "We have a couple hours, I'd say. I'll go make arrangements for the other room while you pack up your things."

That reminded her of the rucksack that was being sent from the hotel in Bruges. She explained what had happened, and then added, "Please make sure the hotel here knows that it's coming."

"No," he said.

She was startled at his brusque refusal. "I beg yours?"

"No. We don't want any attention drawn to you. This hotel won't even know which room you will be in. They will think you are right here, in room twenty-six."

"But Salvadore, you can just tell them not to reveal to anyone where I am. Except to Nico, of course. Surely they would honor such a request."

"We can't take the risk that one of the hotel employees might give us away, however innocently. Remember, Fuentes didn't get where he is by dancing to anyone else's tune but his own. He will use any method to get information, to get what he wants."

"But what about Nico?"

"Don't worry. I'll get word to Nico for you."

Grudgingly, she conceded his point. "So I have to stay holed up in a hotel room until this is all sorted out?" She thought she must sound petulant and was half-embarrassed by that.

He grinned at her tone. "That's right. That's exactly right. I'm glad you've finally got it."

She wrinkled her nose at him even as he rose from the chair and stretched. "Get your things together." He glanced at the piles of paper on the desk filled with page after page of her even scrawl. "You can pass the time by writing," he suggested. "How about a good description of what a *cabrón* Eduardo Fuentes is? See if you can capture his charming personality." There was a lilt of humor in his voice.

She stood as well and looked up into his eyes. "I've already done that," she said with no trace of answering humor. "It's not a pretty picture. No light, not even shadows. Only darkness." She frowned in concentration. "I never thought anyone could exist in this world without some layers, some contradictions. No matter how good a person is, there must always be a flaw of some kind, a weakness. And conversely, no matter how bad, how evil, there must be some redeeming value."

"And Fuentes' redeeming value?" Salvadore asked dryly.

"That is what I cannot understand," she said. "There is none. From what I have both seen and heard about him, from what I know, he is evil. Completely evil. Greedy, clutching, self-serving and self-centered. Murdering, whether directly, doing it himself, or by ordering someone else to commit the deed. Or by enslaving people with his filthy drugs. For no other reason than to make more money. For what? To assist others? To improve lives? No. To feed his own lust to acquire, his own lust for power."

Salvadore was transfixed, silent.

She didn't stop. "To acquire things that do not, in the end, belong to him. He's a cheat, a liar, a despoiler."

Salvadore frowned. "Despoiler?"

"Well, a thief, only worse. Someone who not only steals, but who – who ruins. Who corrupts and destroys." She raised both hands, palms up. "What satisfaction can such a person achieve? How does it feel to 'own' something that in reality belongs to someone else, whether a person or a culture or a country? How does it feel to take a life, or to destroy a life?" She fixed him with her sapphire eyes. "Salvadore, when he tries to destroy Raúl's life with the drugs, he's also destroying yours, and your family's."

His voice was hoarse. "Sylvia. I know this."

Again she heard his pain. She took his hand. "And yet you refuse to be beaten by him. You refuse to let him have Raúl."

"Yes." It was but one word. But it spoke volumes, both about Raúl and about Salvadore. And perhaps about Fuentes, and the ugly, indelible stain that he left on so many lives.

She nodded.

A faint line appeared on his forehead. "Tell me something, Sylvia. About Nico. Why does he pursue Fuentes so relentlessly? What's his motive? What drives him?"

She considered his questions. Really, it was Nico's story to tell, not hers. But the truth was, Salvadore had earned the right to know. "I think the explanation should ultimately come from Nico," she said. "But I can tell you the life-shaping event that turned Nico into a man driven. It's not unlike your own. Nico's father was killed in a motorcycle crash, by a man driving a car that ran a red light. That man was high on drugs. Afterwards he didn't even remember what he had done. And he was utterly devoid of any remorse."

"But Nico remembered," said Salvadore.

"Yes. Nico did remember. How and why. And since then, it has been the sole purpose of his life to track down and remove the people involved in the drug business, at any level."

"Until now," said Salvadore.

Sylvia didn't understand. "I beg yours?" she said.

"Until now," he said again. "I think that DiCapelli now has another purpose that motivates him, beyond his obsession with the underbelly of the drug world."

Still she didn't follow his meaning, and if he had any intention of elucidating her, the moment vanished with the quiet knock on the door, and the hotel employee's voice. "Room service, *het blauwtje de* Duncan."

Salvadore quirked a brow at her and she went to the door. The blond young man with the tray studiously ignored Salvadore's presence as Sylvia moved aside some of the papers on her desk so he could deposit the tray there. He removed the silver covers from the plates, revealing a hefty steak sandwich and a salad with tuna, and small pots of coffee and tea. Then he removed himself from the room and closed the door silently behind him.

Salvadore rose and took a look at the food on the tray. "How might you presume to know what I would like to eat?" he asked with exaggerated primness, in a fair imitation of her words to him.

She laughed. "Just try it. If you don't like it, I'll order something else."

That light banter eased the intensity of their conversation, and they took their food and drinks to the chairs and settled in to eat while chatting companionably. But there was nothing leisurely about this meal. Salvadore ate the steak sandwich quickly, as if he were either very hungry or in a very great hurry, or both.

Then he took his empty plate and cup back to the desk. "I'm going to arrange for your room," he said. "Get yourself packed and ready."

Leaving his leather jacket in a heap on the floor, he stepped out of the room. She heard him test the door to ensure it was locked before he took himself off down the hallway.

CHAPTER **29**

It was a long and dreary journey from Bruges to Amsterdam. As Nico had known would happen, the taxi dropped the three of them at the Bruges train station at nine thirty-two, precisely seven minutes after the *snel trein* had already slithered out, bound for Amsterdam via Antwerp. Although it had been his own fault that they were late, that did not stop Fuentes from berating the taxi driver, who nonchalantly collected his fare and then as he pulled away from the curb, blessed Fuentes with a gesture that had to be Italian in origin, it was so expressively direct. Its meaning was unmistakable, but there was no obvious counter-response. Its glib insouciance served to further infuriate Fuentes. So next in line had to be the hapless ticket agent. That patient man suffered Fuentes' abuse in silence while changing the reservations from the nine twenty-five to the eleven forty departure for Amsterdam.

Nico had half expected Fuentes to abandon the train altogether and just hire a car, but inexplicably the Colombian did not. Perhaps he was trying to be unpredictable, in case someone was on his trail. Someone like Salvadore San Martín, thought Nico with grim satisfaction. In any case, the three of them took seats in one corner of the station where the still cantankerous Fuentes berated the weary Raúl for everything under the sun. But oddly, Raúl still seemed preoccupied and did not respond to Fuentes' abuse. This served to even further exacerbate the vile temper of the drug lord. So he started in on Nico, cursing and threatening, his voice rising above the normal din of the busy station. Nico chose to follow Raúl's example, and ignored the tirade with a studied boredom that he made no attempt to disguise.

At length, apparently having had enough of Fuentes' obstreperous behavior, an exasperated transit guard strode over to their corner and told

Fuentes in no uncertain terms to tone it down. Even as Fuentes responded with an obscenity in Spanish, Nico wondered whether he might attempt to break away under cover of this diversion. But Raúl was watching him rather than the furor that Fuentes was creating, and his hand was still in the pocket of his denim jacket. Nico didn't quite trust him not to use the weapon even here in a crowded public train station. And then the guard spoke one last word of admonishment to Fuentes and left them. If there had in fact been an opportunity to escape, it was as quickly gone. With a sigh, Nico settled back into the uncomfortable plastic chair, glanced at his watch, and closed his eyes.

The two hours dragged by, Raúl half-dozing and Fuentes alternately staring at the ceiling and muttering obscenities at no one in particular. And then the predictable *snel trein* suddenly turned unpredictable. It was two minutes after twelve when the eleven-forty train finally hurried into the station, unloaded and boarded passengers, and pulled out six minutes after the noon hour. What was the world coming to, thought Nico. Twenty-six minutes late. But he kept his observations to himself, having grown bored with his sport of baiting the foul-tempered Fuentes. Besides, he would have to agree with Robert Louis Stevenson. To travel hopefully is a better thing than to arrive. In this case, at least.

Raúl took the seat next to the window. Fuentes lowered himself beside him and pointed Nico to the window seat directly across from Raúl. Very nearly Nico made to create yet another scene by protesting that he didn't like to ride with his back in the direction they were heading. But he decided at this point it just wasn't worth the hassle.

Poor Raúl managed to get his first real sleep on the train. He leaned his dark head against the window and was out before the last car on the train had slipped out of the station. Fuentes let him sleep, not out of any kindness, Nico was sure, but probably because he wanted the young man to be rested and alert by the time they reached Amsterdam.

Nico thought the ride tiresome, but at least Fuentes had finally shut up. So Nico closed his eyes and feigned sleep, pondering what might be going to happen next.

He was eternally grateful that he had caught that glimpse of Salvadore in Bruges. If he had still been torn with worry about Sylvia, this trip might well have been unbearable. He had confidence in Salvadore, that he would figure out where Fuentes was headed. And that Salvadore would protect Sylvia. Strange how the two of them had gone so quickly from suspicion and mistrust, to competitors for Sylvia's affections, to warriors engaged in the same cause for similar motivations. It was an unfamiliar sensation to have a partner of sorts. In the high Andes mountains of Colombia, in the remote and dangerous villages and in the murky Amazon rainforests thick with tangled undergrowth, Nico had worked entirely alone. It was a vulnerable position for an operative of his organization, but it was a necessary precaution against discovery. Nico could melt into the trees, into the shadows, and no one had known he was there. Except, ironically, perhaps for Salvadore. If Fuentes or one of his vast network of associates had discovered Nico, he would already be dead.

A dangerous position, yes, but vastly satisfying to know that the ultimate goal of this often frustrating work was to plunge Fuentes and his organization into a flaming pyre of defeat.

Of course, Nico had worked with other agents of his own organization, but on individual assignments, on a temporary basis. And for the most part, those colleagues of his shared the same basic ideals, the same commitment to the goals of the organization. But never had Nico worked with someone not only whose values matched his own, but whose passion for what is right and what is *not* right was also the same. He and Salvadore San Martín shared a single-minded determination to seek out and destroy the leeches who fed on the life's blood of a decent, civilized people, who with no conscience would destroy lives for nothing more than the accomplishment of their own gratification, their own greed and power. He guessed that the word to describe it would be *selfish*, but somehow that didn't seem strong enough. Perhaps Sylvia could suggest a more descriptive one.

In any case, Nico knew that now he trusted Salvadore completely. With his own life, and more importantly, with Sylvia's. He let his mind wander for a bit, imagining her in Amsterdam, anxious, fretting over her confinement – he bloody well hoped she was confined! – and worrying about him and about Salvadore. He recalled his clumsy attempt to speak to her of his feelings, of his hopes and dreams of their future, and how he had felt when Salvadore had interrupted them. He still didn't know what his primary emotion had been at that moment, fury or relief. He started to shake his head at himself, his own inconsistencies, his difficulty in expressing his own feelings. And then he remembered that he wanted Fuentes to think he was asleep.

Unobtrusively, he watched Fuentes through his lashes, waiting for any sign of inattention. With Raúl out of commission and Nico apparently sleeping as well, and the monotonous smoothness of the train's movement across the flat terrain, perhaps the drug lord would drop his guard, if just a bit.

He should have known better. Fuentes' hand never left the pocket that held the pistol, and his attention remained fixed on Raúl and Nico and the other people in the immediate surroundings of the sleek rail car. Never once did the Colombian so much as glance out of the window to see the horizontal, early-autumnal countryside flash by.

Raúl roused a bit when the train slowed for the stop at Antwerp. He blinked as if confused, then from habit, his gaze went to Fuentes to test the drug lord's mood. But it didn't stay there. Rather it slid to Nico, and his countenance still had that indecipherable, preoccupied expression. Apparently his nap had not given him any rest from whatever demons were riding him.

Since their train was late, they barely made the connection. They piled aboard and hadn't even taken their seats before the train shot from the station, no doubt trying to redeem its now-tarnished reputation of punctuality. Raúl claimed the window seat once again, gave one last contemplative glance at Nico, and passed out.

And again Nico feigned sleep. He could not really plan for anything, since his day was completely at Fuentes' whim. He could only be ready to react to whatever happened. Improvisation. It was something he did very well.

So if planning would accomplish nothing, he might as well make good use of his time in another way. He would think about Sylvia. Salvadore should be back in Amsterdam with her by now, watching over her. A few days ago, that would have been worrisome. No, more than that. It would have made Nico's gut clench with both concern for her safety, and with an unfamiliar jealousy. But not now. Now it brought him relief, that there was another line of defense to protect Sylvia from Fuentes and his violent intentions. Her safety wasn't only his responsibility just now. He had a partner. It was a bloody good feeling.

Without knowing he did so, he grinned. And across from him, Fuentes shifted in his seat, and his hand moved in his pocket, suddenly alert.

Well, damn. Nico closed his eyes and subsided, not moving again until the *snel trein* rumbled into Station Centraal.

Amsterdam. He should have felt tense. But in truth, he felt only anticipation, and the suspense of getting off the train and facing whatever presented itself. He had only two goals. Kill Fuentes and keep Sylvia safe. The rest had to belong to Salvadore.

CHAPTER 30

Nearly half an hour had passed before Salvadore deigned to appear at Sylvia's door once again. She was impatient, having taken less than ten minutes to pack her few things. She didn't have her rucksack, as it was still in Bruges or in transit so she had stuffed everything into a hotel pillowcase and placed it next to the door, Salvadore's leather jacket draped on top of it.

She let him into the room and watched as he scanned it quickly. "Change of plans," he said, almost apologetically. "I guess if we're going to convince the hotel staff that everything is normal and you're still here in room twenty-six, then some of your things should probably remain here as well."

"All right," she said. She handed him his disdained black leather jacket.

He tossed it carelessly onto the bed. "I'm staying here," he reminded her.

"Well, even so, your jacket should not be here, should it? If you want everyone to believe that I'm still in this room."

He gave her a cheeky grin. "Maybe the employees and the other guests will think that I'm staying here with you. I'm sure the guy who brought up the room service tray already thinks that."

She smiled back at his impertinence. "Or not," she said. She returned her attention to the pillowcase and sorted through her clothes and toiletries and manuscript papers. She arranged a few things around the room and stuffed the rest, including the papers, back into the pillowcase.

"All right," she announced. "I'm ready. Where do I go now?"

He flopped down into one of the chairs as if the room already belonged to him and hooked one knee over the upholstered arm, his booted foot dangling. "Well. You have five choices."

"Five choices? I thought you were going to get me a room."

Again his white teeth flashed in a grin. "I did. This old monstrosity that Nico picked out for you has sixty-four rooms. Fifty-nine were already taken, including those belonging to you and Nico."

"And?"

"So I took the remaining five."

She raised a brow. "Bit expensive, isn't it?"

"Sure," he said. "But I'll pass it on to Fuentes as a business expense. Or maybe to Nico."

"Why did you do that?" she asked. "To confuse anyone who might be wanting to know which room is mine?"

He nodded approvingly at her logic. "Yes. That is one good reason to have taken the last five rooms."

"But there is another reason," she said, watching him even as she perched herself on the edge of the bed.

"Oh, yes. When Fuentes arrives, he will no doubt want rooms at this very hotel where he assumes 'the action' is to be. But he will find that none is available. And none will become available in the next few days either, as I have asked to have any that are vacated to be reserved for my so-called colleagues."

"A waiting list."

"Exactly. Our friend Fuentes will not be happy that there is no room for him here at the inn, so to speak. I'd guess that he likely has been in an extraordinarily foul mood all day thus far, and it's only going to get worse when he arrives here in an hour or so and doesn't get his way yet again."

"Is it a wise idea to bait him like that?" asked Sylvia. "Isn't it rather like teasing a wild elephant or something? Tweaking the tail of a lion?"

Salvadore snorted even as he swung the foot attached to the leg that was hooked nonchalantly over the arm of the chair. "Ask Nico," he said. "He's the master. I'd bet he's been baiting the *hijo de puta*, the son of a whore, ever since he took on Nico as his unwilling guest." And he told her the tale that the two hotel employees in Bruges had so cheerfully related, and Fuentes' resulting sour temper.

A faint line of concern disturbed Sylvia's brow. She stood and crossed the room and looked down at Salvadore where he was sprawled in his chair. "Should Nico be doing that?" she asked somewhat anxiously. "This baiting thing? Won't it just make things worse?"

"Likely there are two answers to that. First, Nico probably thinks that things can't get any worse, so he may as well have his sport. You must know by now, Nico can have one hell of a mouth on him when he gets into the mood to be sarcastic."

Sylvia knew from her observation of Nico in Czechoslovakia that this was true, but still she looked doubtful. "And the other reason?"

"Nico is smart. He wants to leave a trail behind, stretching all the way across Belgium and the Netherlands if possible. To be noticed, to be remembered. Should he happen to disappear, someone will remember having seen or heard him." Salvadore raised one hand as if in instruction. "If it weren't for the fracas at the hotel over breakfast, the employees might never have told me that 'that rude man' was headed for Amsterdam via the *snel trein*."

Realization dawned. "So Nico isn't just doing this just to annoy Fuentes?"

Salvadore grinned. "Oh, I expect that the pleasure of annoying Fuentes is an amusing and gratifying side benefit for Nico, even if it's not the main reason for his doing it. Icing on the cake, as you say in English. Besides, a roaring lion doesn't bite. Maybe."

Suddenly pensive, Sylvia settled into the chair next to Salvadore. "Can I ask you a question?" she said.

"Shoot," he said in a fair adaptation of American slang, but he looked a bit wary.

"Why doesn't Fuentes just, well, just –" Her voice trailed off as she found herself unable to articulate the untenable idea.

"Why doesn't Fuentes just get rid of Nico and be done with it?" he asked gently.

"Yes," she said, grateful for his understanding.

He pondered for a moment, considering his words. When he spoke, his demeanor was thoughtful and his words came slowly, as if speaking them was difficult. "Fuentes is a manipulative and ruthless *cabrón*. A bastard who likes to have his game, like a cat playing with a mouse before it, well –" He didn't finish the simile. "He is also after me. And maybe after you, although I don't know exactly why he would want you." He frowned in concentration. "I'd guess that the rules of this particular game provide for the three of us to be brought together before Fuentes finishes his dirty work."

Sylvia recalled her previous experience with the predatory drug lord when she and Nico were at his mercy in Czechoslovakia. She gave an involuntary shiver. No doubt Salvadore spoke the truth. She herself had observed firsthand this sadistic behavior in Fuentes, where he seemed to have a compelling need to flaunt his power and his control over something as very basic as the lives and deaths of his victims. She wondered what it was in his makeup that would cause this gratuitous, petty meanness to become such an integral part of his dark and twisted nature.

She realized then that Salvadore had been watching her, and she flushed slightly. He leaned forward and she thought he was going to touch her, perhaps take her hand. But he did not.

"Fuentes is coming to Amsterdam to play out his deadly game, Sylvia. But over the past months, Nico and I have grown quite accustomed to his tactics. Big egos make big mistakes. When Fuentes makes his, Nico and I will be ready."

"You have a plan, then."

Salvadore grimaced. "We really can't have a plan, not with Fuentes calling the shots. But we can anticipate, and we can react. Typically Fuentes would have an array of his hired goons dancing attention around him, but I've seen none of them this time. Only Raúl." He didn't miss a beat as his brother's name crossed his lips. "That's unusual, and I don't know the reason for it. In some ways it makes him more dangerous, as he apparently doesn't have a lot of backup and may have to act more precipitously than he usually would. Or maybe with his overinflated ego, he thinks to take us on singlehandedly. But in another way, it makes him rather vulnerable. He's got Nico, that is true, but he doesn't have me. And he doesn't have you. Furthermore, we know his next move. He's coming to Amsterdam, via the *snel trein*. But he doesn't know that we know. And he doesn't know that we're here waiting for him, not for certain."

She was quiet, watching and listening.

"So we can anticipate him, be ready for him," continued Salvadore. "We can watch Nico's back, try to get him away. And with any luck, together we can put Fuentes down, once and for all, like a rabid dog."

"And Raúl?" she said, almost involuntarily.

The shadow crossed his face, making his coffee-dark eyes seem older than his years. "Raúl goes home," he said simply. "For good. One way or the other, this time Raúl goes home for good."

Sylvia wasn't sure what he meant, but she heard both the sadness and the determination. She thought perhaps he intended to say that this time Raúl was going home to stay, whether willingly at the side of his brother, or dragged cursing and protesting by that same determined brother. Or cold and still and forever returned to the bosom of his family, albeit with no life left.

Well, she thought, whether Raúl was under the control of Fuentes and the drugs, or whether he was dead and buried and mourned with a finality that only death can bring, in either case he would be dead to his family. She, if anyone, could understand the desperate if guilt-ridden *relief* that even a violent and untimely death can bring to those who still love, and who still suffer.

CHAPTER 31

Fuentes waited until most of the other passengers had left the first class rail car before he rose from his seat. "Let's go," he said. "Raúl, stay close to DiCapelli."

Raúl nodded but didn't utter a word. Fuentes led the way, with Nico deliberately crowding his heels and Raúl bringing up the rear.

"I feel like the filling in a bloody Colombian sandwich," Nico grumbled. The uneventful train ride had refreshed him, and he was once more ready to chew on Fuentes' predictably foul temper.

"*Cállate*," Fuentes said over his shoulder as they exited the train car onto the platform, and made for the Amsterdam station. "Just shut up."

Nico ignored the admonition. "You and Raúl are the bread, and I'm the lettuce and tomato and ham," he went on. "And I suppose your damned guns are the mustard and mayonnaise. It's getting tiresome."

"Your mouth is what's getting tiresome," Fuentes snapped as they debouched into the station. It was crowded, with masses of people milling about, tourists and businessmen and families with tired, squalling children. "*Mierda*," muttered the drug lord as he tried to push his way through the throng. *Shit.*

"Probably there are more late trains," observed Nico, helpfully obsequious, his mouth as annoyingly close to Fuentes' ear as he could manage. "You know how it is. Once they start running late, it's difficult to get caught up again. Missed connections, and all that. It's the same with airplanes and airports. We're lucky to have made our connection in Antwerp. It was bloody close."

Goaded yet again, Fuentes shot him a furious warning look but said nothing, apparently not wanting to make a scene in such a crowd.

Nico gave him a cocky grin, and then turned to look back at Raúl. "Keep up with us, Raúl," he said. "Wouldn't want you to disappear. Your big brother would never forgive me if I let you get lost in a damned train station."

"DiCapelli, shut the hell *up*," Fuentes hissed. He continued shoving his way through the crowd, democratically making no apparent distinction between man, woman or child, until they finally reached the door. Once outside in the pristine sunshine of the afternoon, he led them to where the taxis waited for arriving passengers. They approached the first cab in line. Raúl climbed into the front, and Nico and Fuentes took the rear seat. Nico was very nearly going to complain about the trite sameness of the seating arrangements, when he decided to allow the Colombian to upstage him.

"Hotel Amstel Grand," Fuentes said to the driver as he checked the sharpness of the crease in his dark slacks. He gave Nico a self-satisfied smirk, pleased with his one-upmanship at having known the hotel where Nico was staying.

But Nico only grinned, even as the driver twisted in his seat to make sure he had heard Fuentes correctly. "Excuse me?" he said.

"Hotel Amstel Grand," repeated Fuentes in some irritation.

"But, sir," the driver began.

"How difficult can this be?" growled Fuentes. "Do you know the hotel, or not?"

"On Korte Niezel?" the driver asked, sounding tentative.

"Of course," said Fuentes. "How many damned hotels called the Amstel Grand can there be in Amsterdam?"

"Oh. Only one, I'm sure," said the driver. He gave Nico a glance and a shrug. "All right," he said.

"Move it," said Fuentes. "I don't have all day."

The taxi eased into the traffic. Two minutes and three blocks later it slid to a gentle stop directly in front of the Hotel Amstel Grand.

Nico was still grinning.

Fuentes swore, whether at him or at the driver, Nico couldn't be certain. "*Cristo*, DiCapelli," he said in annoyance. "You might have told me that it was just a few blocks to the hotel from the train station."

Nico took an aggrieved tone. "Well, I had no idea where we were going, now did I? It's not like you share information with me."

"You heard me tell him the name of the hotel," said Fuentes through clenched teeth.

"How could I know there was only one Hotel Amstel Grand in Amsterdam?" protested Nico. "Until the driver mentioned it, of course." His voice lifted, querulous now. "Besides, you didn't ask me. And I wasn't about to interrupt your conversation with the driver, because you've been so testy today." He appealed to the young man in the front seat. "Hasn't he, Raúl? Damned testy, if you ask me. I don't know how you put up with this crap all the time."

Raúl's dark gaze was averted, but the crease was still in his brow.

"DiCapelli." Fuentes' voice was rising ominously.

"And anyway," Nico went on, motioning towards the bemused Dutchman behind the wheel of the taxi, "you told the driver that you didn't have all day. I'd think you would be appreciative that he got us here so quickly. You're never happy, are you? Must be a miserable way to live."

"Just get the hell out of the taxi," said Fuentes, his voice rising a few decibels more. "How much?" he said to the driver, managing no more civility than he had when he had spoken to Nico.

"Ten guilders," the man said. To Nico, the driver sounded rather satisfied to impart this shocking information.

"Ten?" said Fuentes in disbelief. "For a few blocks?"

"Minimum charge," the driver said. This time his voice was most definitely satisfied.

Fuentes swore again and dug into his wallet. "I've got no damned Dutch guilders," he said.

"Pop into the hotel and exchange some of whatever you have," suggested Nico. "Colombian pesos, I presume? *Dio*, Fuentes, you bitch about the price of everything. First the breakfast in Bruges, and now the taxi. What's your problem? Are the profits from your drug business down? Maybe you should step up production. Or negotiate a better deal through the Black Peso Money Exchange. What is that illegal international banking system giving you for your U.S. dollars from the cocaine? Colombian pesos that are about forty percent below the legal exchange rate?"

Raúl was unmoving in the front seat, but again Nico could sense the coiled tension emanating from him.

At this point, Fuentes had worked himself into a fury. "I told you to get the hell out," he shouted. "Raúl, get him out of here."

Rolling his eyes, Nico obliged. He climbed out of the taxi at the same time as Raúl and stood on the curb waiting for Fuentes, his arms folded across his chest with an exaggerated patience.

Fuentes opened the door and started to get out.

"My fare," said the driver implacably.

Fuentes gave him another expletive. "Wait here," he said. He disappeared up the steps of the hotel.

In a few minutes the Colombian was back. With ill-grace he shoved ten guilders through the window at the driver.

"You forgot the tip," Nico pointed out.

"Screw the tip," snapped Fuentes.

"*Dio*, how rude is that?" Nico said. He dug into his jeans pocket and took out a couple of guilders. Handing them through the window to the driver, he said, "*Dank u wel.* Thank you." The driver grinned as he accepted the coins, gave him a salute, and drove off.

Nico turned to Fuentes. "Oh, damn," he said. "I must have forgotten that I had guilders. Sorry about that. Well, anyhow, let's check in."

"You're already checked in," said Fuentes.

Nico lifted a brow in disbelief at Fuentes' audacity. "Well, *merda*, you and Raúl aren't staying with *me*. I don't have a bloody suite. Just a room."

Fuentes was nearing his limit, Nico could tell. "Keep him close, Raúl," the drug lord said. "We'll get a suite." He climbed back up the steep stairs and into the opulent lobby of the Hotel Amstel Grand.

He strode over to the reception desk where he had probably just gotten his Dutch guilders to pay the taxi driver a few moments ago. Nico saw the resigned expression on the hotel clerk's face as Fuentes advanced. He figured the young Dutchman had already borne the brunt of the Colombian's overbearing personality.

Without bothering with the courtesy of a greeting, Fuentes said, "I want to book a suite."

"Do you have a reservation, sir?" asked the young man, pushing his blond hair back from his high forehead as he prepared to shuffle through the cards that were neatly filed in a small wooden box on the counter.

"No," said Fuentes, as if it didn't matter.

The clerk relaxed a bit. "Sorry, sir, but we don't have any suites available."

Fuentes gestured sharply in his impatience. "Well, a room, then."

"No rooms, either."

"What do you mean, no rooms?" said Fuentes furiously. "For the right amount of money, hotels always have rooms. I have money, and I want a room. Now."

"Actually, I have no rooms for any amount of money," the clerk said. If he had been trying to sound sympathetic, he failed spectacularly. "There's a waiting list. In the event that any accommodations should happen to come open, they are already taken."

Planting both hands on the reception counter, Fuentes leaned forward and shoved his flushed face very close to the clerk's. "I want a room. No. I want a *suite*. In this hotel. And I want it *now*."

The clerk didn't pull back even an inch from Fuentes' aggressive stance. He opened his mouth to speak, but Nico cut across him. "Eduardo," he said. "I have a suggestion."

"DiCapelli, shut up!" Fuentes' roar echoed across the lobby.

Nico shrugged. "All right," he said. "But remember, you were pissed off at me over the taxi ride. You're a bit of an ass when you're pissed off. I'd rather not repeat that experience."

Fuentes slammed his fist down onto the counter hard enough to ruffle the papers and make a pen jump. "What is your damned suggestion, then?"

Nico's face lit. He leaned confidentially towards the clerk even though he was speaking to Fuentes. "Well, maybe this nice man can ring up the people in the suites and see if we could share them. There's always too much room in a suite anyhow. Like the one we had in Bruges. It's wasted space. I already have a room, but maybe you could stay in one of the suites, and Raúl in one, and –"

"*Cristo*, DiCapelli. Shut the hell *up!*" Fuentes ran a hand across his face in frustration. He thought for a moment. Then he said to Nico, "We'll use your room." He turned back to the clerk and jerked one thumb in Nico's direction. "Which one is his? Give me the key."

The clerk glanced at Nico's now-impassive face and then back to Fuentes. He lifted his hands and shoulders in a gesture of helplessness. "Sorry, sir. That information is private. We don't give out the numbers of the rooms of our guests. And certainly not the keys."

Livid, Fuentes turned back to Nico, his teeth bared. "Which damned room is yours?"

"No way," said Nico, taking his most stubborn stance with feet planted apart and arms crossed. "I'm not telling you. You're not using my room for your filthy business. This is a nice hotel. They wouldn't approve."

Fuentes' hand moved to his jacket pocket even as all of Raúl's muscles tensed. Nico wondered where the young man's breaking point might be.

"We can finish this right now," said Fuentes.

"Do it, then," said Nico in his most baiting tone. He gestured towards the frowning hotel clerk. "What are you going to do with your witness? And who is going to clean up the blood on the carpet here in the lobby?" He paused for effect, and then said, "Oh, of course. Raúl. He always does your dirty work, so that you don't stain your Dior suit, or ruin your manicure."

The clerk was beginning to show some signs of agitation at what appeared to be imminent violence in his heretofore pristine lobby. Fuentes' face was so purple that Nico wondered if the drug lord was about to succumb to a stroke, or perhaps a heart attack. An encouraging thought, but probably too good to be true.

But whatever else he might be, Fuentes was not stupid. If the clerk raised the alarm, he would certainly have an even bigger problem than the tall, lean, and eminently obnoxious form of Nico DiCapelli, just now propped negligently against the wall next to the reception desk, having abandoned his deliberately stubborn stance. Nico DiCapelli, with his damned big mouth. Fuentes glanced around the vast lobby. "Over there," he said, pointing to the far corner. "We need to regroup."

"Don't worry," said Nico to the clerk as he turned away. "He's always like this. It really doesn't mean anything. Even if you'd had a suite available, he still would have found something to complain about."

"DiCapelli," Fuentes said between his teeth, the warning clear to everyone.

And at last, apparently even to Nico. *"O-kay!"* he said. *"Cristo!"* He gave one last glance and a shrug at the clerk and made for the corner of the lobby where Fuentes had directed him. He threw himself down onto the same upholstered chair that he had used when he and Sylvia had been there. Fuentes took the chair that had been Sylvia's, and Nico considered telling the drug lord that watching Sylvia curled up in the chair for a nap was infinitely more agreeable than seeing the Colombian sitting there glowering. But he didn't want to bring her name into this twisting, out of control atmosphere. Even to mention her might somehow draw her closer to danger. He wondered where she was at this moment, and Salvadore as well. Close by, of that he was certain.

He glanced unobtrusively around the huge lobby for a sign, any sign.

And Raúl, silent as a Golem, watched him, studied him, from his place where he stood braced against the wall, his left hand never leaving the pocket of his denim jacket.

CHAPTER **32**

Sylvia had settled herself and her few things in room number sixty-three on the sixth floor after having been unceremoniously deposited there by Salvadore. Well, perhaps settled wasn't the right word. She was bored. No. Not bored, restless. Not restless, frantic. Frantic for word about Nico. Where was he? How was he? And where on earth had Salvadore taken himself? He had some nerve abandoning her in this remote room with a quick, overbearing order to "stay where I put you."

She had been waiting alone for hours and *hours*. To confirm this, she glanced at the clock on the small table next to the bed. Well, all right, she had been waiting alone for fifty-two minutes. But indeed, it had been a very long fifty-two minutes.

Taking another turn around the room, she wished there was more area in which to pace. And then her scattered thoughts were captured and focused by a quick knock on the door.

"Sylvia!" said Salvadore softly.

She unlocked the door and he slid inside and closed it quietly behind him.

Her eyes were glued to his face, searching for information.

He was grinning. "They're here," he said.

She felt her pulse quicken. "Nico?" she said. "And Raúl?"

Salvadore grimaced. "And Fuentes," he said. "Unfortunately."

"Yes. Of course." Still she watched him. "Where are they?"

"In the lobby, in one corner."

"Because no rooms are available."

"Exactly." Even given the seriousness of their situation, his eyes snapped humor.

She said, "Did they see you?"

He gave her a disgruntled look as if she had just insulted him. "No. Of course not."

"Not even Nico?"

"I don't think so. I couldn't take the chance."

"Salvadore, what should we do now?"

"Well, perhaps we need a plan after all." He leaned against the closed door and crossed his arms. "I think we must figure out how to separate the three of them. I need to isolate Fuentes."

She didn't have to ask why. Even so, she gave a small shudder. Without a doubt, Salvadore had the same violent intentions toward the drug lord as did Nico. She wondered which one would get to Fuentes first. Perhaps it didn't matter.

"All right. What do you want me to do?" she asked.

"Oh, no –" Salvadore began, but she cut across him.

"Don't even think of telling me that I'm to stay here in this out of the way room," she said, planting her fists on her hips. "There is no way that you alone can manage to separate them, and you know it."

He wanted to deny it. But he knew she was right. *"Mierda,"* he muttered. "DiCapelli is going to have my ass in a sling if I let you leave this room with Fuentes running loose in the hotel."

"You have no choice."

He took in her belligerent pose and gave her a sour look. "I know," he admitted.

She relaxed, but only a bit. "So what's the plan?"

"A diversion," said Salvadore.

"What kind of diversion?"

"Just now they're in the far corner, away from reception," he said thoughtfully. "Fuentes and Nico are seated; Raúl is standing against the wall. At least that's how I left them."

"I assume they are armed. Fuentes and Raúl, I mean."

"Well, not ostensibly. But yes, I think we can assume that they are, since it's hardly likely that Nico is with them because he's enjoying their company. Raúl's left hand stays in the pocket of his jacket. And his stance is by no means a casual one." Salvadore frowned. "There is an odd kind of tension in him."

"Of course there would be," Sylvia said. "I mean, given the circumstances."

Still Salvadore frowned as if trying to make sense of something that perplexed him. "I don't know."

"Don't know what?"

"There is something about Raúl that is bothering me," said Salvadore.

"What do you mean?"

"I'm not certain. I thought in Bruges, in the brief instant I saw him, that something was not, well, not right."

"Salvadore," said Sylvia softly. "Do you mean he's on the drugs?"

"Maybe." But then he shook his head. "No. I don't think so. Not while he's working." He frowned. "It's not that. I don't know what it is."

"And now that you've seen him here?"

"I don't know," he repeated. "I can't explain it. It's just a feeling that something is not right with him."

"Well, I suppose perhaps it doesn't matter just now."

"It matters if I'm going to try to predict his actions and reactions, and those of Fuentes," he contradicted her.

"Salvadore, I think we must assume that neither Fuentes nor Raúl will welcome any diversion that might free Nico."

"Of course. You're right," said Salvadore, but still he frowned at her.

"So what does this diversion look like?" asked Sylvia.

Salvadore's brow cleared. "Well, since you insist upon being a part of this."

She nodded decisively.

"Then perhaps we should both enter the lobby at precisely the same time, but from opposite sides. I'll come charging through the main door from the outside –"

"Like an avenging angel," she said. "And I will trip the light fantastic down the main staircase. Like Scarlett O'Hara."

He raised one brow. "Like who?"

"Never mind."

"And when we simultaneously spot each other, we will make enough noise to raise the dead," Salvadore went on. "If Nico is as quick as I think he is, he will take advantage of the distraction. And," Salvadore pointed one long index finger at the tip of Sylvia's nose, "you will then *immediately* run back up the stairs and to this room."

"But Salvadore –"

"Immediately. You will not stick around to see what happens. You will not take it into your head to do anything, well, anything –"

"Precipitous?" she suggested.

He nodded emphatically. "Do you understand me?"

Her eyes narrowed at his peremptory tone. "And what will you do?"

"Depends."

"On what?"

"On what Fuentes does." He shrugged and pushed himself away from the door. "Or Raúl, or Nico."

"Doesn't sound like much of a plan to me," she observed.

"Do you have a better one?"

She smiled and gave over. "Well, no."

"Then we're set."

She nodded, but put out one hand. "Salvadore," she said.

"Yes?"

"Will Fuentes fire a weapon in the very public lobby of this very staid hotel?"

"I don't know," he said frankly.

"Will Raúl?"

His brow creased. He did not speak, and his shrug was half-hearted.

"Well, we will know soon enough," she said. "Let's go."

CHAPTER 33

Nico sprawled loose-limbed in the overly-soft chair watching as Fuentes deliberated his options. He wondered fatalistically why the Colombian didn't just finish him off and be done with it. Why traipse around half of Europe with such an obvious liability as his unwilling and mouthy hostage? Ah, the arrogance of the *bastardo*. He must think he was somehow invincible. Well, thought Nico ruefully, maybe he was. After all, Nico was the one being dragged from pillar to post, whether he wished it or not. And in the company of the inscrutable, completely unpredictable Raúl.

He gave another glance in that one's direction. Sure enough, Raúl was still studying him. But this time, instead of his gaze sliding away, it caught Nico's eye and stayed. Still searching, but now more obviously determined to find an answer to whatever damnable question was plaguing him.

Nico may have looked as boneless as a fat, purring tabby cat, draped as he was on the heavy padded chair with long legs stretched out carelessly. But in fact he was poised and ready for the well-orchestrated diversion when it blazed across the vast lobby like a clash of fire and ice, lightning incarnate. A harbinger of the violent storm to come.

In the same second that Sylvia swept dramatically down the wide, curving marble staircase like *La Belle Dame*, or perhaps a grand lady from imperial Europe, Salvadore burst through the main door with more noise than finesse.

"Salvadore!" Sylvia shrieked in a voice that should have shattered the crystal of the Bohemian chandeliers.

Salvadore stopped dramatically in mid-stride as if shocked into an immoveable and petrified pose. *"Cariña,"* he crooned then, his arms spreading wide as if he expected her to run to him and throw herself into his embrace.

Nico metamorphosed from a snoozing, lethargic domestic cat to a sleek jaguar on the hunt. He catapulted out of the chair and flung himself across the lobby. Not towards Sylvia. Towards Salvadore.

He had no idea how Fuentes and Raúl might be reacting in that moment. He only knew that he had to draw them away from Sylvia. Their thoughts, their actions. Their weapons.

Yes, their weapons. He fully expected to hear the roar of the illicit handguns echoing in the pristine lobby, to smell the acrid scent of burnt gunpowder. Even more compelling, he expected to feel the bullets strike him square in the back. If he could still expect to feel anything at all after that particular event. Or at least to hear the confounded scream of displaced air as the bullets whined past his ear.

But he smelt and heard and felt none of this. Rather he reached the main door at precisely the same instant as Salvadore, who had done an abrupt about-face. The two of them crashed through the opening before the astonished doorman could react, and debouched into the narrow, cobbled Korte Niezel. "To the rear," said Salvadore even as one went left, one went right, and they both vanished up the dim, narrow alleys that flanked the hotel.

Less than a minute later, they met up again on Boomsteeg, directly behind the Hotel Amstel Grand. In the pre-twilight shadows, their eyes locked, black coffee on hazel-green. Then Salvadore grinned. "This way," he said, grabbing Nico's arm to pull him along the alleyway and to another street, Geldersekade, that followed a turgid canal.

Nico resisted. "Sylvia," he said in a low voice.

"Come *on*," said Salvadore urgently. "We've got to have a few moments of quiet to talk. She's safe enough."

"What in bloody hell was she doing in the lobby with Fuentes there?" demanded Nico, sounding more accusatory than he had intended. But *cristo*, the unexpected sight of her had shocked the bejesus out of him.

"*Mierda*," muttered Salvadore as he continued to drag Nico along the street. "I *told* her you would have my ass in a sling. Give me a break here. You, of all people, should know how she is. We needed to create a diversion. She thought it wouldn't be much of a diversion if I just happened to pop in through the front door to pay my regards to Fuentes."

Nico grimaced and walked beside Salvadore somewhat more willingly. "Bloody hell. Her greeting for you might have taken the paint off the walls of the discreet Hotel Amstel Grand."

Salvadore grinned again, but his vigilance did not waver. He shot a careful look behind them even as they walked.

"What happened back there?" asked Nico. "I couldn't glance back and risk drawing attention to Sylvia. Where is she, Salvadore?"

"I told you. Safe. I think. I hope. Fuentes, as usual, was thinking quickly. He sent Raúl after us, and he headed in the direction where Sylvia had taken flight."

"*Merda*," swore Nico, but Salvadore raised one hand.

"She bolted for her room," he said. "That was the plan. Hell, she *agreed* to do that," he added, as if suddenly wondering whether she had kept her part of the bargain.

"To the second floor?" said Nico. "Number twenty-six?"

"No. Sixth floor, room sixty-three. I moved her, but anonymously. No one knows she's there. Except us," he added.

Nico quickly digested these facts. "So, she's to wait in this room on the sixth floor until – what?"

"Until one or both of us comes to fetch her. Fuentes can't know she's there. Nor Raúl."

"Ah, yes. Raúl. So where is your brother now?"

Salvadore gave another glance down the alley behind them and increased his stride. "Fuentes sent him after us," he said again. "I saw him do it. I heard him."

This time Nico glanced back as well. "So Fuentes went after Sylvia and sent Raúl after us."

"So it would seem."

"Fuentes seems pretty confident that Raúl will perform as directed."

Salvadore shrugged.

"Even regarding his own brother," added Nico.

"So it would seem," said Salvadore redundantly, in what sounded like a grim parody of himself.

CHAPTER 34

Precipitously abandoning her *La Belle Dame* act, Sylvia whirled around and bolted up the stairs at a dead run, taking the steps two at a time. Her last quick glimpse at the lobby below showed Nico in flight, heading away from her. Again.

She reached the sixth floor breathless and in record time, and shot down the hallway towards room sixty-three, the key clutched in her hand. Just when she reached the creaking lift, the door swung open.

Without hesitating, she ran on past the lift, ignoring whoever might be arriving. She had the key in the lock and her fingers on the doorknob when an ungentle hand grasped her wrist. She looked up, startled, and gave a gasp with whatever little breath she had left.

Eduardo Fuentes.

It was as if the past two months had never transpired. He looked exactly the same as he had when he had abandoned Nico and her to their ultimate fate in Czechoslovakia. She might have seen him only yesterday.

She jerked her arm away from him, catching him off guard for a moment. "Don't touch me!" she said sharply.

"Then don't move," he said. In that moment she saw the wicked-looking little pistol in his hand.

She didn't move, but she kept her eyes glued to his face for a sign of his intent.

"Well, well," he said. "Kind of you to meet me here." He glanced at the key in her fingers. "Go ahead. Open the door. I'll join you."

"You're not invited," she said, surprised to hear her own voice. It was calm, even matter of fact.

"Too bad," he said. "I couldn't get a room here, and DiCapelli wouldn't share. So I guess I'm your guest for awhile."

"I said, you're not invited."

Fuentes' temper shifted as he glanced up and down the empty hallway. "Open the damned door," he said. "Now."

He shoved the muzzle of the gun against her neck, a round, cold circle of steel, hard enough to bruise.

Without choices, she obeyed, turning the key and pushing the door open. Roughly he shoved her inside, pausing long enough to remove the key from the lock and then closed the door. He pointed to one corner and said, "Go over there. We will wait for Raúl to bring his brother and that damned DiCapelli."

"Raúl doesn't know we're here," Sylvia said obstinately. "Neither does Nico."

"But I would guess that Salvadore knows."

"Perhaps. But he wouldn't tell Raúl."

Fuentes' grin was rather like a wolf baring its teeth. Sylvia decided that it didn't much improve his looks. "He will have no choice in the matter," he said. "Raúl has a weapon, and he knows how to use it."

Since Sylvia thought that Fuentes was probably right she didn't bother to argue. She went to the corner that Fuentes had indicated and leaned against the wall.

Fuentes' impatience was patently obvious. He kept opening the door a crack to look up and down the hallway, and then would close it again, muttering what were unmistakably obscenities, some directed at Nico, some at Salvadore, and some even at the absent Raúl.

When a person at last appeared in the hallway, Fuentes was not pleased. He shoved the door open and Raúl slipped inside. Alone.

"Where the hell are DiCapelli and your brother?" snarled Fuentes, barely waiting for the door to close.

"Gone," said Raúl, lifting one shoulder. "I no find." Then he caught sight of Sylvia standing in the corner. The dismayed consternation that flashed across his face was gone in an instant, and his expression remained blank.

"Damn you, Raúl," said Fuentes.

"They run," Raúl said simply. "I no can find."

"You idiot! At least you could have found one of them."

Raúl's shoulder lifted again, but he did not speak.

"All right," said Fuentes in exasperation. "I'll go find them. You stay here, with her." He waved the pistol towards Sylvia. "And Raúl, keep your damned weapon on her every second, do you hear me?"

"I hear," said Raúl, drawing his handgun from his pocket and pointing it in Sylvia's general direction. "When you come back?"

"When I find either Salvadore or DiCapelli," snapped Fuentes. He placed his small pistol into the pocket of his suit jacket and slammed out of the room without further comment.

CHAPTER 35

Several blocks from the hotel, Nico and Salvadore halted their precipitous flight. "Over here," Salvadore said, indicating a low brick wall that ran along the canal. He sat himself down on the hard surface, taking care that he could observe in all directions, even though they were in the deep shadows of the overhanging branches of a tree. It was quiet along the narrow street, with few passersby. The air had the heavy, sweet scent of impending evening, and no breeze stirred the leaves above them.

Nico lowered himself onto the bricks next to Salvadore. "We've got to get back to Sylvia," he said in an urgent undertone. "I don't like leaving her alone, not with Fuentes on the prowl."

"I know," Salvadore said. "But there's no way he will find her. He can't search every room in the hotel."

"In my long and eventful history of observing Fuentes, he always seems to have the devil's own luck," said Nico sourly.

Salvadore nodded. "That he does. Even so, it's difficult to believe that he can locate her, at least very soon."

"Assuming that Sylvia actually did stick to your plan," said Nico.

"*Our* plan," Salvadore objected.

Nico nodded. "Damned imprecise English language with no plural 'you.' Yes. Your plan, and hers. Even so, that doesn't mean that she stuck to it."

Salvadore gave a grimace. "There is that," he admitted. "But what else would she have done?"

"God knows. Depends on what might have popped into her head. She's got one hell of an imagination. She might have dreamed up some scheme to ensure we make good our escape. Thinking, of course, that we couldn't possibly manage on our own."

"I *told* her to follow the plan *exactly*," Salvadore said, exasperated.

Nico rubbed his eyes. He was feeling a bit weary and wishing that someone else was in charge of this madness. "What now?" he asked. "Is there a back way into the hotel? I don't think we want to risk the main entrance and the lobby."

"Through the kitchens," said Salvadore. "They take deliveries along one of the side alleys. Might be a bit awkward getting through, though."

"I wish I knew this hotel better," Nico said. "Stupid of me not to have scoped it out when I arrived the first time. I hadn't realized that my stay here would be anything more eventful than just a holiday."

Salvadore grinned. "I scoped it out," he said. "As soon as I discovered you were going to be staying here. I made a very thorough job of it."

Nico shook his head. He still could hardly believe that he and Salvadore had been tracking each other for the past months. "So, how do we get to room sixty-three?"

"Through the kitchens, up the back staircase that is used only by the service people, housekeeping and so on. Then down the hall, and *viola!* There will be Sylvia, waiting patiently for our expected arrival."

Nico snorted. "Waiting, yes. But maybe not so patiently." He slid off the wall and glanced up and down the alley. Still there was no one. "Lead off," he said to Salvadore.

The two of them walked side by side back towards the hotel, watching for any unexpected movements in the shadows.

CHAPTER 36

Standing with her back braced against the wall, Sylvia watched her captor. Raúl was seated on a chair near the door, leaning back with his legs crossed. He seemed to be completely unaware of her presence.

She could sense some strong emotion emanating from him, but what? He was not unduly nervous. Nor did he display the changing personalities, the see-saw extremes of charm and menace, of humor and brusqueness, that she had observed when she was held as his hostage in Bruges just the day before. Rather he seemed, of all things, contemplative. He did not have his pistol trained on her as Fuentes had ordered him to do. The weapon was balanced across one thigh, held casually and pointed at nothing in particular.

She shifted against the wall and spoke. "I wonder where Salvadore is right now," she said.

He blinked, as if he had forgotten she was there. But in the next instant, she had his full attention. "Salvadore be okay," he said. "He always be okay."

She shook her head. "I don't think so," she said. "Not this time."

He frowned, she thought perhaps in concern. "What you mean?"

"I mean, I think Fuentes intends to harm him."

Raúl nodded his understanding, but was apparently unmoved. "Yes, Fuentes intend. But he never get Salvadore."

Sylvia wondered what that meant. "But, Raúl, you helped Fuentes find Salvadore and Nico."

The young man shrugged. "Of course," he said. "Because Fuentes want."

"But Salvadore's your *brother*."

"I know. But Fuentes never get Salvadore. Salvadore smart."

With one hand she brushed her hair back away from her face. "Fuentes is dangerous," she said. "Dangerous to Salvadore."

"Danger, yes," Raúl agreed. "But not to Salvadore."

Sylvia felt her insides tighten. "To Nico?"

Now Raúl frowned again, contemplating. "I not know. Maybe I think he not danger to DiCapelli."

"But I believe Fuentes wants to kill both Nico and Salvadore."

Raúl nodded. His reply was matter of fact. "Yes. Of course. He want Salvadore and DiCapelli to be die – to be dead."

"But Raúl," she began.

"I *say* you." He tapped his cheek just below one eye with his forefinger for emphasis. "Salvadore smart. More smart than Fuentes. Maybe DiCapelli smart too."

"Raúl," she said, her voice very soft. "Why do you work for such a man as Fuentes? For money?"

His eyes darkened and took on a troubled look as he glanced away. When he brought his gaze back to hers, his face was slightly flushed. "Sylvia, I –" He stopped and began again. "Yes, of course. For money, a lot of money. But also Fuentes give me, well, give me the drugs if I work for him."

"I know," she said.

"You know this?" She could see the shame weighing heavy on him, but this time his gaze did not waver.

"Salvadore told me."

His flush deepened.

"Raúl, what you do, the way you live, is your business. But you are hurting your brother by it."

His dark eyes widened in disbelief. "No. Salvadore strong. I no hurt my brother."

"You hurt him," she insisted.

He shook his head.

"He loves you, and you hurt him. He *told* me."

Raúl didn't speak for a time. When he did, his voice was low. "I no want hurt Salvadore."

"But you do." She was gentle, seeing the pain that deepened the crease in his brow. "He wants you to be safe, with your family. Not with the likes of Fuentes, not using the drugs."

Raúl shook his head again as if to somehow deny what he surely knew was the truth.

"Salvadore knows that you are destroying your life and your future." She put out one hand towards him in an appeal. "And in the process, you are destroying him as well. His life and his future."

"But Salvadore strong," he said barely above a whisper. "Not like me. Salvadore *strong*. Salvadore always be strong, even as *chico*. As boy."

"Don't you see, Raúl? A man can be as strong as you say and still be hurt. Every day, every night that you are under the control of Fuentes and the drugs, you are hurting him."

He closed his eyes for a moment as if to shut out the stark truth. "I love my brother. I no want hurt him."

Her response was cut off by the door being thrust open. Fuentes, in a fury, stormed through and slammed it shut behind him. *"Hijos de puta!"* he swore violently. "Those sons of a whore. They've disappeared." He turned on Raúl. "This is your doing, you little *cabrón*."

Raúl stood up and eyed him, unflinching. Even so, Sylvia shook her head as if to ward off the onslaught. "You must know that they will not leave here without me," she said. She almost added, "And not without Raúl," but thought better of it.

Fuentes appeared to consider her words for a moment. "You'd better hope so," he said, the threat abundantly clear. "Not that it will do you a damned bit of good." He turned his attention back to Raúl. "At least you managed not to lose her," he said.

Raúl observed him, and then almost as an afterthought, he belatedly lifted his weapon. He shrugged in a somewhat disinterested fashion. "I no lose her," he said. "As you see. She is here."

With another curse, Fuentes threw himself into the chair that Raúl had vacated. *"Maldición,"* he swore. "Damn it to hell."

CHAPTER 37

Nico and Salvadore ducked into the shadows of one of the alleys along the side of the Hotel Amstel Grand. As Salvadore had promised, there was a set of wide double doors where kitchen deliveries were made. He tested one of the large metal handles. It was unlocked. "Here we go," he said to Nico.

He pulled the door open and stepped inside as if he had a legitimate reason to be there. Whistling tunelessly, he jammed his hands into the pockets of his jeans and sauntered through the busy place. Nico followed suit, studiously nonchalant.

Salvadore kept up a nonsensical conversation with Nico over his shoulder, in Spanish. Both men managed to look entirely astonished when a large, apparently overheated man in a tall white chef's hat and stained apron began gesticulating in their direction and speaking rapidly, first in French and then in Dutch and then in English. Clearly he was ordering them out of his kitchen, and just as clearly they were completely bewildered as to his intent.

Salvadore lifted both hands palms up in an exaggerated Latin gesture. *"Cómo?"* he said. *"Hay una problema?"*

The other kitchen employees stopped what they were doing, willing to be entertained by the spectacle of the chef's rising agitation and the confused expressions of the two intruders.

The preparations for the evening's dinner were well underway and when Salvadore gestured expansively as if to protest the chef's aggressive and unwelcoming attitude, his outflung arm collided with a waiter carrying a tray that was loaded with food. There was a violent crash of china as the entire mess landed at the chef's feet like a bizarre offering to a pagan god.

"Ah, *disculpe!*" Salvadore exclaimed. "Sorry!"

At the top of his substantial voice, the chef cut loose with a string of what were clearly French invectives. Salvadore returned his insults volubly and just as noisily. In Spanish.

Nico grinned and threw in a few of his own favorite expletives. In Italian.

Chaos reigned for a few moments as the assaulted waiter stared in horror at the pile of food and broken china splattered across the floor. The chef took one step forward into the mess, his wicked-looking carving knife raised and his round face red with fury. Salvadore grabbed Nico's arm and pointed to a door across the crowded kitchen that apparently opened into the dining room. The two men bolted for safety, ducking past the gaping employees and away from the still-roaring chef.

"Subtle," murmured Nico as they halted at the swinging doors and peered into the dining room, ignoring the very loud argument that was ensuing between the chef and the unfortunate waiter.

Salvadore shrugged. "And I always thought that the Dutch were such a placid, civilized people," he said. "I'd bet that chef is a Frenchman."

They both scanned the dining room. There were a few guests there, but nobody that they knew. At least neither Fuentes nor Raúl. Or Sylvia.

They stepped through the two-way swinging door and Salvadore led the way across the dining room, but before they reached the opening that led to the lobby, he made a quick left turn towards a narrow, unobtrusive door. "Room service and housekeeping," he announced, not slowing his stride as he shoved it open and they stepped through. The hallway was narrow and poorly lit, with black and white squares of tile on the floor. It seemed to go the entire length of the hotel before a shadowy flight of narrow wooden stairs appeared before them. They took the steps three at a time, rounding each landing to climb again.

But halfway up between the second and third floors, their progress was impeded by a stout, chocolate-skinned woman with greying black hair that was pulled back into a tight bun. She was toiling up the stairs carrying a huge armload of towels and was quite out of breath. She gave a start at hearing their approach behind her, and stopped, completely blocking their way. Then she began to explain to them with rather more words than necessary that they were not allowed in this particular area of the hotel. Since she couldn't gesture with her hands, she tried to make her point with her substantial chin, even as she chattered on in whatever her native language was. The resulting effect was somewhat quivering and grotesque, and Nico stifled a laugh.

"*Por favor!*" exclaimed Salvadore in his most gentlemanly voice as he stretched out his arms. "Let me carry those for you."

The woman shook her head vigorously and then, perhaps remembering the steepness of the stairs, she handed them over. Still talking nineteen to the dozen and now gesturing with her hands, she led them at the pace of a lazy snail up the stairs until they reached the fifth floor. There she stopped at the landing and, pushing the door open, she stepped into the hallway. She reached out her arms for the towels. Salvadore swept her a gallant bow and handed over his burden with a wink. She giggled and started off down the hall, apparently forgetting to remind them to stay out of the service stairwell.

They ducked back in and took the last narrow flight in a few seconds. Cautiously Salvadore opened the door a crack and peered through. The carpeted, well-lit hallway was empty. "Room sixty-three," he murmured, and the two men stepped through the opening.

In short order, they had reached their destination. Nico put his ear against the door and listened for a long, tense moment. Then he took one step back and looked at Salvadore. "Ah, *merda*," he said, his voice barely a whisper. "Fuentes is in there."

Salvadore froze and his brow creased in disbelief. "But how?"

Nico lifted one shoulder in an *I don't know* gesture, observing Salvadore even as he calculated quickly.

"And Sylvia as well?" Salvadore murmured the question.

"Don't know." Nico's shoulder lifted again. His eyes narrowed. "I don't suppose you happen to have a weapon, do you?"

In answer to the barely-heard question, Salvadore dropped one hand into the pocket of his jacket. The much-hated SIG Sauer pistol flashed a dull silver in the hall lighting.

"And a key?"

The next flash of metal from the same pocket was an old-fashioned key for the old-fashioned lock.

Nico nodded his approval and dipped his head towards the door. "Let's go pay a visit," he murmured.

He took the key from Salvadore and, as silently as possible, slid it into the lock. Thanks to the well-oiled maintenance of this expensive old hotel, the bolt slid back without a sound.

Pocketing the key, Nico met Salvadore's grim gaze one more time. Salvadore's nod was barely perceptible.

Nico shoved the door open with such force that it crashed into the inner wall and nearly recoiled back into his face.

There was a hesitation, a split second no longer than it took to draw one breath. Nothing moved. Nico took in the tableau: Fuentes. Raúl. Sylvia.

Then in one long stride, he and Salvadore stepped through the opening, and Nico kicked the door shut with his heel. The sound of the slamming door seemed to echo through the confined space, shattering the frozen shock of the room's occupants.

CHAPTER **38**

Nico glanced around the small room. It was a tight fit for five people, especially with three of them armed. He and Salvadore were standing side by side just inside the closed door. Fuentes was halfway down the wall on the right side, braced in front of the chair he had abruptly vacated, his nasty little pistol raised and pointed at Nico. His dark face was a mask of shock and fury. Raúl was against the wall directly opposite Nico and Salvadore, and his weapon was also trained in their general direction. And Sylvia stood near the foot of the bed to Nico's left. Her eyes were fixed on him, sapphire bright, and he saw her certainty. Now that he was here, everything would be all right. He hoped fervently that it was true.

He felt the faint tremor of claustrophobia that he always experienced when a situation seemed to be whirling out of his control, but he shook it off and slipped into his rôle.

In an exaggerated fashion, Nico made as if he were scoping out the room, examining the furnishings and all the walls, floor to ceiling. Then he gestured expansively toward his partner as if to draw attention to him. Salvadore was standing with feet apart and knees slightly bent. He held his own weapon in both hands, steady as a rock, pointed directly at Fuentes' belly.

Nico scowled and shifted his body into a more arrogant stance even as he crossed his arms over his chest. "So, Eduardo, old man," he said in his most insolent manner. "What have we got here? Looks like a Mexican standoff. No, make that a Colombian standoff."

"Two guns against one?" said Fuentes, clearly pleased at the prospect. "Not very good odds for you, DiCapelli."

Nico shook his head and gave Fuentes an exasperated look as if the drug lord had just uttered something incredibly stupid. "I've just said that it's a *standoff.* You know what a standoff is, don't you? *Merda*, I'd lay odds that even Raúl knows what it is." He turned his attention to Raúl. "Do you?" he asked earnestly.

Raúl didn't move a muscle and didn't react in any way. Nico noted that the barrel of the young Colombian's weapon was as rock steady as his brother's. But it was pointed at the door somewhere between Nico and Salvadore. Interesting.

Nico felt Sylvia watching him, knowing she must be wondering what he was doing with this ridiculous sideshow. Well, what he was doing was trying to keep Fuentes off balance, to find a catalyst – any *deus ex machina* that might bring matters to a head and provoke a confrontation that would force an end to this battle, this blood feud. An end in favor of him and Salvadore, and thus in favor of Sylvia.

Fuentes was dangerous enough, but Nico thought that he could anticipate his actions and responses fairly accurately. But Raúl? He had to be even more dangerous because he was completely unpredictable. Nico figured he wouldn't flinch at putting a hole into him. But would he actually kill his own brother? Nico couldn't be sure. Even so, he had to proceed with the half-baked plan that he had concocted in the last three seconds.

He sighed at the apparent lack of response from Raúl and turned back to Fuentes. He uncrossed his arms and planted both fists onto his hips. "A standoff, Fuentes, is where one side faces down the other with equal firepower. A deadlock. Perhaps you understand what a deadlock is?" He managed to sound hopeful. *"Punto muerto?"* he prompted in Spanish.

Fuentes' eyes narrowed at Nico's blatant sarcasm. "I don't see equal firepower here," he said.

"The equalizer is that Salvadore has his weapon trained on *you*. So there's no doubt as to who is going to go down first. Do you comprehend? Then there will be only two guns left. A standoff."

"Raúl will remove Salvadore," said Fuentes. "Make no mistake about that."

Well, it was a risk. It was a substantial risk, but Nico was fast running out of options and ideas. "Raúl would never shoot his own brother," Nico stated flatly, infusing as much certainty into his words as he could. He felt Raúl's intense gaze move to him but kept his attention on Fuentes.

Fuentes snorted his contempt. "You're more of a fool than I would have thought, DiCapelli. Raúl is *mine*. I own him, body and soul."

"No, you don't," Nico contradicted. "He belongs to Salvadore. And to his family in Quinchía, in the mountains of Colombia."

"You don't know what the hell you're talking about." Predictably, Fuentes' temper was heating up. "Raúl is mine and has been for some time. *La mano izquierda.* My left hand."

"Not anymore." Nico raised one hand and pointed across the room to the subject of their argument, who stood silent and unmoving, not even altering his expression. "Raúl belongs to Salvadore," he repeated. He shot a glance at Raúl. That young man's dark gaze was riveted on Nico, but his weapon was still trained on the door. Not on Nico. And certainly not on Salvadore.

"*Cállate la boca,* DiCapelli," snapped Fuentes. "Just shut the hell *up*. I'm damned tired of your mouth."

Nico lifted one shoulder in an eloquent, *in your face* gesture. "And I have no damned intention of shutting up," he said. "I'm damned tired of your being such an ass, and I'm telling you, it's a standoff. Haven't you ever watched the old American cowboy movies? Even odds make it a standoff, by definition. Everybody knows that."

But then his brow creased as if in confusion. "Oh, wait. *Merda.* Maybe the word is showdown. Like the Showdown at the OK Corral." He contemplated for an instant and then shook his head decisively. "Nope. A showdown is more like a final confrontation. This is definitely a standoff."

And then he favored Fuentes with his most insolent grin.

CHAPTER **39**

It must have been the insufferable grin that finally did it. In the space of a breath, Fuentes' barely-controlled composure snapped. "All right, DiCapelli," he said, a savage edge to his voice. "Have it your way, then. Don't shut up. You will enter the gates of hell with your mouth still running, I have no doubt. But just now, you're not going to hell. She is." He waved his pistol in Sylvia's direction. "And after she's been dispatched, I will keep you around for awhile longer, to give you time to think about how perhaps you might have prolonged her life, or even saved it."

Nico tensed. The *bastardo* meant it. Inexorably, the muzzle of the small weapon moved towards Sylvia. "Raúl," Fuentes hissed. *"Cuidado!* Watch DiCapelli."

Raúl gave an obedient nod. And then with a swiftness that should have been impossible, that gave neither Nico nor Salvadore even half a heartbeat to react, the young Colombian launched himself at Sylvia, tackling her to the floor. No sooner had the two of them made their violent crash-landing on the edge of the carpet, than Raúl twisted his body. His handgun swung up and pointed directly at Fuentes.

On instinct, the drug lord ducked, and in that second a vast range of emotions flashed across his arrogant countenance. Shock that this day was somehow turning on him like a dull domestic pet unaccountably becoming feral. Disbelief that the slavish Raúl had suddenly and inexplicably slipped free from his self-imposed prison. Fury that DiCapelli might yet again be snatching away control.

But he hadn't survived this long without having developed some very quick reflexes. *"Hijo de puta!"* he snarled even as he steadied himself and took the originally intended shot, but now to where Sylvia had been knocked to the floor.

Ah, but Raúl was still with her. Even as Nico hurtled himself forward to seize the drug lord, to somehow spare Sylvia, even as Salvadore leapt into the line of Fuentes' deadly fire, Raúl's handgun settled all accounts. It spat vengeance and mortality at the same second that Fuentes' pistol roared.

A tiny red flower blossomed in Fuentes' forehead, dead center. The Colombian's expression registered an almost ludicrous astonishment for a split second, even as his own bullet screamed past Salvadore, one scant inch away from retribution. Then Fuentes crumpled, in one moment of eternity going from a ruthless, self-assured monster to a heap of useless clay taking up space on the floor of room sixty-three of the venerable Hotel Amstel Grand.

Nico's ears rang from the deafening explosions that reverberated in the small space. He looked around frantically, trying to determine what exactly had happened, where Sylvia was. Then he realized that she was still trapped beneath Raúl's sprawled body. But it wasn't she who was pouring blood into the carpet. Rather, Raúl had taken the hit. In what might be considered a fair exchange for what Fuentes had intended, the bullet that had been meant for Sylvia was lodged instead in Raúl.

There was one breathless second in which no one spoke or moved. Then, "Raúl!" cried Salvadore in anguish for his impending loss. And in his next breath, he whispered, "Rulo, *mi hermano,* my brother," and took one agonized step forward.

Raúl twisted his head and raised it a mere inch to look up at his brother. "No, Salvadore," he said. *"Estoy bien."*

"No, you're *not* okay," said Salvadore, going down onto his knees beside his brother. "That *cabrón* shot you!"

"Yes, but I think only leg." Raúl shifted his weight so that Sylvia could move. "Hurt like hell," he added.

"Sylvia," said Nico softly. He was crouched on his haunches next to her and realized that he was holding one of her hands. He couldn't remember having taken it.

She smiled up at him, and then glanced to where Raúl had brought himself rather shakily to a semi-sitting position. The young Colombian looked stunned. His shoulders were hunched forward and his eyes were half-closed against the pain.

"Raúl," Sylvia said. She reached out and touched his arm with her free hand. "Thank you."

His expression softened. *"Claro,"* he said. And then he added earnestly, "I need you be safe. *Entiendes?* You understand?"

She didn't understand, but she nodded and smiled.

"Sylvia," said Nico again. "Are you all right?"

"Just a bit shaken," she assured him. "But please, now you must see to Raúl."

"Raúl," said Salvadore. "*Cristo, mi hermano*, you're leaking blood all over the carpet. The management of this hotel is not going to be very impressed with the condition of this room."

Raúl looked at his brother somewhat cautiously, as if measuring his mood.

"I'll have a look at your leg," said Nico to Raúl. But first he rose and crossed the room to where Fuentes was sprawled in his own coagulating blood. He knelt and touched the Colombian's throat to check for life. "Dead," he announced to the room in general, "and good riddance." He scowled. "I guess it *was* a showdown, after all. A final confrontation, rather than a standoff. *Merda*. I do hate it when I'm wrong." Then he returned to where Raúl waited, ashen-faced and tense with pain.

Somewhat shakily, Sylvia clambered to her feet. As gently as they could, Nico and Salvadore managed to remove Raúl's boots and jeans even as the young man attempted to stifle a groan. Sylvia stripped a sheet from the bed to toss over him. Together, the two men examined the wound. They spoke simultaneously.

"Ah, *mierda*," said Salvadore.

"Ah, *merda*," said Nico.

Ah, shit. This was definitely not good.

Raúl looked first at one and then the other in some apprehension. "*Qué?*" he said. "What is?"

"Sylvia, could you get all of the towels from the bathroom?" said Nico. "He's losing a good deal of blood. And bring another sheet, one that we can tear into strips. I think that we need to fashion a tourniquet of sorts."

"Artery?" asked Salvadore. He sounded calm, but Nico could feel the controlled tension that emanated from him.

"I don't think so," said Nico. "The entry wound is too central in the thigh for an artery." Very gently, he raised Raúl's leg. The Colombian gave an involuntary gasp at the sharp pain that jolted through him. Nico could find no exit wound on the other side.

He looked into Raúl's pale but stoic face. "The bullet hit you in the front and center of your left thigh," he said in Spanish. "I'd guess it's lodged against the bone. Odds are good that the femur – the thigh bone – has been broken."

Then he addressed Salvadore, switching to English. "I think this is going to require surgery, both to remove the bullet and to fix the shattered bone. But first we've got to get the bleeding stopped. And then we've got to get him the hell out of Amsterdam, and fast."

Salvadore didn't ask why. He knew why. A dead man and blood all over the carpet in a room at the stolid Hotel Amstel Grand was not good for business, nor for the city's pristine reputation. Instead he said, "To where?"

"London," said Nico.

"How?"

"Private jet. No immigration process, no questions. My organization can provide a safe house and a surgeon, and then can get both of you out of Europe."

"To Colombia," said Raúl. He was speaking to his brother. "To Quinchía, to home. Salvadore, I want go home."

"Oh, yes, Raúl," said Salvadore. "I'm taking you home. Your family is waiting for you."

Raúl sagged a bit then, his pain and exhaustion and the shock of this day's out of control events weighing heavily. Salvadore wrapped a protective arm around his shoulders as Sylvia approached with a stack of towels in her hands and another sheet draped over one arm.

"Lie down now," said Nico. "We're going to put you back together again."

Raúl looked confused, but Nico ignored that. He settled in to business, grateful for the training that his organization had provided for him in emergency first aid. Specializing in violent injuries, given the nature of his work. God knew he had gotten a good bit of practice in the field. Well, he would put it to use now.

With Salvadore's help, he tore the sheet into strips. He knotted one long length very tightly around Raúl's thigh just above the oozing wound. Then using the towels, he cleaned as much blood as he could from the injury. He grimaced his approval as the flow of blood slowed.

"Sylvia, fold one of the small towels into quarters," he said. After she had done so, he took it from her and pressed it to the wound, tying yet another strip of sheet around the leg to hold the towel in place.

"A compress," he said to Raúl in Spanish. "To help stem the flow of blood."

But he might as well have spoken in ancient Greek. Mercifully, Raúl had fainted.

Nico worked rapidly, the urgency of their situation chewing at the edges of his mind even as he focused on Raúl's damaged leg. They must not be found here. One inviolate rule in his organization was *never get caught*. There would be too many questions from the Dutch authorities that could not be answered. Nico couldn't quite believe that the shots had not been heard, but no alarm had yet been given. At least he could hear no running feet, no pounding at the door, no pulsing sirens.

He glanced over at Fuentes' corpse and then across Raúl's prone form to Salvadore. "One hell of a shot, our Raúl," he said. "Damned instant reflexes and one hell of a shot. Thank god."

Salvadore looked down at his unconscious brother. "He has always been that way," he said. "Even when we were boys, growing up in the mountains near Quinchía. Quick as a snake striking and an excellent shot. But this time he used his talents for the right cause." His gaze went to Nico. "Why?" he asked as if in contemplation. "Why now?"

"I don't know, Salvadore," Nico said as he used the last clean towel to wipe the sticky, darkening blood from his hands. "Maybe because he's been off the drugs for awhile?"

Salvadore frowned. "But he's been off them before, and for longer periods of time. And it hasn't changed his – his alliances." He shook his head. "Why now?" he repeated.

Stiffly Nico got to his feet. "I expect we won't know until we talk to him," he said. "And that won't be very soon, as I think he's going to be out for awhile." He shook his head. "But it's just as well. When he comes back around, he's going to be in a great deal of pain. And I don't have anything to give him to relieve it, as my rucksack is still in Bruges."

"What happens now?" asked Salvadore. "I think we need to get the hell out of this room, and out of this hotel."

"Right," said Nico. "Shall we move to my room, or Sylvia's?" Anywhere, he thought, as long as it was away from this damning confirmation of violence.

"Too risky," said Salvadore. "We'll have to carry Raúl. And we don't want to leave any evidence that ties this mess to you or Sylvia."

"I know," Nico said. "But I don't see a lot of other options. I'm not too keen on having room service show up to serve four people and a corpse."

Salvadore gave a slight grimace and reached into the pocket of his jeans, pulling out four keys. "We're on the sixth floor now, right?" He sorted through the keys, and selected one. "How about the fourth floor? Room forty? Away from our good friend here," – he gestured towards the body – "but not too close to where you and Sylvia are registered as staying on the second."

Nico's astonishment was clear. "How in hell did you manage that?" he asked.

"Later," said Salvadore. "I'll tell you once we get to room forty. For now let's get out of here." He stepped to the door and, opening it cautiously, looked up and down the corridor. "No one," he said to Nico as he closed the door again.

Nico eyed the unconscious Raúl. "Think we can pass him off as a drunk this early in the evening?"

Salvadore looked skeptical. "He's a bit bloodied up to only be drunk," he observed.

"Maybe he got so drunk that he fell over a chair, or down a flight of stairs," Sylvia said.

Both men stared at her as if startled to discover she was still in the room.

"The two of you get Raúl's clothes back onto him," she said. "And then, Nico, you go wash your hands. They're still bloody. You shouldn't have used the last clean towel to wipe off the blood."

Nico looked at Salvadore and started to say something about bossy women, but Sylvia was apparently already off in another direction. She was, of all things, studying Fuentes' sprawled form. "I wonder," she said thoughtfully, "if we could make Fuentes' death look like a suicide. Maybe we could take his gun away and put Raúl's near his hand."

As macabre as her proposal was, Nico felt a smile tug at one corner of his mouth. The creative imagination at work. He felt suddenly like a character in one of her novels.

Salvadore was frowning, considering her idea. "I don't think that will work," he said finally. "I believe it might be a bit difficult to shoot oneself straight on, in the center of the forehead."

"Raúl's fault," said Nico. "He should have shot him in the temple. In the right temple, since Fuentes was right-handed."

"Wrong angle," said Salvadore. "An impossible shot from where Raúl was in relation to Fuentes."

Sylvia looked at them both as if they had suddenly taken leave of their senses. "So a suicide won't work?" she said. "What, then?"

"Getting out of here, and now," said Nico, abruptly back to business. "Let's get Raúl ready for a stroll."

With difficulty, the two men got Raúl's jeans back onto him, and then his boots. The jeans were a bloody mess, but there was nothing for it. Salvadore picked up Raúl's handgun and shoved it into the pocket of his own jacket even as Nico stepped back over to Fuentes' body. He knelt and then methodically went through the pockets of the dead man's clothes, taking care to touch only the edges of whatever he found. There was nothing of interest. A British passport, no doubt a fake, with Fuentes' name and photograph. A wallet with a few credit cards and some Belgian francs and a few Dutch guilders. So. The drug lord was traveling light. *Had been* traveling light. Perhaps he still was, to more quickly make his way straight to hell.

Nico stuffed the items back into Fuentes' pockets. Then he reached into his own jeans pocket and pulled out a folded handkerchief. Carefully he moved aside the blue cloth to reveal a small plastic bag filled with a fine white powder.

"What's that?" asked Sylvia.

"Cocaine," said Nico. "Excellent quality, too. Colombian. Only the best for Eduardo Fuentes. Street value of this little bag of poison is about ten thousand dollars U.S." Without touching the plastic, he slipped the bag into the pocket of Fuentes' jacket and stuffed the handkerchief back into his own. Then he added, "I'm damned lucky that Raúl didn't find it when he frisked me, looking for weapons."

Salvadore looked stunned for a moment, the obvious question on his lips. But then he shrugged his approval. "So rather than Sylvia's suicide theory, we have a disagreement among some of the esteemed members of the I.A.D.R. The International Association of Drug Runners. I like it. Nice touch. It is – how do you say –"

"Apropos," supplied Sylvia. "Both relevant and opportune."

Salvadore nodded. "Right," he said. "Shall we take his gun?" He pointed to the small weapon lying as if abandoned next to Fuentes' body.

"No," said Nico. "I think we leave it. It provides an interesting prop to this little tableau, don't you think?"

He rose and stepped away from Fuentes' body. With one of the bloodied towels, he made his way through the room, wiping down every spot in the room where anyone might have left a fingerprint. He gave one last glance around to ensure that he had not missed a single particular. "Details," he said aloud, echoing what one of his trainers had drilled into him. "We live or die by the details."

"Cristo," said Salvadore as he watched Nico work. He posed the question that he might have asked when Nico had produced the cocaine. "What exactly is it that you do for a living?"

"Later," said Nico, and then he parroted Salvadore's own words. "I'll tell you when we get to room forty. Are we ready to head there?"

Again Salvadore opened the door and looked up and down the hall. Still it was vacant.

Holding it only by its edges, Nico removed the "do not disturb" sign from the doorknob and moved it to the outside of the door. "Maybe that will buy us a bit more time," he said to Salvadore.

Salvadore nodded. "Okay. Let's go," he said. He handed the key to room forty to Sylvia, and then he and Nico knelt beside the unconscious Raúl.

"Come on, my drunken friend," said Nico. The two men carefully lifted Raúl. With the comatose man's arms draped across their shoulders and his head hanging forward, they supported his dead weight, half-carrying and half-dragging him from the room.

Sylvia closed the door behind them and then tested the knob to ensure it was locked and the "do not disturb" sign was still dangling in place.

"Wipe the knob, Sylvia," said Nico over his shoulder.

She obeyed, using the tail of her shirt, and then followed.

"Go ahead of us," said Nico. "And call up the lift. If anyone is on it, speak to them so that we know to turn away. Then you get on, just as normal, and go down. But come right back up."

She nodded her understanding and punched the call button. When the lift arrived, she pulled open the door. The car was empty.

"Good," said Salvadore. "Come on."

They entered the small space with some difficulty given Raúl's inert condition, and the fact that the lift was designed for only three people at a time. Sylvia punched the button for the fourth floor. The ancient lift car gave a lurch and started down.

"Sylvia," said Nico. "If anyone is on the fourth floor, you get off, but we will stay on. We'll go up to the fifth floor, and then right back down to the fourth."

"Okay," she said.

The lift clunked to a stop and Sylvia drew back the safety door. She pushed open the outer door and stepped out. Nico and Salvadore heard her speak brightly. "Oh, hello!" she said, even as she pulled the safety door closed and then shut the other firmly behind her.

Salvadore punched the button for the fifth floor. The lift continued downward.

"*Mierda*," he swore. He pushed every button on the wall of the lift, including the emergency stop, but it continued its inexorable descent.

"Block the door," Nico said urgently.

The lift stopped at zero, the ground floor. As Nico propped the limp Raúl upright against the back wall of the car, Salvadore kept a firm hand on the door. They could hear the bellman on the other side wondering aloud why the door would not open, even as Salvadore repeatedly punched the button for the fourth floor. At last the lift creaked back into motion, this time upward. It stopped at the fourth floor.

Nico braced himself as the door swung outward, opened by whomever waited in the hallway.

"Welcome back," Sylvia said calmly, pushing back the safety door. "How nice to see you again. Please come with me." She directed them off the lift and, a few doors down, to room forty. Nico gave a long sigh of relief when the door closed behind them and Sylvia had locked it.

The room was substantially larger than room sixty-three had been, with a huge bed situated against the wall. They took the still-unconscious Raúl to the bed and gently lowered him upon it. Sylvia brought a light blanket from the closet and covered him against the inevitable coldness of shock.

For a moment, Salvadore gazed down at the pale, still face as if even yet he couldn't believe that his brother was not only alive, but that he had turned on Fuentes and had bitten the very hand that had fed him the poison.

Nico glanced at him and then headed for the telephone on the desk. "I'm going to call my contact at my organization," he said. "He's going to have to help us mop up this mess." But then he grinned. "Attila is going to be very surprised and pleased that we at last managed to take out Fuentes. As long as we can get out of here undetected, that is. Mustn't leave a mess. He doesn't much like it when I do that."

Salvadore frowned. "Won't the hotel have a record of any calls made from this room?" he asked.

"Oh, yeah," said Nico. "But it won't do them any good. When I place the call, I'll use a code that will scramble the number. Neither the hotel nor the police will ever know which country was called, let alone what number."

"And which country are you calling?" asked Salvadore.

"The U.K. London." Nico picked up the receiver and punched in a series of numbers. There was a very short pause while the call was connecting. Then Nico spoke, rapidly, clearly, to the point. He described what had happened, and said that Fuentes was dead. This announcement resulted in a good deal of racket on the other end of the line during which he held the receiver away from his ear and raised one brow at Salvadore and Sylvia. And then he told his contact what they needed. He was explicit and comprehensive. They needed *out*, by whatever means, and immediately. Out of the Amstel Grand, out of Amsterdam, out of the Netherlands. To London. They needed a safe house. They needed a surgeon for a gunshot wound and probable serious fracture of the femur. There was more, but the rest could be arranged after they were in London. "I'll call back in fifteen," said Nico, and he hung up. There had been no mention of the very distinctive name of his contact. Attila indeed.

Salvadore and Sylvia were staring at him.

"Nico," said Salvadore. "Who in *hell* do you work for?"

"We've got fifteen minutes before I call back," Nico said. "I'll tell you, but only if you tell me how you ended up with the keys to so bloody many rooms in this hotel."

Salvadore's smile was faint, but it was there. "You first," he said. He pulled a chair next to the bed where Raúl lay as still as a corpse. Sitting down, he put one hand protectively on his brother's forearm.

Sylvia was already seated on the small couch at the side of the room. Nico lowered himself next to her and took one of her hands. He felt the tremor that went through her at his touch. "You okay?" he asked.

She nodded, mute.

He put an arm around her and pulled her tightly against him even as he kissed the top of her head. Salvadore looked away.

And then Nico described his organization, World Designs Ltd., and what he did for a living. An independent group, operatives working for no specific country or nationality. Only for truth and justice, for a kind of moral rightness. It should have sounded hokey, but it didn't, coming from his lips.

As an example, he told Salvadore of the incident in Czechoslovakia where he had met Sylvia and had crossed paths yet again, and almost fatally, with Eduardo Fuentes. The drug lord had been there to buy some stolen jewels and artifacts from a former Communist leader whose plan had been to sell the heritage of his own country and then get himself abroad where he could live the rest of his life in luxury on the spoils stolen from his people. But that one never got out of Czechoslovakia alive, and he never delivered the priceless antiques to Fuentes. Because Nico had stolen them. And when they turned up again, they were in Prague, at *hrad* Pražské, Prague castle, where they were assumed to have been all the time.

Salvadore was astonished at such a story, at such an operation. "How in god's name did you know about this organization, this work, to get such a position?" he asked.

Nico smiled. "I knew nothing of them," he said. "Out of necessity, practically no one does. After I graduated university, I took an exam to see if I might qualify for the U.S. Foreign Service. Before I ever found out the results, my organization contacted me with a job offer. They somehow had access to the test results and tried to snag the, well, the –"

"The top candidates," Sylvia said.

Nico raised one shoulder. "The top candidates," he agreed. "Before they could commit elsewhere. So that is how I came to do what I do."

"But why did you decide to do it?" asked Salvadore.

"I had ample opportunity to question the recruiters for my organization. They knew I was a bit, well, *rabid* in my opinions about drug lords, drug runners, drug users."

Salvadore cast an involuntary glance at the oblivious Raúl. "Because of your father," he said.

Nico shot him a look of surprise.

"I told him about your father, Nico," Sylvia said. "I thought he deserved to know."

Nico smiled at her and nodded. "You were right. Since he spirited you away from Bruges and to safety, he did deserve to know." His attention went back to Salvadore. "My father's untimely death, and the resulting loss not only to me but to my mother, set into motion a new direction for my life. I became obsessed with somehow 'making a difference' in the world. And one way to do that is by penetrating and destroying the shady underworld where the drug lords operate."

"I understand," said Salvadore.

"Of course you do," said Nico. "Because of Raúl."

Salvadore looked at Raúl again and his hand tightened on his brother's arm. "Do you think that we actually have him back now?" he asked meditatively. "Now that Fuentes is dead?"

"You know as well as I how difficult it is for someone to kick the habit of the hard drugs," said Nico. "But I think you should allow yourself to hope. The choices that were made here today by your brother were his own choices. He was not coerced into behaving as he did."

Salvadore nodded. "He made a split-second decision, and he made the right one."

"He made the right one, that is true," said Nico thoughtfully. "But I'm not so certain that it was a split-second decision. I watched him change during the events of the past several hours. He was preoccupied, with something weighing on him."

"I know. I saw it too," said Salvadore. "But what?"

Nico rubbed his chin. "Well, I can't say for sure at this point. But I was riding Fuentes pretty hard all the time. I think Raúl was at first shocked, not only at how I was behaving towards Fuentes, but also that I seemed to get away with it, even when Fuentes' temper was at its foulest. Maybe Raúl had come to believe that Fuentes was somehow lord and master, and infallible. Maybe he believed that he had no choices. And maybe he just stopped believing that."

"And," Sylvia said softly, "while the two of us were waiting in that room upstairs for Fuentes to return, I told Raúl that he was hurting you, Salvadore. Hurting his brother. He didn't want to believe it. He thought you must be too strong to ever be hurt, and too smart to ever be in danger from Fuentes."

Salvadore said nothing, but he moved his head slowly from side to side even as he studied Raúl.

"I will say one thing." Nico sighed, and ran a hand across his beard-stubbled face. "I and my organization really mucked up with regards to you, Salvadore. We usually do a better job of obtaining and interpreting information. I expect Attila will chew on me for not figuring out your rôle in this little adventure a lot sooner than now." As if the mention of his contact had reminded him, he gave a quick glance at the watch face on the inside of his left wrist. "Fourteen and a half," he said, getting up and heading for the telephone again. "I'd better call Attila. He gets ever so cranky if I'm late. Not as cranky as Fuentes, of course. But you still owe me the story of the hotel keys, Salvadore."

This time the phone call was longer, and Nico made notes on the pad of paper provided by the hotel. At last he hung up and turned to Salvadore and Sylvia. "Okay," he said. "The private jet has already departed London for Amsterdam with six on board, including a doctor. They're going to get us out of Amsterdam. We need to leave as few traces as possible of our being here."

"With the exception of the inconvenience of Fuentes taking a nap upstairs?" said Salvadore dryly.

"Well, there is that." Nico grimaced. "Too bad there isn't a garbage chute in this creaky old place, for easy disposal. Fuentes is just going to have to be one of those messy little 'loose ends' that Attila hates so much." He waved one hand as if dismissing his contact's expected irritation. "Anyhow, Salvadore, tell us about all those room keys."

Salvadore obliged and Nico started laughing. "You can imagine Fuentes' reaction at finding no suite available, at any price," he said. "That was a stroke of genius."

"The trouble is," said Salvadore, "I'm afraid that I attracted too much attention to myself in the process. I mean, booking all those rooms."

Nico nodded. "What passport did you use when you reserved the rooms?"

"Actually, I didn't use any, as no one is yet 'officially' checked in," said Salvadore. "The arrangement I made with the hotel was that I would deliver the room keys as my associates checked in. I'm just the front man." Then he added, "But I don't know what you mean by 'which passport.' If I had used one, it would have been the only one I've got."

"Colombian?"

"Of course."

"We'll have to fix that."

"Fix it?"

Nico raised a brow. "Well, yeah," he said. "You need to have a couple extra passports, and from different countries. So that in the future when you're involved in little escapades like this, you can't be traced afterwards."

Salvadore eyed him. "You're serious."

"Oh, I'm serious all right," said Nico. "My organization could use talent like yours." He gestured towards the still prone form on the bed. "And Raúl's as well, if he can kick the drugs. I still can't believe how bloody quick he was. Never seen anything like it."

Then Nico suddenly changed direction. "According to Attila, some of the operatives that are coming with him will collect our things while we make our disappearance. I rather left a trail behind me, all across Belgium and the Netherlands with my big mouth chewing on Fuentes. Intentionally, given the circumstances." He pulled a face. "But I'm not sure Attila will agree with my approach, now that we know the final outcome. He's rather keen on hindsight, I'm afraid. For now, I'd like things to settle down a bit. Maybe you and I should just vanish, Salvadore, and let the hotel figure out that we've disappeared after we're long gone. That poor clerk may wish he had given Fuentes a suite after all."

"Well, in a way, he did," said Salvadore. "Not a suite, that is true, but a room at least." He gave a slight grin, but it held no humor. "Not at all Fuentes' style. What a low-life way to depart his world of luxuries."

CHAPTER **40**

Just over two hours later, the high-low wail of an ambulance siren announced the arrival of what Nico had called his Special Emergency Response Team.

A short ten minutes ago, an apparently stricken Sylvia had hysterically informed the hotel staff through bitter tears that she had called for an ambulance because she had had a fight with her boyfriend and he had gotten drunk and passed out in room forty and that she was *sure* he had alcohol poisoning because he had done it before and *oh!* she just *knew* that he was going to die if he wasn't taken directly to hospital and *immediately* but wasn't it just *too* embarrassing and would the hotel *please* handle the incident discreetly?

Of course the hotel would handle it discreetly, she was assured.

Nico later praised her fine acting ability and the fact that she had delivered the entire litany without pausing to take a single breath. And then he had observed cynically that the hotel wouldn't want to handle it any other way than discreetly, as they were even more concerned about their pristine reputation than about her distress.

In any case, the ambulance came to a shrieking halt, subsiding at the back of the hotel. The two attendants with the stretcher trolley were delivered by a hotel clerk – discreetly! – to room forty. A sharp rap brought Sylvia to the door. Hustling the clerk out of the way, the medics entered and closed the door firmly in the young man's curious face.

The pair of them very nearly made a caricature of sorts, and in her mind and imagination Sylvia immediately began sketching them with words. They were both wearing very proper Dutch medic uniforms of crisp white with blue piping, but there the resemblance ended. One was tall and thin, his face nearly cadaverous. His hair was thick and wavy and completely white, and he carried with him a quiet authority. The other was short and rather rotund, and his completely bald head gleamed in the glow of the overhead light. He was entirely unprepossessing. The round blue eyes in his round cheerful face were twinkling at Sylvia as if he knew exactly what she was thinking. She blushed slightly. He gave her a wink and turned to Nico.

When he spoke, his voice was entirely unexpected. It was a deep, powerful bass, and as soon as he had uttered two words there was no doubt at all as to who was now in charge.

"Well, DiCapelli," he said, his unmistakable English accent as prim and proper as the queen herself. "What in bloody hell have you got yourself up to now?" He gave a quick sidelong glance at Sylvia. "Pardon my language, Miss Duncan," he said. "Nico seems able to inspire me to my worst manners." Then as quickly, he turned his attention back to Nico. "Well?" he demanded.

Nico put one hand to his heart in a theatrical gesture. He lifted his other hand palm up in exaggerated supplication, and threw back his head. "Attila! You cut me to the quick! I, who have delivered up the vile Eduardo Fuentes to place as an offering at your honored feet."

Salvadore and Sylvia stared at Nico in astonishment, and the tall, white-haired medic looked somewhat bewildered, but the object of his histrionic appeal was apparently unimpressed and thus unmoved.

"Knock it off, DiCapelli," said 'Attila.' This very un-British expression sounded oddly incongruous coming from his lips. "You're not going to work me over with that vituperative mouth of yours like you undoubtedly did poor old Fuentes."

Nico was as suddenly serious. He dropped his arms and his pose. "Jonathan, I wasn't expecting you. Pretty high level response, isn't it?"

Jonathan, previously Attila, started to speak, but Nico cut across him. He pointed to Sylvia. "Sylvia Duncan you know," he said. "Know about, anyhow." The long finger moved to Salvadore. "Salvadore San Martín." And to the still, pallid form on the bed. "Raúl San Martín. Our wounded hero of the hour. Raúl took out Fuentes for us."

The tall, thin man moved suddenly, lifting an official-looking black leather bag from the stretcher and stepping directly for the bed. Salvadore moved automatically into a defensive posture.

Jonathan raised one hand. "Doctor Japie Bosch," he said. "He needs to have a look at this esteemed Raúl."

"My brother," Salvadore said, as if that explained everything.

Apparently it did. "Ah," said Jonathan.

"Jonathan is my contact at the organization," said Nico, stating the obvious.

With Salvadore hovering protectively, the doctor pulled back the light blanket that covered Raúl. "Help me get these out of the way," he said to Salvadore, indicating Raúl's jeans and boots. His accent was heavy and sounded very Dutch.

While the doctor was working over Raúl, Jonathan and Nico conversed in low voices. As promised, Jonathan had brought along four other operatives who were in the process of going through the rooms of Sylvia and Nico and retrieving their things, hopefully including the few things that had been left in Bruges. They would handle checkout and payment for the rooms. The operatives would stay in Amsterdam for awhile to keep an eye on the investigation that would soon be launched, and to mop up Nico's damnable mess, as Jonathan termed it.

Salvadore gripped his brother's hand while the doctor gently removed the bloody strip of sheet and the folded towel that formed the compress on the wound. Next the tourniquet was loosened. He inspected the torn flesh. "Your work, Nico?" he asked.

"Yes," said Nico.

"Nice job."

Before Nico could thank him for the compliment, Jonathan spoke, his voice dry. "Well, Nico, so you did manage to pick up something useful from your training."

The doctor ignored this by-play. "Did you check to see if there is an exit wound?" he asked.

"I did," said Nico. "There's not."

"I see. Thus your suggestion that surgery would be indicated. A probable shattered femur."

"Exactly," said Nico.

The doctor continued his examination, checking blood pressure and heart rate and the shallow breathing. "How long has he been unconscious?"

Nico said, "A couple hours, at least. He fainted while I was working on him." He frowned. "Seems like he's been out for a damned long time. Shock, do you think?"

Salvadore tightened the grip on his brother's hand. "Raúl will be okay, no?" he asked, concern making his accent heavier than usual.

The doctor nodded. "I should think so. We'll get him into surgery immediately."

"Jonathan," said Nico, now with some urgency. "It won't take the hotel staff long to figure out that this isn't actually Sylvia's room."

"You're right," said Jonathan. "Let's get out of here. Come on, Japie. Move it."

"I'm going to give him an injection against pain in case he awakens while we're transporting him," the doctor said to Salvadore, again ignoring Jonathan's brusqueness. "And we will need to get a blood transfusion started as soon as we can. I don't suppose you know his blood type?"

"AB negative," said Salvadore. At the doctor's surprised expression, he added, "We're the same. AB negative. Blood type is required on all official identification documents in Colombia."

"A good idea," said the doctor approvingly, even as he administered the injection for pain. "But AB negative is one of the more rare types. We will need to call ahead to London to ensure that it's ready to go."

On that comment, Raúl's slack body was gently transferred to the stretcher, covered snugly and securely strapped.

"Very good," said Jonathan.

"Okay," said Nico. "Sylvia will go with you, appropriately upset and concerned for her comatose boyfriend. Salvadore and I will meet you at the airstrip. The one to the east?"

Jonathan nodded his acquiescence even as he stepped to the door and opened it. The same young, blond hotel clerk was still stationed there, anxiously twisting his hands. "We must take the stairs," Doctor Bosch said to him in perfect Dutch. "You will go with us. To show us the way. Discreetly, of course."

If that young man detected any irony in the last few words, he gave no sign. In a relieved voice he said, "This way, please."

The doctor and Jonathan, in their rôles as ambulance attendants and medics, followed him with the trolley bearing the unconscious Raúl. The young man's bloodless face was nearly as white as the small pillow that supported his head. Sylvia stepped mournfully after them, the very picture of anxious dejection.

Nico and Salvadore waited in the room until the tragic young lovers had disappeared down the wide hallway and onto the wide staircase. "Okay," said Nico. "We're out of here." They headed for the back stairs, hoping not to run into any of the hotel employees.

Even as they debouched into the long narrow hallway on the ground floor, they heard the wail of sirens start up again. "There goes Raúl," said Salvadore. "*Cristo*, I hope he's okay. I wish I could be with him."

"He's in good hands," said Nico. "We use only the top specialists in every field, including medicine. Doctor Bosch is from South Africa. Hence his impeccable Dutch accent. His native language is Afrikaans. We're lucky he was in London just now. I expect that he will be Raúl's chief surgeon."

They reached the door and passed into the now-crowded dining room. The plaintive reverberation of the ambulance siren was already fading into the distance. But then came the sound of other screaming sirens, apparently advancing towards them, and at an alarming rate of speed. Their shrill sound was both nagging and accusatory.

"Uh-oh," said Nico. "If that means what I think it does, we'd better get moving. Someone has apparently been mucking about on the sixth floor."

"Lobby or kitchen?" said Salvadore.

"Kitchen, I think," Nico said. "Let's go bid that French chef a good evening."

Moving casually so as to not attract undue attention, they crossed the dining room and slipped into the kitchen. The first person they encountered was the waiter who earlier had had his tray toppled by Salvadore. His eyes widened and his mouth opened as if to challenge them. But Nico drew one finger across his throat in a brief expressive gesture and shook his head. The waiter subsided. Nico and Salvadore slipped through the room and, undetected by the chef, stepped out into the alleyway.

They looked up the narrow street in the direction of Korte Niezel. It was ablaze with bright red strobe lights flashing from police cars, and the pulsing sirens echoed eerily down the alley where they stood.

"Well, well," said Nico. "I do believe that Eduardo Fuentes is about to check out of the Hotel Amstel Grand."

"I'd guess the police will have the hotel completely sealed off in about sixty seconds," Salvadore said.

The two men sprinted down the alley, away from the chaos at the front of the hotel. With Salvadore leading the way, they took the same route along the dim canal on Geldersekade as they had earlier that evening. Now the turgid waters were a flat black, reflecting the darkness of the night. Suddenly the Colombian made an abrupt left turn up a side street. Nico followed.

Halfway up the block, Salvadore halted next to the black Buell motorcycle that was chained to a lamppost. "Taxi?" he said to Nico, one brow quirked.

Nico grinned. "Damn, but you're good," he said.

In a heartbeat Salvadore had the machine freed of its moorings and the black helmet on his head. With a flick of his thumb, the beast roared to life. Nico swung aboard behind Salvadore and the motorcycle shot forward. "Where to?" Salvadore asked over his shoulder.

Nico directed him down darkened cobbled streets and over innumerable canals. By illegally snaking in and out and between cars, and taking one-way streets in whatever direction they wished, in less than fifteen minutes they were at the east edge of the city, and the flashing light of a diminutive control tower showed them the rest of the way to the private airstrip.

There was nothing there except for one small but sleek jet plane, its engines idling impatiently, but with no lights. "Where the hell is the ambulance?" asked Salvadore, searching the darkness.

"Come and gone, I'd guess," said Nico. "Probably Raúl is already on board. Let's go to the plane."

The Buell rumbled across the smooth black tarmac, and Salvadore stopped directly next to the plane. A light flicked on and Jonathan's round face appeared in the open doorway at the top of the steep stairs. He rolled his eyes. "Really, Nico. Can't you do anything in a conventional manner?"

Nico hitched one brow. "Room on board for Salvadore's beast?" he asked as he slid off.

"No," said Jonathan. "We'll have to have it shipped." He motioned to a man who waited somewhat nervously next to the control tower. "Take this monster," he said. "Where do you want it to go, Salvadore?"

"Quinchía, Colombia," said Salvadore. "I'm taking Raúl home." With some reluctance he handed over the Buell and the helmet, and he and Nico climbed the stairs and ducked into the plane. Nico pulled up the stairs and expertly secured the door.

Clearly this aeroplane was intended for medical evacuations. Raúl and his stretcher were securely strapped onto what looked like an immoveable hospital cot. Salvadore, relieved with the apparent professionalism of everyone concerned, settled into a seat next to his recumbent brother where he could watch the doctor at work and keep one hand on Raúl's arm.

"Jonathan," the pilot called back from the open cockpit. "The control tower just sent a message that no planes are to be allowed to depart from any airport in the Netherlands until further notice, including Schiphol and all private airstrips. Some kind of emergency in the city."

"Did you respond?" asked Jonathan.

"Not yet," the pilot said.

"Don't, then," said Jonathan. "Get this piece of tin into the air."

The jet's running lights flashed on and the sleek machine started to taxi down the runway even as Nico strapped himself into the seat next to Sylvia and took her hand. The radio in the cockpit squawked shrilly in a frantic mixture of Dutch and English, at first with admonitions and urgent orders, and then deteriorating into furious threats. It was clear to everyone what the agitated voice in the control tower was saying, but the pilot was unresponsive. The plane accelerated at an astonishing speed and then lifted off smoothly. As the ground fell away beneath them, Jonathan said, "Well, bloody hell. Excuse me again, Miss Duncan. But I don't suppose we'll be able to use this particular airstrip again, not very soon at least." He gave an exaggerated sigh. "Sometimes, Nico, you do leave behind such a damnable mess."

CHAPTER 41

Five days later, Nico and Sylvia were relaxing at one of his organization's locations, this one in north London. It was a huge old Victorian place, with thirty-something rooms. Although it had been built over one hundred forty years ago, it was in nearly-perfect condition. A vast lawn spread out on all sides, the even greenness interrupted by the black trunks of ancient spreading oak trees and flower gardens not yet beginning to fade. Not a bad caravanserai, Nico had observed. The irascible island weather, which had been rainy and gusty for some days and which Nico had impertinently compared to Jonathan's temperament, was for once behaving.

Raúl had regained consciousness on the flight to London while the doctor was in the process of connecting an IV to his arm. Salvadore and the doctor had conversed in low tones for a time, with Salvadore translating for his brother.

Upon their arrival in London at yet another private airstrip, Raúl had been transferred via ambulance to the Blackheath Hospital, where he underwent surgery on his damaged leg. As Nico had surmised, the femur had been shattered, and the operation was long and difficult. Salvadore had inquired whether this particular hospital might have been chosen for its specialists. But Jonathan responded that his organization used their own specialists, and that Doctor Bosch would be joined by two others who had been flown in for this express purpose. He said further that they used this particular hospital because it was a private one and allowed outside surgeons to use their very up to date equipment and operating theatres. Afterwards, Doctor Bosch assured the brothers that Raúl's leg, given time to heal properly, would be right as rain. Nico had to translate that particular idiom for them.

"Appropriate that the English idiom would reference rain," said Salvadore sourly, thinking that the sunshine of the Colombian Andes was long overdue and would be more than welcome.

But as it turned out, Salvadore's determination to take Raúl home to Quinchía was not to be. No sooner had the small jet hurtled into British airspace than the alarm was raised. Salvadore and his Buell had most definitely been noticed in both Amsterdam and Bruges. He was wanted for questioning in the untimely death of Eduardo Fuentes, a not so upstanding citizen with a questionable British passport and a nasty little packet of illegal drugs in his Dior suit jacket. With that rather obvious tip-off, it had taken no time at all for the Dutch authorities to figure out that perhaps Interpol might be interested in their fast-breaking but increasingly messy case and the late *Meneer* Fuentes. Nico was also wanted by the authorities for the same purpose, but it wasn't likely that this particular British passport would be traced. Well, hell, another perfectly good passport down the tube, Nico had remarked without much concern.

Perhaps the Netherlands had no extradition agreements with Colombia, but Salvadore had to disappear for awhile. So he and Raúl and presumably the black Buell motorcycle had been delivered to Buenos Aires, Argentina, with new Argentine passports and for Raúl, at least one would hope, a new life. For if Raúl had a new life, then at long last so did his brother.

Thus Salvadore and Raúl were removed from London via private jet, from a private airstrip in London to another private airstrip in Argentina. (Jonathan was exceedingly fond of private airstrips, Nico confided to Sylvia within Jonathan's hearing, upon which that gentleman reflected somewhat caustically that he was going to run entirely out of private airstrips that he could use around the world if Nico continued to cut an incapacitating swath through them.) So Raúl had been taken from the Blackheath Hospital in London directly to the *hospital* Británico in Buenos Aires, his determined brother and Doctor Japie Bosch at his side.

The day after they left, a long cardboard tube was delivered to Sylvia. Astonished, she opened it, and out slid a beautiful print of Vincent van Gogh's *Crows over the Cornfield*.

CHAPTER 42

So this particularly lovely almost-autumn afternoon found Nico and Sylvia sitting together on a blanket that Nico had tossed onto the slightly damp grass in the shade of the oaks in the gardens of the vast estate. They were eating French Brie on fresh, crusty Italian bread and sipping an imported Argentine Malbec, with a toast to the good health of Salvadore and Raúl. The deep red of the wine in the Waterford crystal goblets absorbed the cerulean blue of the sky. They conversed casually, and when they ran out of observations and comments, the silences between them were gentle and comfortable.

During one such lull, Sylvia reached out and put her hand over one of Nico's. "May I ask you something?" she said, her voice suddenly a bit shy.

"Of course," he said. "Ask away."

"Remember that first morning? I mean when you arrived to Amsterdam and we met in the dining room?"

He smiled at her. "Yes. I do remember."

"Well, before Salvadore interrupted us, you were going to tell me something."

She felt his hand move under hers but was not dissuaded. "What was it, Nico? What had you been going to say? It seemed at the time to be, well, to be important."

"Oh, yes," he said. "It was important."

"So will you tell me now?"

He looked off across the lawn and then up at the cloudless sky. He shifted on the blanket and leaned forward, taking both of her hands in his. "It had to do with you and – and me."

"What about us?"

"Well, you see, Sylvia, what I had wanted to say –" He hesitated and then tried again. "Well. Ah, *dio*."

She gave him a tiny frown. "I don't believe I've ever seen you quite so without words, Nico," she said. "What is it? What's wrong?"

"Oh, nothing is wrong. It's just that – it's just that, well, nothing has seemed to matter so much before."

"So much as what?"

"So much as *this*."

Still the tiny frown was on her brow and he lifted one index finger as if to erase it.

"Please, Nico."

He dropped his hand and struggled to get his thoughts together, to give voice to the words he had rehearsed to himself at least a thousand times. Taking a deep breath he said, "Sylvia, I have spoken to my training officer and to Jonathan. I mean, about you."

"About me?" She was surprised. "Whatever for?"

"Well, about my – my relationship with you."

The small frown had deepened. "You need your organization's permission just to see me?"

"No! Of course not!"

"Well, what about then? What business have they with me?"

He tried again. He must get this right. "Sylvia, please understand. Most, if not all of the agents in my, ah, organization leave when they, well, when they get married. Or at least they don't take active assignments anymore."

He thought he saw realization beginning to dawn in her eyes. At first he was relieved, but then he was perplexed because he thought he could read pain there.

But maybe he was wrong, as he often was with her, because she gave a slight smile. "And you don't want to leave your organization," she said. "Or to give up your postings."

Relief again. "Right," he said. "Oh, I knew you would understand." But then once more he was confused, because he thought he saw that damnable pain again. And worse, he could see the beginning of her slow but inexorable withdrawal from him. He felt absurdly panicked. "Sylvia, don't!"

She looked startled. "Don't what?"

"Don't withdraw from me! Not now!"

She refused to meet his gaze. "Please, Nico. I don't think –" She faded off.

"You don't think what?" He grasped her chin in his fingers as if he would force her to look into his eyes.

His touch was insistent, but still she refused, keeping her eyes lowered, the honey-colored lashes brushing her too-pale cheeks.

"Sylvia, please! Look at me!"

As if with a great effort, she forced her sapphire eyes to meet his green-hazel ones. *Merda!* He could nearly see his reflection in the unshed tears that shimmered there. "Sylvia," he said gently. "I don't understand."

If she had blinked, he knew the tears would have started a narrow track down her face. But she didn't.

"Sylvia," he said again. "I don't *understand*."

Her voice was barely a whisper. "So, Nico. What did you need to talk to your organization about? Your trainer, and your – and Jonathan?"

It was his turn to look startled. What in bloody hell was she talking about? "Well, Sylvia, because I want to marry you, of course."

She stiffened. "To *marry* me?"

"Of *course*," he said again. He sounded, of all things, disgruntled. "Whatever bloody else would I mean?"

All she could manage was a choked, "Oh."

Adroitly, he took advantage of her being seemingly disconcerted. "I told them about your writing. They already knew about it, of course. Well, we have been exploring the idea of doing a better job of documenting our work. Cultures, changes, trends. Absorption of ideas. Threats, both internal and external. And I felt that with your talent you could chronicle it. Not on the actual assignments, of course. But you would be involved in the advance planning and the debriefings."

She still hadn't quite found her voice. "Chronicle it," she whispered.

Porco mondo. Damn it all. She wasn't usually so obtuse, he thought irrationally. "Sylvia, good god. Aren't you listening?"

And then to his consternation, the brimming tears spilled free and traced an uneven, brilliant path down the pale softness of her cheeks. His heart twisted within his chest. "Sylvia, *mia cara.* Please. *Don't tell me no!*"

To his dismay, she was shaking her head. "Sylvia, dammit! Sylvia, please, *listen* to me!"

"Oh, Nico, are you asking me to marry you?"

He looked at her as if she must surely have lost her mind. "Bloody hell," he began.

And then a smile burst through her tears and she began to laugh.

Merda, he thought. She *has* lost her mind.

"Yes," she said.

He blinked. "Yes?" he said.

"Yes."

He stared. "Yes, what?"

"Yes. I will marry you, Nico."

He became suddenly very still. "You will?"

"I will. And I will chronicle every step of the way as you chase drug lords and steal treasures and charge headlong into whatever other madness you manage to concoct."

He blinked again, this time to clear the blurring of his own vision. "Sylvia," he said.

"Yes?"

"You said yes?"

"Yes."

"Yes, that you will marry me?"

"Yes."

And then she was in his arms and hard against his body and his face was buried in those wild Wyoming honey curls, and he was whispering, *"Ti amo, ti amo,"* and thanking whatever saint it was that looked out for thieves and liars and mercenaries.

CPSIA information can be obtained at www.ICGtesting.com
Printed in the USA
LVOW122234031211

257705LV00002B/70/P